THE HUNT FOR MARA LAYIL

THE HUNT FOR MARA LAYIL

by E.J. ROSTEN

Manuscript by Amber J. Keyser

RELIUM MEDIA

Published in the United States by Relium Media LLC.
www.angelpunksaga.com

ISBN-13: 978-0-9853521-3-4

Blessing of the Blade Guardian

As you wielded the Blade of the Sacrifice, may my knife fly true.

As you enforced the Covenant, may my heart beat true.

As it was in the Before, may all Offspring live true.

Prologue

THE WORLD OF THE ELEVEN

Five thousand years ago the Age of Embodiment began with the White One and the Eleven, who brought the element relium from the Before into our world. As the children of the Eleven and their human mates slipped into the stream of history, they were known by many names. Among themselves, they are the First Born. Their descendants, the Offspring, are found in every culture around the world.

They are almost human—but not quite. The relium coursing through their veins gives them strengths unknown to man. Their participation in the human world is limited by the Covenant, which forbids the Eleven and their descendants from killing each other, bearing children together, and manipulating the will of humans.

Each family developed a line of scribes bound by a blood curse and tasked with recording family secrets and lore. Only the Keeper of the Lines knew every twist and turn of their complex genealogy, keeping the cipher-locked secrets in the closely guarded Book of Tracings. As the number of Offspring grew, the Eleven established the Crimson Scribes to govern their vast legacy.

Many array themselves around the Eleven. The Amyclaean Guard are sworn to protect them and enforce their will. Monks in the order of *Pro Lapsis Astra* dedicate themselves to praying for these Fallen Stars. And more ominously, the Hidden Eye, on a holy mission to eradicate abomination, is hunting them around the globe.

Now, in our time, their world is crumbling. Will the children of the Eleven return to the Before or will revolution sweep the globe?

One

MARA

TORU'S ISLAND, NORTHEASTERN JAPAN

Mara crouched at the top of the cliff, listening for sounds of pursuit over the roar of the ocean. She'd ripped her jeans climbing up the snow-covered rock. Frigid night air wafted up her leg and throbbed through the soles of her combat boots. Thin clouds scudded across the moon.

She stomped the blood back into her feet and rubbed the knotted muscles in her forearms before turning her attention to the target—an ancient, pagoda-topped fortress that dominated the small island. A biting wind whipped through the battlements, but there was no sign of life.

So far, so good. Toru Itou didn't know she was coming.

Mara snatched another look over the precipice. The three guards from the security station at Toru's boat slip sprawled unconscious where she'd left them at the base of the rock face. They'd been easy to surprise. The island was like freaking Alcatraz, ten miles from mainland Japan and ringed with cliffs.

They probably didn't have scrawny blonds tackling them very often.

Besides, they were human. Not much of a challenge for Offspring like her. If that were the extent of Toru's security detail for the biolab, this would be easier than roller derby. Mara peered at her nails, bloodied from the climb, and tore off a jagged bit with her teeth.

After more than a month on the run, she'd lost track of the days, but December was almost over. Maybe it was New Year's Eve. *Crack the champagne, boys.* Mara ran a hand through her short, spiked hair. Back in Portland, women were painting their nails and primping their curls. Their dates were hoping to get laid. Even Mara's own decidedly wilder friends would be cooking up a party that involved loud music, spur-of-the-moment tattoos, and possibly a midnight ride down Burnside on kiddie bikes.

Mara pulled the collar of her leather motorcycle jacket up to block the cold and blew on her hands to warm them. This tour-de-Japan wasn't exactly the party she'd hoped for, but at least she wasn't locked up. This time last year she'd been fresh meat, facing twelve months in Cascadia Correctional Facility. It was a helluva place to turn eighteen. The only good thing about it had been Ethan.

Light-brown skin, curly hair hanging in his brown eyes, reflexively reaching for his longboard even though those assholes who ran Cascadia wouldn't let him keep it in lock-up much less ride. He was one of the few people in group therapy—otherwise known as blowhards talking about feelings—who hadn't been afraid to look her in the eyes.

Ethan was always calling your bluff, tough girl.

Even freezing her ass off, she grinned. They'd been released the same day. Mara had been sure Ethan was going to kiss her on the front step of Cascadia. She was leaning in for it, eager after all those months without a hand on her body. Getting beat up in the prison kitchen didn't count. Of course, Momar pulled up to get her a few moments too soon.

You owe me one, Ethan Skylar.

Mara's awareness of the biting wind and darkness faded as grief swirled through her like bile. Momar Singh—aloof, exacting, steadfast—the part bodyguard, part stiff-upper-lip man-nanny had raised Mara and her little brother, Max, while their parents squinted in their stupid microscopes.

Momar was all the father I needed and now he's dead.

Mara shook the tears out of her eyes like a dog after a bath. She wanted things different. *But they're not. Not by a long shot. If you can't do what you came here for, Max is as good as dead too.* Even now, after a very brief period of hope at Momar's funeral, her brother had relapsed and lay in a deep coma. Only a steady transfusion of the blood she'd collected from Sinioch Moreau kept him alive.

And the healer was running out of blood.

Because I killed Sinioch.

She hadn't meant to kill him, but when Sinioch had threatened her brother ... A rush of remembered rage filled Mara. Sinioch hadn't stood a chance. For that crime, she'd been sentenced under the Covenant that governed all descendants of the Eleven.

So much for second chances.

Mara jerked off her leather backpack and unzipped it. She'd removed her gauntlets for the climb but felt naked without them. As she pulled out the eight-inch tubes, she watched the way the surface of the slate-colored metal roiled and churned, devouring the moonlight.

They weren't iron or silver but relium, and far more precious than gold. *And deadly.* Mara knew that better than anyone. At her touch, a gauntlet sprang open lengthwise. She pushed the sleeve of her jacket above her right elbow and slid her arm into the slot. The metal pulsed like a beating heart and closed around her forearm, rippling as it molded to her flesh.

She was Offspring—mostly human but not quite, and the relium of the gauntlets responded to the same element in her blood. Mara grimaced as she put on the left gauntlet. These relics had been bought with sacrifice. As a rule, Mara didn't go in for all that save the world crap, but for Max ... She felt a catch in her throat. *Yeah, I'd drag myself onto a burning pyre for the little dude.* The cold in her bones deepened, and it wasn't just the freezing night or the looming fortress.

"Stop it," she muttered to herself. "Get your ass in there."

The monk and the healer who were taking care of Max were convinced that the Offspring, Toru Itou, was holding Mara's mother here. Mara's job was simple—break her out and bring her home where she could get to work finding a cure for Max.

Mara wrenched on the backpack and sprinted from the cliff edge to the foundation of the fortress. A broad set of stairs spat her out into the main level, an immense open-air room that shoguns had used to review samurai troops long ago. Her snow-covered boots left slushy splotches across the glossy bamboo floor.

The upper levels were only accessible by a narrow stairway, but the old structure had been retrofitted with a belowground bunker serviced by an elevator, its stainless-steel door like a robot biting through the ancient walls. The last guard she'd poleaxed before climbing up here had said her mother was in something called Block Eighteen.

Mara jammed the down arrow with an icy finger and waited, edgy and impatient.

She hadn't seen or heard from either of her parents in over a year. They'd disappeared the same night she'd been arrested and sent to Cascadia. If she wasn't so pissed, Mara might have been worried.

Still, being minutes away from some gushy reunion with her mother made her stomach churn. What would she say? *Thanks for letting me rot in detention. Really appreciated the eleven months, two weeks, and three days of awesome!*

The elevator hummed to a stop, and Mara tensed, but when the doors shushed open on silky hydraulics, it was empty. She entered and mashed the only button with her palm. From the time it took for the elevator doors to open again, Mara guessed she was pretty far underground. *Block Eighteen must be some kind of lab. Just the place to find Mom revving up a centrifuge and muttering formulas.*

For as long as she could remember, her parents had been holed up in research facilities, studying the blood of Offspring to find out why they lived longer and healed faster, why some could heal the sick, and others kill with nothing more than a touch. And her parents had created, whether on purpose or by accident, the toxin that even now was worming its way through Max's body, incapacitating the relium in his blood, and killing him slowly but surely.

Mara sucked in a breath, realizing she'd been clenching her fists so hard her nails had cut bloody half-moons into her palms. *Max is the only reason I'm here. I don't give a crap about Mom.* The elevator doors opened. Mara slid through them, ready to pound anyone who so much as glanced at her, but the bunker was empty as a morgue.

Cold enough for corpses.

A shiver rippled through her.

Offspring. She was sure of it. For the past month, she'd been hounded, chased, and attacked, and if she'd learned anything—other than it was almost always better to hit first and ask questions later—it was this: Mara knew in her blood when others of her kind were near.

My own personal alert system.

She scanned the cinder block walls of the bunker. Her breath billowed in the antiseptic, blue-lit air. Long banks of stainless-steel drawers were stacked five high and five across. Numbered blocks of twenty-five drawers each filled the cavernous room.

This is no lab.

Other than a faint hum that seemed to emanate from the drawers, Mara heard only the low thump of her beating heart. She oriented herself to the numbering system and walked down the aisle toward Block Eighteen.

The sensation of accelerated blood flow that alerted her to the presence of other Offspring was faint, almost smothered. No attack was imminent. Block Eighteen was cold storage, not a research lab.

The drawers in the block were unmarked. She picked one at random and gripped the handle. The sharp, die-cut edges bit into her palm. Her reflection in the polished metal surface grimaced back like a small, ferocious animal. The blue light reflected off the stainless-steel studs that dotted her ears from top to bottom. Snow still clung to her shoulders.

I don't want to know what's in there.

A shudder drove through her.

What are you gonna do? Go home and sit by Max's bed while he dies?

Mara realized she'd been holding her breath and let it out in a long hiss. Even in the cold, her hands had gone slick with sweat. She wiped them on her jeans and checked to make sure the gauntlets were secure on her forearms.

Okay. Let's do this.

Mara took the handle again, this time in both hands, and pulled.

The drawer slid out with a soft sigh. She flinched backward, half expecting the contents to leap out at her.

She forced herself to look down.

The albino girl, wearing a threadbare sundress, was young— maybe eleven—about the same age as Max, and like him, her muscles were stiff and contracted in some kind of predeath rigor mortis. *She's been dosed too.* The hum was louder now, and Mara noticed an electronic panel on the inside wall of the drawer. Snaking from the panel into the vein inside the girl's left arm was a clear tube through which dripped an occasional pulse of crimson fluid.

Blood from a First Born.

Mara fought the urge to retch.

The blood of the first generation born to the Eleven and their human mates was far richer in relium than that of Offspring, whose genetics had been diluted by more generations of outbreeding with humans. It was the only thing strong enough to counteract the toxin and prevent immediate death.

She slid her hand under the girl's back.

Bony stumps protruded from each of the girl's shoulder blades. The unscarred skin stretched taut over them and gave an odd tilt to the girl's chest, pushing her rib cage up as if she were on the verge of levitation. Mara flexed her shoulders and felt her leather jacket pull tight against the matching stumps jutting from her own back. The deformity, an evolutionary remnant of their ancestors, marked them as Offspring.

"I knew it," she whispered to the still face.

Mara swiped at her eyes with the back of her hand. She wanted to find an empty drawer and shut her own damn self in, but that would do shit for Max. Instead, she went back to the search.

A Black man lay inside the next drawer, his bright cotton tunic still stained with blood from whatever struggle had brought him here. His bloodshot eyes bulged sightlessly at the ceiling. Hope trickled out of Mara. The guard had said, "Your mom's in Block Eighteen, lower level." Now she understood the mockery in his voice.

I should have broken his butt-ugly jaw.

Mara leaned against the wall of drawers, her breath coming into rhythm with the hum of the stasis machines. She had no doubt that her mother was lying in one of these drawers. She didn't need to see it, did she? There was no point.

If you can't help Max, I don't care how you got here.

It was her own fault that she was lying like a mummified mermaid in a freak show.

"I don't need you," Mara muttered as she began wrenching open the drawers.

An old woman in a sherbet-orange housedress. A gaunt man with Russian mob tattoos. A round-faced Mexican woman who smelled vaguely of roses. Each face stared at her, rigid and unseeing. A tremor raced up her spine.

"If you didn't want an Offspring daughter, you should have a married a goddamned human." Mara slammed the drawer shut and the clangs reverberated through the bunker, ricocheting off metal and concrete.

"I hate you! I hate you!"

But she opened every drawer.

Her mother, Veronique, was in the last one, green eyes staring, no longer beautiful. Her hands were frozen in rigid claws, and Mara could imagine her scrabbling at the slick metal, buried alive. A fitting fate for a recluse. She'd been kind but not motherly and, like an old-fashioned doll, both hollow and brittle.

Mara's breath came in shallow, desperate bursts, and she fought the urge to pull her mother's body from the suffocating drawer.

There's nothing you can do.

She should go, and go quickly, before someone discovered the guards she'd knocked out and came looking for her. Instead, she reached toward her mother's face. Mara cupped her cheek, feeling the constricted muscles under her skin.

"Mom?" she whispered. "Wake up."

Nothing. Of course not. She'd been an idiot to expect a response.

You couldn't wait to have me out of the house.

It had been a long time since her mom had done anything for her.

Well, I couldn't wait, either, but you should've been there for Max! He's just a kid!

Mara's arms fell to her sides, as heavy and lifeless as the bodies in the drawers. Max was her responsibility now. She was his legal guardian. *I love him!* True enough, but in the dark bunker, Mara had to admit she'd been hoping their mother would take back the job. *Eighteen is too young to be someone's parent.*

"You've been a shitty mom," she whispered.

Mara was bone-weary.

Always fighting and running and never getting anywhere.

As she pushed her mother back into icy darkness, the click of the latch sounded as final as the slice of a guillotine.

Two

ETHAN

MONASTERY OF PRO LAPSIS ASTRA, PORTLAND, OREGON

Ethan's head throbbed like he'd been bludgeoned with a mallet. He lay in a narrow bed in a windowless room, sucking hot, stale air. In the dim light of medical displays, he saw a drawn curtain dividing the room. From the other side came the sound of slow, regular breathing.

Did I crash my board?

He rummaged through a jumble of images, trying to remember. It was a fractured, violent collage. None involved flips or ollies. All involved Mara. A month ago, they'd been released from Cascadia, and he'd been swept into a series of events so strange that they seemed more hallucination than real.

Ethan liked things that made sense. Give him code or hieroglyphs, a Rubik's Cube or a jumbled pile of Scrabble tiles. He would find the pattern, decipher the message, make order out of chaos. And stay in control. Unlike him, Mara was ...

Reckless.

Infuriating.

Fascinating.

The two of them were as different as a wolf and a Labrador. Maybe more. Yet he couldn't walk away. She was an unsolvable puzzle.

Irresistible.

From the moment he'd met her at Cascadia, her mystery dogged him. How had she managed to come out on top in a fight with three bigger inmates? Why did her black eyes fade and heal so quickly? What was that thing that happened during group therapy when it seemed to Ethan that time had stood still around them?

He had to figure her out.

So he'd stuck with her when all the shit had gone down, and here was the truth—against all logic, his intuition said that she was his second chance.

I'll take her on faith.

Hurried footsteps sent his head pounding again. Against the backlight of an open door, Ethan could make out two figures— a stolid-looking man with a bushy beard and a slight, graceful woman. A thrill sped through him like a fast descent on a vert ramp in the skatepark.

"Mara?" he asked.

"It's just me and Abbot Greb," said the woman as she turned up the lights. Ethan pushed himself up on one elbow, craning his neck to see past them.

Mara had to be there!

But it didn't take long to see she wasn't.

Mara might look small and delicate, but she could fill space like an enraged wildebeest. If she were here, he would know it.

"Where is she, Hiroko?" he asked, sweeping shaggy brown hair off his sweaty forehead and grazing a huge lump. "Ow!"

Hiroko nudged him flat and leaned over, comparing the size of his pupils. "Take it easy. You hit your head really hard. Let me see what I can do." Her cool fingers skimmed his temple, and immediately the pain eased.

"Where is she?" he repeated. "I told her I'd stay with her!" He wasn't cocky enough to believe he could keep Mara out of trouble, but he sure wanted to try.

"I am sorry that I couldn't send both of you," said Abbot Greb, lowering himself into a chair. His drooping eyelids blinked over eyes milky with cataracts. "I'm an old man. Even shifting to send Mara was nearly too much for me."

Hiroko turned her attention from Ethan to the abbot, fussing over him, taking his pulse.

Send us both? Where? Ethan's anxiety cranked up. *1 plus 1 is 2. 1 plus 2 is 3.* He cycled through the Fibonacci sequence in his head until he could trust himself to speak. *2 plus 3 is 5. 3 plus 5 is 8.*

"Shifting is not what you would call a smooth process," the abbot continued. "No doubt the morning news will report a seismic tremor centered near here. That's why you fell and got knocked out. I am sorry."

"Where's Mara?" Ethan asked.

Abbot Greb pinched the bridge of his nose. "Japan."

"Japan?" Ethan fell back onto his pillow and stared at the ceiling. She was half a world away. *5 plus 8 is 13. 8 plus 13 is 21.* What was he supposed to do now? Go back to the apartment he shared with his mom and see if she was drunk yet? *I have got to move out.*

"She must find her parents," said the abbot.

"Max doesn't have much time," Hiroko added. "I'm barely keeping him alive."

She pulled back the curtain separating the room and leaned over the motionless body of a boy. Ethan sat up, head swimming, kicked off the sheet, and reached for his jeans.

"How is he?"

Hiroko smoothed the blankets over the young boy. "I don't know what more to do for him."

Mara's brother was small for his age, with a smattering of freckles across his cheeks. His hair was darker than Mara's, and Ethan knew he had a crooked smile, one dimple, and was a serious ringer at Mancala.

My kind of kid.

Max's face was a twisted mask contorted by overcontracted facial muscles. He reminded Ethan of an exhibit at the science museum he'd seen last summer: human forms stripped of skin to show the underlying musculature. This was not the boy who'd flung himself into Mara's arms when she'd been released from Cascadia. Not by a long shot.

"Mara hasn't heard from her parents in over a year," Ethan said. "Their son is dying. Where the hell are they? If they cared, wouldn't they be here?" From the sour expression on the healer's face, Ethan could tell she shared his less-than-stellar opinion of the Layils, but the abbot smoothed the rusty-orange robe over his knees and peered at Ethan from under bristly eyebrows. "It is possible that they are being detained against their will."

13 plus 21 is 34. 21 plus 34 is 55.

Ethan stared at the abbot in disbelief. "Did you seriously just zap her to Japan? To break her parents out of some prison? Alone? We have to find her!" Ethan's mind churned through a series of possible networks where he could track her. "If she has her phone on, I could hack the geolocation protocols—"

"Do you know what Mara is?" the old man interrupted.

Ethan's problem-solving ground to a halt. "Yeah," he said, shrugging, "she's freaky."

A laugh bubbled out of Hiroko. "You can say that again."

Abbot Greb cleared his throat, and Hiroko look chastised.

"Try again," said the old man.

"She's different because she's descended from ... um ..." Ethan trailed off, hesitant to sound like a new-age loony.

"From the Eleven," the abbot said. "Some call them angels."

Ethan rubbed the back of his neck, embarrassed for the old man. *Mara is no angel.*

"In the Before, they were ethereal," the abbot continued, "but they chose embodiment, manifested earthly forms, and slipped into the stream of human history."

"Why?" Ethan asked, even though he might as well have asked why Cinderella's carriage manifested from a pumpkin.

But the abbot was dead serious. "They wanted to know the human condition."

"And mess it up," Hiroko muttered.

The abbot turned his clouded gaze in her direction. "You sound like Sinioch now, advocating for the termination of the Covenant."

"You know what they say about good intentions," she said, touching the transfusion bag hanging above Mara's brother. "Do you really think the Eleven wanted this?"

Ethan heard the bitterness in Hiroko's voice. Mara had echoed it when she'd been convicted of violating one of the three oaths that governed the descendants of the Eleven. That she'd killed Sinioch while trying to protect Max didn't seem to matter.

And now Mara was as good as dead, unless she'd managed to stay ahead of the people hunting her. Sinioch's widow wanted revenge, and Armaros, the last living member of the Eleven, wanted to lock her up for the rest of her life.

"No, Hiroko." Abbot Greb sighed. "I don't think they wanted any of this."

"So you agree that the Covenant has failed our kind?" she said, trying to pick a fight.

"The only thing that matters right now," Ethan interrupted, "is finding Mara. She needs us." His mind whirred back into search mode. "I'm gonna find her."

"What she needs most," said the abbot, "is a new Scribe."

"Mara will never accept another," said Hiroko.

Ethan looked away, his own emotions and memories of Momar still raw. He knew Hiroko was right. Momar had been immeasurably more than a Scribe. The first time Mara had shown him pictures of herself as a little girl perched on Momar's broad shoulders was the first time he saw a crack in Mara's emotional armor. She never got outwardly mushy or anything about Momar, but from everything that happened, how he died in her arms after sacrificing himself to protect her, Ethan knew no one could replace him.

"We must make her understand," explained the abbot. "A Scribe from the Singh family has served the Layil family since the 17th century, keeping their history and guarding their secrets within the family Record."

"She loved him," Ethan ventured. "But even after everything he did for her, dying for her—wasn't his job to protect her? To be her bodyguard?

"No," said Hiroko. "Each bloodline of the Eleven has unique abilities. Scribes teach new Offspring to channel them."

"And definitely kick ass," offered Ethan.

"If necessary," said the abbot. "But knowledge is often more powerful than skill with a blade."

Thanks, Yoda.

"Are Scribes human or Offspring?"

"Human," said Hiroko.

"She won't want anyone but Momar," said Ethan.

No one can replace a dead man.

"I know." Hiroko stood, double-checked the monitors over Max's bed, and reached for the messenger bag she'd set by the door. "But I'm going to Seattle to see Momar's nephew anyway."

"Mara must have a Scribe," rumbled Abbot Greb.

"I'm going too," said Ethan, shrugging on his jacket and grabbing his board from the corner of the room. Hiroko shot him a relieved grin.

"You should be less involved, not more," the old man protested. "It's too dangerous."

"If Momar's nephew is all human, all the time, just like me, then I'm going. Come on, Hiroko." Ethan tugged on her elbow and led her out the door before the abbot could argue, but as he left Max's room, a rush of anxiety filled him.

"Why would the nephew want the job?" Ethan asked.

Hiroko stiffened. "It's important, an honor. Generations of Singh and Layil ... linked together ..."

Ethan raised his eyebrows. "Sure. Whatever. You're welcome to get all protocol droid on me, but we're talking about Mara. She's not exactly a cake assignment."

Her bristle un-bristled. "Why do you want to help her so much, Ethan?"

How do I answer that? Sticking with Mara was asking for trouble. So why was he compelled to help her? He shrugged and held up his hands in mock defeat. "I guess I hate cake."

Hiroko was still laughing as she led him out of the monastery. Ethan flipped his board under one arm and hoped, for the Scribe's sake, that he was one tough son of a bitch. You'd have to be to play on Team Mara.

THREE

Mara retraced her steps to the elevator and returned to the main level. Its echoing emptiness was more ominous now that she'd seen what lay beneath. Her mother was a dead end. *Bad joke. Sorry, Mom.* But seriously, couldn't she ever catch a break?

Hiroko had told her to find her parents—that dynamic duo of craptastic parenting. Abbot Greb had pulled a Dumbledore and zapped her here. He thought both of them were on the island. Mara rubbed her shoulders and stifled a groan. Now she'd have to penetrate the upper levels and look for dear old Dad.

It couldn't be any worse than finding Mom, could it?

Since the elevator only served the belowground portion of the fortress, Mara would have to take a narrow set of stairs. *If it feels like a trap, it probably is one.* But she was ascending before she could talk herself out of it. On the second floor, the low, heavy-beamed ceiling nearly scraped her head, compounding her claustrophobia. Instead of windows, the thick stone walls had open vertical slits every few feet. Long ago, archers would have manned the slits and left the surrounding clifftop piled with bodies.

Easy pickings.

The next staircase was on the opposite wall, and although the room, lit by murky moonlight, appeared to be empty, Mara wasn't about to cross in the open. Instead, she pressed her back against the wall and slid along it toward the next flight of stairs.

One second there was cold stone against her back. The next, she was stumbling backward into a hidden alcove cut in the wall. Something bumpy pressed against her shoulders, and when she looked down, narrow, pointy-toed leather boots stuck out on either side of her own scuffed Dr. Martens.

Mara wheeled, punching as she turned. Her fist connected with a lumpy mass. *Straw?* Unbalanced, Mara fell back on her butt and looked up to see a stuffed suit of samurai armor and spiked helmet toppling toward her.

She cursed, threw her hands up, and flinched away from certain impalement.

Time! I need time!

A hot liquid sensation flowed from her palms toward the helmet. The muscles of her arms screamed as if she were holding back a heavy weight, but no impact came. The spike didn't puncture her hand or skull. Mara opened her eyes.

The helmet had stopped in midair as if caught by the shutter-click of a camera. The armor, woven from strips of leather and flattened squares of silver, hung suspended above her. The boots were frozen in midcollapse near her own feet.

Reaching for the helmet was like pushing her hands through dense mud. In slow motion, she plucked it from the air and placed it beside her with a clunk. She eased the armor onto the floor, relaxed, and the boots finished their crumple with a soft whisper of leather on wood.

Before Momar had told her who—or was it *what?*—she was, Mara had thought there was something terribly wrong with her. By the time she was sixteen, weird things had begun happening around her. She was never sure if the world was speeding up or if she was slowing down or vice versa, but she was usually out of sync.

The few friends she'd had growing up accused her of messing with them and faded from her life one by one. In the year leading up to her stint in Cascadia, the only people she hung out with were too drunk or high to notice when she got freaky.

When Mara had been released, Momar explained that she was Turning—coming into her abilities as Offspring—and that she was descended from Armaros through her father. She'd inherited Armaros's ability to manipulate time, which explained a whole lot of crap. Momar had promised to train her, but with him gone, she was flying blind. Again, Mara felt the pressure of tears at the back of her throat.

Mara looked at the scarecrow samurai lying on the floor. Just now, as the armor had fallen, instinct had kicked in. Good thing too, or she'd have lost an eye. *Maybe I'm not completely hopeless.* Leaving the splayed body behind, Mara crept up the stairs.

Larger, grated windows let more light into the next level. Its walls were lined with display racks. One side bristled with high-tech weapons—shock wands, handheld lasers, and stun guns. The other held rows of shiny medical instruments—clamps, scalpels, scissors, saws. The fortress was half sci-fi lab of the damned and half museum of torture.

Dude needs some serious interior design help.

One more set of stairs. More artifacts. But the weapons and surgical instruments on display here were older and more barbaric. A standing display case stood in front of her. On the other side was an immense door. Because of the low ceilings, it was nearly as wide as it was tall, and looked so heavy that it might take a rampaging elephant to push it open. Her blood thrummed in response to something on the other side of the door. *Offspring—Toru probably.* The threatening presence drew her forward.

As she approached the standing case, Mara's senses blasted into overdrive, and she stood dancer-like on the balls of her feet. There was something in there she *had* to see. Keeping the door in her peripheral vision, Mara scanned the contents of the case. An ancient scalpel rested on black velvet, tagged and labeled, museum-style. Its thin, delicate handle attached to a leaf-shaped blade, razor-sharp on all sides.

She bent closer, pressing her hands against the glass. Instantly, the gauntlets rippled against her forearms, tightening their grip. At the same moment, the scalpel flowed as if momentarily molten. *Relium. Without a doubt.*

Both relics solidified, and a jangling tidbit of some Asian pop song rang from the other side of the door. She heard the solid thunk of a drawer closing. The song stopped midlyric, and a man spoke. "*Hai?*" He paused. "Yes? Toru here."

Might as well get it over with while he's distracted. Mara took a deep breath. *Let's see how good he is at multitasking.* She darted around the display case, set her shoulder against the heavy door, and crashed her way through. Surprise on the face of the man behind the desk transformed into a honeyed grin. He rose, a phone pressed to his ear.

"In fact," he said to the caller, his dark eyes on Mara, "she has just this moment arrived."

What the hell? It was Mara's turn to gape. *This guy was expecting me?*

Toru hung up, set the phone on the desk, and sauntered around it. Mara backed out of the office until she was up against the display case, gauntlets pulsing. Toru leaned casually against the other side of the desk, watching her through the open doorway. He looked about forty, but she knew enough about Offspring to know he must be much older.

She scowled at him.

"What?" Toru asked, his voice lazy, his gray eyes sweeping over her body. "No hellos? No introductions?"

"*Konichiwa.*" Mara forced the Japanese greeting through clenched teeth.

Toru brushed the asymmetric cut of his slick black hair away from a wide-set eye. "Oh, how lovely. Japanese from my little American visitor." Everything about him was *GQ* perfect—from the sleek Italian leather boots to the silk shirt, cashmere sweater, and Nehru-style jacket, all in shades of silvery gray.

"Take your time getting pretty today?" Mara snarled.

He waved a thin hand, blowing her off. "I'll take that as a compliment coming from you."

"Who was on the phone, Toru?" She hoped he'd think she knew more than she really did.

"Oh, Mara-chan, you were listening in." He gave her an oily swoon-over-me look. "Why, it was our friend, Aeda Moreau."

A flash of fear stabbed through Mara. She'd shaken Aeda off the trail in Portland, hadn't she?

Toru stepped toward her. "She really wants to see you."

"I'll be sure to text when we're done here."

Toru's glance swept over Mara again, more probing than lascivious this time. Mara revised her opinion of him. *Handsome? Yeah. But deadly.*

"Do you like my collection?" he asked, taking another step forward.

Mara sidled to her left, circling to put the display case between them. "It's kinda morbid, actually."

"Tools of war, tools of healing. Wonder why?"

"You should try *Star Wars* figures."

Toru laughed, slapping his thigh in exaggerated humor. "Good idea!"

In an instant, he leapt over the case, slamming Mara into the wall and causing artifacts to clatter against their hooks. As he backed away, Mara flew to her feet and moved to put the case between them again.

"This," he said, gesturing to the scalpel in the display as if nothing had happened, "is the pride of my collection."

"How nice for you," snapped Mara.

"You don't seem to appreciate its value." They circled the display case like boxers.

"I want to know where my dad is."

Toru gave an almost girlish titter. "What? Didn't enjoy your reunion with Mommy? Hoping Daddy can fix your baby brother?"

"You're a monster!"

"Daddy's busy helping Aeda, you see. I know they'd both love to see you again. Why don't you wait inside my office and I'll arrange it?"

"Why don't you go to hell?" Mara rammed into his chest, sending them both tumbling to the floor. On his feet faster than she believed possible, Toru grabbed a length of iron chain from a hook on the wall.

"Now *this* is a very useful weapon." He held it out, leering. "*Manrikigusari,* we call it. Strength of a thousand men."

Before Mara could blink, the chain became a circle of silver whirling in Toru's hand. She thrust her left arm forward to block, but like a viper, the chain wrapped itself around her wrist.

"Aren't you tricky?" he hissed, the thud of metal on metal echoing through the room. The chain wasn't relium but it bound her wrist so tightly she couldn't break free.

With a swift jerk of the chain, Toru hauled her forward until they were nose to nose. "What are you wearing? The relium calls to me."

"You need to brush your teeth, old man." Mara swung a punch with her free arm, snapping Toru's head back. He dropped the *manrikigusari* and crumpled to his knees against the wall.

Mara fumbled to dislodge the triple-wrapped chain from her arm, but before she could free herself, Toru rose with a *katana*, the curved sword of a samurai, in one hand and a rhino-sized tranquilizer dart in the other. Mara hefted the chain and wondered if she'd be able to use it without knocking herself out.

Toru tilted his head toward the case while keeping his eyes on her. "The scalpel on display is made of relium. Very handy for killing Offspring and First Borns. But you know all about that, don't you?"

Mara set the chain spinning in front of her. "Sinioch tried to kill my brother," she snarled.

Toru flung the dart. The collision with the spinning chain sent both weapons flying. Toru ducked the dart as it sped back in his direction. Mara ran for the wall of weapons. Her fingers grazed the bone handle of a short-bladed *tanto* knife, but it clattered off the wall, out of reach.

Light glinted off the blade of Toru's *katana* as it flashed toward her. She turned and threw both arms up to block her face. Preceded by an increased thrumming through her veins, blades sprang from her gauntlets, slicing their way through the leather of her jacket as they emerged and stopped the *katana* with a fierce clang. She thrust downward, twisting the sword from Toru's hands. It clattered across the floor and Mara stepped forward, forearms raised.

Toru backed toward the case, alarm coursing across his face. "So you're going to kill me too, just like you killed Sinioch? Who's the monster now?"

Anger blazed through her. "He was! He attacked my brother!" Mara flung her palms forward and a wave of force rolled out with the blast of a volcano. Toru flew into the display case, which erupted in a hailstorm of glass.

Mara slumped, staring at Toru's limp body. Exhaustion replaced fury. With a *snick*, the gauntlets' blades retracted. All she wanted to do was go. There was no help for Max here.

As Mara edged toward the stairs, Toru's eyes flicked open. "Stop."

She froze.

"Why not … finish … the job?" His fingers scrabbled through the glass, blood streaming from many cuts.

"I'm not a monster," she whispered.

With effort etched all over his face, Toru pulled himself up, leaning heavily on the edge of the shattered case. Mara slunk backward onto the first step.

"I collect the tools of samurai and healers because I am of the line of Otohime." As the words left his lips, he sent the relium scalpel whirling toward her. Warned by the relium in her veins, Mara dodged as it left his hand, but still it slammed into her left shoulder with a terrifying thunk.

Mara shuddered as pain stabbed through her arm. "Good for you," she grunted.

Toru fell against the case. "Most know us … for our ability … to heal the body. They think that is our only … gift."

"You'd make a shitty healer." Mara shut her eyes and wrenched the blade out of her arm, suppressing the scream that rose in her throat.

Toru's face slid into a sour grin as he raised one hand toward her. "But really … Otohime was the master of the body. And to master ... means both to heal," Toru made a slicing motion through the air, "and to harm."

Mara gasped as pain ripped through her right side. She clutched at her jacket feeling for a blade, but there was nothing.

"Shit!"

A hot bloom of blood soaked through her shirt. What the hell had he done? Mara struggled to keep her feet.

"You see," he groaned, "we ... control ... the body." Toru crumpled to the floor, weighed down by his own injuries. "I could ... kill you."

Darkness swirled at the edge of her vision. Mara forced it back.

"But," Toru continued, "Aeda ... she wants to do it. Slowly." A slightly strangled laugh burbled from his lips, along with a mouthful of scarlet bubbles.

Streaming blood and clutching the crimson scalpel, Mara stumbled down the stairs.

"Don't worry ... about me," he choked after her. "The ... children of Otohime ... heal quickly."

FOUR

AEDA

PAN-NATIONAL HAEMATOLOGICAL RESEARCH CENTRE,
CHIANG RAI, THAILAND

Aeda swept a strand of black hair from her brow with one long fingernail. It was hot for January, and the sticky air irritated her even more than the preposterously slow *tuk-tuk* carrying her from the apartment to the lab. Compared to the sweeping lines of the skyscraper where she and Sinioch had lived and worked in Portland or the ancient pagoda on Toru's island, this facility was a squat architectural nightmare. Its advantage was the location near the poppy fields of the Golden Triangle. Being able to produce the heroin that she and Sinioch distributed up and down the West Coast had been one of Sinioch's more brilliant business decisions. Without the middlemen, they made far more money to put into their revolutionary work.

Sinioch.

At every turn, something reminded her of him. She was dangerous with grief.

Anger rose in her, studded and ugly like a tank, and she squeezed the metal railing of the *tuk-tuk* until her slender hand blanched. Under the pressure, the railing snapped, sending a metal shard into her palm.

"Damn it!"

Reaching the lab, the driver pulled to the curb and turned for payment. Horror washed over his face as he watched Aeda pull the shiny splinter with her teeth and spit it out in a red-tinged spray of saliva.

"This should cover it," she snapped, thrusting a fifty-*baht* bill into his hand.

The armed guard in the lobby nodded to Aeda without looking at her directly. She was beautiful but hard-edged, the kind of woman to admire only from a distance.

Up close was too close.

Aeda passed through a second set of doors into the air-conditioned offices of her so-called research centre. The Thai government thought the Moreaus ran a facility to study blood-borne diseases and granted them level-five secure storage status. Most government inspectors were too freaked out that their eyeballs would explode from stray Ebola virus to check the goings-on in the building very closely.

Of course, we do study blood—of a sort.

Her first stop was the office of the head of security. Guleed Awaale had come to Aeda through underground channels in Mogadishu and could probably bench press a piano.

"Any trouble?" she asked.

His smile exploded at her, a shark-like mouth of perfect teeth, the canines filed to points, gleaming against his dark face. "No trouble. Very boring," he said in a voice far too musical for what the man was capable of.

"You're watching for Dr. Layil's daughter?" Aeda fully expected Toru Itou to contain her, but she wouldn't let down her guard until she had the girl's body in hand.

"Don't you worry. If Blondie shows up, she will go down." He grinned at her.

"Excellent."

Once in the seclusion of her office, Aeda's thoughts turned again to Sinioch. Not that they were ever far from him—or from Mara Layil ... his murderer. Aeda itched to have her hands around the girl's throat. Her men had come close to capturing her several times in the month since Sinioch had been killed, but somehow Mara kept eluding her.

She is powerful and growing more so.

The Amyclaean Guards that Armaros sent after Mara were constantly underfoot. Plus, the girl had help from that damnable Abbot Greb. The monks of Pro Lapsis Astra were supposed to *pray* for the descendants of the Eleven, not pick favorites, but Abbot Greb was bending all the rules for that Mara. *Self-righteous old man!* Aeda wanted to gouge his rheumy eyes out.

A dark yearning bloated her. She wanted Sinioch. She'd loved both his fury and his fire. A reddish haze obscured Aeda's vision. She clenched the arms of her chair.

Get the girl. Obliterate her. Achieve his vision. It's what Sinioch would have wanted.

A jolt of pain from the fresh wound in her palm cut through the haze, a pinprick of clarity. Aeda clawed her way back into control. The important thing was capturing that punk and finding out why she was so special to Armaros.

Armaros! Aeda spat on the floor. *Her disembodiment can't come fast enough for me.*

Sinioch would have ferreted the answer out. The right pressure here. Some painful persuasion there. He'd always done the *fieldwork*, as he called it. Coop him up too long and Sinioch would begin to prance like a racehorse yearning for the track. Aeda ran their operation from the office and lab. He ran the streets.

A perfect partnership.

From the moment they'd met, both knew it was time for Offspring to come into their own. The Eleven had chosen free will, but the bureaucracy they'd spawned was more like the US tax code, an infernal rat's nest for the damned. *My god, the Covenant is nothing but rules and oaths—the suffocating constraint of it all.*

When Sinioch had rallied others to join his revolution, he'd paced the room extolling the freedom to express the fullness of their powers. "We are so much more than human!" he'd cried. "Why be subject to human limits?" He'd swept them into his vision of a greater purpose—to rule, to thrive, to dominate. She'd fallen in love with him all over again that night.

And then that little bitch killed him!

Aeda punched a button on her laptop and pulled up the security footage of his death for the hundredth time. There, in black and white, was the penthouse of their skyscraper in Portland. Sinioch crouched over the Layil boy, checking his pulse. He rose quickly. The recording had no sound but clearly something alerted him. He strode on long, powerful legs to a set of floor-to-ceiling cabinet doors. He threw them open to reveal a dark metal chest plate and leg greaves. As Aeda watched her husband strapping on the armor, a deep ache tightened in her chest.

It felt too intimate, yet she kept watching.

Then Mara—*that monstrosity!*—burst into the room and threw herself between Sinioch and the boy. They spoke, an angry confrontation lost in the soundless recording.

Aeda wished she could have held on to his last words.

It wouldn't have been enough, but it would have been something more than she had now.

In the clip, Sinioch's attack came faster than Aeda could have imagined, even though she knew his gifts in every way. Wrapping his arms around the girl, Sinioch shot upward, breaking through the glass dome at the top of the building and out of range of the camera. For several moments, the screen was filled with shards of falling glass; then the camera picked up a Japanese woman creeping toward the boy.

Aeda's lip curled in a sneer.

Hiroko Mori, Abbot Greb's youngest and favorite healer. *She'll be the second to die. After Mara Layil.*

Aeda braced herself for the end.

Preceded by another shower of glass, Sinioch and Mara plummeted from the sky, limbs entwined like lovers. The impact shook the camera. When the footage stabilized, there was Mara, pulling her bladed gauntlets from Sinioch's chest. Aeda felt the gashes as if she bore them herself. Blood poured from her husband's chest, pooling on the floor.

"No!" Aeda whispered, pressing her hands against the computer screen.

Make it stop!

The healer slid on her knees through Sinioch's blood. She siphoned off the liquid pulsing from his wounds, filling vial after vial.

You are no healer!

Rage rushed through Aeda as if it were a living thing—seeking, twisting, filling, a darkness large enough to fill her and spill over, obliterating all light. She gripped the edge of the desk until she felt the wood bite into her fingertips.

The tumult swept through her.

Mara Layil will pay.

In blood.

FIVE

PETRA

HIGH COUNCIL COMPOUND OF THE ELEVEN, ISTANBUL, TURKEY

Petra Adler, a muscular woman with short-cropped, blond hair, topped the tower stairs and stood at the stone railing. From the fortified wall that surrounded the High Council Compound, she could see the Bosporus twisting like a muddy green python from the Black Sea, through Istanbul, and into the Sea of Marmara.

Above her, a low-lying bank of clouds threatened rain, or maybe snow, if the temperature dropped any lower. Below her, the city hummed and buzzed, the sidewalks crowded with pedestrians bundled against the winter bluster. Petra could just make out the crowded street market where Mara Layil had slipped through her fingers—an unforgivable failure. And one she'd spent the last month trying to rectify.

How could one young woman be so hard to find?

Prayerfully, Petra touched her throat and the hilt of the relium knife at her waist. Like all members of the Amyclaean

Guard, she had been ritually pierced. Twin rods of relium passed on either side of her windpipe and screwed into diamond-shaped plates, front and back. It made speech excruciating, but what they lost with their voices, they gained in position. Since the death of the Blade Guardian, the rest of the Eleven relied on the Amyclaean Guard to mete out justice. To Petra, her piercings and the knife were signs of loyalty to her beloved Armaros.

And Armaros wanted Mara Layil returned to the High Council Compound.

Where is she?

For thirty years, Petra had been coming to this spot to think.

When the Eleven had chosen ancient Byzantium for their central meeting place over two thousand years ago, it had been a dusty crossroads, hardly a city at all. As Petra watched a red tugboat nudge an oil tanker through the maze of ship traffic, she wondered if they foresaw how the seeds they'd sown would grow.

Below her, in the interior courtyard, several members of Petra's elite, twelve-member guard were in the practice yard throwing knives at moving targets. A cluster of Crimson Scribes in their distinctive yellow and red robes emerged from the residence wing, heading for the office block. The oldest family lines had personal Scribes, of course, but as the number of Offspring around the world grew, the Eleven saw the need for governance and established the Crimson Scribes. They, along with numerous lower-tier assistants, liaisons, and support staff, managed the day-to-day oversight of the loosely connected First Borns and Offspring.

As head of the Amyclaean Guard, Petra worked closely with Matthias de Alba, the head of the Crimson Scribes. They'd been an effective team for many years now. On the surface, everything appeared to be business as usual, but all Petra could think about were the cracks in the foundation of her world. They'd been growing for a long time, she realized, surely since the death of Tur'el, the second to the last member of the Eleven, over a century ago.

Mara Layil was an earthquake, shaking everything to the core and threatening all that Petra believed in. Since the beginning, her world had been bound by the Covenant.

Simple rules. Good rules. Clean like the cut of a honed blade.

Offspring were forbidden three things: to kill each other, to bear children together, and to manipulate the will of humans. After the Embodiment, Tamel was the member of the Eleven tasked with enforcing the Covenant. When he broke with the rest of them, justice was left to the Amyclaean Guard.

For the fifteen years Petra had served as its head, her job had been clear—enforce the Covenant to the death. Petra didn't relish killing, but she believed in order and in the legacy of the Blade Guardian. Mara Layil had broken the Covenant when she killed Sinioch Moreau and should, by all rights, die. Yet a month ago, Armaros had commuted the girl's sentence from death to life imprisonment served under Petra's watch.

The question—why?—needled Petra. Every thought she had circled back to that question. *Why spare Mara Layil?*

The only precedent had been the Twins—the children of a forbidden union between two of the Eleven, Javan and Serac. What was a third generation Offspring like Mara Layil compared to the Twins?

A gnat to an eagle. A worm to a cobra.

Sparing an insignificant Offspring did nothing but encourage the rogues who wanted to break from the Covenant altogether. There were too many of them. Petra kneaded her broad shoulders with calloused hands. A longing filled her to see the thrones in the High Council Chamber. She needed to remember what was sacred and precious about her world.

Petra descended from the fortified wall, nodding curtly to the murmured greetings of those she passed on the way to the chamber. No one expected an Amyclaean to answer. The circular room was empty. Flat winter light streamed through a central skylight in the ornate, domed ceiling and fell upon the statue of the White One.

The life-sized angel had been carved of snowy marble. The tips of her wings were so thin that the light glowed through them. As always, Petra had the impression that the White One was about to spread her wings, lift her sad face to the sky, and return to the Creator through the skylight. Petra ran one finger down the cold cheek. *Somehow she manages to look kind too.* Reflexively, Petra wrapped her arms around herself, feeling her uniform tighten across the stumps on her shoulder blades.

Arrayed around the White One were the carved thrones of the Eleven, each engraved with the symbol of its occupant. Former occupants, she should say. Only one remained—silver-haired Armaros, the Time Weaver—the center of Petra's universe. All the meaning she needed, Petra found in Armaros. In her presence, Petra trembled like a child. Her praise was a gift. Everything Petra did, she did for Armaros and for the Covenant.

I do not doubt her!

Armaros had a reason for leniency.

She wanted Mara Layil.

Petra grimaced at the sting of her own failure. When Mara had been sentenced in this very chamber, Armaros had looked at Petra and said, "You will keep her safe." Petra had nodded, then …

I should have bound her.

For weeks, there'd been no sign of the girl; then she'd shown up in Portland only to disappear all over again. *By the Blade, I will get her back.*

Footsteps interrupted Petra's thoughts. She turned to see Shiraz, a member of her Guard and also a monk of *Pro Lapsis Astra*, waiting by the door. By way of greeting, he touched his throat and blade, and she returned the gesture. Shiraz held out his smartphone, indicating that she should look. He was one of the youngest Amyclaeans and a self-proclaimed gearhead. The email was from a monk in the Portland monastery.

Mara Layil had been there! Adrenaline shot through Petra. Shiraz's source had seen the young woman enter the abbot's private sanctuary but had never seen her leave. *That old badger! He'd sent her somewhere. Where?* Petra eyed Shiraz. She had always trusted him, but she didn't know if Abbot Greb's allegiance had turned anti-Covenant. If so, that could mean a shift in loyalty for the entire order of *Pro Lapsis Astra.* She'd have to watch Shiraz more closely.

In the past, the monks had never been closely aligned with the Eleven but had offered succor to any Offspring in need. If they were hiding Mara Layil, Petra was determined to find out. She dismissed Shiraz and headed to the archives.

Armaros wanted the girl kept here at the High Council Compound.

And what Armaros wanted, Petra would make happen.

Or she'd die trying.

Six

MARA

TORU'S ISLAND, NORTHEASTERN JAPAN

We heal quickly ...

Toru's words followed Mara down to the ground level.

She hoped the same was true for her. Otherwise, she was done for.

Mara crossed the broad expanse of bamboo floor, compressing the gash on her side. The stab wound on her shoulder throbbed. Blood was soaking through her shirt, and Mara could feel its warmth seeping into the top of her jeans. Woozy with blood loss, she stumbled for the exit. At the top of the pagoda's main steps, she faltered and fell onto her knees. The scalpel she'd been gripping slipped from her fingers. Red droplets splattered the white museum tag and snowy ground.

"Pick it up."

A man's low voice rumbled over her.

"Who's there?" Her own voice sounded very far away. She squinted into the darkness trying to find the speaker, but turning her head was like pushing through wet concrete. Nothing moved. There was no sound except the far-off whoosh of waves against the rocky shore.

Mara picked up the scalpel. "I'm so cold."

While she'd been inside the fortress, it had begun to snow. Minuscule flakes settled on her leather jacket like a bad case of dandruff. It had been as cold as a witch's tit down in Block Eighteen, but it was bone chilling outside, and a bitter wind had come up.

Mara shivered violently and collapsed into a drift.

"Get up!"

The brusque command roused her briefly. She fumbled for the handrail, vaguely registering a new rush of blood from her side, but her eyes were closing again.

"I'm tired."

"Sleep will kill you."

Who was this jerkwad?

Mara forced herself upright, clutching the railing. She was pretty sure it was carved into an angry-looking sea serpent, but maybe both the voice and the monster were hallucinations. The stairs swam before her eyes, and each step down gave her the sensation of falling. She had to find a boat and get off this wretched island. Blackness crept into her vision, blotting out sight.

"That's right. Keep moving, you little shit."

Mara swung her head blearily from side to side, shuffling along the seawall. "Who's there?" she mumbled through the thick rebellion of her tongue. A wave hit the rocks five feet below. She looked down, stupefied, unable to process wave-water-ocean before crumpling to the ground again.

Lying on her back, Mara tried to force the random firings in her brain into some sort of order, but the snowflakes falling on her face distracted her. They were soft, like feathers, like a kiss. Ethan would touch her like that, one finger tracing the lines of her face.

"That the best you can do?"

Momar?

No.

Momar is dead.

She'd seen him fall. A mushroom cloud of grief filled her. With every beat of her heart, blood surged from Mara's side. The muffled sound of the waves matched the rush of blood—*shush, shush, shush*—whispering *let go, let go, let go.*

"No, you don't." A dark shape slid into view. Her gauntlets pulsed hard against her wrist bones, shocking her out of the stupor. She knew she should fight, but her limbs were rubbery and useless like the tentacles of a beached squid.

"You're bleeding out."

Mara fought to keep her eyes open.

The hooded man crouching beside her had a craggy face and cheeks dark with stubble. He bent forward, blocking the snowfall, his breath warming her face. "You must slow time around those wounds, Mara Layil. Turn the blood."

Don't tell me what to do!

She wanted to bite him. Instead, a guttural moan snuck from her lips, and her head lolled to one side. The icy touch of damp rock on her cheek jolted through her.

"Help ... me." The plea escaped without her permission. How could she *turn* the freaking blood? Her control over time was helter-skelter under the best circumstances. And these were not her best circumstances. What did time have to do with blood anyway?

The man let out a harsh chuckle. "If you don't have the balls to save yourself, then I won't waste my time on you."

Blood and time, time and blood. The red current gushing from her side was the scarlet rush of a broken hourglass, seeping far too fast to clot. It was like watching a river. If she stared at the opposite shore, the flow was continuous. If she fixed her eyes on one section of water, it seemed to freeze.

With every ounce of strength she had left, Mara pointed her attention to the opening on her side. Stop! She focused on the sliced edges of flesh, the chalky hint of bone, the metallic smell. Slowly, so slowly it could have been another hallucination, the fatal flow ebbed, clotted, stopped.

"Yes, that's it. That's better."

The shadow tipped back on his haunches. Snow fell on Mara's face again, sticking in her eyelashes. The man plucked at the edge of her jacket. He lifted the bottom of her t-shirt and peered at the bloody gash now rapidly clotting over. His closeness sent a thudding cascade through her veins. "Precious stuff, this blood of yours. I'd hold onto it better if I were you."

Mara struggled to summon control of her numb body. Finally, she forced her tongue to work.

"Who … who are you?"

He laughed again, this time with real humor in his hard voice.

"Last time we met, you called me an asshole."

What? She'd never felt such a powerful pull from any Offspring before. *Who is he?*

Mara inhaled. Filling her lungs sent pain spiking through the edges of her wounds. She focused on shallow puffs until the pain dulled.

"You're still an asshole," she muttered. "Whoever you are."

"You're the one who broke the Covenant."

Her brittle bravado shattered. "I didn't mean to … to kill him," she whispered. "I had to protect my brother. And the gauntlets …" She lifted her right arm but only had the strength to hold it for a second. "I didn't know they had blades."

"Listen, Mara Layil." He bent close, blocking out the sky once more. "You're a first-rate screwup, but I'm offering you a second chance. You're in no position to argue. If Toru catches you, he will give you to Aeda, and even Armaros, as much as I love her, is determined to have you under house arrest for life. With your pedigree, that could be a very long time. I'll get you off this island, but remember ..." His lips brushed her ear. "You will owe me."

Owe you? Not fucking likely. No matter who you are.

But the words wouldn't form on her frozen lips.

"Oh yes," he continued, threat growling in his throat. "And I will collect."

Seven

ETHAN

SINGH RESIDENCE, SEATTLE, WASHINGTON

When the Amtrak train stopped in Tacoma, Ethan woke up to find Hiroko handing him a white to-go cup. "I bought you a latte."

"Thanks." He burned his tongue on the first slurp and then sipped more carefully.

Hiroko settled back down. A misty drizzle gave the impression they were traveling through dirty white gauze.

"Hey, look at the graffiti over there," said Hiroko, drawing his attention to a freight car on the neighboring tracks. A Day-Glo orange bat perched on a grinning, green skull. Jagged, foot-high letters spelled *SMASH*.

"Cool bat," Ethan said.

"Look at that symbol." In the lower right corner, like a signature, was a stylized *W* in black paint surrounded by a circle. "An Offspring painted it."

"You know that because ...?"

"That's Tur'el's symbol," Hiroko explained. "Only one of his descendants would leave that mark. The families of the Eleven are, shall we say, very protective of their bloodlines. Kind of like the British royal family or something. Anyway, there's a symbol for each of the Eleven. The White One had a symbol too, of course, but she didn't leave any descendants. If you know what you're looking for, you'll see the signs."

"What happened to the White One?"

"Ah ..." Hiroko sighed, the corners of her lips drooping. "It's a sad story."

Ethan sipped his coffee. "We're not in Seattle yet. Hit me."

"Well, the old stories say the pain of embodiment was terrible. The Eleven and the White One ended up pinned to the ground by horrible metal wings. She couldn't stand to see her brothers and sisters suffer so she had them build a great fire, and she pulled herself into it. As she burned, the relium wings melted. That's what her brother Tamel used to forge the Blade of the Sacrifice. That's how he freed them. He's called the Blade Guardian because of it."

Ethan grimaced at her, his stomach churning at the grotesque story. "She burned herself alive so he could make a sword and chop everybody else's wings off?"

"Pretty much," said Hiroko.

"That is gnarly."

"Yeah, and that's why the White One has no descendants. I'll show you her symbol."

Hiroko pulled a notebook and pen from her bag and drew a circle with a stylized X in the middle and something like a flaming comet heading straight for it.

"What about the others?" Ethan asked.

Hiroko kept sketching. "This is the one we saw in the gang graffiti, Tur'el's symbol. This one belongs to Armaros. She's the only one of the Eleven still alive. I'm descended from Otohime. This is hers. Azza, Serac, Javan, Tamel ..." Hiroko named them as she drew. Each encircled symbol reminded Ethan of Japanese kanji. Exactly the sort of thing that someone might choose for a tattoo. "... Agabos, Minaios, Shen, and Hrminir."

"That last one's a mouthful," said Ethan.

Hiroko laughed and then turned serious. "Speaking of mouths, here's another symbol you ought to know if you're hell-bent on sticking with Mara." She drew a wide-open eye, but instead of a pupil, it held a mouth.

"That's creepy."

"This symbolizes the Hidden Eye. They're humans who hate Offspring—think we're abominations." Hiroko wrapped her arms tightly around herself. "They hunt us down and kill us."

"For real?" he asked, wondering if there was anyone *not* trying to get Mara.

Hiroko nodded. "They say we're perversions."

No wonder Mara's kind kept a low profile.

In Seattle, Hiroko hailed a cab, and as they drove toward the neighborhood called Queen Anne, Ethan scanned walls, billboards, and signs, but he only saw one—Tamel's symbol worked into the logo of a high-end knife shop.

Hiroko shifted in her seat so she could look him in the face. "You didn't answer my question back at the monastery."

"Uh … question?"

"Why are you still in this?"

"You mean with Mara?" he asked, feeling a warm rush up his neck. He ducked his head and pretended to look out the window.

"She's in so much trouble," Hiroko said.

Ethan flipped the question back at her. "Why are *you* in it?"

Hiroko fiddled with the strap of the bag. "I met Mara right after she got out of Cascadia. Momar had brought her to Abbot Greb to learn about being Offspring. I only Turned a few years ago myself," she explained. "It started right after my twenty-second birthday, and it was horrible. I thought I was going crazy but my mom was right there, explaining everything and guiding me."

Parents parenting? I don't know anything about that. Ethan's dad had walked out when he was a baby, and his mom had a beer bottle fused to her hand.

"When I saw Mara, my heart went out to her. I mean, there she is, freaked out, quills bristling. Abbot Greb, who *is* a nice man, yells at her. So she bolts. And I ... I followed. I didn't want her to be alone, you know."

Yeah, I do.

"You met her in Cascadia, right?" Hiroko looked at him expectantly.

"That I did. First week of lockup. Matching orange jumpsuits. Same group therapy."

During his first session, Mara, with two black eyes and a swollen nose, had been flanked by empty chairs. Ever since Capri, one of the other inmates, had bashed her face in with a pot, the rest were giving Mara a wide berth. Only crazy people messed with Capri.

I must've been one sick son of a bitch.

Even that first day when she'd looked like crap and had cussed out everyone in the room, he'd liked her. She wasn't sucking up to Mr. Mandel, the counselor, or getting all woo-woo-touchy-feely with the therapy crap. She didn't *share,* either—thank god—but somehow managed to cut through everybody else's bullshit.

"Why was she in there?" Hiroko asked.

"Mara's story in group was that she'd hooked up with a sloppy drunk from Reed College who had a stash of weed in a stolen car." Ethan shook his head, a perplexed look on his face. "Doesn't add up, though. She got twelve months for that. What I did was worse, and I only got six."

"Will you tell me what you did?" Hiroko's face made it clear he could say no if he wanted to.

Ethan stared out the window. "I was a serious hacker. Part of a group called YouKnowMe."

Hiroko quirked an eyebrow.

"It was our jab at Anonymous," Ethan explained. "Anyway, we took on a challenge from this guy in Vegas to crack the traffic control systems in a major city and redirect traffic—actual cars, you know—to create a pattern that could be picked up by satellite. Best image wins. When I froze traffic in the final pattern, it gridlocked the city."

"I remember that," said Hiroko, shaking her head in disbelief. "The news was going crazy, blaming it on crossed wires or something. You shut down Portland."

Ethan pushed his hair off his forehead but hit the bruise, winced, and pulled away. "I know. There was an ambulance trying to get to the hospital. The driver decided his only option was to turn the wrong way down a one-way. He hit a woman crossing the street."

"Oh no."

"And she died."

Hiroko leaned heavily against her seat.

"I know. I turned myself in as soon as I heard." Six months wasn't enough to pay for a woman's life, but it was start.

"You couldn't have known that would happen."

Ethan waved her silent. *No sympathy.* Mara hadn't handed him any. When he'd told his story to the group, Mara had said, "You're bat-shit crazy to have turned yourself in," and they'd nearly come to blows over it.

From the moment he met her, Mara Layil was picking his scabs.

They rode in silence for a few blocks.

"I don't know anything normal about Mara," Hiroko said.

"Well," Ethan offered, "she likes old vinyl and Enfield motorcycles."

And she has a wicked smile.

The cab pulled to the curb. The twin rooflines of a massive brick mansion rose like pyramids over the thick, concealing hedges. Anyone standing at the gables would have a mind-blowing view of the bay. It was about as far as you could get from the rundown, two-bedroom apartment he and his mom shared in North Portland.

"I'm guessing a Scribe gets paid more than your run-of-the-mill admin," he said, jerking a thumb toward the house. "I'd be one too, if this is where you get to live."

Hiroko gave him a funny look.

"What?" Ethan demanded.

"Her Scribe is supposed to live with her," said Hiroko.

"Live with her?" Ethan didn't like the sound of that. "So you brought me here to pick up some guy who's gonna go live with Mara?"

"Well, not like that," said Hiroko. "Come on."

Ethan followed Hiroko up a narrow path of paving stones that wound through the fanciest gardens he'd ever seen. Even in the dead of winter, waxy white flowers shone against shiny green leaves. The huge front door dwarfed Hiroko. Peering through floor-to-ceiling windows, Ethan could make out white marble everywhere and mirrors in brushed metal frames.

Hiroko straightened her green coat, patted her already-flat bob, and rang the bell.

A low resonant gong sounded through the house.

Just as Hiroko was about to ring again, they heard a man's voice through the door. "Get that, will you, Dalmeet!"

"I'm not your butler!" screeched the reply.

Ethan caught a glimpse of a slender figure darting through a hallway. The sounds of a shoving match filtered through the thick door.

"You've got to be kidding me," Hiroko muttered. She rang the bell again and then pounded on the door.

A huge, barrel-chested Sikh flung it open. Crisp, carved muscles stood out from his expensive t-shirt and more expensive jeans. He was in his midtwenties and wore a turban and ritual blade.

Damn, he looks just like Momar!

Behind him, a younger man pulled himself to his feet and brushed off his perfectly ironed khakis. Clearly, the two were brothers, but the younger was thin and fine-featured where the older was linebacker material.

The larger man's eyes roved over Hiroko. "What have we got here? Pole dancing to go?"

Mara would punch him for that.

Hiroko kept her cool. "I am Hiroko Mori. This is Ethan Skylar. Are you Taan Singh?"

"Absolutely."

"We knew your uncle Momar," said Hiroko. "I'm really sorry for your loss."

The man shrugged. "What do you want?"

"We come on behalf of the Layils."

At the name, the younger brother stepped closer to the door.

"You have no business here," Taan said, his mouth twisting in a sneer. "The Singhs are Unbound. Don't waste my time."

Ethan couldn't believe that Hiroko wanted *this* guy to *live* with Mara.

"Let's talk inside," said Hiroko. It wasn't a question.

Taan moved to shut the door on them, but his brother slipped past him. "Come in," he said, taking an elbow in the ribs from his brother. "I'm Dalmeet Singh. Momar's other nephew."

"Is Mara still alive?" asked Dalmeet, leading them into a living room big enough to hold Ethan's entire apartment and gesturing for them to sit.

"Of course, she's alive," Ethan snapped, pissed that anyone would even suggest the other possibility.

"For now," Taan drawled, draping himself over the couch like a lion. "You here to talk about her funeral arrangements?"

Funeral arrangements? What a dick!

Ethan wanted to rip the bored expression from the guy's face. Instead, he forced himself to breathe deeply. *2, 3, 5, 7.* He cycled through a sequence of prime numbers. *11, 13, 17, 19.* Losing it wouldn't help Mara.

"No one's ever eluded the Amyclaean Guard for this long," said Dalmeet. "It's only a matter of time before they find her."

Not if I can help it.

"I've heard that Aeda wants revenge." The prospect seemed to amuse Taan as if Mara's troubles were a reality TV show he could watch from his cushy living room. "An eighteen-year-old Offspring with zero control over her abilities against Aeda Moreau. That's bad shit."

"Which is exactly why she needs a Scribe," said Hiroko, staring the man down.

"And that's exactly why I'm saying no," Taan replied. "I'm not Uncle Momar, and I'm not going to die for that girl."

"Succession, Taan," said Hiroko, "that's what I'm talking about. You're next in line."

Dalmeet was the textbook definition of clean-cut. He hardly looked old enough to shave, but as Hiroko spoke, Ethan saw a hungry look in his eyes.

Taan has everything, and Dalmeet wants it.

"Don't threaten me about succession," said Taan, his voice rising. "I'll repeat this slowly so you can get it, lady. The Singhs are NOT bound."

"What's he talking about?" Ethan asked Hiroko, feeling Dalmeet's attention turn on him.

"Who is this?" Dalmeet said, pointing at Ethan. "He's not from a Scribe line. He's not Offspring, so you shouldn't tell him anything. We shouldn't even be talking in front of him. It's against protocol."

Hiroko hesitated for an instant.

"Don't you think it's a little late for the *I'd tell you but I'd have to kill you* routine?" asked Ethan.

"Oh, go ahead," Taan teased. "Let's break all the rules. Dalmeet's just being fussy."

"Scribe families and the Offspring of the Eleven have always had a special relationship," Hiroko began.

Taan burst out laughing. "Special? Oh, that is rich!"

Ethan resisted the urge to pick up the iron floor lamp next to him and bludgeon the idiot.

Hiroko ignored him and went on. "Most Scribe families are bound to their Offspring family by a blood curse. You serve or you die."

"Except the Singhs," Dalmeet broke in. "We serve by choice."

"Damn right, we do," said Taan, "and you can take all this crap about succession and shove it up your ass. The Layil girl doesn't have a chance."

"Your father disappeared searching for the Blade Guardian. Your uncle spent his life protecting the Layil family. Does that mean nothing to you, Taan?"

"I don't have a death wish."

"She needs your help!"

"Mara is damaged goods," said Taan.

Not as damaged as you're gonna be. Ethan's hands clenched into fists.

"Barely even Turned, and she's broken the Covenant," Taan continued. "First violation in hundreds of years. Why would I touch that?"

Hiroko gaped at him.

"Besides," Taan continued, "I haven't seen the Record since I was ten years old. Maybe Momar went senile and lost it. Without the Record, I couldn't help her even if I wanted to."

Ethan stood and pulled Hiroko up after him. "This is pointless."

Hiroko clutched her bag to her side, examining Taan for some scrap of decency.

You'll wear your eyeballs out.

Taan lounged back in the couch and gave Hiroko the once-over. "But you're kind of cute, little lady. Now if it was you needing a Scribe, that would be a different story."

Hiroko scowled.

"Taan, you're a prick," said Dalmeet primly.

Ethan tugged Hiroko's arm again. Taan was a first-class bonehead and the younger one was nothing more than an insecure, second-rate second brother. Neither had a damn thing to offer someone like Mara.

And they'd better not move in with her, either!

EIGHT

DALMEET

SINGH RESIDENCE, SEATTLE, WASHINGTON

Dalmeet couldn't tear his eyes away from the messenger bag. Hiroko hadn't taken her hands off it for a second. The way she clutched it, you'd think it held a winning lottery ticket, a newborn baby, or the Record of the Layils! *Jackpot indeed!* The Record was here, within his grasp. Momar hadn't lost it, he'd kept it from Taan.

Never in a million years did Dalmeet think he'd get the chance to be a Scribe. Of course, he'd hoped and prayed, but only a fool would actually think it possible. He was fourth in line after Uncle Momar, his father, and Taan.

Always Taan in the way—taller, stronger, revered. *But never smarter. The fool turned down Hiroko's offer! Now's my chance.* The door slammed shut behind Hiroko and Ethan. They were leaving and taking the Record with them.

Not if I can help it!

Hiroko and Ethan were about to turn the corner by the time Dalmeet caught them.

"What do you want, pretty boy?" Ethan asked, turning so quickly that Dalmeet nearly fell on him. That wouldn't have been a bad thing. Ethan was handsome with that utterly unique combination of features that some mixed-race people had.

Recovering his balance and straightening his black turban, Dalmeet blurted, "*I'll* be her Scribe."

They stared at him.

"I'll be her Scribe," he repeated. "I'd be honored."

"But Taan is the rightful successor," said Hiroko. "He's been trained."

Yeah, right. Dalmeet bit back the pissy comment that rose to his lips. *Agree with her. Agree to anything.*

"True," he said, nodding genteelly, "but you have no idea what a terrible student he was. Good at all things physical, but I'd bet you ten bucks he can't even name the Eleven." Dalmeet stepped closer. "I can be her Scribe. I know the language of the Record."

"What's he talking about?" Ethan asked Hiroko.

Dalmeet caught himself in the middle of an eye roll. Pissing Ethan off wouldn't help his cause. "The Record is the Layil family history. It contains the collected experience and knowledge of all the Scribes who have ever served them. Some of those secrets and that knowledge was shared with the Keeper of the Lines and added to the Book of Tracings, but that was long ago," he explained.

"So if we've got that," said Ethan, "why do we need you?"

Dalmeet willed his voice to stay steady. "The Record is written in a cipher devised by the Layils' first Scribe—my Singh ancestor. No one but a Singh can read it. So you do need me, you see?"

Ethan's face remained expressionless, but Dalmeet thought he could detect a spark of interest in his dark eyes. *His beautiful dark eyes.* Hiroko moved closer to Ethan. Neither seemed likely to let him get near Mara Layil.

But they're more vulnerable than they look.

The healer was young—twenty-four or twenty-five at most—that meant the more experienced Offspring had shied away from the Layil problem. Ethan Skylar's jeans were cheap and frayed at the bottom. The skateboard tucked under his arm was long overdue for new wheels. Probably he'd grown up poor and had a worldview too narrow to understand how dire things were for Mara.

Dalmeet doubted she even knew they were here, negotiating something that could affect her forever. *And could affect me forever too.* Dalmeet's heart raced in his chest. He was so close!

Finally, Hiroko spoke. "How could I possibly trust you with the Record? You've not been vetted."

"You trust him." Dalmeet inclined his head toward Ethan. "He's not even Offspring. I'm guessing he got roped into all of this by accident and is just along for the ride." The look on Hiroko's face proved his point, and Dalmeet clasped his long, fine fingers, waiting.

"Look at him," Ethan said to Hiroko, "Mara'd have to babysit this guy."

The door of opportunity was closing.

"I've trained in *gatka* since age five. I can fight barehanded and with a kirpan." They didn't need to know that Taan handed him his ass nearly every time they sparred. "I'm a decent shot too," Dalmeet continued, hoping Ethan wouldn't call his bluff by picking a fight.

Hiroko turned her back on Dalmeet and pulled Ethan toward her. "You can't understand how many secrets there are among our kind," she whispered. "Only a Singh could know enough to help her."

Dalmeet watched the gray water of the bay, holding his breath.

"But how do you know he even knows anything?" Ethan whispered back.

I know enough to help her, especially once I have the Record. That part was no bluff. Dalmeet struggled to keep his face neutral. Out of the corner of his eye, he saw Hiroko's shoulders twitch in a helpless shrug. She was his, he was sure.

"I don't know," said Ethan. "I don't like it. You saw that house. He's spoiled, probably wears silk underwear. Definitely not Mara material."

Damn it, they're cotton. Heat rushed up Dalmeet's neck and cheeks, but he couldn't afford to lose his cool now. He had to get Ethan on his side. The Singhs had served the Layils for centuries in all kinds of underclothes. He was a Singh! History was his pedigree. How could he make an outsider understand the import of that?

The rain resumed, cold on his face. At any moment Hiroko and Ethan could leave. What would Dalmeet have then? Taan's constant ridicule, a fast track to law school, and a pathetically normal future.

Death was preferable.

They were starting to walk away. Dalmeet had to say the right thing, right now! He had to put everything on the line or be barred from the world of the Eleven forever. He would swear by anything, do anything ...

"I'll renew the Binding," he called after them.

"What?" Hiroko turned back and grabbed Dalmeet by both arms. "By the Blade, do you understand what you are saying?"

A tremor rushed through him. *The Cursed Bond.* Of all the Scribe families, only the Singhs had been freed of the ancient ties. Hadn't his father scorned the other Scribes who labored under the death curse of the Binding?

But the free status of the Singhs had not saved his father from the Hidden Eye or Uncle Momar from Aeda's thugs. Heavy, sodden grief sliced through Dalmeet. Only his uncle had seen the possibility of death claiming so many Singhs. Only his uncle believed that Dalmeet should be trained. Uncle Momar would want him to help Mara, even if it meant the Binding.

"I do." He forced himself to sound casual, though terror raced through him. Even if he survived the Binding, those hunting Mara would be after him as well, but she was his only chance to be more than a second brother.

More than a nobody.

Dalmeet shook off Hiroko's hands and looked straight at Ethan. "I will be Bound."

All CPUs ran on overdrive behind those eyes, and Dalmeet realized that he'd underestimated Ethan. He was more than a muscled hottie. He was analyzing Dalmeet, calculating his benefit to Mara. Dalmeet stood still under the assessment. How far would Dalmeet go for a chance at the life he'd always wanted? *Pretty damn far.*

Finally, Ethan's lip twitched upward. He made six-shooters with his hands and pointed them at Dalmeet—*boom, boom.* "You know, Mr. Straight-and-Narrow, we're a bunch of outlaws."

"So how do I trust you?"

Ethan shrugged. "You don't."

"I'll tell you what," said Dalmeet, his eyes boring into Ethan's, "let's share the risk. I'll do the Binding if you do it too."

Ethan's eyes probed his. Finally, he extended his right hand. "All right."

Hiroko intercepted the handshake. "Stop it, Ethan. I know you want to help Mara, but you don't know what you're doing.

The Binding will change you. It was only for Scribes, and no one even does it anymore. It's too dangerous."

"You said he was human like me."

"Yes, but only death can break the Cursed Bond."

"I don't care," Ethan snapped, breaking free of Hiroko's grasp. "You said she needs a Scribe. This will get her one. And a spare too."

Dalmeet saw a yearning in Ethan's face that matched his own. Excitement swept through him like a runaway train. Ethan brushed past Hiroko and again extended his hand toward Dalmeet. "We do it together." His voice was husky and hard.

The heat and crackle of a lit sparkler flared in Dalmeet.

He tightened his grip on Ethan's hand.

This was more, so much more, than he'd ever hoped for.

Or ever feared.

NINE

MARA

MORIOKA, NORTHEASTERN JAPAN

Snow filtered down from the charcoal-clouded sky. Mara sprawled at the end of an alley between two rows of warehouses. When the flakes cleared the rooftops, they skittered and flicked from side to side, caught in random updrafts of warm air escaping cracks under loading dock doors.

She reached toward consciousness.

How had she gotten here?

Her stomach growled.

I'd kill for noodles.

A low rumble of laughter rolled through the alley. It was enough to jack up her adrenaline and wake her fully. Mara hauled herself into a sitting position. Acid-hot fire jabbing through her wounds brought back her chummy tête-à-tête with Toru. Mara scanned the narrow alley.

Who's laughing?

Everything was deserted. It was the dead of night in an industrial district.

Behind the whisper of snow, silence expanded like shadow.

Her bones ached with cold. Her wounds burned. Her thoughts were fuzzy and confused. Another minute passed. She noticed the subdued reverberation of traffic on a far-off highway. It reminded her of waves and the cloaked figure who had talked to her on the island.

They had talked, right? Maybe he'd drugged her? Again, quiet laughter filled the alley.

"What is so damn funny?!"

The laughter stopped.

Mara tipped her head back and peered into the falling snow. "Great," she muttered. "I'm the butt of some cosmic joke."

She rubbed her eyes. Her brain was ultrascrambled. Whether she should chalk it up to blood loss, starvation, hypo-freaking-thermia, or good old paranoia, she didn't know. Did she really have a dark-robed stalker? Or was she totally losing her mind? Mara flashed her middle finger in the air for good measure. The mystery man could suck dog balls.

I'm so tired.

Death by cold was supposed to be painless.

Don't be a baby. Make a plan.

Warmth, food, sleep.

That's what she needed—and she needed them in exactly that order. Bonus points if she could take off her boots and make sure there were still toes attached to her feet. Ignoring the pain in her shoulder, Mara reached an exploratory hand inside her jacket to check the more serious wound. Her t-shirt was stiff with dried blood. She pulled it up, wincing as the icy air displaced the tiny bit of warmth clinging to her skin. Toru had carved a five-inch slice that started on her right side, an inch below her bra, and traversed her belly almost to her navel. *So much for bikinis this summer.* As if the stumps on her shoulder blades weren't bad enough.

On the upside, the edges of the wound had already started to heal. A thin seam of delicate pink tissue, so new it seemed ready to melt, showed the path of a future scar. Rapid healing was one advantage to being Offspring, though she was pretty sure that if she weren't Offspring, she wouldn't get her ass kicked so often.

Moving slowly to avoid dislodging the fragile skin, Mara rose to her feet. The effort left her panting and lightheaded. *Warmth, food, sleep. And don't die.* It was a good plan. Mara patted her forearms to reassure herself that the gauntlets were in place and fiddled with the strap of her backpack until it was secured away from her shoulder wound.

"Okay. Execute."

The laughter—more felt than heard—returned and with it the thrum of her blood. From the rhythm in her veins, Mara was sure that the Offspring, or whoever it was, was physically far away. How he sent his humor into her head like this, she didn't know, but she got the joke.

"Execute the plan," she clarified. "Me, I prefer to live."

As soon as she was moving, the presence of her invisible stand-up comic faded away completely. She was alone. Mara took unsteady steps to the end of the alley, which opened onto an equally empty avenue. Widely spaced streetlights illuminated the snow-filled air at each corner, but otherwise, no light came from the warehouses. Mara took corners at random, not bothering to keep a mental map of her route. Since she had no clue where she was, it hardly seemed to matter.

With each step, she repeated her mantra. *Warmth, food, sleep. Warmth, food, sleep.* Dark block after dark block, she walked, no longer bothering to brush snow from her face, never stopping, knowing that if she did, a restart would be impossible.

Warmth, food, sleep.

Half-asleep, Mara turned a corner and walked straight into a square of golden light glittering through a steamy cloud of noodle-scented air. She stopped, wobbling on her ice-cube feet. Surely this was a hallucination. Nobody cooked noodles in the dead of night in a deserted neighborhood, did they?

But there was a shop door, propped open a few inches. The rich smell of broth and udon enveloped her. Mara's stomach roared, and she strode inside—*caution be damned.* As she entered, Mara caught a glimpse of herself reflected in the steamy windows. She had the bloodstained, waif-zombie look nailed. She prayed that the woman behind the counter would serve her because Mara doubted she had the strength to actually kill for the noodles.

The plump noodle lady was so short she could hardly see over the edge of her gigantic wok as she gave the noodles in the pan a final swirl before tipping them out on a plate. The woman stared vacantly over Mara's left shoulder as she stuck a pair of chopsticks into the center of the heap of noodles and handed the plate straight to Mara. Was she sleepwalking? Sleep-cooking? The noodle lady didn't seem all there.

Who cares! The noodle shop was sauna warm, and Mara was starving. She eased her backpack onto her lap and sat gingerly on the stool. Garlic-scented steam swirled over her frozen cheeks as she crammed a huge twist of hot noodles into her mouth. They hung from her lips like worms, the most delicious worms she'd ever eaten.

Smiling and nodding, the noodle lady washed and dried the wok. She walked to the front of the shop and turned off the neon signs. She locked the door carefully, and then with a soothing blur of Japanese and much flapping of hands, the woman told Mara to finish eating and proceed to the back of the shop.

Mara stared at her, nodding stupidly, still shoveling noodles into her mouth. The dumpling of a woman smiled a sweet, vacant smile and disappeared through the blue and white cloth hanging at the back of the kitchen. Mara scanned the shop, looking for some sign of her mystery man. Maybe he had something to do with all of this?

That's not reassuring.

Still, every instinct in her body said she was safe, so within minutes, Mara had wiped down her own plate and ducked through the rough fabric curtain. The room behind the kitchen was small, hardly the size of her closet back home, which she had to admit, was a really big closet. One side of the room held a dresser, a shelf with photos, and two cushions for sitting. Two narrow futons nestled on the other wall. The noodle lady was already asleep in one of them, snoring gently. Through a cracked door, Mara glimpsed the bathroom. Not part of her original plan, but now that she saw the facilities, she realized it had been a long time since she'd gone. *New and improved plan—warmth, food, pee, sleep.*

That done, Mara unlaced her boots, leaving them on the tatami mat next to the noodle lady's pink sandals, and peeled off her sodden socks.

She had toes. Thank the freaking gods she had toes!

Warmth—check; food—check; pee—check. Now to sleep.

Mara eased herself onto the futon and rubbed life back into her feet. She took off her leather jacket and blood-soaked jeans and pulled the blankets up over her shivering legs. She unlocked the gauntlets and zipped them into her backpack. *I'm sorry, Momar. I know you'd want me to leave them on.* Constant readiness had been the drill since she was very young, but her arms ached. *Don't get your turban in a wad. The noodle lady's all right. Anyway, I'm too tired to fight.*

Mara curled into a tight ball around the backpack and burrowed into the blankets.

I wish you were here.

And what she meant was that she wished she were a little girl again.

Momar would tuck her in, smelling of oranges and clove. He'd call her his favorite tornado. All would be right with the world.

It had been a long time since she'd felt like that.

Ten

PETRA

HIGH COUNCIL COMPOUND OF THE ELEVEN, ISTANBUL, TURKEY

Petra arrived at the knife range an hour before she expected the other members of the Amyclaean Guard to gather and receive their assignments for the week. She was unsettled. Maybe combat practice would clear her mind.

Before taking up the first practice blade, she bowed her head, caressed the piercing at her throat and the hilt at her waist, and silently intoned the Blessing of the Blade Guardian.

As you wielded the Blade of the Sacrifice, may my knife fly true.

As you enforced the Covenant, may my heart beat true.

As it was in the Before, may all Offspring live true.

She straightened the row of practice blades. Made of Damascus steel, each replicated in length and heft of the relium blades carried by the Guard. They didn't pull tight to the bearer's hand the way true blades did, but practicing with the real thing was unthinkable. Relium was the rarest element on Earth.

After Tamel, the Blade Guardian, had forged the Blade of the Sacrifice from the White One's wings, he made relics for the rest of the Eleven out of their own wings—armor for Azza, a crown for Armaros, a set of scalpels for Otohime. The resonance of each relic was attuned to the blood-based relium of its bearer. Thus, in the hands of Agabos, the spearheads forged from his own relium flew truer and more lethally than if thrown by anyone else. Petra touched her own knife again. She wielded it like part of her own body because of decades of training and because both she and the knife were of Hrminir's line. Siblings of a sort.

In the millennia before the birth of the Twins, Tamel had sometimes, at the request of his brothers and sisters, given the relics new forms for only he, among the Eleven, could reforge relium. When he broke with the others, his last act had been to take a relic from each and forge a knife. These were the blades now born by the Guard. One member from each family line. Eleven weapons of justice. The twelfth—the one carried now by Shiraz, who represented *Pro Lapsis Astra* on the Guard, combined the metals of all the other lines.

The knives would outlast their current bearers and hold their current forms. With the Blade Guardian gone, no relic would be reforged again.

Air hissed as Petra's first throw hurtled toward the target. *Damn.* It hit nearly a half an inch from the center of the mark. *So much uncertainty. So much distraction.* Petra strove for an ordered mind and a steady hand. *Feel the blade—focus.* For the rest of the hour, she practiced until every blade hit dead on.

As the Guard gathered, Petra used several practice knives to pin a world map to the target board. The eleven men and women she'd trained clustered around it. She wasted no words, and they asked few questions. Each utterance was painful because of the piercings in their necks so they'd learned to read each other in silence as much as possible.

Petra jabbed one finger at their current location in Turkey.

"Layil," she rasped. "Lost."

Several pairs of eyes darted toward Semo, a huge Samoan with a romantic streak, and Liesl, the woman currently breaking his heart. They'd failed to catch Mara on the streets of Istanbul. It didn't do to have dissent—or sex, for that matter—among the Guard. Incompetence had no place here. Petra would separate them on this mission; she hoped that would reduce the chance they'd botch anything else.

"*Pro Lapsis Astra* helps her." Sweat beaded along Petra's forehead with the strain of speech. She pointed to the locations of all known *Pro Lapsis Astra* monasteries. If Abbot Greb was helping Mara Layil, then perhaps he had sent her to one of the other outposts.

Wordlessly, Petra divided her Guard, sending her three most reliable back to the United States to stake out Los Angeles, New York, and Portland. Two, including Liesl, would go to India, and three were dispatched to the monasteries in Europe. She'd go to Japan with Robaire and the other lovebird. Shiraz would stay here until she was confident that he would put the mission of the Amyclaeans above his vows to the monastic order.

"Girl ... is ... trouble." Robaire forced out the words, a hint of his French African accent still detectable through his constricted vocal cords.

The table on which the practice blades lay ready was engraved with the symbols of the Eleven and the White One. Lightly, Petra tapped Armaros's symbol—a circle containing a slash mark like a thin feather and a swirling, interrupted figure eight.

Immediate understanding flashed across his dark face. *We serve Armaros.*

But Petra knew that, like her, all members of the Guard were struggling to understand the logic behind Armaros's actions. Death was paid for with death. That was the way of it and had been for over five thousand years.

She looked at Robaire, tapped the symbol again, and swept one hand down in a final, quelling motion. *We follow orders.* A hint of disdain flashed through his eyes, but he gave a curt nod.

Petra dismissed them, catching the tortured look that passed between Semo and Liesl. She retrieved her map and turned back in time to see Robaire stop near Semo. There was something furtive in the look that passed between the two men. It raised her hackles, which was not something to ignore.

They walked shoulder to shoulder toward the main doors. *What are you up to?* Petra turned toward the women's sauna, but once she was out of sight, she raced into an alcove from where she could see the main doors to the practice grounds. Seconds later, Robaire and Semo exited, walking swiftly. They turned right toward the kitchens rather than toward the chambers of the Guard. Petra shadowed them carefully. The smell of fresh bread and the heat of the ovens filled the passageway.

Fifty feet past the kitchens, the corridor dead-ended at the freight dock where trucks delivered produce and supplies to the compound. A monitor mounted near the metal garage door to the docks displayed live footage from the security cameras outside. As Semo and Robaire peered at it, Petra slipped toward them and into the narrow slot between the trash compactor and the huge recycling bin.

This is crazy. These are my men.

Her men continued to stand before the monitor like statues, backs to her, hands identically clasped. She'd trained these men. Fought with them. In the Guard, they were as one, weren't they?

Movement flickered on the monitor. On the other side of the closed garage door, a delivery truck backed into position at the loading dock. Robaire and Semo continued to watch the monitor without opening the door. The driver climbed down from the cab and circled into sight.

When he opened the back of the truck, Petra expected it to be full of boxes, maybe bags of flour or rolls of toilet paper. She bit back a gasp. The last thing she expected was to see Matthias de Alba, the aging head of the Crimson Scribes, standing in the empty cargo space of the vehicle.

He lives here. Why is he skulking in the back of a truck?

But clearly, her men expected him.

Robaire hit the red button above the monitor and with a screech, the garage door rattled open. Petra pulled her head back into the rotten-smelling alcove. She could see half of Matthias's face and the backs of Semo and Robaire. They skipped all pleasantries.

"Were you followed?" Matthias asked in a low voice.

Although she was only a few feet away, Petra strained to make out his words.

Robaire shook his head.

It was clear to Petra that they'd picked their meeting place carefully. The security camera ensured they'd know of an approach from outside and the hubbub from the kitchens covered all conversation.

"Armaros pardoned the girl," Matthias said urgently.

Semo nodded, touching himself on the chest. *I know.*

"This undermines all of us—Amyclaeans and Crimson Scribes alike," said Matthias. "We uphold the Covenant. We guide the Offspring of the Eleven. We must remain strong."

Petra knew there was discord. For some Offspring family lines, allegiance to Armaros and the Covenant chafed. They resented the constraints it placed on their exercise of power out in the world.

"The rogue families will see Armaros's decision to pardon the girl as a sign that she is weakening," Matthias continued.

Impossible!

"If we are to avert a civil war, we must move forward with the plan of succession immediately."

Matthias leaned closer to Semo and Robaire. Petra pressed her cheek against the sticky side of the recycling bin, pushing forward as far as she dared. She half heard, half read his lips.

"We may need to urge things forward."

Her men nodded, complicit.

Realization hit her hard.

By the Blade, did they mean ...?

"The Covenant must be upheld, even if that means removing Armaros." Matthias's eyes burned. The glint in them scared her.

And Petra Adler was not easily scared.

Eleven

ETHAN

MONASTERY OF PRO LAPSIS ASTRA, PORTLAND, OREGON

It was close to midnight by the time Ethan, Dalmeet, and Hiroko returned to the monastery, but there was no talk of sleep. Ethan was not about to give Dalmeet a chance to back out. Or give himself one, for that matter.

Hiroko's studio apartment in the monastery was a mash-up of manga and medical school. Ethan checked out the life-size, cutaway models of a heart, brain, and the nasal-sinus system perched on stacks of graphic novels. Jars of dried herbs stood beside a set of mouthwateringly perfect plastic sushi.

"Wait for me," said Hiroko. "I'm going to get Abbot Greb."

Dalmeet sat stiffly on one of two straight-backed chairs at a round table, staring at Hiroko's messenger bag and incessantly pinching the crease of his khakis.

Ethan leaned against a bookshelf. "You can relax. It's not going anywhere."

"The Record is an incredibly important document," Dalmeet spluttered. "The collected knowledge of generations."

"How old are you? Sixteen?" Ethan growled. He pulled out the other chair, flipped it backward, and straddled it. "Kinda young for the knowledge of generations, aren't you?"

"I'm almost eighteen. You can't be any older."

Ethan shrugged. "Nineteen."

"You go to college?" Dalmeet asked.

"Nah. What about you? Must suck to still be in high school."

"I graduated early from Seattle Prep," said Dalmeet.

"Aren't you special?" Ethan knew he was being a dick, but everything about this Singh guy was getting under his skin. The fancy house and perfect clothes. The know-it-all attitude. That he might be living with Mara.

"I was an advanced student."

Ethan stood up so quickly he knocked his chair over. "What's that supposed to mean?"

"Nothing." Dalmeet waved a hand dismissively. "Forget about it."

Ethan picked up the chair and tried to master his irritation by pretending to study the books on Hiroko's shelves.

I'm nervous, that's all.

In spite of his bluster, Ethan was rattled about the Binding.

Hiroko said it would change us. How?

After a minute of silence, Dalmeet cleared his throat. "So you're from Portland?"

An olive branch.

"Born and raised," Ethan muttered.

More silence. Ethan wasn't in the mood to make it easy.

Dalmeet tried again. "Sisters? Brothers? Maybe one as delightful as mine?"

Ethan chuckled before he could help himself. Maybe Dalmeet wasn't quite as snobbed-up as he thought. "Just me and my mom." He rolled his shoulders, trying to shed the feeling he had something to prove. *She more than makes up for your brother.*

"Dad in the picture?" Dalmeet asked.

"He's in Alabama somewhere. He's hard to keep track of. Moves a lot."

"How long has he been gone?"

Ethan considered him. Dalmeet didn't have a trace of snark on his face, and Ethan remembered Hiroko saying that his dad had been killed looking for the Blade Guardian. "Forever. My dad found Portland too white-bread and fatherhood too time consuming." *And Mom's too hard to live with.*

"So he's Black and your mom's white?"

"He was sober. She's a drunk."

Shit! Did I just say that? The connection he'd felt building between him and Dalmeet evaporated. Why did this conversation expose his every shortcoming?

"New topic," snapped Ethan, smacking his hand against the wall harder than he meant to. Dalmeet flinched, his chair legs skidding backward with a screech.

Where the hell is Hiroko?

Ethan crossed his arms over his chest, glaring at Dalmeet.

Dalmeet composed himself and held his hands in the air like he was surrendering to the police. "Why don't you tell me how you met Mara?"

Great. One fun topic to another.

"We were in detention together," said Ethan. "At Cascadia Correctional."

"Detention?" Dalmeet tilted his turbaned head, looking like he'd smelled something foul. The anxiety swirling in Ethan's belly boiled into flat-out pissed.

"Yeah, jumpsuits, manacles, shooting hoops in the yard," Ethan snarled. "We made shivs at craft time. You got a problem with that, Richie Rich? Don't think I'm good enough for Mara?"

Dalmeet rose, leaning over the table toward Ethan. "I don't have a problem. In fact, I thought you might actually have something to offer her—besides being a thug."

Any effort at calm flew out the window, and Ethan was grabbing Dalmeet by the collar of his crisp white shirt and hauling him across the table. "Like you do with your fancy pants and fancy house? What do you want from her?"

"Not to get laid!" squawked Dalmeet.

Ethan wrenched him closer. "What do you know, you little shit?"

Half strangled by his shirt, Dalmeet fought to speak. "Enough to know that during the Binding, you'll wish you were a dead man. It's a lot of pain for a piece of ass."

"Mara is not a ..."

"Ethan Skylar!" Hiroko yelled, the door slamming as she entered the room.

Ethan released his grip, and Dalmeet fell into a chair, gasping.

1 times 1 is 1. 2 times 2 is 4. 4 times 4 is 16.

Control. He prided himself on control.

Why are you losing it?

It hardly mattered if this twerp thought he was a meathead.

Abbot Greb entered on Hiroko's heels. Ignoring the scene they'd interrupted, the abbot clasped Dalmeet's hand in both of his. "Mr. Singh, I am so very glad that you have come."

"Uh ... I ...," Dalmeet stammered. "I'm the ... My brother was detained. So I ..."

Abbot Greb dropped his hand and instead grasped his shoulders, pulling Dalmeet close.

"You came," he said. "The honorable blood of the Singhs is yours to claim. There is no birthright on courage."

Abbot Greb fixed his rheumy eyes on Ethan. "The Binding is no simple oath. It is not for you to consider lightly."

But for Dalmeet, it's a sign of courage? Ethan straightened and shrugged back his shoulders, regaining control. "I've considered. I'm doing it anyway."

"Why?"

"There were certain ... trust issues," Hiroko explained.

The abbot silenced her with a gesture. "Ethan, you've seen things that would cause any sane person to run away. Why choose this?"

"I want to help Mara. She's my friend. She needs a Scribe, apparently. And he won't go through with the Binding unless I do."

The abbot sighed deeply. "It will change you."

"I told him," Hiroko blurted.

"You didn't tell me how."

"We will be stronger, faster, and live longer." Dalmeet seemed to grow taller as he spoke. "We'll be more Offspring than human."

The abbot was right. Ethan didn't know what he was getting into. Any sane person would run away. But he could sense that even in Mara's crazy world, there was underlying order even if all he saw were questions. *Why had the Eleven embedded themselves in human history? Were they playing a game? Was she—under the skin where it really counts—all that different from him?* Between the inexorable pull of a puzzle and his utter fascination with Mara herself, there was no way he was backing out.

"Look," said Ethan, afraid that the abbot would send him away, "I'm willing to take the risk, and Mara needs all the help she can get, right?"

No one spoke.

Ethan could see the four of them reflected in windows turned to mirrors by the blackness outside. Dalmeet inscrutable, Hiroko already on his side, and the abbot deliberating.

Don't send me away.

The faint warbling call of a screech owl filtered through the glass.

"Come," said Abbot Greb, leading the way out of the room. "We will make the Binding."

Ethan and Dalmeet walked side by side, separated by a prickly distance. Hiroko pushed past them when they entered the room where Max still lay on his hospital bed. Wires and tubes connected his thin body to a high-tech panel of medical equipment.

While Hiroko checked Max's vitals, Ethan rested one hand on the boy's shoulder.

Poor kid.

"Excuse me," said Dalmeet. "Is this the Binder?"

Ethan and Hiroko looked up.

Dalmeet pursed his lips and sucked air through his nose, giving him the pinched look of a peeved society lady. "This boy is damaged. He's ruined as a Binding agent. If the metalloproteins in his blood aren't in the proper conformation, they won't function. If you think I will risk ending up like that," he gestured to Max's contorted, frozen face, "well, you're wrong. I won't do it."

"What the hell?" Ethan clenched his hands into fists.

"What are you? Some kind of cowboy?" Dalmeet snapped. "His blood is poisoned! Who knows what he could do to us!"

"All I know is that Mara needs us and so does Max!"

Hiroko stepped between them. "Dalmeet, have some faith! I would never put you at risk like that. I know Max's blood is poisoned. I brought you here because this is the only space with the right equipment." She paused. "Mara is the Binder."

Dalmeet narrowed his eyes. "I thought you said no one knew where she was."

Hiroko held up one hand and turned toward the gleaming panel of medical equipment. She snapped on a pair of nitrile gloves before opening a small metal storage unit. Cold air billowed from the refrigerated compartment. She pulled out a palm-sized bag of blood and laid it on a stainless-steel tray. All eyes were on the thick, red liquid. Beads of condensation formed on the surface.

"It's Mara's," explained Hiroko.

Ethan felt queasy. He was about to receive something that Mara didn't know she was giving. Abbot Greb lowered a rough, wrinkled hand to the bag as if giving it a benediction.

"How?" Ethan choked out the words.

"When Max began to really go downhill," the abbot said, "we thought Mara's blood might bring him back. She banked this before she went to her trial in Istanbul."

"Let's get it over with," said Dalmeet. "I understand it's terribly ... unpleasant."

Hiroko pulled two chairs from the corner of the room and gestured for them to sit. Dalmeet straightened his collar and turban. He pulled the kirpan from his waist sheath and bent his head to the hilt, eyes closed. Ethan collapsed into his chair and stared at Dalmeet's body curved in prayer.

Ethan's throat felt tight. The room was way too hot. He pushed his knuckles into his eyes until bursts of color exploded against his lids. He wished he could pray, but his faith hinged on the natural laws of the universe. So instead, he counted.

1, 2, 3, 4

The numbers built a pattern on the inner surface of his mind.

5, 6, 7, 8

"Ethan?" Abbot Greb's gruff voice slid through the numerical grid.

Dalmeet had resheathed his blade and was sitting ramrod straight. Hiroko wheeled an IV pole from the corner of the room and slid it into place between the two chairs.

"When Mara's blood is transfused into you," Abbot Greb explained, "the metalloproteins in her blood will overtake your own hemoglobin. They will assume all oxygen transport for your body. It takes time, a few minutes, maybe more. During that time, you will feel like you are suffocating."

Ethan's fear spiraled higher. Not trusting his voice, he jerked his head once to show he understood.

"Once Mara's blood is entrenched, your life is in her hands. If she chooses to withdraw it ..." Kindness suffused both the abbot's voice and his pause, but Dalmeet, emotionless, brought down the ax.

"You die."

"Withdraw it?" Ethan didn't see how that was possible.

"A fully Turned Offspring, well trained and equipped with a relic, can pull her own blood out of someone Bound to her."

Ethan's stomach clenched. His first cellmate at Cascadia had slit his wrists with a smuggled-in razor blade so Ethan had a pretty good idea just how much blood was in the human body. "Do it," he grunted.

Hiroko stood between them. Splitting the outflow tube from the blood bag, two IV lines looped in her hand. Ethan caught Dalmeet's eye, curious if he too was afraid.

Dalmeet gave him a weak grin. "I hate needles."

Another olive branch.

Ethan leapt at the truce. "So do I," he said. "You're sure about this?"

Dalmeet nodded, his highbrow attitude gone. *He's not all softness and show.* Maybe they could join forces after all.

Ethan extended his hand. "Blood brothers?"

A squeeze rippled between them, and Hiroko placed the lines that would complete the Binding.

Mara's blood flowed into the tube, pushing the saline in front of it.

Ethan sucked in air and prepared to be smothered.

The first thing he felt was cold. Ice poured into his arm.

And then his lungs seemed to implode, crushing the air out of him in a last burst of breath. His head swam. Burning began behind his eyes. Fire scorched through his skull and buffeted the length of his body. The room faded from view. He knew nothing but the hot, dark, crushing absence of air, as if his head were wrapped in slick plastic, filling his nostrils with industrial stink.

Ethan's heart galloped in his chest trying to outrun certain death.

Panic unhinged his limbs and broke his control. A thousand nibbling piranhas tore at his flesh. Sweat poured down his face. He was a pile of bloody chunks. *I don't want to die.* What was that prayer his mother used to slur through drink and despair? *Even though I walk through the valley of the shadow of death, I will fear no evil ...*

Ethan grabbed his lifeline.

9, 10, 11

How long will it take?

12, 13, 14

How long can I last?

15, 16, 17

So this is what it's like to die.

18, 19, 20

Pain burned through his veins and arteries. It ate through his hands and feet. His guts were drenched in boiling oil. His flesh was dead.

21, 22

His mind—erased.

23

His heart—obliterated.

Nothing was left.

Not even numbers.

His first breath after death came in a desperate, heaving gasp.

25

Air poured into him.

26

Enough air so that Ethan thought he might actually be floating.

27, 28

He breathed and breathed and breathed.

It was over.

I am not dead.

He sat in the same chair, in the same room, in the same body, shuddering uncontrollably. Ethan could hear Dalmeet gasping and wheezing. Hiroko kneeled between them, one hand on his knee and the other on Dalmeet's. Her frightened gaze darted back and forth. A clipped chuckle burst from Ethan's lips.

"Ethan!" Hiroko startled and fell backward onto the floor. "What's wrong? Talk to me!"

He patted her head, breathing deeply and long, grateful for the way his lungs rose. He breathed out just as gratefully.

"You," he said to Hiroko, "look like you're watching tennis."

Dalmeet laughed too, no longer snarky and self-conscious, but like Ethan, grateful to be breathing at all.

Twelve

AEDA

PAN-NATIONAL HAEMATOLOGICAL RESEARCH CENTRE,
CHIANG RAI, THAILAND

Aeda couldn't believe that Mara had broken into Toru's stasis facility and made it off the island alive.

Incompetent fool!

Toru was lucky he'd told Aeda the news over the phone. In person, she'd have damned the Covenant and snapped the imbecile's neck like a twig. He'd had the gall to suggest Mara'd been eaten by sharks. *Unlikely.*

Still, Aeda ordered her head of security to double the guard. She'd believe the girl dead when she had a corpse in a bloody pool on the floor. Barring that, she'd settle for Mara in a drawer next to her mother.

Which I can arrange in a heartbeat. Aeda smirked as she envisioned what it must have been like for Mara to find her mother at Toru's. *Didn't get what you expected, did you, princess? Come find Daddy next.* Aeda couldn't wait for that reunion.

Mara's parents were experts in the blood lore of the Eleven, a branch of study that had flourished since the Middle Ages, when surgeons in black cloaks were administering leeches for everything from runny noses to nightmares. Da Vinci had drawn the intricate anatomy of the heart, and Harvey had traced the circuitous path of blood within the body. In every physical detail, humans and the descendants of the Eleven matched. It was Azza's Offspring, Rudolfo Gori, whose blood transfer experiments revealed that the unique abilities of Offspring resided in their blood, but his methods were crude. It took the modern techniques of molecular biology to reveal the true nature of their power.

"I think it's time to visit my favorite scientist," Aeda announced to her empty office, pushing back from the desk. "Time for thumb screws." Her crimson lips stretched across her face like a gash as she smiled. Sinioch wasn't the only one who could apply pressure.

Aeda's lizard-skin stilettos clicked like a Geiger counter up the stairs to the second level. Airlocked double doors protected access to the particulate-free cleanroom, which stretched the entire length of one side of the floor. Inside, it was lined with laboratory tables and air purification hoods. Centrifuges, amplifiers, and sequencers whirred and clicked. Several scientists were at work in bunny suits, as they called their head-to-toe white protective gear.

She rapped on the window until one of the scientists looked up. Through his face shield it was impossible to gauge his response, but it seemed to Aeda that Dr. Paul Layil hesitated for a moment before holding up one finger, gesturing for her to wait while he came through the airlocks.

You made your deal with the devil, my dear.

The Layils' early research had been conducted at a university medical school where they were professors, but ethical restrictions blocked their experiments on humans. *Everyone has a price.* Sinioch and Aeda had offered them a sparkling lab, unlimited resources, and test subjects, both human and Offspring. In exchange, the Layils developed a new way to process opium that resulted in heroin undetectable by current drug tests.

"Ah, there you are," said Aeda, as Dr. Paul Layil, minus the bunny suit, exited the final airlock.

He nodded, stiff backed.

She tapped her fingers against her thighs.

Go ahead. Give me the cold shoulder. As long as I get what I want ...

"I'd like a progress report," she said.

"The storage facility is functioning perfectly." His voice was flat and expressionless. "We've titrated the drug more precisely. It requires a much-reduced transfusion to maintain the subjects."

"But you need a little more of my special contribution, don't you?" asked Aeda. "Veronique surely does."

Without waiting for a response, she led the way into the lab on the opposite side of the hall. The dimly lit room consisted of a series of medical bays. In each lay a body contorted with unnatural rigor.

The fruits of your labor, Doctor.

While the Layils had pursued a method for turning Offspring powers on and off at will, they stumbled on the toxic protein that bound to blood-borne relium and induced a degenerative coma. Sinioch had immediately seen its potential as a nonlethal—and non-Covenant-breaking—means for them to deal with Offspring who interfered with their heroin trafficking business, keeping them conveniently out of the way.

Aeda walked past the motionless subjects. Heart tracings zigzagged across monitors. Electronic leads sprouted from foreheads and chests. Silicone tubes, pulsing with crimson liquid, snaked into ports on their inner arms.

You filled the stasis chamber with our enemies, my love, and I will put them to good use. I promise! As she thought of Sinioch, a wrenching ache coursed through Aeda, but no sign of her suffering touched her perfect features as she entered the alcove set up for blood donation and perched on a chair with padded armrests. She rolled up the sleeve of her silk blouse and presented one thin, pale arm.

"For your wife, then," she said, soothing and sibilant.

Paul Layil did not look at her. Instead, he gloved up and cleaned her skin with an alcohol-soaked cotton ball. He tied a rubber tourniquet above her elbow and slid a needle into the purplish vein at her inner arm. Aeda sensed that he did not want to touch her. As soon as blood was flowing through the donation tube, he backed away.

"What is the status of our new project?" she asked.

"We are still experiencing some ...," he paused, grimacing, "complications."

"Complications?" she mimicked. "What a tidy, clinical description of your botched attempts."

"We were ... making excellent progress until ... until you took Veronique," he stammered.

Aeda stared at him blandly. It was fun to watch him squirm.

"She was integral to the work."

"The work was going too slowly," said Aeda with sugared sweetness.

Paul's voice rose. "You didn't have to dose my son!"

"We thought you needed extra incentive."

"Incentive?" he spat. "My son is eleven years old."

"Exactly. And if you perfect the device, then you will be able to wake him as well."

Every muscle and tendon in Paul's neck constricted, and Aeda wondered if she'd pushed him too far, but he mastered himself, unclenched his fists. Dr. Layil was indeed a smart man.

Attacking her was as good as killing his wife and son, and he knew it.

"Get this thing out of me," she snapped, pointing to the line in her arm. "You're bleeding me dry."

Paul removed the needle and taped a pad of gauze to her inner arm, watching the last drops flow into the sterile pint pack. He began to pull away, but she grasped his forearm with one, viselike, manicured hand. When the bones were a hair from snapping, she leaned in close.

"I have a great deal invested here. Let me remind you of our agreement."

"I haven't forgotten."

Aeda detected a hint of defiance under his polite tone. "Let's refresh. Without reanimation and control, your beloved Veronique stays in the drawer, and Max never turns twelve."

Fear swept over Paul's face.

Good. He should be scared.

"They never did anything to you," he whispered.

Aeda flushed. The anger, always so close to the surface now, ballooned within her. Her skin itched with the need to devastate him.

"No," she said, quiet as a looped snare, "but your daughter did."

THIRTEEN

ETHAN

GREENWAY APARTMENTS, PORTLAND, OREGON

By the time Ethan stumbled into his apartment, it was nearly three o'clock in the morning. Hiroko had offered him a guest room at the monastery, but Ethan wanted to be alone with his thoughts. The flickering light of the TV on mute illuminated the shabby living room. On the coffee table, empty beer cans competed for space with old magazines and an overflowing ashtray shaped like a porpoise.

His mom was passed out on the torn brown couch.

Well, mostly alone.

Ethan knelt beside her, careful not to dislodge the empty Folgers coffee can that propped up one corner of the sofa. The cat sleeping beside his mom opened one eye, mewed, and hopped down to rub against his leg.

"How's it purring, Abacus?" Ethan scratched her under the chin, glad to see that the near-death experience back at the monastery hadn't made him unrecognizable to his cat.

I don't feel any different.

He said as much to Abbot Greb before he left. All he got in response was more mumbo jumbo: "You will."

Whatever. I'll believe it when I see it.

Ethan shook his mom's shoulder.

"Hey, Mom, you should go to bed."

Pattie Skylar pushed herself to a sitting position, rubbing her eyes and pushing stringy brown hair back from her pinched face.

"Where've you been?" Her voice was raspy from menthols, and her sour breath enveloped him. This binge had been a long one.

"You know," he shrugged, "around."

Bleary-eyed, she patted him on the shoulder and then wobbled toward her bedroom. Halfway down the narrow hallway, she turned back. "You're a good boy, Ethan. Get out of here." That was the best parental guidance she had to offer.

I'm trying. Good god, I'm trying.

Ethan had been making decent money for several years, building web-based security systems for online customers, but when he got locked up, his mom had gone on a bender and lost her job. Fifteen grand in savings down the hole paying her rent while he was in Cascadia. *Gonna take at least three months to make that back.* And if he couldn't get her back on her feet, moving out might be a long time coming.

Ethan crossed the stained blue carpet to the kitchen. Abacus had clawed it to shreds near the door between the two rooms. A long snaggle of yarn caught on his sneaker, pulled taut as he stepped over overflowing bags of accumulated beer cans, and snapped back, delighting the cat. She tangled with it while Ethan excavated a can of Friskies from a pile of cigarette cartons. Abacus abandoned her carpet snarl as soon as she heard the pop of the metal lid.

He opened the fridge. A jar of Greek olives, a greasy-edged, to-go container from the Chinese place down the street, and a loaf of bread with green fur. His stomach flip-flopped.

"Wanna share your Friskies?"

When she ignored him, Ethan took the olives and retreated.

Unlike the rest of the slowly decaying apartment, his room hummed with an orderly march of bits and bytes. Banks of video monitors, linked processors, hard drives, keyboards, and consoles lined the walls on metal racks—extensions of his brain. From here, he could turn cogs and heft levers—all digital, of course—and worm into whatever system he desired.

Ethan shrugged out of his jacket and jeans and sat on the edge of the bed in his boxers and T-shirt. Exhaustion throbbed through him, but he had a constrained, cagey feeling. After the constricting pain of the Binding, being inside his small room was making him unusually claustrophobic.

And, since Cascadia, he hadn't been able to shake the feeling that YouKnowMe was watching him. Turning himself in had not endeared him to the more anarchist members of the group.

Screw 'em.

He didn't need them. For as long as Ethan could remember, he'd taken care of himself. He'd managed the strain of his time in lockup better than most guys because he was good at being alone. Mara was too. He'd seen that side of her in Cascadia, the way she didn't look to anyone else to complete her. Whether she was sitting alone sketching the other inmates or balls-out manic, Mara was comfortable in her own skin. That quality had drawn him to her with inevitable force.

Like gravity.

Everything that had happened today was because she tugged at the very fibers of his being. Fibers now awash in her blood. He shifted uncomfortably, his conscience troubled by what he had done.

Abacus mewled outside the door. Ethan's bed creaked as he rose to let her in. He flicked off the light, lay back on his bed, and the cat curled up on the pillow next to him. Over the hum of hard drives and the whir of cooling fans, his mom's snoring echoed through the thin walls.

As Ethan slid closer to sleep, he became of aware of his own beating heart. The fluid that this muscle pumped through his body was no longer entirely his own.

I am not alone.

Mara was there—inside of him, closer than anyone had ever been. It was so ... so ...

Ethan struggled to find the word.

... intimate.

Desire flooded him, tinged with guilt.

He wanted her. Now he had her. And she didn't even know.

He hadn't had a chance to ask for her blessing.

Fourteen

MARA

MORIOKA, NORTHEASTERN JAPAN

Mara stayed with the noodle lady for four days. The woman was perky with the daytime customers who crowded the noodle shop, but she treated Mara with absentminded distraction. They didn't talk. Not that Mara really felt like talking, but being ignored made Mara feel ghostlike, and at one point she patted herself down to make sure she was, in fact, still there.

Weird.

She didn't see the cloaked man again, though she definitely felt his presence. It wasn't a creepy, stalker thing. He seemed protective—and a little amused by her. Mara was sure the noodle lady acted under his influence and doubted if she would even remember the scrawny, beat-up stray she'd taken in.

At the same time, Mara was bone-deep positive that she was safe, so she ate noodles, slept, and waited for her wounds to heal. The speed of her recovery was freaky fast. Every few hours, Mara checked the stab wound and the gash on her side. Each time, the bruising across her midriff had faded, and the edges of the wounds sealed in a shiny pink line of scar tissue. By the end of the third day, she could stretch and twist without pain.

By morning on the fourth day, it was time to go.

The clothing situation was dire. When she'd first stumbled into the noodle shop, Mara'd stripped off her blood-soaked clothes and tossed them in the corner of the room. She'd been wearing an old pink nightgown borrowed from the noodle lady ever since. It hung on her thin shoulders like a giant pillowcase and swished around her knees.

Mara plucked her balled-up t-shirt off the floor and took it into the bathroom. *Disgusting.* Her blood had dried rusty and thick in the fabric. She doused the shirt in the sink, scrubbing at it with a bar of hand soap.

Freaking hopeless. I'm gonna look like a slasher victim.

The sound of sizzling pans and the clanking of plates came from the front.

The presence of the cloaked man filled her. He was laughing again.

"Screw you," she murmured to the empty room. "Go spy on someone else for a change."

The feeling of safety left with him, and Mara was immediately on edge. The square mirror over the bathroom sink was hung at noodle lady height and only showed the bottom half of Mara's face. The reflection grimaced back at her.

Actually, I am a slasher victim. That would be funny if she didn't keep replaying Toru's words. *Who's the monster now?*

"Shut the hell up!"

A questioning burble of Japanese responded.

"Shit," Mara muttered, opening the door to the bathroom. The last person she wanted to yell at was the noodle lady. Mara emerged to the receding slip-slap of the noodle lady's pink rubber sandals and the closing swish of the curtains separating the apartment from the kitchen. A pile of neatly folded clothes perched on Mara's futon.

A perfectly starched and ironed white school uniform blouse with puffy sleeves. Navy-blue pleated skirt. Shiny black patent leather Mary Janes. *You've got to be kidding! I'm eighteen, not five.*

Silent laughter reverberated through the room. Whoever this guy was, he had a warped sense of humor and a serious fashion fetish.

"You forgot the lollipop, pervert," she told the ceiling.

At least she could save her jacket. The lining was nasty, but she could deal with that. Mara emptied her backpack looking for the Swiss Army knife Max gave her for Christmas last year. Next to the sweetie-pie schoolgirl outfit, she piled her wallet, passport, dead phone, a pack of Black Jack chewing gum, and the relium scalpel Toru had left in her shoulder. Its museum tag was tattered and splattered with blood, but she could make out the carefully printed collection number and address for the

Pan-National Haematological Research Centre in Chiang Rai, Thailand.

The plan, though admittedly pretty lame, was to look for her dad in Thailand.

Using the two-inch blade of her pocketknife, Mara hacked out the bloody lining of the jacket and cut off the blouse's dainty sleeves. The skirt and oh-so-shiny girly shoes were a total no-go, but the frilly knee socks she could handle. Mara slipped on her bra followed by the shirt, leaving it untucked, and wriggled into her filthy, blood-splattered jeans and combat boots. Mara's gauntlets felt momentarily cold as she clicked them into place, but as the relium flowed around her forearms, it warmed to her flesh.

I'm fashion forward. Toss a Catholic schoolgirl and a Harley Davidson into a blender, she'll come out all glam like me.

Mara ran a finger along the gauntlets. The seams had completely disappeared. There was no sign of the blades that had emerged during her fight with Sinioch and again with Toru. *How did that happen?* If there was some sort of mechanism concealing the blades, she couldn't find it. And anyhow, she didn't think she'd done anything to release them.

They were there when she needed them, though.

There was no forgetting the sight of sharp metal buried in Sinioch's chest. The queasy roil of guilt in her gut was immediately swallowed by hot anger.

He'd tried to murder her brother!

She'd kill him again if she had to.

Mara reloaded her backpack. She was tossing the ruined t-shirt and jacket lining into the wastebasket when the noodle lady came in, retrieved the blood-stained garments, and packed them carefully in Mara's backpack.

"What are you doing?"

The noodle lady burbled in Japanese and patted the top of the pack.

"You want me to take this crap with me?"

The noodle lady nodded and left as suddenly as she'd come.

"Yuck," Mara said. "Am I supposed to be saving tampons too?"

She left the clothes in the pack but hated leaving the sweet woman. Being taken care of had been a nice change of pace.

Yeah, from my whole life.

Mara zipped up her jacket, did a final survey to make sure she hadn't forgotten anything, and pushed through the curtain into the noodle shop. She blew the noodle lady a kiss before merging with a stream of men and women heading to work in the surrounding factories.

The cold bit her cheeks and snuck through the slashed holes in her jacket. She puffed out her breath and patted the near-empty wallet in her pocket, dodging a group of schoolgirls in more respectable versions of her own uniform. She'd split from the noodle shop with the bare bones of a plan. Now the logistics made her head swim.

She had to get to Tokyo and then Bangkok.

If she used her ATM card to replenish her cash, someone—either Aeda's thugs or the Amyclaean Guard—would probably find her. Ditto if she tried to recharge and use her phone. It was no coincidence that Mara hadn't shaken off her pursuers until her battery died.

If only she had Ethan.

He'd fire up his tricked-out tablet computer and conjure up a plane ticket for her. Mara wrapped her arms around herself. Whether that was to stay warm or to pretend he was hugging her, she wasn't sure.

Immediately, she felt stupid and selfish.

Who in their right mind would want to hitch on to her train wreck?

No wonder she was always alone.

Snow began falling. Already her toes were icy, and she longed to return to the noodle shop. Mara stopped at the corner to get her bearings. Electric wires crisscrossed the space above her in no predictable pattern, caging in the sky. Then through the traffic she saw an elevated train track and headed for it at a run, giving an elegant man in a natty business suit an inadvertent body check.

"Sorry," Mara panted, stopping to pick up his briefcase.

"You should be careful," he said in precise English.

Whatever. I'm gonna freeze to death out here.

"Wait!" she called after the man. "Do you know where the train station is?"

He pointed down a side street.

"Can I get to Tokyo?"

"The Tohoku Shinkansen, the bullet train, will take you right into the city. Did you know your lips are blue?"

Mara bit back the snark on the tip of her tongue and sprinted toward the station. Inside it was toasty warm and smelled of citrus and fish. Mara blew on her reddened hands and stamped her feet to goad circulation. She checked the schedule. Forty-five minutes to departure. There was an ATM right by the ticket counter. A squat, menacing machine.

You've watched too many spy movies.

If she accessed her bank account, it would take a while for them to find her, right?

Well, maybe I'll wait a bit longer.

Ten minutes before the train was due to leave, Mara sidled up to the ATM and withdrew the maximum amount. She slid the Yen into her wallet and eyed the crowd warily, but there wasn't a whiff of Offspring in her vicinity. She chose a window seat in the middle of the car on the left side, breathing a sigh of relief when the doors shut in a huff of hydraulics.

Luck's on my side for a change.

She had several hours before anyone could get their mitts on her.

Mara curled up in a window seat. The woman next to her was listening to Tokyo pop, the tinny beat escaping her headphones in wispy rhythms. When the train sailed into Sendai, Mara was half-asleep. A blur of passengers moved on and off the train. Vaguely she registered the absence of pop music and the open seat next to her.

The express train sped on.

Twenty minutes outside of Tokyo, the train stopped at Omiya. When the doors closed, a frisson of warning arced through Mara like an electrical wire spewing sparks. She bolted upright, scanning the car. The doors at both ends opened simultaneously. In the front loomed an enormous Samoan. Behind her, a tall woman with a blond crew cut and a Black dude with biceps the size of bowling balls blocked the aisle. All wore gray ribbed sweaters with high collars and black suede patches on the shoulders and elbows. Three sets of eyes locked on Mara.

She recognized them immediately—her buddies from the Amyclaean Guard.

Shit. So much for lying low.

Mara stepped into the aisle.

A few passengers looked up from their papers and smartphones.

The Amyclaean woman stepped forward, beckoning to Mara.

"You want me to go with you?" Mara said, dripping sarcasm.

She nodded.

"I don't think so," said Mara, considering the windows. They didn't open. Besides, leaping out of a train moving at two hundred miles per hour didn't sound like the greatest idea in the world.

The Amyclaeans closed in carefully.

"Back for more, huh?" Mara said, stalling.

A cacophony of voices—terrified, confused, angry—burst from the other passengers. One young man jumped in front of the biggest Amyclaean, gesturing for him to leave Mara alone. When he ended up flat on his back three rows down, the rest of the passengers plastered themselves against the windows as far from the aisle as they could get. The Samoan cracked his knuckles. The other dude gave Mara a smile that said, "Come here, dinner."

She'd wipe that look off his face.

"You should talk more," said Mara.

The woman took another step forward.

"Conversation—it's a dying art." Mara crouched, a hurricane of power circling through her. She channeled its flow, releasing it through her palms. The woman and her burly boyfriend dodged too late. They were blown backward and smashed into the rear row of seats with a thudding crash. A woman behind her wailed like a banshee. Three others burst into tears. Like frenzied ants, the other passengers scrambled over the backs of seats, past the prone bodies of the two guards, and shoved their way through the rear door.

The Samoan lunged for Mara.

She whirled on one heel to find him inches from her nose, arms closing in for a lung-crushing bear hug.

Slow down!

Mara struggled to stop the passage of time around her. *Stop, stop, STOP!* His tree-trunk arms were inches from her ribs. *Toothpicks, nothing but toothpicks.* Less than an inch from her, his arms stuttered to a stop like a dying windup toy.

The immense strain of holding everything back filled Mara. Darkness swam at the edge of her vision. A few more seconds and she'd pass out for sure. *Use his weight.* Mara released everything at once. Her legs collapsed. She dropped to the floor as the Samoan's arms closed around nothingness. His momentum returned, and he toppled forward. Mara pushed herself on her belly through his legs.

She scrambled to her feet. For a big dude, he sprang up more quickly than she expected. And he was pissed. A hysterical mob of passengers pressed their smartphones against the window of the rear door. Train-spotting loonies. They'd escaped the car only to come back for dramatic footage? But she didn't have time to worry about them. Instead, she brought her fists in front of her face, sent another power blast through her feet, and launched herself into the air toward the Samoan.

He crouched and leaned to the side, taking the blow on his left shoulder. He staggered back but managed to snake his right arm around her waist, dragging her toward him.

Mara twisted and writhed against the fleshy weight of his arm. Behind him, the other two were coming around. Fear sent her thrashing into overdrive. She threw herself against his injured shoulder. He let out a strangled cry. His arm faltered, and Mara wrenched herself free. She slashed toward his throat with one forearm. The gauntlet thudded into his neck with a searing clang of metal on metal. *What the hell? Was he wearing a dog collar?* The man gave a guttural cry of pain, his eyes rolled back in his head, and he collapsed in the aisle.

By now, the big woman had regained control of her limbs.

Mara scrambled backward and dashed for the front of the car. The passengers on the other side of the window saw her hurtling toward them and fell on top of each other in their frantic attempts to get away. Mara wrenched open the door dividing the cars and dove through it. She searched for some way to block the door to the car. The blond woman vaulted over her companion. *Come on. Come on.* Mara willed the blades to emerge from the gauntlets.

Nothing.

Roaring in frustration, Mara punched the door. Just before her fist connected with steel, the metal of the gauntlet flowed over and encased her clenched hand. The force of her blow left a fist-shaped crater in the door, derailed the opening mechanism, and jammed it in the closed position. On the other side of the glass, disbelief filled the woman's face while Mara looked from her fist, no longer covered by the gauntlet, to the door and back.

Sweet!

The Amyclaean unsheathed a knife clearly forged of the same metal as her gauntlets. As Mara watched, the woman used the knife to cut through the door like it was tissue paper.

Who made that piece of shit? Munchkins?

Through the train-car windows, Mara could see downtown Tokyo. Skyscrapers rose mile upon mile like shiny teeth. The train rushed toward the city. She was almost there.

So close.

A person-sized slab of metal door crashed toward Mara with a thundering boom. The blond woman kicked it away, and the jagged-edged steel skittered under a row of seats. Mara backed away, her eyes darting to the windows and the white sky above Tokyo.

Mara tensed and raised her fists.

The woman made a strange, hacking cough like a cat with a hairball and then spoke in a voice so damaged, Mara could hardly make out the words.

"It doesn't ... have to ... be like this."

"Tell that to your friend who tried to squeeze me to death," Mara snapped.

"Come. Alive." The effort it took to form words clouded the woman's face. Beads of sweat stood out on her brow. "Armaros granted ... life."

"Prison?" Mara spat.

"Life."

"Screw that." Mara threw a punch.

The woman blocked it without even blinking. Mara tried again. This time the woman caught Mara's fist and held it. Mara grabbed their clasped hands with her free one and swung herself up on the woman's arm. She pulled her body into a tight ball and slammed into the woman's torso.

In a tangle of limbs, they crashed to the floor. Mara could see the two men coming to their leader's aid. *I have to get out of this train!* She elbowed the woman under the chin and scrambled free. Nothing mattered more than getting out—not the height of the elevated track, not the speed at which they were hurtling toward Tokyo.

Mara raced away from the Amyclaeans.

Where's the emergency exit? Stewardess?!

Mara heard the snick of blades extending from her gauntlets and instantly knew what to do. She threw both arms up in front of her face, changed trajectory, and dove straight toward one of the huge side windows.

As the blades hit the thick, tempered glass, the window exploded. Mara felt a hand clutch at her heel, then lose hold. Instantly, she followed the shards of glass, straight into free fall.

FIFTEEN

PETRA

AMYCLAEAN SAFE HOUSE, TOKYO, JAPAN

The bare bulb hanging from the center of the room quivered wildly as the metal door slammed shut behind Petra. She ran her fingers through the inch of blond stubble on her head, taking in her damaged team.

By the Blade! She'd anticipated the girl's moves. She'd had her team strategically placed in Japan before the girl was even located, and still they'd blown it. She'd blown it.

What a colossal disaster.

Robaire pressed a folded t-shirt to his face, trying to staunch the blood streaming from his cheekbone. When that girl blasted him across the train, his face had collided with the arm of a seat. Semo cradled his left arm against his yard-wide chest, eyes screwed up in pain.

Petra strode to the Samoan's side, put one hand flat against his chest and seized his left wrist in the other. She gave a swift, violent jerk. With an explosive *POP*, the shoulder joint snapped back into place.

Semo tipped his head toward the ceiling, mouth open in a strangled roar, and then fell forward on the table, breathing heavily. Beside his labored heaves, the only sound in the room was the steady drip of blood from the drenched cloth in Robaire's hand. Petra stood nearby until Semo raised his head from the table and nodded his silent thanks. She then began circling the room. Robaire replaced the saturated t-shirt with another cloth and sat silently, watching her.

She'd lost the girl a second time. An unforgivable failure. Mara Layil was an out-of-control child, barely Turned. How hard could it be to capture her?

Damn near impossible, it seems.

Petra glanced at her cell phone, hoping she could conjure up a status report from Istanbul. Immediately after the debacle, she'd notified Tokyo-based agents of the Council, who were already tracking what happened to Mara Layil after she fell.

Robaire coughed, and Petra's thoughts turned to the conversation she had overheard. She wished she could crack into their skulls and haul their thoughts out on the table.

What are they planning?

For thousands of years, the Amyclaean Guard had served the Eleven faithfully, and these two had been with her for decades. Still, with only Armaros left, loyalties were shattering on all sides.

They're my men, aren't they?

She sat between them. Like all Offspring, they would heal quickly. By morning, the cut on Robaire's face would knit, and Semo's arm would be sore but functional. Robaire removed the cloth from his cheek and asked a question with his eyes. He too wondered what had happened to Mara Layil.

"Yes," she rasped, surprised to realize that not only did she believe the girl survived, but she hoped she had. They'd know soon enough, but for now, all they could do was wait. After a few moments, she gestured toward the cots against the far wall, and both men went to rest. Petra was too pissed and twitchy to sleep.

The girl was stronger than I expected. Much stronger.

Most third-generation Offspring had a fraction of her abilities and only a sliver of her grit. *Jumping out of a high-speed train! That took nerve!* Petra couldn't help but admire Mara's refusal to surrender.

Without warning, the door swung open, clanging angrily against the concrete wall. Petra dropped into a defensive crouch, but before her heart reached fighting speed, a wave of drowsy calm scented with jasmine swept over her.

An elderly woman strode into the room with quick, determined steps. Her long silver hair shone like a ray of moonlight against her black clothes.

Armaros!

"Petra." Her liquid voice held no hesitation despite her extreme age. "Rise, child. And you, Semo and Robaire." The men had prostrated themselves on the floor at the woman's entrance. The initial calm evoked by Armaros dissolved, and Petra's heart began to race. Her failure to capture the girl had led to this—a personal rebuke from the last living member of the Eleven. Armaros was the gravitational center of the Amyclaean Guard, yet they rarely saw her, and she never followed them into the field.

"I am not here to yell at you," said Armaros. Instead of the disappointment Petra expected to see, her mentor's expression was kind, tender even.

"Don't ... deserve ... forgiveness," Petra stammered.

Armaros radiated serenity.

Near divinity.

For unmeasurable years, Armaros had inhabited the Before, one with all things. In her mortal life, she had lived over five thousand years—lifetime upon lifetime of experiences.

Blessed be the Sacrifice.

Armaros looked at the three of them with luminous silver eyes, gestured for them to sit, and circled the table.

"Let me ease your minds," she said, her voice a warm, scented breeze.

She stopped behind Petra, hands alighting on her shoulders like songbirds.

"My Petra, when you took the Guard's oath before me, I was blessed. You have fulfilled my every expectation. The Covenant has been safe in your hands."

Blessed! The word enveloped Petra. *I am not a failure.*

Armaros moved to Semo, speaking to his concealed heartbreak with the rustling tone of autumn and comfort. "You miss your dear one." His broad frame trembled under her touch. "Some say that love is an echo of the Before when the Eleven were intermingled. They are right. We wove in and out of each other like a symphony, both whole and part of the whole. Separating from my other selves was"—the air in the room changed like pressure before a storm—"painful."

A great sigh wracked Semo's chest.

Armaros moved to Robaire, and icy air smelling of snow swept through the room. "I hear the whispers that soon I will follow Tur'el in death, but I am still with you."

Petra wondered at the wash of emotions on Robaire's face, a mixture of expectation and doubt, but then as Armaros completed her circle of the table and stood before them, the air in the room changed again, becoming hard-edged and antiseptic. As a unit, the Amyclaeans snapped to attention.

"I have changed my mind," said Armaros in clipped, brisk tones.

Relief flooded Petra. The Layil girl would get the punishment she deserved after all. The ambiguity of the commuted sentence would be replaced by clean, clear law. "By the Covenant!" she rasped.

"I am not talking about execution," said Armaros. "You will all return to the Council." She might as well have slapped them. "Immediately."

Petra raised a hand in protest.

"I am not abandoning the Covenant, Petra Adler. I am trying to leave this world intact, and I am asking you to trust me now. I will take care of the girl myself."

Armaros leaned into Petra, "Call home the Guard. You must keep them united." She straightened, nodded brusquely like a general dismissing her troops, and left them gaping in the harsh light. Petra stared after Armaros, missing the pointed look that passed between Semo and Robaire.

Sixteen

ETHAN

GREENWAY APARTMENTS, PORTLAND, OREGON

Ethan downed another Red Bull and adjusted his headphones. The hard-driving rhythms of Skrillex underscored his frantic typing and drowned out the nonstop text alerts on his phone. For the past four days, he'd been looking for Mara. He had to find her.

He'd started by hacking the cell network and pinging Mara's phone, but she'd either been smart enough to ditch it or the battery was dead. It would have been the easiest way to find her, but lots of other people were going to be looking too. No doubt all of them were tracking her credit cards. He was too, but he had other tricks up his sleeve.

Ethan knew he was a damn good hacker and had put together a smoking if ugly set of hardware. *I'll find her first.* Dalmeet had insisted on putting out feelers among the other Scribes so that if anyone found her, he'd know. Ethan doubted that was going to be the ticket, but he wouldn't turn any help away.

He brushed Abacus off the desk and tweaked his hack on Mara's social media feeds. She certainly wasn't posting updates, but perhaps she'd gone to someone for help, someone from her online circle of peeps. *Long shot, but what the hell.*

His phone buzzed so wildly, it jiggled itself off the bed. Ethan swiped it from the floor and read Dalmeet's text. <u>Your passport is ready</u>.

<u>Thanks</u>, he typed back. <u>That was fast!</u>

<u>I've got a few skills</u>. Ethan could hear the snark behind the text but also the humor. In the last few days, he and Dalmeet had formed an edgy alliance through a steady stream of messages. The shared experience of the Binding had drawn them together. Not that they were talking about it, but finding Mara was something they could both get behind.

Ethan checked the search results he'd been grabbing from ATMs in Japan. Nothing. Ethan paced the room and noticed his longboard tilted in the corner. He was itching to ride, thinking that speed and the focus it required might purge his body's memory of the Binding, pain that still caused him to shudder involuntarily every few minutes.

He texted Dalmeet. <u>I've still got the shakes. You?</u>

<u>Yes</u>.

<u>Will it stop?</u>

<u>Yes</u>.

<u>Dude ... a little more detail please</u>.

Nothing.

An alert exploded from one of Ethan's computers, distracting him from the tremors in his limbs. Ethan pulled off the headphones, scooping Abacus out of his way again.

"Shut down that damn noise!" his mom called through the door. "What are you doing in there?"

"Working, Mom!" Ethan killed the sound output and heard his mother shuffle off to the fridge for another beer.

Working at cracking into the Japanese transportation grid.

He'd hit a firewall that was fighting back, hence the flashing red screen. *Just a tweak here … and BOOM, I'm through.*

His phone buzzed—Dalmeet again.

Hiroko's freaked. An Amyclaean showed up looking for Mara.

A what?

Offspring. Enforcers of the Covenant. Navy SEALs on steroids.

Ethan's anxiety ratcheted up.

Nice. They seen Mara?

NO. We do NOT want them to find her first.

Where are you, Mara Layil? Ethan desperately wanted to see her. He wanted her to know he had her back.

I'm on it, he texted Dalmeet.

Streaming lines of data poured down the monitors, numbers and letters blurring together in a haze of caffeine and sugar-fueled sleeplessness. Ethan knew he should trust the code he'd written to work its magic and was on the verge of forcing himself to sleep when the data stream froze and another bright red warning box popped up.

Yes!

Mara's credit card had been used at a train station in Morioka, Japan, a little over three hours ago. *She's alive!* A thrill buzzed through him, followed immediately by irritation. *Shit!* By using the card, Mara had made herself way too easy to find.

"Mara, when I find you, I'm gonna wring your neck."

But Ethan had what he needed: *Tokyo* and *train.* The keyboard rattle-tapped madly as he began hacking the video feeds from every transit station between Morioka and Tokyo. He shot off a text to Dalmeet—<u>She's alive!</u>—and then began mining every social media site for cross-referenced locations and visual data. Images flickered rapidly across three of his screens. Coordinates scrolled down the others.

With others on the hunt, it wouldn't be long before she was found. While the hard drives churned, he stuffed his highly modified tablet computer, extra batteries, and Wi-Fi-device detector into his backpack along with some clothes. They had to be ready to move.

When he turned back to the bank of computers, Ethan gasped. "No way!"

He'd had a facial recognition hit from the Morioka train station. The time stamp, corrected for time zone, was ten minutes after Mara had pulled the cash. A grainy image showed Mara pushing through the turnstile toward a train.

Ethan's heart beat double time. To find her destination, he tightened the parameters on his search, his breath coming fast. Once the algorithm initiated, he slammed out a quick message to Dalmeet.

Found her in Japan! She got on a train 3 hours ago.

Dalmeet's response was immediate. We're coming.

Bad idea. Having Hiroko and Dalmeet in his shithole apartment was not high on his list of activities. Ethan peeked out his door and looked into the living room. His mom was sprawled on the couch watching TV.

I'll come to you, he texted back.

You have no car. We'll leave from your place.

Ethan groaned, but Dalmeet was right. He couldn't leave the computers until he'd pinpointed Mara's exact destination anyway. He took two minutes to fill a bowl for Abacus and taped a note to the refrigerator reminding his mom to feed the cat while he was gone. He copped one of his mom's beers and girded himself for their arrival. Not something he was looking forward to.

Twenty minutes later, one of the computers whistled. A URL on YouTube was racking up hits so fast it made his eyes cross. Posted only thirty minutes earlier, the clip already had over a thousand views. The caption read "Crazy American Girl."

That sounds about right.

Ethan clicked *play* and popped it to full screen.

He squinted at the blond girl in the footage. *Holy shit.* He watched, clenching the arms of his chair. He replayed. In the split second it took the screen to refresh, the "likes" had nearly doubled. The thing was going viral.

After a fourth viewing, Ethan scrolled through the flurry of comments, including debate about special effects, doctored video, and heartfelt convictions that the girl in the video was either a mutant or a space alien.

That's so Mara.

The comment that stopped him cold was the one linking to a suicide prevention site. *She wouldn't do that, would she?*

Ethan was still stressing when Dalmeet and Hiroko knocked.

"I'll get it, Mom!" he called, but she stumbled to the door, swinging it open before he could make it out of his room.

"Yeah? Whatcher want?" she slurred. "You Jehovah's Witnesses? Mormons?"

Ethan groaned, wishing he could pause, rewind, redo.

No dice. Suck it up, sucker.

Halfway across the living room, Ethan saw them through the open door. Dalmeet's face was a careful mask. Hiroko was blushing on his behalf.

"Hey, guys." Ethan rubbed the back of his neck and looked at the floor. "Mom, I've got this."

She swayed in socked feet, clutching the doorframe to stay upright. "These your friends?"

"Yeah," said Ethan, realizing that she hadn't bothered to put her robe on properly. The left side of a dingy, overlarge bra was on display. *Oh Christ.* "Come on, Mom. You can go back to bed."

His mom pointed at Dalmeet. "You're wearing a turban!"

I am never going to live this down. Ethan braced himself for Dalmeet's indignation and disdain.

"Yes, ma'am." Dalmeet's words were gentle. "I am a Sikh. I wear the dastar to remind myself to stand tall and be proud of my heritage."

Ethan tore his eyes from a crusted stain on the carpet. Dalmeet wasn't making fun, not at all. Hiroko stepped forward, supporting his mom's elbow with one hand. "Come on, Ms. Skylar, I can help you with that headache." His mom let herself be led away, and Dalmeet followed Ethan through the detritus in the living room.

"I'm sorry," Ethan said, "for the mess, for my mom, for ..."

"Don't worry. I wear a turban. It stands out."

"But ..."

Hiroko rejoined them in Ethan's room. "At least she won't have a hangover."

"This time," Ethan muttered.

"Hey," said Dalmeet, "Chill. Remember what Abbot Greb said ..." He dropped his pitch to match the old man's gravely tone. *"There is no birthright on courage."*

Hiroko laughed, and Ethan felt the tension ebb from his shoulders.

"Show us what you've got," said Dalmeet, gesturing to hacker command central.

Ethan slid into his desk chair. "You're not gonna believe this."

Hiroko and Dalmeet clustered around him as he replayed the clip. The cell phone video had been shot through thick glass. The user had a touch of the shakes—*Mara has that effect on people*—so the frame jiggled periodically. There was Mara, looking waifish, fighting with a huge man in the center aisle of a train car. At first, it seemed he would crush her in a brutal hug, but then there was a strange, static moment like the feed had frozen or something.

That wasn't it, though, because there was still audio in frantic Japanese.

The person with the camera shrieked as the big man collapsed with a crash. For a split second, the girl looked straight into the camera.

Hiroko let out her breath in a nervous burst. "That's definitely Mara."

Dalmeet's tense body leaned into the display. It was the first time he'd seen Mara, Ethan realized. He wondered if this would be enough to send him running.

"I can see Uncle Momar's technique in the way she fights."

He's not freaked. He's analyzing. Maybe Dalmeet was his kind of guy after all.

On the screen, a tall, tough woman regained her feet, shaking her head as if to clear it and blocking the camera's view of Mara. Hiroko clamped a hand on Ethan's shoulder.

"That's Petra Adler, the head of the Amyclaean Guard!"

"How did they get there so fast?"

Dalmeet shook his head. "They must have been waiting for her in Japan."

The woman chased Mara up the aisle into the next car. It looked like Mara had managed to block the door, but just as quickly the woman was using a knife to cut through the glass and metal like it was paper.

"How the hell is she doing that?" Ethan asked.

"Relium," said Dalmeet, not taking his eyes from the screen.

The crash of the door was followed by an explosion of glass. The videographer shrieked. The screen turned into a jumble of blurred motion and rapid-fire narration in Japanese.

When it stabilized, Ethan could tell the owner of the phone had it facing out the window of the train. Against the backdrop of the Tokyo skyline, they saw a black and blond blur plummeting through space. In the final seconds of footage, the blur slowed in midair and resolved into the figure of a girl floating downward as if supported by an invisible parachute. Just before she hit the ground, the video cut out.

Without a word—and without loosening her death grip on Ethan's shoulder—Hiroko replayed the clip. When it stopped, in a grainy, far-off still of Mara suspended ten feet from the pavement, Hiroko sat down heavily on the edge of Ethan's narrow bed.

"She hovered," Ethan said.

Hiroko looked as confused as he felt. "I know."

"She's a direct descendant of Armaros," said Dalmeet.

Ethan stared at him like he'd just announced Mara was half lizard. "She jumped out of a bullet train a hundred feet in the air going three hundred miles per hour. Who cares about her freaking genealogy?"

"Top speed is closer to 278."

Hiroko flashed a warning look at Dalmeet, who held up his hands in defeat.

"What do you know about Armaros's bloodline-specific abilities?" Dalmeet asked Ethan.

"About as much as I know about belly dancing."

"Well, it's complicated."

Ethan rolled his eyes. "What about Mara isn't complicated?"

Hiroko gave a worried chuckle.

"When the Eleven became mortal," Dalmeet continued, "each brought a hint of the strengths they'd borne in the Before. Armaros's could work time. That's why they call her the Time Weaver. That's what she's passed down to Mara."

"I still don't get it," said Ethan.

"I don't totally get it, either," Dalmeet admitted. "According to the Record, events occur in both time and space, but all points in timespace exist simultaneously. Time is not a river flowing by. It's an environment events pass through. Armaros can enter it at will. I think Mara may have blipped out to save herself from falling and then blipped back in to land."

"Whoa," said Ethan, "I think I've seen her do that time-hiccup thing."

"What?" Now it was Dalmeet's turn to be confused. "When?"

Ethan waved his hands in the air as if he could gather together the confusing memories and force them to make sense. "I thought she was just messing with my head."

"I'm sure Mara would never do that," said Hiroko.

"I can't remember very well," Ethan continued, "but a couple of times when we were together, weird things happened. Like we were slowing down while everything else was going faster. Or maybe it was the other way around." Ethan shook his head. "It freaked her out. She thought she was losing it."

"She's newly Turned," said Dalmeet. "Without guidance, there's no way she's got good control. She's dangerous."

"I already know that," Ethan said, turning back to the computers and changing his search parameters to focus on the coordinates near Mara's new location. It took an hour, but eventually he found her.

"That's the Narita airport feed."

It was Mara, for sure.

He synched location and time with every passenger manifest.

"Bangkok!" he said. "She's boarding a plane to Bangkok!"

Time for a field trip to an ass-kicking.

Seventeen

AEDA

PAN-NATIONAL HAEMATOLOGICAL RESEARCH CENTRE, CHIANG RAI, THAILAND

The latest report from Dr. Layil had been promising. Aeda drummed her long nails against her desk, wishing Sinioch were here to see her triumph. A shudder rippled through her. Ever since his death, she'd felt slightly unhinged.

Is this what grief does?

The explanation did not sit well. She was neither delicate nor overly concerned with personal attachments. She'd have described her marriage to Sinioch like that of predatory cats—tigers, maybe, or jaguars. They both liked being alone, prowling the edges of their shared territory, edging the boundaries ever outward, and coming together in dark, frenzied couplings, only to part again.

They didn't sit around in sweatpants and watch romantic comedies.

He should be here. A new era is coming—one without the Covenant controlling our every move. In his absence, her very blood felt explosive, ruination bursting out of her pores. *I'll destroy that little bitch.* Aeda leaned back in the leather chair and closed her eyes, imagining her hands around Mara Layil's neck. The squelching sound of twisting ligaments and the gunfire cracks of separating vertebrae; those were the noises she wanted to hear.

An alert from her laptop jolted her from thoughts of revenge. She composed her face before accepting the video call from Matthias de Alba.

"Matthias," she said, his name coming out in a low growl. Everything about the pompous old man, from his floor-length robes embroidered with gold to his elaborate ritual tattoos, annoyed her. It was the 21st century, not the Middle Ages! Who dressed like that?

"Are you alone?" he asked.

Aren't I always alone now?

"Yes," she said, remembering to soften her voice and let sadness trickle behind her eyes. She needed the old fool on her side. "Forgive me for saying so, Matthias, but you look worried."

Matthias glanced out of the frame of the video camera. As far as Aeda could tell, the room he occupied was empty, but the nervous movement told her that he wanted this conversation secret. *Interesting. Since when has the Head of the Crimson Scribes needed me for private counsel?*

"Armaros has called off the Amyclaean Guard."

"What?" This was unexpected. Even if Armaros had commuted Mara Layil's death sentence, Aeda expected the Guard to recapture her. "They're no longer hunting the girl?"

Without the Amyclaeans in the way, I can take her!

"Armaros told them she would take care of Mara Layil herself." Matthias cleared his throat.

Not if I get there first. The Time Weaver is over five thousand years old. Half dead.

"Then surely, Matthias," Aeda soothed him, "justice will be served."

He frowned. "Armaros's dedication to upholding the Covenant seems to be … ah … waning."

"The Covenant has served us for millennia," Aeda replied. "Yet Armaros has been lenient before—one or twice."

The old man shifted uncomfortably in his seat and lowered his voice. "May I speak freely?"

"Of course." Aeda leaned in toward the camera.

"I know the Layil girl is one of Armaros's direct descendants, but leniency sends the wrong message. There are Offspring who would see the Covenant rescinded."

The old fool has no idea that I intend to tear it to shreds!

"The anti-Covenant forces may use this," he continued, "as a justification to destabilize everything we have built."

Your comfortable little bureaucracy, you mean.

"Matthias," said Aeda, wrinkling her beautiful brow in concern, "I know you and the rest of the Crimson Scribes do as much as you can to ease the weight on Armaros's shoulders, but—though she will always be our inspiration—perhaps even she is ready for some ease in her old age."

"I wish that Armaros would agree to step down from the Council." Matthias looked truly pained. "She will not, even though many of us are willing to step up."

"Hmmm," Aeda murmured, proceeding carefully. "That is too bad. Even I can see that our kind would be well served with someone like you looking out for us. Can you see no way to encourage her to step down?" She set the question between them as if it were a sleeping baby.

"I believe," Matthias began, but amended, "we believe that to secure the Covenant, there should be succession." He wiped beads of sweat from his forehead. "There may only be one way."

Wild joy surged through Aeda. The scales were tipping. How Sinioch would have relished this moment! Supercilious Matthias de Alba, squirming like a spitted frog, was so overawed by the power of the Covenant that he was willing to sacrifice Armaros, its primary defender. He could not be playing more perfectly into Aeda's plans.

"You know, Matthias," she said, "I have the utmost respect for you—utter confidence that in your hands, the Covenant would endure."

His eyes bore into hers, trying to read the subtext of her words. "Does that mean I can count on your support?" he asked. "Are you willing to act?"

More than you know.

"For you? Yes."

As Matthias tugged at the neck of his robe, Aeda noted a tremor in his reliably steady hands. Slowly, he reached into a hidden pocket and drew forth a dark coil of wire. Aeda's blood surged. She knew exactly what that was—a relium relic and the only thing that could kill one of the Eleven.

"You should come now," he whispered. "All of the Amyclaeans are away from the Council."

You have sold your soul, Matthias.

Aeda didn't spare a thought for her own.

Everything was coming together—the support of the Crimson Scribes and the absence of the Guard. Aeda fought to keep her face solemn.

She would go, but what of Mara? If she showed up in Thailand as Toru expected, Aeda wanted to be there. Let Guleed Awaale take her. Surely the head of security could manage the girl. Firsthand revenge was a small thing to trade for the end of the Eleven.

"Very well, Matthias," she said. "But if by my actions, you are raised to the highest position in the Council, I get the girl when she is found."

His chin ducked once.

"You must turn the other Crimson Scribes against Mara. Tell them she's hunting Offspring—first Sinioch, then Toru, and now she's after me. Tell them," Aeda purred, "that she tried to kill her own parents. No one is safe from her."

No one is safe! A powerful urge for domination roared through Aeda. *I will chart the course of our kind from here on out.*

Matthias was sweating more profusely than ever.

You bumbling ninny.

"Put that away," she said, tilting her head at the relium garrote he still had in his trembling hand. "I am coming."

"May the Covenant be upheld as long as Offspring walk the Earth," Matthias intoned.

"May the Covenant be upheld," she repeated. *Let the old man think what he wanted.* Without Armaros, Matthias and his precious Covenant wouldn't last long. As she terminated the call, Aeda felt a dangerous thrill surge through her.

The Age of the Eleven was ending.

Eighteen

MARA

BANGKOK, THAILAND

Mara spent the seven-hour plane ride from Tokyo to Bangkok in a state of constant alert. Her gauntlets had gone through security without a trace of alarm. Disturbing from a TSA point of view but damn convenient for her. Of course, if she could carry relium on board, so could another Offspring. Mara scrutinized the demure flight attendants in crisp navy-blue suits as though they might detonate, scanned businessmen leaning over laptops, and spied on exhausted mothers with sticky-faced toddlers.

With her spiky blond hair and zombie-biker look, Mara felt as if she were wearing a sign screaming, "Attack me."

Or shun me.

Mara listened to three young women across the aisle jabber about backpacking through Asia and smoking weed on Khao San Road. Occasionally the one on the end looked disdainfully at Mara before turning back to her friends. Mara felt a pang as the trio huddled close and peered into their Lonely Planet guide. She'd never had friends like that.

Ethan had been the first person, outside of Momar and Max, who she'd felt close to in years. There's nothing like crisis for bringing people together, and the shit that went down with Sinioch certainly qualified as crisis. Ethan had seen Mara at her worst and still liked her.

That blew her mind.

And if I were normal?

What if she and Ethan could just hang out? She could watch him carve arcs and flip tricks in the skatepark under the Burnside Bridge. Afterward, they could walk to Voodoo Doughnut and get that uniquely Portland version of delicious— a bacon-topped maple bar. Doughnuts made her think of coffee loaded with cream, which made her think of the smooth skin of Ethan's neck. She wanted to bite him right there.

Stop it! You're being an idiot.

Mara pulled off her filthy jacket and kneaded the muscles in her stiff neck, ignoring the way the chick across the aisle wrinkled her nose.

How the hell did he get under my skin like this?

Ethan should be less involved, not more. She'd already dragged him into enough trouble, but she couldn't help wishing he were sharing this row of seats. Maybe playing cards or making fun of the sorority girls next door. *Another dumb idea.*

Mara patted the empty seat beside her. *Everyone near me gets hurt.*

When they landed, Mara elbowed her way off the plane and through the international arrival doors of the terminal. She figured the Amyclaeans or Aeda's men or someone else equally eager to kill her would be waiting, but her doglike instinct to sense Offspring came up empty. Either it was safe, or her inner dog was distracted, sniffing its own ass.

Leaving the terminal, Mara plunged into the hot night and broke into a hacking cough from the stinking fumes of roaring traffic. Spikes of pain shot through her rib cage. Nothing like a bare-fisted tango with three Offspring to add bruises on top of bruises, and free-falling from an elevated train was the cherry on top.

At least I know how to have a good time.

It was nearly nine o'clock, assuming she hadn't screwed up the time change, and Mara wanted to drown her woes in a long shower and then get up close and personal with a pillow. A cabbie in a baseball cap embroidered with tomatoes took her to a hotel near the Northern Bus Terminal.

The next morning, she planned to take an eleven-hour bus ride to the Pan-National Haematological Research Centre in Chiang Rai. It was a long shot, coming here. For all she knew, her dad was in a steel drawer just like her mom. If he wasn't here—or worse, if he was but wouldn't help—she and Max would be screwed up, down, and inside out. The odds reeked, but her brain was too fuzzy with exhaustion to come up with another plan. She had to find her father.

Mara let a skinny bellboy in a lavender uniform lead her up a wide, curving, concrete ramp. The hotel was a converted garage with rooms plopped down where parking spaces used to be. The central car ramps had been left in place for travelers to roll their suitcases up and down. Her room had one mirrored wall, and the rest was entirely decorated in primary colors. Elmo and Cookie Monster would be all over the *Sesame Street* vibe.

Mara locked the door and barricaded it with a bright red dresser, ignoring her body's aches. The window opened and the ledge was wide enough to offer an escape route if necessary. Mara piled her clothes on the floor and worked off the grime in the shower. She fell asleep thinking of the women from the plane heading off together—friends with their arms interlocked, faces giddy, eager for an adventure.

I hope they get mugged.

Early the next morning on her way to the bus station, she wove through crowds of people waiting for buses and ordering food from street carts. On a corner, a man with a twisted leg was calling *Khanom krok! Khanom krok!* and cooking coconut custards on a large metal griddle. A woman in a red Mickey Mouse t-shirt and orange sarong jabbered cheerfully at him.

Stomach gurgling, Mara bought some custards and an omelet chock full of garlic and chilies so hot that tears ran down her cheeks. While she sat on the curb and ate, a brown bird with a bright yellow mask landed beside her and picked at a pile of garbage. When a cell phone rang, the bird mimicked the sound perfectly.

"Wow," said Mara. "You're tricky."

The bird cocked its head at her.

Mara whistled a random tune, and the bird let out a torrent of sounds—burbling notes, excited chattering, angry squeaks, and shrill squeals.

Mara was about to whistle again when the rhythm of her blood changed. She rose, dropped the last of her breakfast for the bird, and scanned the mash of people. Nothing looked out of the ordinary, but an Offspring was coming. The rhythm in her blood was more pulsating and commanding than anything she'd felt. Horses charged through her veins. Whoever approached resonated even more strongly than her stalker friend.

The bird startled into flight as the crowd in front of Mara parted. Down the opened path walked a finely boned, silver-eyed woman with a long braid down her back.

Armaros!

The last time Mara had seen her ancestor was when Armaros had sentenced her to life imprisonment. She'd run then, and damn straight, she was running again. Mara willed speed into her limbs, but before she could bolt, Armaros raised her palm and mouthed the word *stay*. Instantly, Mara was pinioned like a fly in amber. Around her, the crowd continued to flow and gabble, but Mara was frozen in time.

Stop it!

The scream was glued inside her head. No matter how hard she pushed and jabbed at the surrounding space, she couldn't break free. Armaros approached, lifted a delicate eyebrow, and fixed her gaze on Mara. The sweet scent of jasmine swirled around them.

"I've watched you long enough to know you like to run, Mara Layil."

Screw you!

"We are stepping outside of time. It's not a place you can run from."

The woman grasped Mara above the elbow, and Bangkok vanished.

Nineteen

MARA

OUTSIDE OF TIME

The invisible restraints fell away, but Mara's head spun too violently for her to do anything but struggle to stay upright. When the darkness cleared from her vision, she was standing on an expanse of gold sand that stretched as far as she could see in every direction. In the distance, the sandscape melted into the near-white sky in a sloping curve. It was like being inside an egg.

The roaring sensation in Mara's blood was gone, and she was short of breath. She pressed her hands against her chest, expecting the rise and fall of her lungs and the pounding of her heart.

Nothing.

Her heart wasn't beating! Panic raced through her. "Where are we? Am I dead?"

"What?" Armaros laughed, turning her gaze from the milky sky to Mara's. "Of course not. Outside of time, your heart ceases measuring your life."

"Great, that clears things up."

How do I get out of here?

"If you try to run, you'll end up back at yourself."

Very Zen, bitch.

"Are you taking me to prison?" Mara asked.

"That depends on you."

Mara squinted at Armaros. *What was the old bat hinting at?*

A knowing smile twitched across the woman's face. Almost as if she knew what Mara was thinking. "It's time we got to know one another. Your grandfather, Christopher Layil, is my son, which makes you my great-granddaughter."

"So I've heard, but haven't you had like hundreds of kids? You're not exactly making the rounds for our birthdays."

"We're on the same side here."

"Family's never worked out great for me."

"Whose fault is that?"

"Theirs!"

Armaros tilted her head to one side like she didn't buy Mara's argument.

"My parents never had time for me," Mara protested, "or for Max, either."

"Being an adult means doing what you must rather than what you want."

"That's crap parenting."

"By the Blade, child, they love you even if you don't realize it. Sometimes love means protecting children from themselves."

"What's that supposed to mean?" Mara bristled. "I'm not a child."

Armaros waved one hand dismissively. "It's time for you to grow up, Mara Layil. If you want your freedom, you need to earn it."

"Earn it?!" Mara's hands balled into fists, but she managed to keep them glued to her sides.

"Stop thinking the world revolves around you and your problems. I am the last of the Eleven that survives. My children—those multitudes you referred to—and the children of my brothers and sisters are on the brink of a crisis they can't even imagine. I will secure their safety—your safety—before I pass."

"But ..." Mara began.

Armaros stopped her with a glare. "From here, we are stepping to a different point in timespace—the year 3360 of the Embodied Age—humans call it 290 BC. You must understand the threat." She pressed her bony fingers into Mara's wrist. The sand and pale sky vanished.

They stood at the edge of a circle of newly quarried standing stones. Within the circle a great crowd jostled and pushed to see what was happening on a huge stone table in the center. From the way her blood soared, Mara knew that all were First Born or Offspring.

Four forms—a tall, swarthy man, an auburn-haired beauty, and two children—were chained with relium upon the table. Children? They were like no children Mara had ever seen. They were three or four years old, male and female, she realized, though so identical that it hardly mattered. Their skin was unnaturally pale, like cave fish. Even their hair was pearly white. When they turned their heads, Mara expected to see the pink eyes of an albino. Instead, they had solid, glossy white orbs. No pupils, no irises.

Repulsed, Mara would have drawn away, but Armaros's fingers clamped down upon her wrist. Mara felt momentarily grateful for her great-grandmother's presence. "What are they?" she whispered.

"The Twins—Lilya and Eleon—the children of my other-selves, Javan and Serac." Armaros nodded toward the bound man and woman. "Watch."

The noise of the crowd increased as nine people made their way through the crowd. They arrayed themselves in front of Javan and Serac. Mara's eyes widened as she recognized a much-younger Armaros among them. "That's you?" she prodded.

"This was the last time all of the Eleven were together in life." Mara heard the tremble behind her words and recognized grief. "Oh, Azza," Armaros whispered as one of the Eleven stepped forward. The crowd dropped into uneasy silence as the muscular man addressed Javan and Serac.

"My brother, my sister, against all of our laws, you have birthed these abominations."

A low hiss emanated from the creepy children, and their weeping mother, Serac, strained against the chains until blood streamed from her chest and arms.

Azza continued, stone-faced, "Though we shared perpetual union in the Before and though we love you deeply, your breach is unforgivable."

Javan roared murderously, pulling against his chains. Violence swirled through those gathered like the chittering of venomous insects. Some called for justice, others for mercy.

"It has been decided. You are banished from the High Council. You are forbidden to see each other in this lifetime, and the product of your union will be terminated." Azza summoned another member of the Eleven and addressed him. "Tamel, as the Blade Guardian, it falls to you to mete out justice."

In their bondage, the slender child-forms of the Twins began to glow, starlike and luminous, pulsing with fear.

Not fear but anger. Mara scanned the crowd. *Do none of them sense the rising threat?*

With a silky sibilance, Tamel unsheathed a terrible sword, over a meter long and honed to an edge that seemed capable of dividing the world in half. Tears covered Serac's exquisite face in a wet sheen. Her bloodied chest heaved. Javan was rigid with defiance. The Twins pressed shoulder to shoulder, their pupil-less eyes fixed on Tamel as he raised the sword.

Mara held her breath. The crowd fell silent.

Then the Twins spoke.

Tamel froze, blade raised.

Their mouths moved in unison. Their voices harmonized in a minor key that reverberated through those gathered. Their words were not the words of children. "You left the Before for love." The Blade of the Sacrifice trembled in Tamel's grip. "Is this an ending or a beginning?"

Both—it's both. Suddenly, Mara was afraid for all of them.

"Do it!" screamed Azza. The crowd erupted, howling for vengeance.

"I will not kill the innocent." Tamel sheathed the Blade and turned to go, his words still echoing off the standing stones, but Azza blocked his path.

"Where do you think you are going?" he snarled.

"In honesty, my brother-self, I do not know, but I will be your executioner no more."

"And what of the violators?" Azza demanded. "You are the Blade Guardian!"

The glow that emanated from the Twins intensified into white-hot fire burning from their core. A shock wave burst out of them with an ear-splitting *BOOM.* Several of the standing stones toppled, crushing Offspring and sending great clouds of grit into the air. The Twins snapped the chains binding them like so much rotten string and turned on Azza.

In horror, Mara watched hundreds of relium cords spring from the Twins' bodies. The tentacle-like appendages whipped through the air, snaking around Azza, pulling him down, cutting off his screams, and crushing him to death.

Quick as anything, the young Armaros leapt onto the stone table behind the Twins. She plucked a relium crown from her brow and pulled on it with both hands. It grew larger and larger until she held the enlarged crown, arms outstretched, like a giant hula hoop.

In the midst of the pandemonium, Armaros slipped the hoop around the Twins. As it engulfed them, they vanished. The hoop shrunk rapidly, closing the opening that Armaros had carved between time and not-time. When it was the size of a ring, Armaros slid it on her finger, crumpled to her knees beside Azza's corpse, and wept.

Mara was lying nose down in the glittery sand, ears still ringing from the explosion but aware of silence. Her pulse was gone. Armaros, old once more, sat cross-legged beside her, waiting.

Mara sat up, brushing sand from her face. "What happened to the Twins?"

"I used the Circlet of Moments to remove them from the timeline of our world. I sent them to a place like this—outside of time."

"A prison."

"I'd think that you of all people would appreciate that prison, as you call it, is preferable to death."

I don't know about that.

"If they're locked up," said Mara, "what's this big threat you keep yammering about?"

Armaros frowned at her. "You saw the Twins. Nothing like them has ever existed. They embody chaos—unpredictable, dangerous. They drove Tamel to his death. They killed Azza."

Can't blame them for that.

"For the safety of the Covenant and our people," Armaros continued, "Lilya and Eleon must remain outside of time."

"So what's the problem?" Mara asked. "Seems like you've got it handled."

"I am a very old woman. When I die, the constraints on the Twins will crumble. They will return to normal time. Over the years, their abilities and their anger have grown. They cannot be released into the world."

"Of course, they're royally pissed. Wouldn't you be? Thousands of years in some place like this." Mara let handfuls of gold sand flow through her fingers and rolled her eyes at the flat, nothing sky. "Unless they've died of boredom."

"Mara Layil!" Armaros shook her by the shoulders. "They are dangerous."

"Yeah. Fine. I see that! Use your pretty crown to keep the freaks locked up."

That's what happens to freaks like me.

Armaros pursed her lips. "Therein lies the problem. The Circlet is lost. You will find it and bring it to me. In exchange, you'll have your freedom."

"You lost it?" *I can't fucking believe this.* "How?"

"The last time I visited the Twins, they tried to kill me. During my escape, the Circlet fell from my grasp and into an unmarked point in time. Your Scribe will help you."

Don't go there, Grandma.

"Momar is dead," Mara said, clenching her hands into fists. "I have no one."

"I think you'll find help waiting for you," said Armaros.

Enough with the fortune-teller crap.

"I'll see what I can do," said Mara. As soon as Armaros took her back to the real world, she planned to bogue out and get on with her original plan. "But you've got to stop messing with me."

"I am not messing with you."

"What about on the island? And these stupid clothes?"

Armaros stiffened, riveting her eyes on Mara. "What do you mean about the island and the clothes?"

"Well, I didn't fly from Toru's Island to the mainland, did I? And I don't wear skirts."

Armaros muttered under her breath, brow creased. "I wonder ..." But she brushed away the musing. "I will stop messing with you when you do as I ask. Otherwise, maybe you can join the Twins. I probably won't kick off for another five hundred years or so."

A wave of dizziness engulfed Mara. She swallowed back bile and blinked to clear her vision. Armaros was gone. Mara's hair stuck to her forehead and a trickle of sweat ran between her breasts. The curb was hard under her ass. She tried to stand but her legs wouldn't hold her. Day had turned to night.

How many hours had passed?

Think, Mara, think.

Her memory was jagged and broken.

Motorcycle taxis whined through the street like hornets. A completely new collection of food carts had sprouted up around her. Blue gas rings hissed against metal woks. A woman wielding a wooden pestle pounded a pungent mixture of peppers and pickled crabs. The shrill cacophony of the street made it hard to think. She felt bruised by the commotion.

As Mara tried to draw the fractured bits of herself back together, a telltale ripple swept through her blood.

Offspring.

No, not a fight. Not now.

Still disoriented, Mara swung her head from side to side, searching for whomever it was that wanted to kill her this time. Across the busy road, an electronic billboard alternately blinked images of racy men's underwear and announced, *"Thailand, the Land of Smiles."* A great tourist destination.

Come to Thailand. We'll rip your head off and smile!

Twenty

The flights from Portland to Seoul, Korea, and then on to Bangkok had taken nearly twenty-four hours. Dalmeet's stomach churned with exhaustion, and his teeth felt fuzzy. Even this close to midnight, traffic choked the wide avenue, but the armored body and bulletproof glass of the boxy Mercedes Gelandewagen muted the bleating horns and rumbling diesels.

Dalmeet leaned against the leather upholstery and rubbed his temples. *Thanks be to the White One for luxury vehicles.* His father and Uncle Momar had cultivated relationships within the Foreign Service. Using those connections, Dalmeet, Ethan, and Hiroko had sped through customs and secured diplomatic transport, sparing them a cab ride from hell through the city.

Instead of rear seats, the SUV had three upholstered benches situated in a squared U-shape. A privacy window separated them from the driver. Hiroko dozed in the corner. The healer, who considered Mara some kind of wild younger sister, had no doubt that Mara would accept him as her Scribe, but Dalmeet wasn't so sure.

Calling Mara wild is like calling the ocean damp.

Ethan's face was invisible behind his hair, and his fingers flew over the screen of the enhanced tablet that might as well have been fused to his hands. Mara's hacker had kept to himself since the Binding, but from what Dalmeet had observed, Ethan was both carefully logical and wide open to the inexplicable aspects of Mara and the Eleven. *An unexpected combination.* He'd found Mara through absolutely brilliant hacking that Dalmeet only vaguely understood.

Dalmeet suspected Ethan was in love with Mara. Why else would he have gone through the Binding? He wondered if she shared those feelings. She'd have to be a blind idiot not to notice how gorgeous he was.

"What's up?" Ethan asked, catching Dalmeet watching him.

Love those eyes.

"Nothing." Dalmeet shrugged. "I'm wiped." He patted the Record, which lay open on his lap. "The letters are starting to swim together."

Ethan lowered the tablet to his lap, stretching his neck from side to side. "Making headway?"

The leather-bound Record was far more than a book. Carefully handwritten by Scribe after Scribe, formal accounts of events in the Layils' lives were interspersed with drawings and maps, even scraps of fabric and a bit of tree bark stained dark. A complex cipher protected the family's secrets.

"I am," he said. "Uncle Momar taught me to decode it when I was pretty young, but I'm rusty. Can you take a look at this chart? It's encrypted differently. Mathematical, I think."

Ethan slid closer so he could look at the Record. "Sweet! Let me nab a picture of it. Then I don't have to get in your space while I work on it."

You can get in my space.

Ethan used his tablet to take a picture and then slid back to his original seat.

Dalmeet went back to the Record. In it, his predecessors had recorded their own darkest fears and secret hopes. His mind whirled as he struggled to grasp the many threads, the interwoven stories and the stratagems, some of which would take generations to see fruition. Dalmeet had read enough to know that Mara was part of some plan involving the Layils, Momar, and Armaros herself. The chart he'd asked Ethan to work on was part of it, but damn if he could work out the details.

He needed Uncle Momar.

Even dead, the old Sikh's broad-shouldered shadow towered over him.

I'm no Momar.

He'd barely skimmed the surface of the Record.

What can I be to her? Some scrawny, cut-rate, second-run Singh.

Dalmeet touched the blade at his waist. He'd been trained since youth in *gatka,* but he wasn't any good at it. Not like Taan, who was lithe and fast. Not like Taan, who was born to be a Scribe.

Someone should smack me. I'm her Scribe. Not Taan. Now act like it!

He had no doubt Mara needed the best he could give her.

Between the Guard and Aeda's men, Mara was like Indiana Jones in that Peruvian temple: spiders, collapsing floors, giant boulders, crazy Frenchman, snakes ...

She needs backup, not a self-pitying Singh.

Abbot Greb had warned them to trust no one. Not even the Amyclaean Guard. But Dalmeet knew he needed Mara to trust him. Otherwise, he might end up like the fool Indiana Jones hired, skewered on spikes.

"This chart looks like data for a breeding experiment," said Ethan, handing over the tablet. "A list of generations. Maybe part of the Layils' research."

Dalmeet scanned the work Ethan had done. His mind flew into overdrive trying to make sense of it. In light of Uncle Momar's entries, the chart could only mean one thing. But that was ... *By the Blade ...* Dalmeet leaned against the seat trying to find an alternate explanation.

An alert notification sounded from the tablet. "Hang on." Ethan pulled it out of Dalmeet's hands. "That's the search I'm running on the GPS signals for the cab company that picked

Mara up from the airport." His fingers raced over the screen. "Here," he said. "The cab dropped her here. Let's go!" Ethan nudged him out of the muddle of his thoughts. "Come on, Dalmeet. Give the dude directions."

"Right … uh … sure." Dalmeet leaned forward to tell the driver their new destination.

Ethan woke Hiroko, and in five minutes, the driver was parking the SUV.

"Let's have a look," said Ethan.

"Keep your eyes out for the Amyclaeans," cautioned Hiroko, "and Aeda."

Dalmeet broke into a sweat as soon as they left the chilled interior of the SUV. Sickly yellow bulbs lit the busy night market surrounding the Northern Bus Terminal. At a nearby food cart, a large man in a stained apron was tossing a stir-fry. Vivid flames blazed and a haze of hot chili pepper burned Dalmeet's eyes. Wiping his forehead with a handkerchief, he pushed past a cluster of people waiting to order.

Everywhere he looked, he saw the sleek black hair of the local Thais and occasionally the coarser, brown hair of a Malay from the south. Dalmeet followed Hiroko and Ethan through the noisy crowd, scanning for blond and worrying about what he'd say if they found her.

Hi, I'm Dalmeet, your new Scribe.

They passed a tent full of live chickens squawking out some avian version of a death metal cover.

Hi, I'm Momar's nephew. I'm here to help you.

The incessant pounding of mortar and pestle at the *som tom* cart sent his brain thudding. Surely he could think of something to say that wouldn't make him sound like a complete imbecile!

A piercing yell broke through the singsong noise of the crowds.

English? Before Dalmeet had a chance to register the meaning of the words, Hiroko was in motion. She dodged right, crashing into a booth full of brightly colored sarongs. Ethan leapt the other way and sent a mountain of furry red fruits flying like grenades.

Dalmeet was glued in place by his own confusion until a shrieking blur slammed into his chest and sent him flying into the street.

"Aaaah!" he screamed. "Get it off! Get it off!"

All around him, people screamed, rushing out of the way.

His attacker straddled him, pressing her forearm against his neck. Cars and motorcycles squealed to a stop on all sides.

Dalmeet's blood frothed through his veins.

It's her! A happy thrill filled him, in spite of his pinioned arms and bruising backside.

"Who are you?" she snarled.

With the wind knocked out of him, Dalmeet could do little more than blink at the feral girl threatening him.

"Mara! It's us!" Hiroko crouched next to her, and Dalmeet felt the pressure on his neck ease.

"Easy, tiger." Ethan had a hand on the girl's shoulder.

So this is Mara Layil.

She released Dalmeet's arms and climbed off of him, the savage expression on her face replaced by confusion. "What are you doing here?"

"I love it when a plan comes together," said Ethan as he helped Dalmeet out of the oily puddle of fetid gutter water. Hiroko urged them out of the street and away from the gawkers. Dalmeet leaned against the side of the SUV, gulping air and trying to get used to the way Mara made his blood race.

A side effect of the Binding. I wonder if Ethan feels it too.

Mara paced in a tight circle. She pushed up the sleeves of her tattered leather jacket, and Dalmeet saw the gauntlets. The slate gray metal flowed along her forearms. He'd never seen a true relic before and wanted desperately to touch them, but Mara was firing high-caliber scowls so he didn't move.

"What the hell is going on? Who are you?"

Dalmeet hoped her eyes didn't shoot laser beams. Ethan gave him an encouraging nod. Dalmeet opened his mouth and shut it again. He still didn't know what to say.

Grinning, Hiroko came to the rescue. "Mara, you almost killed us!"

"With fruit," said Ethan, tossing a *rambutan* at Mara. She caught it easily but didn't crack a smile.

"You're not supposed to be here."

Ethan shrugged and flashed her a crooked smile. If she could stay mad with him looking at her like that, then Dalmeet was impressed.

"This is Dalmeet," said Hiroko. "Your new Scribe."

Mara's expression grew even more dangerous. "I don't need a new one."

Dalmeet stiffened. *Nice to meet you too.*

"Let's get out of here," said Ethan, tucking his hand under Mara's arm and leading her toward the SUV. Mara climbed in and occupied one bench, legs spread wide.

Super classy.

Dalmeet sat as far away from Mara as he could and stayed quiet. He wasn't sure what might cause her to detonate. From the information in the Record, he'd expected her to be slightly unstable. Trying to kill him on the first day might be par for the course. So far being her Scribe was big fun.

At least she was glowering at Ethan for the time being. "Something's different about you," she said. "You ... feel ... different."

"Wanna feel me up?" Ethan teased.

"Oh, shut up! Howdya find me?"

Ethan waggled his tablet at her. "Caught you on an airport camera getting in a cab. Hacked the cab company ..." He shrugged. "Child's play."

"You've been spying on me?"

"That was a hell of a good show on the train, by the way." Ethan seemed oblivious to the fact that he was sitting next to a porcupine.

I've got to figure out what makes her tick.

"The train? How'd you know about that?"

"Hey, Mara," Hiroko broke in, "where are we headed?"

"We are not headed anywhere. You are going home."

Does she really think she has to do this alone?

"Like hell," said Ethan.

An internal tug of war played out over her features. She wanted them here—well, at least she wanted Ethan—but she also wanted them gone.

She would have wanted Momar.

"Momar would have wanted us here," said Hiroko and earned herself a laser-blast glare. Dalmeet was impressed that instead of looking away, the healer stared placidly back. Finally, Mara raised her hands in defeat, pulled off her backpack, and rummaged through it.

"Toru Itou left this stuck in my shoulder." She held out a delicate blade. From its handle dangled a crumpled, blood-splattered tag. The current of Dalmeet's blood strengthened, and one look at Ethan's face told Dalmeet that he felt it too—the resonance of the blood, an affinity for relium.

Another relic! Today is one for the record books.

Ethan read the tag. "Pan-National Haematological Research Centre, Chiang Rai, Thailand."

"Let me see your shoulder," demanded Hiroko.

"I think my dad might be there," said Mara, slipping off her jacket and unbuttoning a mangled white blouse. Ethan and Dalmeet stared out opposite windows as Mara sat in her bra, and Hiroko fussed over her wounds.

The Research Centre! Dalmeet's mind whirred. That jibed with Momar's speculations in his last few entries. He pressed an intercom button and gave their driver the destination in a quick flurry of Thai. Once he and the driver had worked out the route, he slid back into his seat to find Mara staring at him like he was some freakish lab specimen.

"You speak Thai?"

"Obviously."

"Why?"

"Um ...," he stammered. "Could you ... uh ... put your shirt on?"

Mara rebuttoned. "Modest, are we?"

Uh ... yes.

Uncle Momar had directed Taan toward the things that would make him a great Scribe—widespread languages such as Chinese and French, multiple fighting techniques, the arcane symbology of the Eleven. He'd given Dalmeet more leeway, given the unlikelihood that he'd ever serve as Scribe. Dalmeet had pretended indifference by learning Thai and Urdu.

Dalmeet pinched the rumpled crease of his khakis, now stiff with the crust of Bangkok gutter sludge. He knew his position hung by a thread. The wild thing sitting across from him in a tattered boarding school outfit was taut and twitchy. At the same time, he was drawn to her. She was his entrée into a world of mystery and power. He wanted to hold the scents of this world to his face and breathe deeply.

By the Blade, the blood of the Eleven runs in her veins.

And now mine.

A thrill shivered through him.

I have to make her need me. It's not too late.

She hadn't kicked him bodily from the vehicle … yet.

"About your dad," Dalmeet began, "from what Momar wrote in the Record, I think you're right. He might be up north."

"You knew Momar?" she asked quietly.

"He was my uncle."

She stared down at her hands.

She misses him too.

He chose his next words carefully. "Uncle Momar trained me in case he wasn't here to help you." He glanced at Hiroko and Ethan, wondering if they were going to rat him out as a spare. No—they were with him.

Mara leaned forward, chin jutting out like a threat. "I don't need your help."

"I think you do."

"Whatever," Mara said, slumping back in her seat. "I'm hungry."

Dalmeet forced himself to ignore the blowoff. He'd take a card from Ethan's deck and observe. Hiroko handed her a bag of shrimp-flavored chips and a Dr. Pepper. Mara leaned into Ethan as he showed her the way he'd hacked into security feeds with her visual profile. Bruises dappled her skinny arms. The skin above her gauntlets was scabbed over.

In spite of her bravado, Dalmeet knew instinctively that she was scared. Whether it was the trace of her blood flowing in his own veins or the weight behind her eyes, Dalmeet felt Mara's growing anxiety. If he couldn't convince her to take him on Momar's word, he'd have to get more drastic. *This is my chance.*

"You're in a lot of trouble," said Dalmeet, keeping his voice low and steady.

She snorted. "What's new?"

"You broke the Covenant. Most people think you should be dead. Armaros gave you a chance, and you took off."

"Thanks for the recap, Mr. Goody Two-Shoes. You planning on taking me back to that old bitch?"

"No." Dalmeet struggled to tamp down his irritation. "I'm planning on keeping you alive, if you'll give me half a chance."

"Give me a fucking break."

He'd absorbed enough of the Record to guess that her Turning was not going well. In his entries, Momar had worried about it since she was fifteen. Mara's powers were growing far faster than her ability to channel them. And if his suspicions about the circumstances of her birth were correct … they were all in over their heads.

But he had to push her.

His gut told him it was the only way.

Push her to the edge so she realizes she needs help.

"Feeling like everything's been going well for you the last few weeks, do you?" he taunted.

"Yeah." Mara looked like she might throw him from the car, but over the pounding of his own heart, he could sense something of her inner state—unsure, off-kilter, unstable. Her tough-girl façade had definite cracks.

"Think maybe you're going crazy? Seeing things? Losing time? Feeling out of control?"

She crumpled the empty bag of chips and dropped it to the floor. The rabid look from when she'd attacked him returned. Mara's body began to sway back and forth.

Fight or flight.

Dalmeet braced himself. He wouldn't put it past her to tear the roof off the SUV as they barreled along going seventy, but he kept pushing. "When you killed Sinioch, did you mean to do that? Or do those gauntlets have a mind of their own?"

Mara's head swung wildly side to side, her eyes blind. The gauntlets writhed and flexed on her arms—one second covering her fists, the next bladed, then resheathed, as she struggled for control.

"I know why it's all happening, Mara!" Dalmeet was yelling now. "I can help you!"

Whether she could hear him, Dalmeet didn't know.

She screamed, guttural and enraged like a trapped animal. Ethan grabbed one of her arms, and Hiroko reached for the other. Dalmeet tensed for her attack, half hoping that the driver would notice something was wrong and let him out. *No dice.* The tinted, soundproof glass muffled all sounds of her rage. The SUV soared north, a steel cage match on wheels.

Mara tugged her arm out of Ethan's grip and sent the can of soda flying. Before it could hit the window, the can stopped in midair. Mara lurched out of her seat, and Hiroko shrieked, but the sound was truncated by a bubble of frozen time, her face contorted and pained.

"Mara, no!" Ethan shouted, but he too hit an invisible wall of time, sprawled flat, and was glued to the floor.

Fear coursed through Dalmeet. Provoking her might have been fatal. Mara whirled on him, eyes rolling, the fabric of time shredding around them. Her hand shot forward and closed around his neck.

The pocket of time around the soda collapsed. The can crashed to the floor, sending a spray of droplets onto Dalmeet's face. He scrabbled at the iron grip around his neck. Black spots dotted his vision. As pockets of time expanded and contracted around them, Ethan and Hiroko twitched like they were being electrocuted.

Mara would kill them all if he couldn't find a way to calm her down. She was looking but not seeing, lost in the maelstrom of her own powers. He both feared her and feared for her. Mara needed him. He was sure she did. From the very edge of consciousness, Dalmeet shoved his knee into Mara's midriff. She flew backward and hit the side of the SUV, which swerved wildly across the lane as the driver finally realized something was wrong and freaked out.

The intercom sparked to life and the driver demanded to know what was going on in a frantic stream of Thai.

"We're fine!" Dalmeet yelled in Thai. "Shut up!"

Mara had slumped onto the bench. Gulping for air, Dalmeet stumbled toward her, grabbing her face in his hands.

"You. Are. Not. Crazy!"

Her eyes flew open, and Dalmeet felt her hanging on his words. *She wants to believe.*

"You're not crazy," he whispered. "I know it. Let me help you as my uncle did. Please."

Tears filled her eyes.

Around them, time rewove itself.

Ethan and Hiroko lay tangled and panting in a pool of Dr. Pepper. Mara, her face streaked with dirt and tears, stared at her hands like they didn't belong to her body. Dalmeet pulled himself onto the seat next to her. His heart was still racing, but the chaotic terror subsided. He put his hand over hers and noticed that they were almost the same size. Ethan and Hiroko pulled themselves back onto the seats.

"I don't want to hurt anyone else." Mara's voice was so soft that Dalmeet could hardly hear her. "Make it stop. Please."

Dalmeet felt her fear in his own veins. He squeezed her hand. "You are the union of two lines of the Eleven. Do you know what that means?"

Mara shook her head weakly, but Hiroko clutched at his arm. "You can't be serious?" she said. "A forbidden union?"

Dalmeet nodded, still shocked by the enormity of what the Record had shown him and stunned by Mara's ignorance of her own heritage. Momar had kept his secret well—too well.

"I'm lost," said Ethan. "Translation, please."

"The Covenant," Dalmeet explained, "forbids Offspring from having children together, but what's clear to me is that Mara was actually conceived in the hopes of uniting the blood lines of Tamel and Armaros."

"By the Blade ..." Both horror and fear swept over Hiroko's face. He knew how she felt.

"That's impossible," Mara said. "My mom isn't Offspring."

She doesn't know.

"Don't look at me like that, Scribe," Mara sniped. "Momar would've told me."

"I don't think so," said Hiroko. "For two Offspring to have children ... It's not only forbidden, it's almost always disastrous."

Mara narrowed her eyes at Hiroko, and Dalmeet braced himself for another explosion.

"What do you mean?"

"Aberrations ... deformities. Usually death."

The sudden, dark silence was like a gaping mouth. More than anything, Dalmeet had wanted to be a Scribe, and now here he was—linked to a girl who'd been crossbred like a dog for a purpose he couldn't begin to fathom.

"Does Armaros know?" Hiroko asked.

He nodded. "I think so."

"Not her! Not the Time Weaver! She's the only one we have left." Hiroko buried her face in her hands.

"Is that why she took me?" asked Mara.

"What?" Dalmeet asked. "Who took you?"

"Right before you found me, I was with Armaros. She found me and took me outside of time. When I got back, a whole day had gone by."

"Outside of time? Why?" Dalmeet's confusion was mirrored in his companions.

"She told me that if I could find some crown for her—she called it a *circlet*—that I could go free."

Dalmeet's mind whirled. *A crown? If Armaros had a hand in planning Mara's birth, she had a reason. If the crown was the reason, it can only be ...*

"The Circlet of Moments—the lost relic of Armaros."

"You can't be serious," said Hiroko.

"I'm dead certain."

"She said my Scribe would help me find it." Without her usual wall of bravado, Mara looked young and forlorn. Ethan slid his arm around her.

He doesn't understand. He doesn't know that we should all get as far away from her as possible.

"We'll find it," Ethan said.

She's cursed.

"That's not all," Mara said.

Alarm bells exploded in Dalmeet's head. *Of course it's not.*

"Armaros told me I had to find this Circlet of Moments so it could be used to keep the Twins outside the flow of time."

The Twins!

Dalmeet pressed both fists against his temples. By the Blade of the Sacrifice, he'd Bound himself to Mara's blood. He'd pledged to be her Scribe. He'd sworn to help her, but he'd never imagined this. Since the Embodiment, no threat was greater than the Twins. They were a singularity—an unknown, potent force.

And they were angry.

TWENTY-ONE

Petra paced the room that had been hers for thirty years. It took exactly six strides to cross the long way and four the short. Her thoughts came in six-stride bursts. The conversation she'd overheard between Robaire, Semo, and Matthias haunted her.

What is this plan of succession?

What do they mean about urging things forward?

By the Blade, Armaros was the Eleven!

Tur'el had passed over a century ago, and the others long before that. In Petra's lifetime, Armaros had been a constant presence—a regal mountain, geologically solid and unmoving. She was the anchor point of their vast family tree. The First Born of the Eleven made up its branches, and their children, the Offspring, were slender twigs, branching this way and that. Petra knew every turn of her own lineage back to Hrminir.

We are family.

Yet even as Petra tried to convince herself that everything was fine, the fear that had stabbed through her behind the kitchens redoubled. *Armaros is in danger.* Her gut screamed the truth of it.

What are they planning?

That was what she needed to figure out and walking a rut in the floor of her room wasn't helping. Matthias spoke of succession. Was he hoping to get Armaros out of the way so he could step into her shoes?

As if he could replace her.

There were rogue family lines that wanted to see the destruction of the Council. They believed the Covenant would die with Armaros and thus would have the most to gain by eliminating her, but from what Petra gleaned of Matthias's twisted logic, he believed succession would insure the perpetuation of the Covenant, not its downfall. Still, the idea was insane. Even at her advanced age, Armaros was more powerful than any Offspring.

An incoming text buzzed her out of her pacing—Matthias.

The coincidence froze Petra in place.

<u>Attend briefing room with all available Amyclaeans in twenty minutes.</u>

All available?

Besides Robaire and Semo, she and Shiraz were the only ones in Istanbul.

I have spread the Guard too thin. Petra had thrown a wide net to catch the girl and only now realized that she had sent her most loyal away. Robaire, Semo, and Shiraz. *I am alone in this.*

As Petra walked to the briefing room, she found the last line of the Blessing of the Blade Guardian running through her mind. *As it was in the Before, may all Offspring live true.* Armaros had known the Before. She had chosen human embodiment. She and the rest of the Eleven had given rise to all Offspring.

Live true.

It seemed a simple motto.

The briefing room was packed with Crimson Scribes and apparently, every aide, archivist, and bureaucrat that Matthias could round up. Matthias himself waited at the front in his formal robes, gray-haired and stern. Petra took her customary place to the right of the podium. Though Robaire and Semo stood against the wall facing her, neither met her gaze.

"I'll be brief," said Matthias after the room quieted. "The Layil girl has escaped from the Amyclaean Guard—again."

Petra stiffened at the insult but waited, expressionless, for him to explain that Armaros had called them off the mission.

Instead, he said, "Mara Layil has gone rogue."

A combination of shocked gasps and knowing mutters filled the space.

"In fact," he continued loudly, "I have reason to believe that Mara Layil is systematically hunting down Offspring and dispatching them. She may be working with the Hidden Eye."

Petra edged closer to the podium, reminding him of her presence. If he had intel on this, it should have come to her first! How dare he insinuate failure from the Guard and then cut her out of the intelligence loop? The Guard and the Crimson Scribes each served Armaros in their own jurisdictions—defense and administration. He was overstepping his role.

Matthias refused to meet her eye. He gave the crowd just enough time to work themselves up before adding fuel to the fire. "Aeda Moreau, the widow of the First Born killed by Mara Layil, is on her way to the High Council as we speak. She is bringing further proof of the girl's unspeakable actions."

Further proof? What proof? By the Blade, that woman could not be trusted.

Petra clenched her teeth and, for the first time in many years, wished she had full use of speech.

"I do not ...," she began, choking out the words.

Matthias raised his voice, steamrolling over her pained rasp. "I've called you together to implore extra vigilance. Mara Layil may attempt to come here, into the heartland of our kind. To guarantee our safety, I am redirecting all members of the Amyclaean Guard to protect ports of entry into Turkey."

Petra's furious disbelief left her even more incapable of words than before.

He'd made a fool of her and now had completely usurped her authority! Worse, he was keeping the Guard spread thin. If he wanted to protect Armaros, he was doing everything wrong.

"Be careful, my friends. Be watchful."

Does he want to protect her?

The doubts that had begun in the corridor beyond the kitchens wormed their way deeper. Matthias pushed past her, and Petra glowered after him as the crowd dispersed into buzzing, worried knots.

You cannot fool me, old man.

In his speech, he had twisted everything. That was the problem with words. They did not have a will of their own. Well, she would not waste her words on him. She would keep her own silent counsel and ferret out the truth.

She touched the hilt of her blade.

The place to start is Aeda Moreau.

TWENTY-TWO

ETHAN

EN ROUTE TO CHIANG RAI, THAILAND

Ethan watched Mara sleep as the SUV rocked over the pitted road. Going over a particularly big bump, the top of her head grazed his leg, riveting his attention to the place where they touched. Spikes of blond hair lay across his jeans like zebra stripes. He fought the urge to smooth it against his thigh. Asleep, she was delicate. The wash of purple under her eyes matched the welter of bruises along her arms. His own arms hurt to look at hers.

Dalmeet had told them everything he'd pieced together about the circumstances of her birth—that Armaros herself had arranged a match between her grandson, Paul Layil, and Veronique, a many-generations-removed Offspring of the Blade Guardian's line. She'd entrusted Momar with the task of keeping Veronique's ancestry a secret.

Why she wanted to join the bloodlines in violation of the Covenant, no one knew, not even Momar. It was a risk on several levels, not the least of which was physical. The Record had revealed a year prior to Mara's healthy arrival, there'd been two miscarriages and the birth of a baby who only lived a few hours, as well as several pregnancy failures between her and Max.

Mara had chewed up this grisly bit of her history and spat it out. She and Dalmeet argued about the Twins until Hiroko had forced a ceasefire. The three of them collapsed into an exhausted sleep, but Ethan was still trying to make sense of the problem they faced. According to Dalmeet, when the Blade Guardian, Tamel, failed to execute the Twins, he'd set something terrible in motion. Now the Twins, if released, were poised like nuclear bombs, ready to destroy everything in their path.

Ethan tried to imagine being asked to execute children. He didn't ever want to meet the person who could do such a thing. He looked down at Mara, her chest rising and falling with each breath.

She wasn't even supposed to be born.

If the Covenant supporters knew the truth, they'd call for her execution all over again.

It wasn't her fault. It didn't make her wrong or evil.

She's Mara.

Ethan hated Armaros for setting her up.

Dalmeet argued that if Armaros wanted Mara to find the Circlet of Moments, she'd better drop everything and do it because Armaros was like a god or something. But if Armaros knew Mara at all, she sure as shit wouldn't have tried ordering her around. On the other hand, Mara was dead set on finding her dad and doing everything she could to save Max before she'd even consider her granny's request. The more Ethan thought about it, the less he understood and the smaller he felt. He couldn't shake the sensation that jaws were closing in around them.

Mara jerked and twisted in her sleep, calling out as if something startled her. Hiroko woke immediately and stroked her cheek, shushing her.

Ethan wished he had the guts to touch her like that. Mara settled without waking, and Hiroko too went back to sleep. Ethan stared out the window at a long stretch of nothing. Dalmeet said it was eleven or twelve hours to Chiang Rai, depending on whether the road was flooded out. An overnight bus trundled alongside them. An attendant was handing out pillows and blankets and the multicolored action of some kung fu video flickered from ceiling-mounted screens.

Ethan wanted to rest, but he was too keyed up. Mara's gauntlets were close enough to make his blood race like he'd downed one too many cups of coffee. The scalpel relic she'd asked him to tuck in his tablet case pulsed with a slower beat, and Ethan felt as if two discordant songs were playing in his body.

Neither he nor Dalmeet had mentioned the Binding.

She has to know sometime.

The secret weighed on him. He felt like a thief, filling his veins with something she had not offered. *I've got to tell her.* Ethan was no psychic, but he could predict her response as surely as he knew each number in the Fibonacci sequence. *She's gonna tear my head off.*

Hungry for distraction, Ethan turned on his tablet. The glow of the screen, the road noise, and the soft breathing of the others filled the back of the SUV. Like he often did when he couldn't sleep, Ethan logged in to *Stack & Scatter* and waited for someone to join.

Ping!

CLOAKED, a player he'd never faced before joined the game.

His own handle was *PYTHAGORAS.*

His opponent laid down the first word—*LISTEN*—for six points. Seriously? Ethan was a top scorer on *Stack & Scatter.* Few players were good enough to challenge him. If six points was the best this bozo could do, then Ethan was doubtful it would be the distraction he needed. *What a colossal waste of an S.*

Ethan searched his letters for a killer word.

The game used letter tiles with the same point distribution as other popular word games but an unbounded board without double- or triple-point squares. You had nine tiles, not seven, and besides linking words in the usual fashion, you could stack tiles on top of existing words. They had to be sequential unless— and this was Ethan's ace in the hole—you could use all nine tiles in one play. Then they could scatter across the board and you got points for nine words in one turn.

The scatter play was how he usually dominated the game.

Ethan's mind rattled through the options for his next move. The letters clicked into place easily. He wanted a word with high points as well as one that would set him up for future plays.

He tapped letters until he'd connected *WORKS* to the *S* in *LISTEN*. Thirteen points. Not stellar, but it blocked the *S* and would leave *W* open to use again.

He looked up from the tablet. Ahead of the SUV on the right side of the road, a cluster of buildings sat in an orange halo of streetlights. An open-air restaurant bustled with people, but the rest of the stores were closed for the night. Even the gas station was closed.

Their vehicle sped on, leaving the lights behind.

Ping!

CLOAKED had changed the *K* in *WORKS* to a *D* for nine points.

Ethan tossed down *NASCENT*. It was only worth eight points, but it was a great word. There was such promise whenever things were just coming into being. He liked beginnings a lot better than he liked endings.

Ethan looked down at Mara again. Beginning at Cascadia Correctional Facility was not what he would have chosen, but he'd take what he could get. He wanted to be as close to Mara as she would let him.

Ping!

Ethan looked down at the screen. *Crap!*

CLOAKED had used his *W* to make *POWER*. Ten points.

"Well, suck on this, *CLOAKED*." Ethan put down *QUARE*. It was an old Irish word meaning remarkable or strange.

And he uses the Q, thank you very much.

Ethan's score jacked up fourteen points.

Waiting on *CLOAKED*, he zoned out on the screen. *Nascent* and *quare*. Mara shifted next to him. He could see the pulse in the hollow of her throat. What would it feel like to place his lips there, to feel her warmth against his mouth?

He tore his eyes away. *Quare* and *nascent*. Strange beginnings indeed. She rolled over in her sleep, jamming her head more firmly in the space between his hip and the seat back. He wanted to pull her into his lap and kiss her, but that was bat-shit crazy. He might as well try making out with a badger.

A ping brought his attention back to the game. *CLOAKED* played and signed off with a flushing sound.

Ethan could not believe the play.

CLOAKED had stacked *INNO* onto *NASCENT*, making *INNOCENT*. Not a big point play, only earned him ten, but damn impressive.

Ethan stared at the screen. *LISTEN. WORDS. POWER. INNOCENT.*

He had the uncanny feeling that they were supposed to go together. Were they some kind of message?

Get a grip. It's a coincidence. That's all.

Ethan shut down the tablet and stared blankly out the window into the darkness, but the words kept rolling around in his head like pinballs, rearranging themselves. *Listen, words have power.* Any pop psychologist knew that. Just because words mean things, there's no reason to think *CLOAKED* had a particular message for him.

Who is innocent?

Was he? Was anyone really?

Ethan slipped in and out of sleep as the SUV plowed into the night. Around four o'clock in the morning, they pulled off at a small town to switch drivers. Ethan woke from a dream, or maybe a memory, of group therapy in Cascadia. Mara had rolled over while they slept and now her arm was draped over his knee. She woke like a cat, stretching, and as she reached overhead, her forearm thudded softly into his chest.

She snatched her hand back and pushed herself upright.

Ethan smiled blearily at her from under his shaggy hair.

Strange beginnings indeed, but he wasn't thinking very innocent thoughts.

TWENTY-THREE

AEDA

PAN-NATIONAL HAEMATOLOGICAL RESEARCH CENTRE, CHIANG RAI, THAILAND

Again, Aeda longed for Sinioch.

Again and again and again.

She was being pulled in too many directions, and the one person she had always counted on to keep her together was gone. If Sinioch were here, she could meet Matthias de Alba in Istanbul knowing full well that when Mara Layil showed up in Thailand, Sinioch would handle her.

At least her head of security had Dr. Layil confined to the lab building. She had no doubt that his loyalty, such as it was, would falter as soon as he saw his daughter. Yet she could hardly sit around waiting on the girl when the time was ripe for her to make a move on the Council. Armaros was poorly guarded right now! The opportunity was far too potent to miss.

Aeda stared at her hands, her thumbs skimming the tops of her fingertips. Back and forth, her thumbs traced a path along them, anticipating the feel of the relium garrote throbbing taut across the wrinkled neck of the Time Weaver.

Your time is ending. I will rise over your corpse.

She breathed deeply and dropped her hands to her side.

For Sinioch.

It was time.

After ensuring that Awaale had redoubled security on the building, Aeda headed to the second floor to check Dr. Layil's progress. He'd had five days to improve on the device.

It had better work.

Three gurneys in the medical unit were full. The bodies lay motionless under white sheets as ventilators wheezed and various other readouts beeped and hummed. Dr. Layil was at his desk in the adjoining office, which now also served as his bedroom. She leaned on the doorframe, watching him scratch formulae on a legal pad and flip through a stack of medical charts. A rumpled cot stood in the corner. Gray-blond stubble shadowed his cheeks.

She wanted progress, and he had been working feverishly since they'd spoken almost a week ago. *Smart man.*

Aeda cleared her throat.

Layil flinched and the pen skittered down his page, leaving an ink slash through his notes.

"Aeda."

If he was afraid of her, his face didn't show it.

He is afraid of me, though—or he should be.

She nodded a greeting. "I require a demonstration, Layil."

"It's not ready." He went back to his chart notes with deliberate precision.

She crossed the distance between them and pinched his upper arm, pulling him to his feet. "Yesterday, I provided you with a new subject. Today—now—you will provide a demonstration."

He jerked his arm out of her grip. "I told you it's not ready. It only works for a short period of time, and the control is rudimentary."

"Is that your professional opinion or are you having a change of heart, Doctor?"

Paul stared at her, not bothering to hide the revulsion on his face.

The urge to reach through the man's rib cage and pull his heart out rolled through her. She could practically see the beating organ spurting on his lab coat. Aeda forced her hands behind her back, pushed down the furious hunger, and regained her self-control.

When she spoke again, the expression on her face was unruffled. She tucked one of her arms into his as if inviting him for tea and said, "I want to assess your progress at the very least. Shall we?"

Paul pulled out of her grasp but led the way to the experiments. The skinny young man on the last gurney had red hair and freckles. His clavicles pressed against the thin hospital gown. One of her scouts had found the kid stoned out of his mind on a beach in Phuket. He was a perfect subject—late generation Offspring with no idea who he was. Of course, he knew who he thought he was and had bored Aeda's scout to tears with his story of taking a year off from college to "find himself" through travel.

The idiot knew he had bony shoulder blades but never wondered if there was something more to those stumps. There were many like him of such dilute bloodlines that they were practically human. No appreciable abilities. Barely a blood response to relium.

And very unlikely to be missed by other Offspring.

"Do it!" she snapped.

Dr. Layil shaved a patch of curly hair from the side of the boy's head with a safety razor.

"Alcohol," he said, gloving up.

Aeda pulled on gloves and swabbed for him, feeling the coolness of evaporating alcohol waft toward her wrist. Dr. Layil ran a line from a pouch filled, Aeda knew, with her blood into an artery at the boy's temple. Once the steady drip was flowing, he taped the pouch to the bare patch of skull; then he locked off the IV in the boy's arm. Next Dr. Layil removed a microchip and remote transmitter from a Steripak. He attached these next to the transfusion pouch with medical adhesive. A six-inch-long black wire with an electronic lead at the end dangled from the microchip. He threaded it through a thin, metal tube.

"Hold this biopsy tube," he instructed. Aeda gripped the metal handle carefully.

"I'll need to move quickly after this part." A device whirred to life in Dr. Layil's hand. He drilled the entrance port for the device through the boy's skull, and a dark trickle of blood flowed into the boy's red hair.

"Now," he said, using the tube that Aeda handed him to insert the electronic lead deep in the boy's brain. "Sterilize again." When she was done, he bandaged the entry point and taped the wire in place.

Aeda felt the tension ebb from Dr. Layil as he checked the boy's vital signs and brain function. "He's fine so far."

"When can we animate him?" Aeda asked.

Dr. Layil hesitated. "It would be better to wait twenty-four hours."

"I don't have twenty-four hours."

"Plug this into your smartphone," he said, handing her what looked like a black sugar cube with a plug for the headphone jack. "Voice activated. Simple commands only."

A thrilling blend of anticipation and bloodlust filled her.

"Wake up."

The boy's eyes blinked open. Green eyes, she noticed.

"Stand."

Lumbering, as if his limbs didn't quite know how to talk to each other, he rose and stood before her.

"Hit him," she said, pointing at Dr. Layil.

The boy lurched forward and threw a miss.

"What are you doing?" Dr. Layil shouted.

"Again."

This time the boy was faster. The blow connected with Dr. Layil's jaw, sending him into the wall.

"Excellent."

A thrill surged through Aeda. She was very close to her goal now, and she wanted to swallow the world.

"Lie back down."

The boy slumped onto the gurney.

She returned the control to Dr. Layil, who stood hunched, wiping blood from his mouth. "Excellent work, Doctor. Later today I will be sending you another subject. Prepare the implant immediately."

TWENTY-FOUR

MARA

EN ROUTE TO CHIANG RAI, THAILAND

Twelve hours is a long-ass time to be stuck in a car.

Mara cracked her knuckles, itching to get away from Dalmeet. Everything about this unwelcome hiccup in her plans irritated her like a swarm of mosquitos. The night before, he'd made her weak. She couldn't afford that. No time for babysitting. Hiroko was Offspring and could hold her own, but the Scribe, who was nothing like Momar, reminded her of all the places she could go wrong. Hell, she didn't even want Ethan along.

Well, maybe I want him a little.

It was nearly noon, and they were on their third driver. Dalmeet had them lined up like dominos. She wasn't sure how since all his directives were in Thai, but she was at least a wee bit grateful he'd spared her the overnight bus. Now, they were on the outskirts of Chiang Rai and heading straight for her father.

The proximity of another reunion sent her stomach into backflips.

For him I'm probably just another science experiment.

Hiroko and Dalmeet couldn't stop obsessing about that freaking breeding chart and what they should do about it. Neither seemed to notice or care about its other meaning. *The chart means he never wanted me, never loved me.* She hated Dalmeet for making her see that.

And his voice ...

Does he ever shut up?

Dalmeet and Hiroko had been arguing about their next steps for thirty minutes.

"She can't ignore Armaros!" Dalmeet protested.

I'm right here, douche bag.

"Watch me," Mara broke in.

"Mara, that's insane. If she wants you to find the Circlet of Moments, you have to."

"You have to," she mimicked and grinned to see him wince.

"Don't you want your freedom? The Amyclaeans will catch you eventually. They always do."

"Guys! Come on," Hiroko pleaded. "Mara wants to drive by the Research Centre. What's the harm in that?"

"What if she loses it and blows the building to bits?"

"I won't!"

Dalmeet arched an eyebrow.

Mara turned to Ethan. "Does he ever shut up?"

Following her lead, Dalmeet addressed Ethan as well. "I thought you were taking me to meet this uberpowerful Offspring, not some reeking street rat who can't control herself."

"That's it!" Mara lurched forward, grabbing for Dalmeet's shirt, but Ethan slid between them and hip-checked her back into the seat. He gripped her tightly around the waist and made a show of sniffing her armpit.

"Ph-ew, you do reek. Lucky you don't look like a rat, though."

Furious, Mara raised a hand to smack him, but Ethan grinned wildly. She dropped her arm, a sucker for that crooked smile.

"Fine. I won't kill him ... yet. Just get me out of this car. My ass hurts and I'm starving."

"We'll drive by the Research Centre," said Hiroko, "then find some place safe to eat and make a plan."

"And shower," said Ethan, poking Mara in the armpit.

"You don't exactly smell rosy," she said, but there was no bite in it.

Other than Dalmeet's conversation with the driver over further directions, they rode in silence. Dalmeet's prodding nagged at her, and Mara wanted to punch something. Should she do what Armaros wanted? Who knew how long it would take to find the stupid Circlet? Max might not have that long. A desperate yearning for home filled her. Max was a sweet kid. He deserved a decent life.

Screw Armaros. Max is the only one who matters.

Mara would find her dad and convince him to help, force him if she had to.

The driver stopped across the street from an ugly concrete building with vertical windows sunk deeply in the thick walls.

"So that's the Blood Bank," she said.

"Pan-National Haematological Centre," Dalmeet corrected.

"I can read."

The opposite side of the street was lined with shops selling pirated DVDs, music, and a blinking array of electronic devices. Everything from TVs to computers to arcade games was up for grabs. Outside of one shop, a bunch of girls clustered on an electronic dance floor, trying to imitate the complicated gyrations of a dancer on the video display. Speakers blared techno-pop and a steady stream of people filled the sidewalks.

"Give me a second to pull down IP addresses," said Ethan, fingers flying on his tablet. "It never hurts to know the neighborhood. Oh good. I've got a building schematic. There's a side door and roof entrance in addition to the main one."

Through the front doors, Mara could see two security guards, but neither looked too tough. Over the roof, construction cranes and steel girders were visible from a building site on the opposite side of the Research Centre.

"Cameras in five locations," Ethan muttered. "Oh, and that one—six total."

"Whoa!" said Mara, momentarily breathless from a sudden change in the current of her blood. *Offspring!*

Ethan looked up from his tablet. "What's up?"

She held up a hand. It took a moment for her heart to accommodate the thundering pulse in her veins. When she could breathe again, Mara plastered herself against a window and scanned the street.

"What's wrong?" Hiroko whispered.

"Someone's coming! He's Offspring. Very powerful."

All eyes turned toward the Research Centre.

A man built like a weightlifter with the darkest skin Mara had ever seen was approaching the front doors. Around his huge bulk, the crowd parted nervously. As he entered the building, Mara could see taut muscles and prominent shoulder stumps under his thin cotton dress shirt. Her gauntlets pulsed.

"Well, that's trouble. Let's get out of here."

"Finally," said Dalmeet, giving directions over the intercom. The SUV peeled away from the curb.

"How did you do that?" Hiroko asked.

"Do what?"

"Know he was Offspring."

"I always know when Offspring are around," Mara answered. "Don't you?"

"Uh, no. It's a little weird."

Ethan leaned forward. "A little weird? 'Cause what? Everything else about her is perfectly normal?"

Mara leaned back against the seat. "I'm a freak among freaks, hacker boy."

"That's not what I meant," Hiroko protested. "It's just that I thought only the Eleven could sense each other."

"Ask the Scribe," Mara said.

"The sensation you describe is not unprecedented."

"Nice vocab. Studying for the SAT?" she snapped.

"Very funny," said Dalmeet. "When the Eleven were alive, they had a shared consciousness, a hive mind. I suppose because you unite two bloodlines, you are capable of sensing the resonance." He stared hard at Mara. "It's fascinating."

"Don't look at me like that," Mara said. "I'm not your lab rat."

"What do you mean *resonance?*" Ethan asked.

"That's what my parents study," said Mara.

I'm their lab rat.

"When the Eleven chose embodiment," Dalmeet explained, "their human bodies were suffused with this new element, relium. It's a biologically active metalloprotein, but its presence in the blood is diluted by outbreeding with humans. That's why Offspring way down the line have reduced abilities."

"That guy who just went into the Centre must not be very far removed from the Eleven," said Mara. "His blood about blew my socks off."

"Are Offspring eventually regular, like any human?" Ethan asked.

"Yup," said Dalmeet. "There are Offspring so far down the bloodline that they don't even know their own histories, especially if they don't have Scribes to maintain their genealogies."

"Lucky them," Mara muttered.

"Will you give it up?" Dalmeet snapped. "You practically killed all of us last night. Do you want that to happen again?"

"No!" She glared at him.

"Do you even understand what you did?"

She rubbed her hands on her thighs, avoiding his eyes. "I lost it for a moment. Won't happen again. Especially if you don't piss me off."

She expected Dalmeet to back away. Instead, he leaned toward her. That took balls. And if she was willing to admit it, Mara had been grateful that he'd fought her last night. He'd given her what she needed to get control of herself. Maybe he was a bit whiny, but she'd seen a sliver of Momar in him last night.

He's got one chance.

Mara met his eyes. "All right then, what's happening to me?"

"Well," he said, "each of the Eleven had a unique form of relium, hence the family traits, but you've got metalloproteins from Armaros and Tamel circulating in your blood. Plus, you've got those gauntlets."

Mara held up her arms. "So?"

"Look at this symbol," he said, pointing to some of the etchings. "Azza's for sure. Relium is almost alive. Between your blood and your relics, you're a Molotov cocktail. That's why the gauntlets do things you don't expect, and that's why when you lose control, time buckles around you."

"Most hybrids die," Hiroko interrupted, "because their bodies can't withstand the antagonistic resonances."

"You just called me a hybrid," said Mara, but her irritation evaporated. She was tired of fighting. "Explain what happened last night. Please."

Dalmeet rubbed one hand across his forehead. "Imagine time is like a blanket. Every moment exists at some location on the fabric. Last night, you were punching holes in the blanket."

"But isn't time linear?" Mara asked.

"It seems like that because events happen and can be ordered in a logical way. An egg on the table. An egg falling. A broken egg. Time is always there but the events move through it."

"That sounds crazy," said Mara.

"But think of the power if you can move through it with control and precision."

"I still don't get what happened last night," said Ethan.

"Mara got mad and stopped events at multiple places in timespace. That's why the soda can froze, and you and Hiroko got caught."

"How do I control it?"

"*Can* she control it?" Hiroko asked.

"Uncle Momar left detailed plans for your training in the Record."

"Okay, then," Mara said. "Can you help me do it?"

Dalmeet grimaced. "It was a five-year plan ..."

Mara lost her grasp on the last straw. *He can't help me after all.*

The SUV pulled off the main road and into a narrow, gated drive. When they stopped inside the walled courtyard of an ornate wooden structure, no one moved. Mara realized the others were waiting for her to lead them, but her limbs felt so heavy. *There's too much to carry. I don't know what to do.*

But she did know either she had to trust them or ditch them—all of them. You couldn't get more earnest than Hiroko, and she knew Ethan had her back, but what about Dalmeet? He bugged the hell out of her. *Is that because he's not Momar?*

"Do you like him?" she asked Ethan, gesturing to Dalmeet. He had a sense about people. A *yes* from him was a *yes* she could trust.

Ethan nodded. "I'd keep him."

Dalmeet glued his eyes to the ground.

The weight lifted. "All right, then." She pushed open the back door of the SUV and let the morning light stream in. She squinted at Dalmeet. "Are you sure you're up for this?"

"Absolutely."

She gestured to the door. "After you, Scribe."

White gravel crunched underfoot as they approached the stairs of the guest house. The roof rose in slender peaks toward the pink sky. Hiroko paused to smell the ivory flowers draping the railings like frosting. Dalmeet was near the top of the steps when Mara called to him.

"Dalmeet?"

All three turned to look at her.

"Yes?"

Mara heard the wariness in his voice but pressed on. "I'm sorry I tried to kill you."

His face broke into a smile. "Ethan said it meant you liked me."

"Oh, Dali," she said, laughing for the first time in a long while. "You're a piece of work!"

TWENTY-FIVE

ETHAN

LAI-THAI GUEST HOUSE, CHIANG RAI, THAILAND

Ethan sat on a shaded porch, which ran the length of the second level of the guest house. He was trying to decode another chart from the Record for Dalmeet, but Thailand was constantly distracting him. In his nineteen years, he'd hardly left Portland, much less traveled the world. His hacker connections stretched to all corners of the globe, of course, but cyberspace didn't buzz and growl and steam like Thailand did.

Music filtered up from the lower level of the secluded hotel where they were the only guests. Ethan suspected Dalmeet had something to do with that. The guy was a whiz at all things logistical and had a seemingly limitless supply of cash. He anticipated their needs. Foreign adaptors for all of Ethan's devices. Prepaid, anonymous cell phones. A triage kit for Hiroko. Clothes, miraculously in styles they all liked. Even more remarkable, he'd wormed his way right into Mara's good graces—most of the time.

They'd had two days to rest up and plan. By now, Ethan knew the layout of the Pan-National Haematological Research Centre inside and out and had a decent grasp on the security detail. He was sure they could get in, find Dr. Layil, and get out.

Well, 80 percent sure.

Ethan set aside his tablet and leaned over the porch railing, breathing in the smell of wet earth and observing a long-tailed, black bird flitting over the stream below. Day-Glo flowers speckled the deep green wall of leaves and vines.

"I could get used to this," said Mara, coming up beside him, shoulder to shoulder.

"Me too."

Her hair was wet, her arms bare and free of the gauntlets.

"What do you think of these?" she asked, plucking at wide-legged, orange pants, which tied in a knot at her waist. "Dali says they're Thai fishermen pants." Her new T-shirt, emblazoned with a Princess Leia-Tank Girl mash-up, barely reached her navel.

They're hot.

He looked back at the stream. "Nice."

"Hmm," Mara said, still messing with the knot. "Dali looks pretty elegant in his. I think I look dorky."

"Clean, though," said Ethan, not trusting himself to look at her.

"There is that!" She shoulder bumped him. For someone about to break into a high-security lab, she seemed pretty relaxed.

"You nervous?" he asked.

"I'm trying not to think too much. You?"

"I'm psyching myself up," he admitted. "To get you into the Research Centre, I need to call in some favors from some old ... friends."

She caught the hesitation. "And?"

"Remember that time in group when I told you why I was locked up?" She nodded. "I promised myself I wouldn't get involved with YouKnowMe again, but I'll need their help to pull this off."

They were quiet for a long time. When the black bird flew off, he asked, "Do you remember what you said in group when we were talking about the woman who died because of me?"

"Do I want to know?"

"You said, 'Who the hell do you think you are? God?'"

She winced. "That was harsh."

"Then you said, 'You're not that powerful. You don't piss in the gutter and cause a tidal wave in Hawaii.'"

"I'm a bitch. Sorry."

"Mara, don't be sorry. I felt like I'd pulled a trigger and killed that woman. What you meant, at least what I thought you meant, was that I wasn't a murderer—just really, really stupid.

I'll always feel responsible, but at least I don't feel totally hateful anymore."

They stared at the stream, watching a leaf spinning in the current.

"Do you remember what else you said?" he asked.

"I said more? Somebody should have shut me up."

"Like anybody could've done that!"

She rubbed her neck sheepishly. "Don't tell me."

"You said, 'Life's a meat grinder. We all come out sausage.'"

"Ewww," she said. "Embarrassing pop psychology."

"I'll make a bumper sticker for your Enfield," Ethan joked.

"I'll hold your hand while you get my wisdom tattooed on your ass."

They laughed, and Ethan felt the tension leave him. This travel thing was okay.

They turned at the sound of footsteps. Hiroko and Dalmeet followed the proprietor of the guest house out onto the porch. Balancing the tray on the edge of an outdoor table, Khun Lek laid out place settings, a platter of fruit, and a pitcher of milky orange Thai iced tea. He indicated for them to sit, brought his hands together in the honorific *wai*, and left them alone.

"You got any tats, Dali?" Mara asked as she poured herself some tea.

Dalmeet gave an exaggerated sniff. "I'm not that lowbrow."

Ethan grinned. It was good to see Dalmeet loosening up and Mara getting more comfortable with him. In the last few days, the four of them had become less like uneasy allies and more like friends.

Except she needs to know.

The tension returned to his shoulders. Ever since they'd found Mara, the Binding had weighed on his mind. He and Dalmeet had argued the pros and cons of telling her. *It'll just make her mad.* True. *Less mad now than if she finds out later.* Also true. For Dalmeet, the question of *when* or *if* to tell her was strategy. For Ethan, it was about trust.

He'd taken something precious without asking.

Never again.

Ethan cleared his throat, cutting through the chatter at the table. "Mara, I've got to tell you something."

"Yeah?" She was still pestering Dalmeet about tattoos and only half listening.

His voice sharpened. "Listen."

Mara stiffened. "What? You wanna confess you got nipple rings?"

He shook his head. Anxiety zinged through him.

What if she hates me?

Dalmeet was practically burning his eyes out in a silent effort to stop Ethan's confession. Hiroko picked at a hangnail. No help from that quarter.

"Spit it out," said Mara. All the ease in her expression had hardened. Shields were up.

Now or never.

Ethan went full out like he was pulling an epic flip at the skatepark.

Do or die.

"Before we came to find you, I agreed to the Binding."

"What's that?" She shrugged. "An oath or something?"

Dalmeet popped out of his seat like he was a corn kernel in an air popper. "Are you serious?" His head snapped toward Hiroko. "She has no idea. I can't believe it." His attention went back to Mara. "Momar didn't tell you anything?"

"Sit down and shut up!" Mara hollered. "Momar was kinda busy—getting killed!" Silence fell around the table. Dalmeet looked like he'd just run over a puppy. Mara was a thousand miles away again, and Ethan didn't know what to say.

"Guys," said Hiroko slowly. "Let's just explain what happened. Mara—" Hiroko waved her quiet before another outburst. "I needed to get you a Scribe. I wasn't sure Dalmeet was the right one, but when he said he'd go through with the Binding, I knew he was serious about helping you. So even though it's not done anymore, I thought—"

Mara's impatience bubbled over. "Stop with the history already. What the fuck is the Binding?"

"I transfused your blood into Dalmeet and Ethan."

Ethan could feel an echo of Mara's confusion.

She still doesn't understand.

Increasingly, he was able to sense many of her emotions. That too felt like a violation. He knelt and took one of her hands.

"I'm sorry. I mean, I'm not sorry I did it. I'm sorry we didn't ask. All I wanted was to help you."

"What are you all talking about?" Mara pulled away and stood stiffly by the porch railing.

"I'll show you," said Hiroko, clearing a space in the middle of the table. "Does anyone have a pocketknife?" Dalmeet produced one immediately. "Give me your hand."

Dalmeet pursed his lips but laid his slender, brown arm on the table. Hiroko flipped it palm up and held his hand firmly. Before he could protest, she jabbed the point of the knife into his thumb and squeezed a droplet of blood onto the table.

"Ow!" He snatched his hand out of her grasp and pressed a napkin to the wound.

The dime-sized drop of blood quivered slightly.

"Now, Mara," Hiroko ordered. "Put your own hands on the edge of the table."

Wary, Mara stepped forward and laid her hands on the mahogany surface like she was playing the piano. Twelve inches away the circle of blood seemed to breathe in and out.

"I want you to focus on Dalmeet's blood and draw it toward you."

Mara squinted at the table, splaying her fingers against its surface.

Like a living thing, the droplet slid toward her.

Ethan felt the pull mirrored in his own veins and in the strain on Dalmeet's face. The vital part of themselves was being sucked toward her. Ethan edged closer. He couldn't maintain the distance between himself and Mara, feeling as if he might be turned inside out by the insistent call of her blood.

When the droplet hit her fingertip, she looked up. The pull ceased. Ethan and Dalmeet fell away from her, panting, but free from the deadly pressure.

"What just happened?" Mara asked.

"The relium in your blood has taken control of their blood. This gives them a weakened version of your abilities—strength, healing, life span. But it also Binds them to you. If you choose to withdraw your blood from theirs, just like you did with the droplet on the table, they will die."

I need to tell her everything.

Ethan pulled himself together. "We can also feel a hint of what you feel when we're close."

Mara looked like she'd swallowed a slug. "You can read my mind?"

Ethan cringed. The last thing he wanted was to invade her privacy.

"No, no. Not like that," Dalmeet cut in.

How can he sound so nonchalant?

"It's like we're super in tune with you. Like groupies."

"Groupies, eh?" She squinted at Dalmeet. "Why would you do that? I can't even carry a tune." Under the casual tone, Ethan could sense her unease. Like a change in air pressure, the weight she felt pressed down on him.

"We were trying to help," said Dalmeet, his voice made thin by her desire to run from them.

Ethan wanted to clasp her hand, reassure her with warmth and touch, but he couldn't cross the barrier between them.

Finally, it was Mara who pulled away. "I can't help it if you guys are idiots." She threw up her hands, exaggerating her do-what-you-want shrug. "But you—" she said confronting Ethan, "maybe you should consider those nipple rings."

A cold trickle of loss slid through Ethan.

The distance between them was uncrossable.

They were one more burden upon her.

TWENTY-SIX

AEDA

EN ROUTE FROM CHIANG RAI TO ISTANBUL

It was late, and the private airport was nearly deserted. Stars pricked a thousand holes in the velvety sky. Heels clicking on the tarmac, Aeda strode toward her jet. She paused at the bottom of the stairs to watch as a stainless-steel refrigerated case the size and shape of a coffin was loaded into the plane's belly. Once the cargo hold was locked, she boarded. Immediately, the single attendant shut the cabin door. Aeda took the drink he offered without looking up and gazed out the window.

Part of her wanted to stay and wait for Mara. Aeda knew bone-deep that the girl would come for her father, and Aeda did so want to be the one to crush her.

Sinioch deserved as much.

A rush of dark hatred followed close on the heels of memory.

Yet if Aeda played her role correctly in Istanbul ... ah, yes! Then that would be something to be proud of. Without even realizing it, Matthias de Alba was on the verge of destroying the very Covenant he so wanted to protect. Without Armaros to champion the High Council and everything it stood for, many First Born and Offspring would rise to join Aeda.

They would thunder for liberation.

They would topple the Covenant.

She would lead them out from the shadows of humankind.

I will rise.

She waved the flight attendant over for another drink. He was human, had bad skin, and smelled slightly sour. Why would the Eleven have actually wanted to live among them? To be like them? It nauseated her. Humans were weak and fragile and limited. Aeda yearned to be free of their filth.

It is time for Offspring to rise! We will sweep humans from the earth and claim it!

Mara Layil would not be a part of that triumph. Aeda would sway the opinion of the Council against the girl, and they would execute her. *Or I will—and with pleasure.* As soon as she'd extracted what she wanted from her favorite scientist, all the Layils would be expendable.

Even if Mara managed to get through Guleed Awaale's security provisions while Aeda was in Istanbul—an unlikely event—it might work to her advantage and motivate Dr. Layil to work harder. His enhancements to the control device were the final part of her plan.

Now to get rid of Armaros.

The flight attendant laid a hand on her shoulder. "Ms. Moreau, seat belt, please. It's time for takeoff."

She pushed him away. "Get me another drink."

He scurried to the galley as the engines roared to life.

Very soon everything she needed would be in place.

Everything except Sinioch. Aeda gripped the arms of her seat so hard, she left dents. She inhaled through her nose, feeling her nostrils pinch together, trying to curb the fury pounding through her.

The plane taxied, accelerated, and rose from the runway. *She'll pay, my darling. I swear it.* After another minute of ascent, the plane banked sharply. A thin arc of orange along the horizon marked the coming dawn. When the Eleven were no longer embodied, Aeda would know true freedom. She felt the strength of her limbs and knew that what she carried in the hold of the plane was but a taste of the power that would soon be at her command.

No restraints. That's what she wanted.

The time was now!

Armaros is fading.

I am not.

Twenty-Seven

ETHAN

LAI-THAI GUEST HOUSE, CHIANG RAI, THAILAND

The next morning, Ethan and the others met over breakfast.

"Today's the day," he announced. "I cracked into Aeda Moreau's email. She caught a flight to Istanbul last night."

Hiroko's brow wrinkled, and she frowned into a steaming mug of hot tea, but Mara fist-bumped him, and Dalmeet saluted, adding, "Finally, a lucky break!"

"Uh, careful there, Dali," Mara said. "Don't forget I'm like the opposite of luck."

"That's why you've got us."

"When do we start knocking heads?"

"Guys," said Hiroko, "this is serious."

Ethan pulled on a straight face, but shitty times required dark humor. They were breaking into a top-security medical facility to find a man who probably didn't want to be found. Paul Layil made Ethan's parents seem downright decent.

"Ladies ..." Ethan drew out the word and earned a grin from Mara. "We gentlemen have a plan."

Mara flopped into a hammock set up in a corner of the porch. Hiroko gulped down the last of her tea and squeezed in next to Mara. "Let's hear it."

"Before I take the security cameras offline, we're gonna make sure they see you trying to get in through the loading dock. We'll initiate Dalmeet's show, and voilà—utter mayhem."

"But actually, Mara," said Dalmeet, "you'll be entering through the roof. The diversion should buy you enough time to find your dad and get him to come with us."

"Your show?" Mara asked.

Dalmeet pointed to Ethan, who explained. "Did you notice all the electronics shops across from the Centre?"

"No, I'm not a total tool like you."

"We're going to hijack the feeds to all those monitors with images of you."

"The security guards are gonna drop everything to watch TV?"

"Not exactly," said Ethan. "Dali's arranged for lots and lots of Maras."

"Goodness, I think one is enough," said Hiroko, getting an elbow to the ribs from her hammock mate.

"All we need is a little dance video from our star attraction."

Dalmeet pulled out his phone and pointed it at Mara.

"Are you cracked? I'm not dancing."

"We only need thirty seconds of footage, tops, then Ethan can loop it."

"No way. I don't dance."

"Come on," said Dalmeet. "A hip-waggle? That's all we need."

He cued up some crazy Indian pop song on his phone and set it on the table. Mara stuck her tongue out at him, but he grabbed her hand, pulling her from the hammock. At first, he was tugging her around the porch like a rag doll, but Ethan started drumming on the table, and before long, Dalmeet and Mara were spinning down the length of porch.

It thrilled Ethan to watch her like this, uncaged and unarmored, abandoning herself to the moment. He tore his eyes from her hips and swung Hiroko into the fray. When they all collapsed side by side in the hammock, Mara's sweaty hair was plastered to her forehead, and Hiroko was laughing so hard she got the hiccups. Ethan replayed the video he'd taken and reignited their hysterical laughter.

"I told you I shouldn't dance," Mara gasped between breaths.

"Scary moves," said Ethan. "That's all I'm saying."

"You're not all that," she teased back, cuffing him on the top of his head.

Ethan poked her in the ribs, relishing the sound of her squeals. *I could watch you dance all day.* He pressed his leg against hers and breathed in the tangy smell of her sweat. *Or all night.* Ethan never wanted to get out of that hammock.

But an hour later, Team Mara was all business.

Ethan's good humor was gone. For Mara, he was going back to YouKnowMe. It was breaking the promise he'd made to himself. She was worth it. He didn't doubt that, but he hoped they wouldn't suck him back in, making him into someone he didn't want to be.

It was time to take control of Chiang Rai's traffic grid.

Ethan reached out to the hacker network, shooting off direct messages. In addition to rerouting traffic around the Centre, he'd need help patching the pirate video of Mara into the hundreds of TVs, gaming kiosks, and computer screens flashing and blinking along the roads around the Centre. He pushed out GPS coordinates and all the IPs he'd poached. After an hour, he'd done what he could.

Nothing to do now but wait—and try not to think about Mara, sweaty and undressed.

Dalmeet had been on the phone nonstop, pulling together his part of the plan. Hiroko and Mara had gone into their rooms to nap. A sudden violent downpour had cleared away the mugginess of midday.

Ethan logged in to *Stack & Scatter*.

CLOAKED's last move stood out starkly: *INNOCENT*. Kind of ironic given the state he was in. Ethan shook away the thought and studied his letters. He attached *SUBTLE* to the end of *INNOCENT*, making it plural and scoring points for both words. Before he'd even placed the last letter, *CLOAKED* pinged in to play.

That's odd. It's like he—or she—was waiting for me.

His opponent immediately stacked, turning *SUBTLE* into *SUFFER*.

Very cheery.

Ethan attached *ERUPT* to the *R*. Within a second, *CLOAKED* changed it to *CORRUPT*. Ethan's next play was *ENTICE*. Words stairstepped across the screen. The unbounded nature of *Stack & Scatter* meant that often games sprawled like this. Some players needed to scroll back and forth, but Ethan was able to keep the entire layout in his head.

CLOAKED turned Ethan's last word into *JUSTICE*.

Seriously? Ethan had never seen a game like this, where random words wove into meaning.

Innocents suffer corrupt justice.

And right there in his hand was *GUILT*, perfectly poised to attach to the *U* in *JUSTICE*.

Guilt?

Ethan's stomach pretzeled. He could tell from the feed of direct messages running in real time along the side of his screen that YouKnowMe was jazzed to have him back in action. They were rapidly taking control of the area around the Research Centre.

Guilt.

He had that in spades.

CLOAKED took *B, L, A,* and *M* and stacked on Ethan's *QUARE* from earlier in the game. That turned the word into *BLAME.*

Innocents suffer corrupt justice—guilt and blame.

Who was innocent and who was to blame?

Mara had said the ocean didn't care if he took a leak. Probably she was right, but as Ethan stared at the words on the screen, he couldn't help wondering who they were for. Like him, Mara had done something abhorrent. She'd killed Sinioch trying to save Max, and punishment had been meted out.

Was that justice?

Or was it once guilty, always guilty?

What about redemption?

TWENTY-EIGHT

DALMEET

PAN-NATIONAL HAEMATOLOGICAL RESEARCH CENTRE,
CHIANG RAI, THAILAND

That afternoon, Dalmeet and Mara tucked themselves into a narrow shop jam-packed with pirated DVDs. Mara waggled a copy of *Blade Runner* at him. "Love this one!"

"Me too." He didn't mention that Mara reminded him of the movie's beautiful replicant, Pris. She hadn't ended well. "Here's one about you," he said, tossing her a copy of *The Fifth Element*.

"Milla Jovovich kicked ass in that movie."

"Like I said—it's your show."

"But I do my own stunts."

The easy banter tamped down Dalmeet's jangling nerves. Working with Ethan the last few days, he'd been swept away by the plan's intricacies and their growing rapport. Even Mara had let her spines down a bit.

He checked his watch.

3:30. Showtime.

"Hey, Mara," he said, holding out his watch, "I gotta go."

"Bathroom's back there," she joked.

All he wanted to do was hide in the bathroom. *This is crazy.* They'd be killed for sure. Fear deadened his limbs.

"Mara, if we don't … I mean … I want you to know … I …"

Ignoring his stammers, Mara draped an arm over his shoulder and leaned toward him until their temples touched. Her pulse beat against his, and the lead weight in his body lifted. Her brash confidence coursed through him. "No worries, Scribey-Baby, it's just like dancing, and you got the moves." She gave him an exaggerated, smacking kiss on the cheek, turned him toward the door, and slapped his butt to send him off.

Fragments of the Blade Guardian's blessing skipped into his head.

May my knife fly true … May my heart beat true …

Dalmeet didn't need the threat of the Binding to know he'd do anything for her. At the door to the shop, he turned back. "Good luck!"

Mara grinned. "Right-o, maestro. Let's rock this flash mob."

Dalmeet headed for an alley to the right. Mara darted through the busy street in a blond blur. Her job was to show up at the loading dock and cause a scene.

At least that part of the plan's a guaranteed win.

And his first job was hardly life-threatening. Dalmeet had spent the last few days visiting teen dance clubs and arcades, rounding up participants for his choreographed distraction. At

3:35, activity amped up in front of the Centre as his recruits wandered through the electronics shops, pretending to browse.

Behind the building, Dalmeet met a pimple-faced man and handed over 10,000 baht for a silver pushcart on wheels. Pastel pink images announced ice cream and popsicles for sale, but the refrigerated unit actually held stacks of "Falcon Girl" t-shirts like the one Mara was wearing and spiky blond wigs. For just over $300 US dollars, he'd be able to dress sixty-five Mara look-alikes. Dalmeet filtered through the crowd, passing out costumes.

Ten minutes to go.

On a rooftop opposite the Centre, Ethan bent over his tablet. Hiroko strolled in front of the Centre, tilting her head to glance through the glass doors. Somewhere down the street and out of sight, Mara waited. Dalmeet handed out the last of the wigs and t-shirts, ditched the ice cream cart, and returned to the DVD shop across from the Centre.

A shiver ran up Dalmeet's spine. The stultifying Singh home was worlds away. And his cocky brother? Let Taan have his big muscles and put-on swagger. Dalmeet had managed to surpass him. He was in the thick of things, not Taan. *I'm the Scribe.*

Hiroko sidled up next to him.

"Everything's quiet inside. Still only four security guards in the front, but one of them is that huge guy we saw the day we cased the Centre."

"Guleed Awaale?"

Hiroko nodded. After Mara's response to the huge, dark-skinned man with shark-like teeth, Dalmeet had made inquiries among the other Scribes. The long litany of anecdotes about Aeda's head of security sounded like the plot summary for a Mob movie. He made the rest of her guards look like teddy bears, and in all honesty, even the smallest of them could crush Dalmeet like a bug.

"Okay, guys," Ethan said, joining them. "I copped video feed from the Centre's roof camera and have it looping through. When Mara hits the roof entrance, they won't see a thing."

"Security inside?" Dalmeet watched as two guards paced the block. Ethan shook his head. "Not on the top floor. I checked the internal cameras again. Dr. Layil is still upstairs with two techs. There's one guard below ground in that morgue place."

"You ready?" Dalmeet asked Hiroko.

She flattened her perfectly straight hair with trembling hands. "I think so."

"You've got this," said Ethan. "Just like driving a stick shift."

Last night he'd downloaded the specs for the construction crane working on the site behind the Centre and taught Hiroko to drive—virtually at least. They all knew she was more nervous about getting past the building crew than operating the equipment. Dalmeet hoped the flash mob would take care of that for her.

Five minutes to go.

Ethan's arm was pressed against the concrete wall so close to Dalmeet's that they nearly touched. Everything pulsed with the sweaty tropical heat. The wall. Their arms. Dalmeet didn't move.

Four minutes.

Hiroko nudged Dalmeet. A reptilian head the size of a sneaker stared at them out of a waist-high pile of trash. A long pink forked tongue flicked in and out, testing the contents of an abandoned plastic to-go container.

"Yuck."

"It's a varanid," said Ethan, glancing over. "They're related to Komodos."

"How can you do natural history at a time like this?" Dalmeet asked.

Ethan squinted at him. "What should we do? Warm-ups?"

"It's warm enough," said Hiroko.

Maybe warm-ups are a good idea. He was going inside the Centre with Mara while Ethan conducted traffic and the flash mob. Dalmeet stretched his neck and fingered the hilt of the blade at his waist.

I hope the Binding has improved my skills.

"All right," said Ethan. His face had gone dead serious. Dalmeet knew he wasn't happy about how spread out the four of them would be. "Let's do this." He forced a grin and cuffed Dalmeet on the shoulder.

"Don't worry." Dalmeet matched Ethan's tone. "I'll keep her out of trouble."

Even Hiroko laughed. "Good luck with that."

She sprinted toward the construction site, and Ethan swung onto a fire escape, climbing back to his rooftop command station.

Two minutes.

Now the tension was so great that Dalmeet could hardly keep still.

He caught a glimpse of Mara waiting at a video arcade near the loading dock—pale, worried, momentarily unguarded. The gauntlets on her thin arms seemed heavy and oversized. How long had it been since she'd seen her dad? Over a year? And to find him here, in Aeda's lab ... well, let's just say they hadn't dared discuss what it might mean.

3:44

YouKnowMe launched the cyberattack. Every streetlight that Dalmeet could see turned red. Mara emerged from behind an old-school Pac-Man game and darted across the narrow street to make a good show of trying to break into the loading dock of the Centre. Horns began blaring from all sides. Over the din, Dalmeet heard yelling from the direction of the loading dock.

She's got their attention.

Right now, Guleed Awaale was probably catching the scuffle on the security monitors and gathering his troops to hit the loading dock from inside. Adrenaline raced through Dalmeet.

Mara would need to extricate herself quickly. He would need to be ready.

3:45

An ear-splitting riff of electric guitar wailed out of every speaker on the street, drowning out car horns and shouts. In a flurry of white, Thai teens—boys and girls alike—pulled the t-shirts over their heads and tucked black hair into punky blond wigs. YouKnowMe simultaneously hijacked hundreds of screens. The street belonged to the mob.

Where is she?

Dalmeet panicked. What if he lost the real Mara—his Mara—in the crush of fakes? But a few seconds later, she was racing toward him, Awaale and his men slavering at her heels.

This is it.

Dalmeet pushed off the wall and joined her, sprinting around the building to the construction site in back. The music intensified to an ear-shattering level. Every screen was flashing a series of brightly colored bursts in time to the frenzied techno beat. As the bewigged teens coalesced en masse around the screens, Dalmeet and Mara were swallowed in the crowd.

Seconds later, Mara's image filled the street like a funhouse full of mirrors. The Mara on the screen began to dance in a hip-thrusting explosion of limbs.

On the street, all the Maras followed suit.

Dalmeet and Mara snaked through the writhing, bouncing crowd, finding Hiroko perched on the seat of a crane. They wedged their toes side by side on the large metal hook and grabbed the chain. Immediately, they were swinging into the air as Hiroko maneuvered them up and over the alley to the roof of the Centre.

The flat tar roof gave slightly under his feet as Dalmeet dropped from the crane. Heat bounced off the surface and sent oily fumes swirling into his nose. Mara bashed open the door with one kick and hauled him inside. He skittered after her, down an iron ladder set in the cinder block walls.

A sterile hallway stretched in front of them.

Along each side of the hallway was a long room with windows so thick that everything inside looked slightly distorted. The whirring sound of air recirculation equipment filled Dalmeet's ears. Half his brain struggled to keep listening for the sounds of pursuit while the other half tried to make sense of what he was seeing through the windows in the room on their right.

He registered the panels of medical equipment—blinking lights, oxygen sensors, the rhythmic zigzags of heart-rate readouts. Even the row of white-sheeted gurneys could be forced into some definition of hospital, as in *a place that makes people better*. It was the shapes beneath the sheets that contradicted reason. They were contorted, warped, deformed.

He pressed his palms and forehead against the glass, breathing hard.

Everything was wrong.

A hand on his arm pulled him down. He tried to slap it away, but Mara hissed at him and pulled harder. Dalmeet crumpled to the floor. Mara crouched against the wall and peered through the wall of windows across the hall. White-suited figures worked on the other side of the glass. None appeared to have seen them.

"Did you see that?" he whispered, jerking a thumb toward the bodies.

"Shhhh!"

"What are they doing in here?"

"I have no idea," she mouthed. "I don't care."

Dalmeet tried to steady his breathing.

Mara stared at the white-suits so hard that if she could ignite them, the place would have been a smoking pile of ashes. Finally, she pointed to a tall man pulling a tray of vials out of deep freeze. "That's him."

White wisps spiraled off the tubes as frost melted into steam. Paul Layil placed the tubes on a black slab table, pulled off his insulated gloves, and set them aside. He moved toward the windows. Dalmeet held his breath even though he knew that with the recirculating air whooshing around them, it wasn't sound that mattered. Only Mara, quivering next to him, mattered. Dr. Layil bent over a drawer, searching for something.

Mara might as well have sported a countdown timer on her forehead. Her agitation was growing every second.

"Keep it together," Dalmeet whispered, even as he knew it was too late to defuse her.

When she made her move, Dalmeet braced himself, but instead of bashing through the wall to her father, she stopped silently before the window, hands raised in supplication, waiting for him to notice.

Dr. Layil continued to fumble in the drawer.

When he finally looked up, he was rooted to the spot, holding a Sharpie in one hand. Through the visor on his white hood, Dr. Layil's lips moved, forming her name—*Mara*. Father and daughter stared at one another. Dr. Layil broke away first. He gestured for her to get down. She hesitated.

Idiot. You should know orders are a bad idea with Mara.

Nonetheless, Mara did crouch, and she remained frozen in place as the doctor replaced the samples in the freezer and spoke to the techs before walking casually toward the airlock. When he emerged, minus the white suit, his face was a mask of worry. He gave a clipped summons and urged them into the room with the gurneys. The room was dim and quiet except for the steady hum of the monitors on the bodies beneath the sheets.

Are they patients? Victims?

Dalmeet shuddered.

Dr. Layil motioned them into a windowless office and shut the door. When he turned toward Mara, his mouth was a hard, threatening line.

I don't trust him. Momar had written of Paul Layil's fixation on unraveling the blood secrets of the Eleven. Dalmeet wondered what lines this man was willing to cross.

"Dad?" Mara's voice came out thin and small.

"What are you doing here?"

"I ... Dad ..." Confusion swirled across her face.

"Dr. Layil," Dalmeet said, "we've come to get you out of here."

"Who in the bloody hell are you?"

"Dad, what's going on? Max is in trouble. Mom is too. I saw her. She's ... she's like them." Mara nodded toward the bodies. "Abbot Greb said you would know how to help."

Emotion twisted the man's face. "Where is Momar? He knows I'm walking a very fine line. He was supposed to keep you clear of all this."

"Clear?!" Her volume jacked up.

Don't lose control. Not here. Not now.

"My uncle, Momar, is dead," Dalmeet said, pressing close to Mara, hoping she'd calm down. "I'm Mara's Scribe now."

"Dead? How?"

"We don't have time to explain. Let's get out of here."

"I can't leave!" he protested. "My work ..."

"Can't or won't?" Mara screeched.

"Do you think I have a choice?"

"Dali has the Record," Mara said, clenching her fists. "It said you joined them. You joined Aeda and Sinioch on purpose."

Dr. Layil rubbed his eyes. "I did," he admitted. "We did—your mom and I—but we tried to get out. That's when Aeda poisoned your mom."

"With the toxin *you* created!" Mara's voice rose dangerously.

Dalmeet gripped her arm, all the while knowing he couldn't hope to hold back a tornado.

"We were trying to create a drug that would let Offspring turn their powers on and off in case their abilities were unpredictable."

He's talking about Mara and Max. Layil knew their mixed bloodlines might cause disaster. Dalmeet hoped Mara wouldn't make the connection, but she was too smart.

"Are you fucking serious? You wanted an off switch for me?" She hurled the accusation at him. "You bred me like a racehorse but wanted to make sure I wouldn't get in the way."

At least her father had the decency to look ashamed. He reached out to her.

"Mara, honey, we didn't set out to hurt anyone. I didn't know Aeda and Sinioch would use the drug on your mom and Max."

Mara slapped his hands away. "Then why are you here working for her?"

Dr. Layil dropped his arms to his sides. "She'll kill you and your brother and your mom if I don't do what she wants."

She'll kill them anyway.

Sympathy and fury warred in Mara's expression. Dalmeet wondered which one would win out. She surprised him by abandoning both, returning to what mattered to her most.

"Is there a cure for Max?"

"Transfusion of First Born blood."

"That's temporary," said Dalmeet. "What's the permanent fix?"

Mara's father flushed. "I've had a breakthrough on that recently. A pellet of pure relium implanted in the heart muscle would act like a magnet, drawing the toxin away from his metalloproteins."

"Excellent! Let's go!" A sheen of hope gave Mara's face a luminous glow, and Dalmeet realized she was beautiful. *At least when she's not scary as hell.* He shared her surging excitement, but some dark thought, not quite realized, niggled at him.

"I ... I can't," Dr. Layil stammered. "Aeda will kill your mother if I don't do what she wants right now."

Mara tensed. "What does she want?"

She and her father stood a few feet apart, but it might as well have been miles. Before he could answer, a clamor rose from the lower floor, and heavy footsteps pounded up the staircase at the end of the hall.

"Quickly!" Dr. Layil hustled them out of the office and into the dimly lit lab. He shoved them into one of the alcoves and pulled the privacy curtain around the gurney.

Dr. Layil met the guards in the hall. "Can I help you?"

"Any disturbance up here, Doc?"

"No, not at all. Just work, work, and more work." The lie flowed easy and smooth. Through his own fear of discovery, Dalmeet tried to figure out what was bothering him. Something Dr. Layil had said was not adding up. But what?

Mara moved toward the rigid body on the bed. She rested one hand on the splayed foot of the gaunt woman. It startled Dalmeet out of his deliberation. How could she be so unyielding one minute and so tender the next? The conversation between Dr. Layil and the guards faded as they walked down the corridor.

"We need to get out of here," Dalmeet whispered.

Mara held up one finger without looking at him. She paced around the body, bending over the woman's face. "It's just like on Toru's island," she muttered. "Offspring. Not dead— waiting."

Dalmeet was buried in his own problem solving.

He said relium was the cure for Max. A relium implant.

The guards passed by the medical bay once more and headed downstairs. Dalmeet peeped out of a split in the curtains and saw Mara's dad speaking through an intercom to the technicians in the cleanroom.

"A collection," Mara said, "waiting."

Relics of the Eleven are the most precious things on Earth. Where will he get the relium?

Mara froze. Dalmeet did too.

At the same moment, they turned to one other.

The Blade Guardian.

"An army." Mara grabbed Dalmeet by the arm. "He's building Aeda an army of Offspring. They're waiting in those drawers, waiting for my father to figure out how to control them."

Dalmeet was practically choking on his own realization. "Mara, about the cure ..."

"I know," she said, repulsed. "He can cure them, but he won't!" She flexed her arms, and the gauntlets rippled like muscles in a horse's flank, angry and ready to rear. "Not even for his own son!"

He didn't want to tell her. How could he tell her? It would kill her.

"I'll make him!" She spit the words out.

Dalmeet blocked her as she stepped forward. He wrapped his arms around her in the tightest, closest embrace he could manage.

"What the hell, Dali?" Mara wriggled her pinioned arms.

He didn't want to tell her, but he had to.

"Even if he would," Dalmeet said, "he can't."

"What?" She pushed away from him. "What are you talking about?"

"The cure ... It requires someone to forge the relium."

"So? We'll find someone to do that."

Dalmeet shook his head slowly. "Only the Blade Guardian can reforge relium."

"I'll find him, then."

Dalmeet felt tears prickle behind his eyes. By the Sacrifice, he loved the way she was willing to take on the world. He cleared his throat and steadied his voice. She deserved the truth, straight up and ugly.

"The Blade Guardian is dead."

"He can't be dead. Max needs relium."

"Armaros is the last of the Eleven."

"Max needs relium," Mara repeated, her eyes filling with tears.

Dalmeet pulled her to him, wishing he could give her another answer.

Twenty-Nine

MARA

PAN-NATIONAL HAEMATOLOGICAL RESEARCH CENTRE,
CHIANG RAI, THAILAND

*T**he Blade Guardian is dead.*

Dali's words roared through Mara, echoing off the insides of her skull. That's why there were tears on her cheeks. That's why her head pounded with *dead, dead, dead.* That's why Dali was holding her.

It's over for Max.

No! Dali's jerking me around. That has to be it.

Max is going to be up playing soccer again in no time.

Dad said there was a cure.

Mara pushed Dalmeet away. "You don't know what you're talking about."

She remembered the day she'd been released from Cascadia. Max had rushed from the SUV before Momar could cut the engine. He'd clung to her in the pouring rain. Her first hug in a whole year. Max and Mara versus the world.

"I'm sorry," said Dalmeet. "I'm so sorry."

Shit! Oh shit! Oh shit!

No Blade Guardian.

No cure.

No soccer.

Never, never, ever.

Her bones were concrete, her heart roadkill.

Never.

At the end of the dead stick that was her arm, she felt a warm, disembodied pressure.

"Come on, Mara. We've got to get out of here."

Dali?

The hand grasping hers, the voice—that was Dali. Though why he thought it mattered if they got out of the Centre did not compute. He pulled her past the body on the gurney, through the curtain, and into the corridor between the labs.

"What are you doing?" her father hissed, pointing to the techs in the cleanroom. "They'll see you."

Mara's anger surged, slicing through her grief like gauntlets through flesh. "I was an idiot to think I could count on you."

"I've tried to protect you."

"And Max? What about him?" Her words dripped venom.

He backed away. "Max isn't dead."

"Oh, no," she said, advancing. "Can't break that Covenant, can we? So what if Mom and Max and I end up zombie soldiers in your precious army?"

A bang grabbed her attention. On the other side of the glass, the technicians finally noticed them and began pounding on the window. One struggled to make a call through his white protective gear.

"We gotta go!" Dalmeet pulled her down the hall. "Now!"

"Let me explain," her father said, clutching her arm.

"Don't touch me."

An alarm screamed through the building.

"Go, go, go!" Mara yelled at Dalmeet. Disappointment suffocated her. She needed to get as far away from her father as possible. Close on Dalmeet's heels, she vaulted up the rungs of the ladder leading to the roof.

Three-quarters of the way to the top, a bullet slammed into cinder block inches from her calf. The metal rungs of ladder vibrated beneath her. Mara craned her neck and saw three security guards at the end of the hall. One held a gun, a whisper of smoke snaking from the barrel. The other two clutched handfuls of blond wigs.

"Get your ass up here," Dalmeet hissed from the roof.

She shook her head. "Change of plan." Maybe she could slow them long enough for her friends to get away. She didn't care what happened after that. Without Max, she might as well go down fighting. "Find the others and get out of here."

Mara dropped back to the floor.

The guard fired again.

Mara directed the full force of her mind at the intervening space. The crack of the gunshot tore through her ears, but the bullet froze inches from her face. She batted it away and the slug clattered to the floor.

"Enough with the guns! She's Offspring!" Guleed Awaale pushed through the other guards. A grin split his face like a gash. "Hey, Blondie!" he leered. "Wanna dance?"

Mara's blood picked up the riptide current roaring in the man's muscled limbs.

"Come on! Have a go at me, asshole!" She'd never wanted a fight so badly. She wanted to pound and rip and tear. "Looks like you've been scalping Barbies," she sneered, tilting her head at the wigs.

He laughed, a thunderous guffaw that bounced off the walls. The guards holding the wigs chuckled nervously. "All right, pretty thing. Come with me. We wait for Aeda." He strode passed her father. "How's things, Dr. Layil? Nice reunion?"

Reunion?

Dad's chosen his side.

"What do you want here anyway, girly?" demanded Awaale.

"There's nothing I want now."

Paul Layil reached for her.

"Don't even try," said Mara. "You lied about everything."

"Please, Mara," her father begged, "I love you."

"Love?"

Dark spots fluttered in her peripheral vision. The lab wavered around her. Mara was red fast and blood furious. The gauntlets sprang to life, sheathing her fists. Timespace shredded around her like wisps of silk.

"I hate you!" she screamed, charging through the fissures of the timescape around her. As she passed, cracks spiderwebbed through the lab windows. Before her father knew what was happening, she was plowing her fist into his stomach, and he was collapsing like an imploded star.

Awaale swung at her, his anvil-like hand connecting with her ribs. She went down, her body careening into the wall and sending chunks of glass flying. Inside the lab, the technicians screamed and blocked the door with heavy tables. The other two guards scrambled weapons. Awaale dove, hands closing around her throat.

"That your best move, girly? No wonder Daddy left you."

Her lungs burned.

She hated Awaale. She hated her dad. She was going to die hating them. The pressure on her windpipe increased. Oozy black shapes crowded her vision.

"Plenty of empty drawers for your friends too."

Really? They had to take everything from her? Was she going to die while her dad watched? The unfairness of it fanned an inner spark that even now guttered like a flame in the wind, threatening to wink out.

Not like this.

Not Dalmeet or Hiroko.

Not Ethan!

The shock wave built in her gut like a hurricane. Nearly gone, Mara threw every bit of herself into harnessing the explosion. Time fractured around her, adding fuel. It was bigger than she was now. It held the histories of daughters, of the abandoned, of the hopeless.

The strength of it might blow her apart. Not that she cared.

Her friends needed her, and they were the only ones who she could still help.

As the power burst exploded from her, Mara had one last second of awareness. Her father screamed her name in an animal howl, her head slammed into the wall, and she fell into the void.

THIRTY

ETHAN

CHIANG RAI, THAILAND

W here's the goddamned truck?" Ethan yelled.

"This way!" Dalmeet veered through the construction site and away from the Centre. Ethan wrapped his arms more tightly around Mara and redoubled his speed. Limp, she seemed inexplicably tiny and delicate. Tremors shuddered through her.

He and Dalmeet had been suspended from the crane when the roof of the Centre blew up. Chunks of concrete flew in every direction, battering the machine, their bodies, and the sun-softened tar like a meteor shower before Hiroko lowered them into the crater.

Dalmeet fought like a monster, holding off two guards with his kirpan while Ethan dug through the debris, flinging suitcase-sized pieces of rubble like they were Styrofoam. Finally, he found Mara's twisted, battered body underneath Awaale's bloody bulk.

Now they were racing toward the SUV, Ethan holding Mara and praying she didn't have a spinal injury. He could hardly see her face through the caked blood and dust.

Wake up and bitch at me. Please!

As they reached the SUV, she moaned. Renewed convulsions wracked her body. Crimson spittle bubbled out of her lips.

Wake up, damn it!

Ethan slid into the back seat with Dalmeet and Hiroko close on his heels. Dalmeet urged the driver to retreat, and they were off in a squeal of rubber.

"Lie her down," said Hiroko.

I don't want to let go.

But Ethan eased her blood-streaked body onto the bench seat. Yielding to Hiroko's ministrations, he sat on the floor next to Mara, head bowed. Hiroko's reliable, competent hands slid along the sides of Mara's face, skimming the grooves in her neck and gently checking the rest of her bashed body.

Ethan prayed the only way he knew how.

1 plus 1 is 2.

1 plus 2 is 3.

2 plus 3 is 5.

3 plus 5 is 8.

Dalmeet thrummed his fingers on his knees. "Is she okay?"

"I'm checking for internal bleeding."

Ethan's fear ratcheted up a notch. "We have to get her to a doctor!"

"Shut up," Dalmeet snapped. "Hiroko's a healer."

"We're in the back of a car, and she's rubbing Mara's head!"

Hiroko was nose to nose with Mara, palpating Mara's face as if she were playing an instrument. Ethan didn't dare to imagine what was happening inside the convolutions of Mara's gray matter.

5 plus 8 is 13.

Thick skulled.

8 plus 13 is 21.

Stubborn.

13 plus 21 is 34.

Pain in the ass.

Before, he'd wanted to figure her out. Now he just wanted her intact.

They'd cleared the outskirts of the city and were skimming south along a narrow road bordered by green fields of rice.

"Where are we going?"

"Someplace safe," said Dalmeet.

"If Aeda's people find her like this—" Ethan began.

Dalmeet was breathing hard. A trickle of blood outlined the edge of his jaw and dripped onto his pants. "They won't."

Ethan dared another glance at Hiroko. With eyes closed and face twisted in concentration, the healer was focused entirely on Mara.

21 plus 34 is 55.

Spasms coursed through Mara. *Please don't let her die.*

When Mara's body finally relaxed, the muscles in her face went slack as if in sleep. The tension eased from Hiroko's body too. "I've stopped the bleeding."

Impossible.

"Hiroko, you're amazing," said Dalmeet.

Hiroko grinned. "That was scary."

Scary? More like freaking crazy!

"The pressure on her brain was going sky high—"

"How do you know she's okay without a CT scan?"

"Ethan, I promise, she's okay now." Hiroko was calm. "You know that I'm a healer, descended from Otohime. We can read the body, influence cell growth and clotting, make other adjustments."

Before Ethan could formulate a reply, the driver turned onto a side road in a spray of gravel. Ethan flung out an arm to steady Mara. The road curved toward a vine-smothered, limestone crag towering above the surrounding farmland.

Ethan couldn't fathom how there could be help here, but time and time again his nose was being shoved in everything he didn't know. Meeting Mara meant stripping down his perceptions of the world. If a half-blind monk in Portland could rip open the fabric of space and zap Mara to Japan, why couldn't there be refuge here?

I trust Dalmeet.

Ethan waited.

At the base of the mountain, the driver stopped.

"Did they follow us?" Hiroko asked.

Dalmeet sprang out of the vehicle and checked the road. "I don't think so."

"Where are we?" Ethan asked.

"I just hope they let us in," Dalmeet said.

With one arm under Mara's knees and the other behind her sweaty back, Ethan pulled her into his chest.

"Hey, guys," Ethan called. "A little help here."

Dalmeet rushed back to the car and steadied Ethan as he climbed out, balancing Mara. Her eyes fluttered, closed, then opened again. "Eee-thaaan?"

Come on, baby. Stay with me.

Mara's head flopped from Ethan's shoulder to the crook of his elbow. She focused on Dalmeet. "You guysh are shoooo cute."

They exchanged a look. *Cute?* Dalmeet was filthy. Ethan could smell the stink wafting up from his own pits. Besides, when did the word *cute* ever pass Mara's lips?

Dalmeet shrugged. "Head injury."

Still the worry that hung over all of them eased.

"She'll be all right," said Hiroko. "She'll be fine."

"I am shooo fiiiine." Mara's words held a touch of her usual bravado, but she lacked head control. Her breath teased Ethan's skin. Battered as he was, Ethan couldn't wipe the grin off his face. He didn't plan to let go of her—ever.

Dalmeet led them along a barely visible path skirting the rocky crag. Steroid-sized ferns bent over the path in a cool, green tunnel. The path ended at a tree growing inside a deep stone crevice. Next to it, a low archway led into the rock. They squeezed inside.

The heaviness of the air demanded quiet. Ethan felt sure they were being watched. An ancient carved Buddha, flanked by burning incense and fresh lotus buds, sat in a stone alcove. Centuries of gold leaf, layered and flaking, obscured its features.

"Whasss that shiny thing?" Mara mumbled.

Dalmeet leaned in. "It's the Buddha."

"A poodle? Niiish puppy ..."

"Where are we?" Ethan whispered.

"It's one of the sacred monasteries of *Pro Lapis Astra*," said Dalmeet. "I'm hoping they'll provide sanctuary."

"You're hoping?" Hiroko hissed.

"Look, I memorized the location of every group in every corner of the world that was loyal to the Layils, but Paul and Veronique kind of fell off the nice-guy wagon, if you know what I mean, and everything's changing anyway."

Hiroko nodded. "Who's loyal anymore? And to what?"

"Okay," Ethan broke in. "Don't trust anyone. Got it. Now, let's do this. She's getting heavy."

Mara raised a limp hand and tried to smack him.

"When we get in, don't mention Abbot Greb," said Dalmeet.

"But I thought they were in the same order," said Ethan.

"He's considered very radical."

"The old dude with the robes and the beard is radical?"

"Very."

As she passed, Hiroko swiped the Buddha's gilded knee and brushed her gold-flecked finger along Mara's forehead. "For good luck."

Dalmeet led them into the tunnel. Light glinting from torches set the smudge of gold on Mara's forehead twinkling. At the end, low benches flanked a closed wooden door. Shoes, maybe twenty-five pair in all, were lined up neatly under the benches.

Great! If they're mad at the Layils, we'll only have to fight a few dozen monks. Dalmeet added his to the lineup. Hiroko followed suit and pulled off Mara's boots as well.

"Hey," said Mara groggily, "thosh are miine."

Ethan kicked off his own shoes.

And we'll have to fight them barefoot. This keeps getting better.

"I can shtand."

Ethan kept an arm around her waist when he set her on her feet.

"Worry wart." Some perk had returned to her voice, but she didn't try to escape his arm.

"Are you sure you can you walk?"

She nodded, but as soon as *she* took a step, her knees crumpled.

Ethan and Hiroko propped her between them, and Dalmeet knocked on the door. It swung open revealing two orange-robed Buddhist monks. Dalmeet pressed his palms together, fingers pointing to the ceiling and bowed slightly, greeting them formally in Thai. *"Sawadee kop."*

The monks led them into a common room carved of solid limestone and lit by hundreds of beeswax candles in gold candlesticks. Half of the room was a library with heavy teak bookshelves and cloth-covered couches. The other half held two long trestle tables and benches. Several men were studying or eating. All looked up to stare at the visitors. A few wore orange robes, but most wore the solid black robes of the Greek Orthodox order and sported grizzled beards hanging nearly to their waists.

"Looks like Halloween," said Mara.

"Shhhh," hissed Dalmeet. "They're not keen on women."

Mara's not exactly the one to charm their socks off.

One of their guides pushed open the double doors at the back of the room revealing a sanctuary of multicolored mosaics and dark wooden pews. Incense wafted out of the room, a heavy, spicy miasma that caught in the back of Ethan's throat.

A black-robed monk bent in prayer before a towering mosaic of twelve stars hurtling from a bright, unreachable ceiling of light. The kneeler nodded as their guide whispered in his ear, bent his head once more, and finally lumbered toward them like a great bear.

Dalmeet began stammering introductions, but the bear ignored him, rounding on Mara like he'd caught her scent. "I know you, child, killer of Offspring!" he roared. "There were brothers of my order present when you defied Armaros the Time Weaver. We know what you are!"

All activity ceased around them.

So much for sanctuary.

Ethan felt Mara tense against him.

We're not ready for a fight.

After all, Mara could barely stand. This was not the time to get hard core.

Come on, Dalmeet. Talk us out of here.

"No, sir," said Dalmeet, "it's not like that. She's badly hurt."

The bear didn't take his eyes off Mara. "Are you bringing war into my place of worship?"

Mara roused herself, cleared her throat. Ethan braced for the tirade.

"No, sir," Mara said, Girl Scout earnest.

Head injury? No shit.

"Why are you here?" the bear growled.

Better come up with something good, Scribe.

"We're here on Armaros's business," said Dalmeet. "A duty for the Eleven."

We are?

"Do you really expect me to believe that?"

"Yes, sir," Dalmeet interjected, turning Boy Scout. "You can check with Armaros yourself. She's called off the Amyclaean Guard and has given Mara Layil a task."

The man shot Mara a withering look. "Since twelve years old, I have served *Pro Lapsis Astra*. I pray for the Fallen Stars. Yet you fall and fall and fall again. You Offspring have very little self-control."

He's got Mara pegged.

Dalmeet stayed ultracalm. "Sir, really, we're not trying to make any trouble. Let us rest a few hours, tend to her wounds, and we'll go."

The old monk glared at him. "What task does this Offspring have?"

You've got him now, Dalmeet. Don't blow it.

"Armaros wants Mara to ..."

What would he come up with?

Dalmeet took a deep breath. "She wants Mara to visit the Twins."

One of the monks behind them actually shrieked. Another dropped his wine glass, sending shards skittering across the stone floor. The bear seemed like he would burst into flames.

"Out!" he roared, pointing his finger at them like the barrel of a gun. "OUT!"

At that moment, Mara pinched Ethan hard just above the waistband of his jeans. He flinched, and she slipped free. He braced for impact, but instead, Mara let out a skin-crawling wail and slumped to the floor. As he dropped to his knees beside her, he caught a glimpse of the bear's face torn between fury and fear. Fear crested over Ethan too. What if Hiroko had screwed up? What if Mara's injuries were worse than she thought?

34 plus 55 is 89.

Hiroko was down on the floor checking her Mara's pulse.

55 plus 89 is 144.

Her hands searched for the cause of Mara's collapse.

Please be okay.

Behind him, Ethan could hear Dalmeet, insistent and indignant, demanding that they find a room for Mara *this instant.*

"Fine!" the bear blustered. Several other black-robed monks burst into a swirl of activity. One tried to lift Mara, but Ethan elbowed him away. He and Hiroko carried her down a stone corridor and into a room, which like the main chamber, had been hewn directly into the rock.

Candles embedded in a decade's deposition of wax lined a chest-high ledge encircling the room. Dalmeet snatched the matchbox out of the monk's hands and shoved him and his dour-faced buddies out of the room. As Ethan and Hiroko eased Mara onto a cot, Dalmeet slammed the door on the curious monks and threw the lock.

Mara opened her eyes at once. "He's a blowhard, isn't he?"

Ethan gaped.

She was faking?

Mara smiled, but her eyes still seemed unfocused. Hiroko palpated her temples.

"Yes, indeed, the abbot is a blowhard," Dalmeet said, lighting the rest of the candles and illuminating the spartan room. In addition to the cot, there were two meditation mats, a low stool, and a narrow table supporting three Tibetan singing bowls.

"Mara, you scared the crap out of us!" said Hiroko.

"Is she okay?" Ethan demanded.

Hiroko flopped down on one of the meditation mats, letting out a relieved, exasperated huff. "She'll be back in troublemaking form in no time. Might be the death of me."

Mara gave a weak chuckle. "It worked, didn't it? Besides, I like Ethan carrying me around."

Well, that makes two of us. Ethan slouched beside Hiroko. "You're a terrible date."

"I know," said Mara.

I didn't mean that.

"Guys," said Dalmeet, pulling the stool close. "We've got twelve hours, tops, before the abbot wants us out of here. This is the best chance we're ever gonna get to see the Twins."

"You're insane," Hiroko blurted.

"I know it sounds crazy but think about it. She can get amnesty if she finds the Circlet."

"I don't care anymore," Mara said. "If I can't help Max, none of it really matters."

The heavy, sweet smell of beeswax reminded Ethan of funerals.

"I've been thinking about that too," Dalmeet continued. "Everyone says only the Blade Guardian can reforge relium relics, but what if the Twins are capable of it?"

Mara's lips softened at the edges. She grasped at the hope he offered. "How?"

"I can't promise anything," he said, "but I've read every account I could get my hands on about the day the Twins were banished. Each text agrees that Tamel had bound them in chains of relium. Before they killed Azza, they broke the chains."

Mara hauled herself to a sitting position. "I saw that myself when Armaros took me back."

Dalmeet nodded.

"So, what you're saying," asked Hiroko, "is if they can break relium, maybe they can make what we need?"

"Exactly! They're very powerful."

"And completely unpredictable."

"Sounds like Mara," said Ethan.

"Seriously," said Dalmeet, laughing, "but I didn't bring us here because we needed the abbot. This monastery is a weak spot between time and not-time, and Mara's going to bust us through to the Twins."

THIRTY-ONE

DALMEET

MONASTERY OF PRO LAPSIS ASTRA, SOUTH OF CHIANG RAI, THAILAND

Dalmeet pressed his ear against the door. The muffled chanting of evening prayer echoed in the corridor. It was nearly ten o'clock. Other than offering bowls of spicy coconut soup and sticky rice three hours earlier, the monks had ignored them.

Now on the verge of implementing what was surely the most insane thing ever tried by Offspring or human, the tension in the room was running high. Ethan sat on a meditation mat in one corner of the room, futzing on his tablet and fuming. Hiroko fluttered over Mara like a mother hen.

Dalmeet wished Ethan wasn't furious with him. When they were on the same page—usually trying to corral Mara—the guy had a way of pulling Dalmeet into the fold. And he had those beautiful eyes.

But Ethan was pissed.

They'd almost come to blows when Dalmeet insisted that he accompany Mara outside of time. The trip, if you could call it that, which Dalmeet was proposing was—he had to be honest— probably doomed. As Scribe, his place was at Mara's side. She'd be lucky to get both of them through the barrier of time. Transporting all of them was simply out of the question, and someone needed to stay behind and run interference with the monks.

And getting back?

They would have to wing it.

Dalmeet had finally convinced Ethan that Mara would need his knowledge of the Twins, but Dalmeet knew it wasn't enough. Even if he could have had a direct download from the Record to his brain, it wouldn't have been enough. The Twins were a black box.

I have so little to go on.

When Mara was just a few months old, Armaros had transported Momar across the time barrier for an *audience—* Momar's word, not his—with the Twins, hoping, Dalmeet supposed, that they would shed light on who or what she might mature into. Instead, the Twins had probed Momar's mind and very nearly sent him back in pieces. His notes—brief, confused, and disjointed—made no sense to Dalmeet. Was Momar even in his right mind when he'd penned them?

One thing was clear, though: any mention of Azza had infuriated the Twins.

We'll be ready for that. Dalmeet was insisting that Mara leave the gauntlets behind.

"I feel naked without them," she grumbled.

"I don't care. They are covered with Azza's symbols and carry the resonance of his blood. You don't want to thumb your nose at the Twins."

"Armaros lost the Circlet trying to visit the Twins," Hiroko added. "We don't want that to happen."

Mara released the armor and stared at the rippling metal in her hands. "I hate this."

"Hand them over." Dalmeet held Mara's backpack open to receive the gauntlets.

"Do they call to you?"

He nodded.

This close to Mara and the relics, the resonance boomed through him. A subtle menace from the gauntlets—more weapon than armor. Mara's increasing nerves, her irritation that Ethan was ignoring her, and the faint subterranean ripples of the timespace around them buzzed inside Dalmeet.

Now is when we cross outside of time.

Mara zipped the backpack and handed it to Ethan. "Don't let that douche bag monk have them." In spite of her cockiness, Dalmeet knew she wanted Ethan to reach for her. Instead, he took the backpack without looking up.

"I've got it."

Come on, man, give her something to hold on to.

She touched his shoulder. "Safe and sound?"

Ethan dipped his chin once, hardly meeting her eyes. Dalmeet knew what that meant too. *He won't move until we come back. If we come back.*

Dalmeet listened at the door again. The chanting had stopped, and slipper-clad feet shuffled down the hallway. Someone paused outside their door but didn't knock and after a moment moved on.

"Time to go."

Mara reached for the door.

"How long will it take?" asked Hiroko.

"I don't know," he said.

Ethan reached for Mara, pulling her down to eye level. "Be careful. Be nice."

Mara scowled.

"I'm serious."

"I can be nice."

Ethan started to say something else, but Mara put a finger over his lips. "Unh-unh. Don't get sappy. I'll be fine. See you soon."

Hiroko embraced her. "May the blessing of the White One be yours, now and forever." To Dalmeet, Hiroko recited a line from the Scribe's Creed. "Knowledge is succor and shield."

Comfort and protection.

Dalmeet was sure they would need both.

He eased open the door. The corridor was empty.

Tiptoeing, Dalmeet led them to the common room, also empty, and into the sanctuary. Oil lamps burned beneath the mural of falling stars. Another lamp flickered at the base of an alabaster image of the White One, her limbs stark and ghostly against the gilt wood. After a few minutes searching, Dalmeet found what he was looking for—a low arched door hidden in the shadows to the right of the altar. It led to the charnel house, a repository for the remains of long-dead monks.

The weight of the massive stone mountain above them increased as Dalmeet ducked through the entry. Mara squeezed in and pulled the door shut behind them. In the cool, dry blackness, he felt her warm breath on his neck. He struck a match, and the flickering light bounced off curved bones, brown with age. It deepened the shadowy holes of empty eye sockets. Teeth gaped at them in row upon row of lipless jaws. Skulls, neatly aligned on narrow shelves, filled every spare inch of the charnel house.

"Shit!" Mara hissed.

Dalmeet chuckled. "When a monk dies, they bury him for three years and then exhume the skeleton. The bones get reburied but the skulls go here."

"Could've warned me!"

"That wouldn't have been any fun."

Mara squeezed closer to him as the match burned out. "And you picked this spot because ...?"

"Can't you feel it?" he asked, lighting another match and handing the box to Mara. "The boundaries of time are extremely thin here."

Mara held her flame up to the row of skulls, studying them. "What's on their heads?"

"Birthday, death day, and name of its owner."

Mara cupped her hands around the curve of the nearest skull. A wave of disorientation swept over Dalmeet, the floor tilting crazy as the flame flickered over bone, which was no longer bone.

A man's face took shape between Mara's hands. Strong brow, broad cheekbones, a flowing black beard. It was a kind face. Mara snatched back her hand, and the bone returned, the life of the black-bearded man distilled to a spidery scrawl of faded ink—*Francis Hagopian 1745-1791*.

The match burned out. In the darkness, Mara panted hard, and Dalmeet's heart raced. The face of Francis Hagopian made him terrifyingly aware of his own bones and their temporary sheath of flesh.

"That was good. I think," he said, rekindling the light.

"Good?" Mara gasped.

"A sign that we can pass outside of time. What you did, was it hard?"

"I didn't do it on purpose."

"I know, but was it hard?"

"I was wondering about old Francis, and it just happened."

"Excellent."

Mara grabbed his arm in a sudden, crushing grip. "Dali, don't leave me."

"I won't. This will work. You're blood of Armaros. Time is on your side."

Mara cleared her throat. "I'm scared I'll lose control again."

"It will be easier without the gauntlets. Relics can enhance certain bloodlines, but others are fundamentally at war with each other. Azza and Armaros were never a good combination."

"Let's get on with it."

This is it. The moment when I truly become her Scribe.

Dalmeet dropped the match and reached for Mara's shoulders. She looped her arms around his and held on.

"Remember how we talked about timespace as a layer with all times always present?" He felt her nod in the dark. "You jumped across it a minute ago with the skull. Think about how that felt, but try to reverse it. I need you to find the edge and jump out."

Could this work? His instructions seemed as stupid as some yogi's guided meditation. Panic buzzed through him. Life and death circled closely in the pitch-black charnel house. The floor-rocking vertigo returned. Death was waiting in those bones. The rhythm of Mara's breathing caught up with him, hijacked his own respiration. He felt a momentary urge to fight her and pull away.

You must do this.

He pushed down the fear and let his pulse match hers. He squeezed her shoulders and felt the heat of her skin on his face. "Don't let go!"

"Never." Mara's entire body quivered, ferocious and determined.

Inside the flow of time, he had one last thought. *I would trust her anywhere.* It surprised him; then light exploded around them, pushing the darkness from the edges of his vision.

THIRTY-TWO

ETHAN

MONASTERY OF PRO LAPSIS ASTRA, SOUTH OF CHIANG RAI, THAILAND

Ethan leaned against the wall. He listened at the door. He fiddled with the singing bowls on the table.

Where is she?

When is she?

He walked to the door and listened again. Thinking about time was a head-trip. What did it mean to step outside of time? And how long would it take Mara to get back?

If she makes it back.

This was Mara he was talking about! Of course she'd make it back.

She had to make it back.

Hiroko was sitting cross-legged on the cot.

"Are you meditating?" Ethan asked, plopping down beside her.

She opened her eyes. "No, I'm trying to ignore you."

"Sorry."

"It's okay." She patted his knee and closed her eyes again. "I'm actually wondering about Tamel."

"The Blade Guardian? If the guy's dead, what's there to think about?"

Hiroko stretched the kinks out of her shoulders. "He was tight with the rest of the Eleven until the Twins were born, but when Azza demanded their execution, Tamel went rogue. I'm wondering why he didn't try to influence the rest of them. Maybe change the way things were done. If he cared so much about the Twins, why not try to free them?"

"Maybe he thought they should be punished but didn't want blood on his hands?"

"Could be."

"Or maybe he got tired of being told what to do—*Reforge this relic! Punish this Offspring!*—that could get on your nerves."

Hiroko considered this. "Scholars agree that Tamel was tired of enforcing the Covenant so rigidly. It's one of the arguments that the anti-Covenant supporters use today. They want a more nuanced interpretation."

"Like letting Mara off on self-defense."

She nodded, and Ethan went back to pacing the small room.

"Maybe he thought that reforging relics gave others too much power," Hiroko mused, going back to lotus position.

Ethan pointed to Mara's backpack. "Her gauntlets move and change shape. Doesn't that mean that the Blade Guardian is still alive?"

Hiroko shook her head. "They call to the relium in our blood, but the relics have a limited sentience. They respond to our needs but without the Blade Guardian, gauntlets will always be gauntlets."

Our blood. Our needs.

There had been no time for Ethan to contemplate the repercussions of the Binding. He couldn't really separate an enhanced ability to feel Mara's emotions from his growing attraction to her. On the other hand, there was no denying what had happened at the Research Centre. The old Ethan could never have lifted those blocks of concrete.

I wonder—

Ethan pulled one of gauntlets out of Mara's backpack. Brushing his fingertips along its base caused the gauntlet to spring open. As soon as his forearm touched the metal, it slithered closed, matching every bump and curve of his arm.

Time for a test.

Ethan closed his eyes, conjuring up an image of Guleed Awaale attacking Mara. His needle-like teeth. His massive hands. Mara ready to attack balls-out, and Awaale diving in for the kill. He allowed his rage to mount and brim over.

No one hurts Mara!

Through the roar in his head, he heard Hiroko, but before she could reach him, he punched the stone wall as hard as he could. A split second before impact, the gauntlet slid over his fist. No pain. He battered the wall until Hiroko pulled him away.

"Enough already! It's dead!"

Panting, he took in the cratered wall, his undamaged hand, and Hiroko's horror. "It responds to me."

I am like her.

Hiroko wrenched his arm toward her and removed the gauntlet. "Are you psychotic?"

It was suffocating in the airless room.

1 squared is 1. 2 squared is 4. 4 squared is 16.

He'd already hurt people, killed someone even with a few keystrokes. But now ... Ethan looked down at his hands.

They are weapons.

I'm a weapon.

A sick feeling slithered through him. "Remember when you told me about those people who hunt down Offspring?"

The worry lines around Hiroko's eyes deepened. "The Hidden Eye."

"Do they think Offspring are evil?"

"Unnatural is a better word, I think. They believe the Eleven should have remained in the Before, in their natural place."

"The Binding made me stronger."

She nodded.

"Did it make me dangerous?"

Hiroko put her arm around him. "You will decide how to wield the gifts of the Binding, and trust me, you're a good man."

I hope you're right.

Hiroko tugged him over to the cot and pointed to his tablet. "Right now, you're our best chance at finding the Circlet of Moments. Start looking for some old crown with Armaros's symbol on it."

I can do that.

He squeezed her hand in thanks, grabbed his tablet, and appropriated a satellite connection. Opening a drawing app, he had Hiroko draw Armaros's symbol—a circle enclosing a feather-like diagonal slash and an incomplete infinity sign. Using it as a search image, he cued up a series of queries, targeting art museums, historical societies, and private collections of Mesopotamian artifacts.

History became as soothing as math.

Thirty-Three

DALMEET

OUTSIDE OF TIME

Dalmeet's legs buckled, and he fell to his knees with a groan—not on stone but upon a firm, supple surface. He squinted. Not dawn, not dusk. The sky was white.

There was no sun outside of time.

Something was missing, something he needed.

"My heart's not beating!" His voice quavered.

"It's okay," Mara reassured him.

"How can it be okay?" Dalmeet felt drunk or sick or both. It took him a moment to realize that they were kneeling on an undulating sea of gold-colored sand. The dunes flowed and rippled around them like waves, though there was neither wind nor tide.

"Remember, I told you about this? Our heartbeats will come back when we go home."

Dalmeet dug through a jumble of memories. In the Record, Uncle Momar had said heartbeats were a clock that did not tick outside of time. *Heartbeats come back.* Mara told him that.

When we go home. Mara said she would get him home. *She will keep me safe.*

Beside him Mara stood, shifting her weight like a boxer to keep her balance on the rolling surface. She brushed glittering flecks from her knees and held out her hand. "Let's do this."

With her help, Dalmeet struggled to his feet. The ground directly beneath him seemed solid enough, but the constant movement of the sand in his peripheral vision was totally disorienting. He didn't trust any of it.

"Hey, Dali, look." He followed Mara's finger, distracted momentarily by the huge sky. *Should a sky be so big? So bright?*

"Dali!" Mara was in front of him, shaking him. "Stay with me!"

"What?" He focused on her face, and the churning feeling in his stomach subsided. "Sorry. This is so weird."

She squinted at something in the distance. "You want weird? Check that out."

A hundred yards to their left, a castle was building itself out of the sand. Battlements with merlons, paired arcades with high arches, and towers frosted in curlicue finials were birthed in a steady sweep of shimmering grains. As they stared, the castle solidified until each grain of sand was frozen in its allotted place, and the immense structure stood solid, imposing, and utterly impossible.

Dalmeet opened his mouth, closed it, opened it again. If his heart could beat, he was sure it would leap out of his chest.

Beside him, Mara's breath quickened. His gasps accelerated to match hers. *We shouldn't have come.*

"What now?" Mara asked.

Thoughts failed to connect in his head and come out as words. Instead, a choked gurgle escaped his lips.

Mara pulled herself together. "We're going there."

"Right," he panted.

Mara slogged toward the castle, and Dalmeet had no choice but to fix his eyes on her back and follow. *She's my only stable thing.* He vaguely recognized the irony. *She's the safe place.* The Twins were in there. He knew it. And he did not want to proceed.

"Holy crap!" Mara yelled, and Dalmeet forced himself to look up.

Like a child's beach creation washed away by the waves, the castle began to collapse. In moments, it was gone. Clouds of sugar-fine sand billowed up from the ruin, filling the air with shimmering motes that caught the light.

"It's gone?" Dalmeet was trying desperately to make sense of what he'd seen, but before he'd made any headway at all, the sand swept into motion again.

Mara grabbed his hand. "We've got to keep going."

He staggered beside her, unable to look away from the frenzied motion in front of them. Great circular walls punctuated with layered arches took shape. The structure sent a path rolling out to meet them. Inches from their toes, the path solidified, and the gigantic sand coliseum gave a final shivering twitch.

Mara squeezed his hand. "Ready?"

"No," said Dalmeet, but they stepped onto the path together. Their feet thumping along it was the only sound above the susurration of the path melting away behind them. Hand in hand, they walked through the great entry arch, which like the path, collapsed as soon as they had passed.

Dalmeet flinched, afraid of being buried alive.

"Don't look back," Mara commanded.

With every step they took, the structure morphed around them. Columns twisted into ancient trees with whisper-thin sheets of sand draped over the branches like Spanish moss. A perfectly pruned hedge grew on either side of the path, each twig, leaf, and flower a pressed composite of grains.

It was here, in the center of a magnificent garden of sand, that they found the Twins.

THIRTY-FOUR

PETRA

HIGH COUNCIL COMPOUND OF THE ELEVEN, ISTANBUL, TURKEY

With her Guards distracted and conveniently deployed around the city by Matthias de Alba, Petra was forced to call on the network of informants she'd cultivated around the world. It was seven thirty in the morning, and she was waiting at one of the guard stations on the high walkway surrounding the compound for her sources to check in. The sun rose behind her, and Petra turned her laptop out of the glare. Both her breath and the steam from her Turkish coffee swirled in the cold air.

It was the first clear day after a week of rain and sleet. In spite of her freezing fingers, Petra couldn't bear another minute inside the High Council compound. Whispers were everywhere. Matthias had managed to convince nearly all the Crimson Scribes and most of the Amyclaeans that Aeda was an innocent victim of Mara Layil's unbridled aggression. Most now considered the girl a murderer and a vigilante. They awaited the arrival of Aeda Moreau and her "evidence" like vultures waiting for a carcass.

Petra tried to imagine what Aeda could bring that would outweigh Armaros herself.

The Time Weaver had countermanded the Covenant and called off the Guard. That implied Mara's innocence or at least absolution. Surely one word from Armaros should bear more weight than a week-long tirade from the Head of the Crimson Scribes. The facts weren't lining up with Petra's intuition, and she knew better than to ignore her gut.

In the past week, she'd collected detailed information about the Moreaus' drug distribution ring in the western United States as well as their vast poppy fields in northern Thailand. The Pan-National Haematological Research Centre was a front for heroin processing and probably something worse.

Petra catalogued her discoveries. While drug running was reprehensible, it was not a violation of the Covenant. Aeda and Sinioch carefully navigated within the strictures of their kind. She'd found no evidence of shared Offspring from the two of them and no direct evidence of murder. If they did indeed dose Maximilian Layil with a toxin as Abbot Greb claimed, they'd been careful to use a drug that induced coma rather than death.

And they don't interfere with human free will. Self-destructive junkies could shoot up all the heroin they wanted. What was it those preachy Americans were always saying? *It's a free country.* The Moreaus were not alone in their observance of the letter if not the spirit of the law. Moral flexibility had made many Offspring both rich and powerful.

It made Petra sick.

As she downed the last of her coffee, a link to a secure video channel blinked into her inbox. The subject line was enough to make her rigidly alert: <u>Blast at Pan-National</u>. Petra hit play. It looked like her source in Thailand was walking through a war zone. After accounting for the fact that Thailand was five hours later than Istanbul, the time stamp showed the video had been filmed earlier that morning.

"You asked me to check on Aeda's operation here," her informant narrated. "This is it, or what's left of it. The explosion happened yesterday afternoon. Police suspect a lab accident."

I wouldn't bet on it.

"All the offices are downstairs. I'm on the second floor where the labs are, or rather, were."

The camera panned to give her a full view. Workmen were nailing plywood and blue tarps across a huge hole in the ceiling. Sun shining through the plastic made the lab seem underwater. Crumpled metal light fixtures dangled from the remains of the ceiling. Piles of concrete jammed the central hallway. Broken safety glass glittered on the floor.

"Look at this." The camera zoomed in on a red splotch oozing from under a chunk of concrete. "Blood—but the police said no causalities."

Her source filmed two workmen pushing a load of plywood off a freight elevator. A man in a white lab coat followed them out. Recognition jolted through Petra. *That's Paul Layil, Mara's father, and Armaros's grandson.*

The informant dropped the camera into a bag slung over his shoulder. The screen was obscured, but the audio was still on.

"Excuse me, sir," he asked. "I'm with the expat paper. Can you tell me what happened yesterday?"

"No." The response was terse and confrontational.

"Sure looks like a bomb went off in here."

Dr. Layil grunted.

"So what do you do here, Doctor?"

From the rustling and motion on the screen, Petra guessed Dr. Layil had brushed past. Her informant called after him. "Eyewitnesses say it was a suicide bomber. A blond girl." Petra heard a door slam, and the camera was lifted back into action, giving another sweep of the destroyed lab.

The camera cut out and restarted, according to the time stamp, thirty minutes later in a ratty hotel room. "First," said her off-screen informant, "you should know that they do process heroin there, but that lab you saw ain't no heroin lab. They're doing something else."

That's not exactly big news.

"Second, I wasn't talking smack to Layil. People did see a blond girl—well, a lot of blond girls, near the building. And third, locals are scared shitless of that place. They say people disappear in there all the time." From the narrator's skeptical tone, Petra knew he thought that was superstitious crap, but she wasn't so sure. "You know how to pay me." The clip ended, leaving Petra drumming her fingers against the desk.

A lot of blond girls? I hope he's not high.

But the disappearances jibed with her other research. Petra pulled up a missing persons list she'd compiled from police sources in Oregon. In the last twelve months, the rate of disappearances had nearly doubled. Everywhere Aeda went, people went missing. It made it hard for Petra to swallow the innocent-victim routine. She planned to do more digging, but in the meantime, Petra could not shake the sensation of imminent danger. What began with the Layil girl was reverberating through their world.

Is she a murderer? The girl had killed Sinioch Moreau, but if her claim of self-defense held up, she wouldn't be targeting other Offspring. *That's what Matthias wants people to believe.* Still, Petra could not decide who was more of a threat to Armaros—Aeda or Mara Layil. *But the threat is real!* Nothing in the world was more important to Petra than protecting Armaros. A battle was brewing over the future of the Covenant, and only Armaros could ensure peace.

Petra shut her laptop and rose quickly. There was no time to waste. She descended the stairs two at a time and headed straight for the High Council chamber. It was Armaros's habit to rise early and greet the day from that venerated place. If Petra was lucky, she'd find her alone. The tall double doors were ajar. Petra's heart raced as she glimpsed Armaros walking the circle of empty thrones. She knocked briskly and Armaros beckoned.

Her silver eyes shone. Warmth flooded Petra.

My true mother.

Petra greeted her with the salute of the Amyclaeans.

"You have worries, my Petra."

Petra nodded, loving the way Armaros knew her so thoroughly.

"More ... security ..." Petra pointed at Armaros.

"More security for me?" Armaros scanned her face. "Don't tell me you believe this nonsense about Mara Layil?"

Petra reddened and shook her head. In her gut, she knew it wasn't the girl, but still the danger against Armaros was real. A single word clawed its way past her piercings. "Mutterings."

Armaros laughed. "Everyone seems to think I am about to die. Perhaps some are even looking forward to it." She fixed a piercing look on Petra, who wanted to say *yes* and *no* all at the same time. Instead, she said nothing.

Armaros approached the statue of the White One, tracing the carved features of her face. "My dear, everyone dies eventually, even me." Her thin shoulders shook slightly.

By the Sacrifice, is she crying?

Armaros turned, and Petra saw that the Time Weaver was actually laughing. Armaros patted her shoulder. "No extra security. Everything will be fine."

She wanted to shake Armaros. She wanted to shout that Aeda was coming and that Matthias planned to *move things along,* but she had no real proof. Before Petra could muster the strength to argue, Armaros smiled at her again, gave the White One a last caress, and left Petra alone with her fears in the echoing chamber.

THIRTY-FIVE

MARA

OUTSIDE OF TIME

The girl, Lilya, and the boy, Eleon, were naked. Pearly hair fell in waves over their shoulders, covering the girl's small breasts. They reclined, eyes closed, on a sand settee, touching skin to skin along their arms and legs. They reminded Mara of Italian statues. Nude and exquisite, but too perfect to arouse.

Are they dead? That would be my kind of luck.

Two thousand years had passed since Mara watched Armaros banish them outside of time. The Twins had grown some but they barely looked fifteen.

How do you grow outside of time? Hell, how do you even survive it?

The hairs rose on the back of Mara's neck. Dalmeet squeezed her hand, trembling.

The Twins' eyes flicked open in perfect unison, sending panic racing through her limbs.

One thing hadn't changed—their eyes.

Two pairs of pupil-less, white orbs fixed on her.

Dalmeet shuddered as if his legs might not hold him. She felt his fear and knew it was taking every bit of strength he had to stand with her. She'd begun to count on her Scribe to have the right words for any situation, but he seemed incapable of speech.

Those eyes sucked at her.

What is it they say about eyes? Windows to the soul? Are the Twins all soul ... or none?

"Mara," they said in unison. "Mara Layil."

Their musical voices urged the sand between them into delicate, writhing shapes. Golden flowers grew and wilted at the passing of her name.

"Right," she said, her voice flat and toneless compared to theirs. "You're Lilya and Eleon. Nice to meet you."

I sound like a rip-roaring lunatic.

"Why have you stepped outside of time, Mara Layil?" The question tugged the sand into spirals. "Don't you know it is forbidden?"

"I don't give a crap about that."

They laughed, a mellifluous trill. "And you brought a new Scribe. We rather liked your last one." Tears burned in the corners of Mara's eyes. "Momar Singh broke the rules too. He came to us about you, Mara Layil." Matching smiles swam threateningly across their blank faces. "He told us much."

"What did you do to him?" Dalmeet said.

His anger throbbed through Mara.

"Do to him?" the Twins repeated, their faces reflecting an angry undercurrent. "You know how long we have been trapped outside of time, denied all but the rarest contact." They paused, linked eyes, and then returned their terrible focus to Dalmeet. "When a visitor comes, we try to find out what he knows."

"I read what he wrote after he came back from seeing you," said Dalmeet. "He was out of his mind. You did something to him."

The Twins shrugged. "Not everyone can withstand being outside of time. You should consider what happened to us. We are the prisoners here."

"But that wasn't Uncle Momar's—"

As one, they rose, setting the sand in motion. Mara and Dalmeet clung to each other, desperate to free their feet from the rolling sand. The Twins skimmed its surface, and at a wave of the girl's hand, the sand garden crumbled.

"Now you will watch," the Twins said, their voices piercing Mara's ears. "You will see what they did to us. You will learn about endings and beginnings."

The ground to Mara's left collapsed. Rushing scree pulled her toward the edge of a great cliff. Unbalanced, she pinwheeled her arms and dove away from the drop. In the rush of sand, Mara heard Dalmeet yelling and saw him reaching for her. Mara thrashed against the dense drifts that clutched at her limbs. Sand reached her shoulders, her neck, her chin. Grit filled her mouth, sucking the moisture out of her tongue, gagging her.

Just as her lungs were on the verge of collapse, a sinewy hand seized the nape of her neck and dragged her to the surface. Eleon gave her a shake like a dog gives a stick and dropped her in a heap. Dalmeet lay gasping before Lilya, his turban lost, his long, black hair full of sun-gold sand. He twitched as if he'd stuck a finger in a wall socket. Mara crawled across the sand toward him.

Lilya prodded him with her toe. "Get up."

Mara put her body between them and lifted Dalmeet's head out of the sand. "Come on," she urged, "I'll help you stand."

"GET UP!" the Twins screamed. The command carried a sizzling, electric shock, which forced them upright. When the voltage waned, Mara put her arm around Dalmeet's waist and held him as convulsions twitched through the muscles in their faces, arms, and legs.

"Beginnings," said Eleon.

"WATCH!" howled Lilya.

Her head riveted on the scene, Mara took in the landscape the Twins created. To her left, a cliff dropped to a protected cove. Far below, waves of sand lapped against rocks festooned with tide pool creatures—barnacles, crabs, seaweed. Beyond lay the sea stretching to the unnaturally upcurved horizon and white sky. To her right, the clifftop was a checkerboard of fields. Each blade of wheat and each bunch of grapes was a perfect replica in sand. Farther inland, the terrain grew rocky and steep. What lay past that jagged skyline Mara couldn't guess. *Probably nothing.* She pulled Dali closer.

"We were born along the Mediterranean Sea," said Eleon.

"Look." Lilya pointed to a grove of olive trees.

With a gentle rasp of flowing sand, four figures swirled into being.

Instantly, Mara recognized the much-younger Twins with their father, Javan, and their mother, Serac. The real Twins spoke with icy menace. "We were happy."

The sand versions of Serac and Lilya walked hand in hand, giggling at some whispered secret. In the silent tableau, Mara could see young Eleon's mouth moving a mile a minute and knew Javan was listening. When his son finished the story, Javan threw back his head, shoulders quaking with laughter. He lifted Eleon under the arms and swung him in a circle. Mara could see Lilya jumping up and down and knew she was squealing, "Me! Me!"

They were happy.

Even rendered in sand, the faces of Javan and Serac revealed their devotion to their strange, otherworldly children.

Mara looked away from the foursome.

Had her family ever been like that?

Had her mother ever viewed her without unease?

Had her father ever seen beyond his calculations?

Dalmeet tugged on her arm. "This is the day they were taken. The rest of the Eleven are coming."

Oblivious to the approaching figures, Javan, Serac, and the children surprised a flock of birds, which took to the air like a spray of fireworks. The children danced below the whirling wings. Nine of the Eleven descended upon them with dazzling speed, pressing the family into a huddle. Azza grimaced, his mouth open in soundless accusation. Armaros wrenched the Twins from Serac's embrace, and Tamel, the sand-etched features of his face set against their protests, threw thick chains around each of them.

Tears prickled behind Mara's eyes. *They were happy. Was that a crime?*

She jumped as the real Twins brought their hands together in a sudden, ear-shattering clap. The scene before them collapsed. Harsh light seared Mara's eyes and a sudden wind drove gritty particles into her cheeks and arms.

"Mara Layil, why are you here?" The Twins stood inches away. She hadn't even seen them move. They were taller than she was. Staring at their satin faces, Mara wondered if they saw as she saw. Did they see how battered and filthy and broken she was? Or did they see more?

Mara was afraid of lying but equally afraid of telling the truth. Mara chose her words carefully. "I came about the Circlet of Moments."

The Twins hissed, "Cursed relic," and sand shot up around the four of them in hundreds of waist-high, needle-topped spikes.

"Be careful," Dalmeet whispered.

Mara threw her shoulders back and stepped closer to Lilya. "Yeah, it's a piece of shit, but I'm looking for it."

"Why?" The harmonics of their joined voices buzzed through Mara's brain as she weighed her options. She was pretty damn sure that the truth would get her killed. Armaros planned to use the Circlet to keep the Twins imprisoned in this place.

"WHY?" they repeated so forcefully that she and Dalmeet took involuntary steps back, stopped only by the spiked barrier around them. Mara cast about for some answer that would keep them alive, but Dalmeet saved her. "Mara is newly Turned. Her abilities are unstable. She needs the relic to help her master them."

The Twins leaned in, and Mara could see the effort it took for her Scribe to hold his ground. "She is descended from Armaros. The witch who trapped us here. Why would we help her spawn?"

"Armaros tried to lock me up too," Mara broke in. "She's not my people."

The look they gave her felt like a full-body X-ray and an airport pat down all at once.

She held her breath.

Finally, Eleon raised his hand, and the spikes melted away. In their place, walls soared skyward. Pedestals of sand grew beneath the Twins. When every grain had found its place, Mara and Dalmeet stood in a sandstone throne room. The Twins lounged above them, fingers entwined and legs tossed casually over the ponderous arms of their thrones.

As an afterthought, Lilya built a bench for them with the twitch of her finger.

"Sit."

Mara shifted her weight to one hip and stuck her chin out, but Dalmeet pulled her down on the bench. "They want to talk," he murmured.

"Or give orders."

"As it happens," said Eleon, "we have watched and listened and searched for the very relic you want. It is of special value to us."

They paused for a long moment, and Mara felt sure they were communicating somehow. She tried to ignore the ever-moving sand in her peripheral vision, but the constant slithering of what should have been solid made her skin crawl as did the way the Twins' bodies seemed sometimes made of steel and sometimes milk.

"We know where it is."

"You do? All right, then, that's good."

"The Scribe is right. The relic will complete your Turning. You'll have full command of your capabilities. You shall use it, and then you will bring it to us."

Of course, they wanted it. With Armaros's relic they could break out, which was exactly what Armaros wanted to prevent.

Her mind spun. *I wish Ethan were here. He'd know what to do.* Mara stared into those opaque eyes. *I'm gonna have to wing it.*

"Okay. Tell me where it is. I'll get my time stuff worked out and bring it straight back."

Dalmeet shifted.

What is he thinking that I'm not?

The thrones dissolved, lowering the Twins to the ground. They stepped apart abruptly. Eleon took Mara's arm in a grip far too tight for such delicate hands. Lilya grabbed Dalmeet.

"What are you doing?" Mara snapped. "Let us go!"

"You, yes, but the Scribe stays with us until you bring the relic."

"What? You're crazy!"

Dalmeet's face was tight with fear, but he nodded. "Do it, Mara. You have to, but be fast. I won't last long outside of time."

"He is correct," purred the Twins. "It's very hard on the body."

Before Mara could argue, Eleon threw her into a tornado of sand. The force of the dervish sucked her into the air. She spun into space. Grit blinded her, piercing her flesh like thousands of tiny knives, and all she could hear was Dalmeet screaming her name.

THIRTY-SIX

ETHAN

MONASTERY OF PRO LAPSIS ASTRA, SOUTH OF CHIANG RAI, THAILAND

Ethan had been fused to his tablet for hours when he heard scraping in the corridor. Hiroko was asleep, curled up on the cot. Ethan listened hard but hearing nothing more, he stretched and decided he should try to sleep.

As he lay down on a meditation mat, the rasping noise returned.

What is that?

Ethan strained to hear, unease growing in his belly.

It sounds like something being dragged.

He crept to the door.

Again, he heard the jerky, intermittent sliding sound of something heavy. It stopped outside the room. Ethan held his breath. He wished he weren't on his hands and knees in front of the door. As quietly as possible, Ethan began to inch away, but a new noise began and he froze in midcrawl. Something hard and sharp scratched at the door.

Claws? Rats? Something worse?

He glanced over his shoulder at Hiroko snoring softly. Ethan had no idea what could be out there, and he wasn't sure he wanted to find out.

Ignore it. That's the smart thing to do.

But the scratching continued and with it a low moan. A subdued, vulnerable sound that brought back the scent of concrete and blood on Mara's face, the feeble warmth of her limp body in his arms, the salty taste of her finger pressed against his lips when she warned him against getting sappy. Again, the whimpering moan of a damaged animal snuck under the door.

Forgetting caution, Ethan unbolted the lock.

Mara was lying face down on the threshold, nearly unconscious. The bloody fingers of her left hand scratched reflexively against the space where the door had been.

Her clothes hung in shreds on her body. She was more naked than clothed, and he could see that her skin was a spiderwebbed network of bloody red lines. One of her earrings had been ripped out of the lobe.

"Shit, shit, shit!" Ethan slid his arms under Mara, cradling her against his chest. Blood oozed from hundreds of cuts, dappling his T-shirt with dark spots.

"Hiroko!" he called as loudly as he dared, and she woke and helped him ease Mara onto the cot.

Mara's eyelids fluttered. "Told you I'd come back," she said in a hoarse rasp.

Ethan pressed his lips to hers for an instant and then pulled back, realizing what he'd done. "Sorry."

She smiled weakly.

"Where's Dalmeet?" Hiroko asked.

"The Twins … they kept him."

Hiroko's eyes filled with tears. "They kept him outside of time? He'll never last. Why would they do that?"

"So I'll do what they want."

Ethan swore. "He's a hostage. Or a sacrifice!" Turning his attention from Mara, he paced the room, violence swirling through him. "I'm going in." He pulled the gauntlets out of the backpack and shook them. "I'll take these. I'll get him back."

Mara tried to push herself to a sitting position, wincing in pain. "Ethan—"

"Don't say anything," he interrupted. "Just take me there. I'll stay in his place if I have to." Hiroko tried to calm him, but he brushed her away and slammed his hands on the narrow table. "Goddammit, I told him I should be the one to go."

"Ethan!" Mara yelled. "Shut up! Do you think I wanted to leave him there? Do you think I meant to?"

Ethan flinched at the outrage on Mara's face and fell silent. *1, 2, 3, 4, 5 …* Of course, she didn't mean to leave Dalmeet. The gauntlets clunked back onto the table. Mara would have killed the Twins before she let them have him.

"I know you wouldn't leave him."

"Damn right, I wouldn't."

"Drop it! Both of you!" Hiroko snapped.

6, 7, 8 … Ethan sat heavily with his head in his hands.

Hiroko knelt before Mara. "Let me look at you. You're a mess."

Ethan watched as she pulled away the shredded fabric of Mara's clothes. She was indeed a freaking mess. Scratches crisscrossed her body. There was something odd—*something familiar?*—about the shape of those cuts. Cogs and wheels in his brain whirred into motion.

9, 10, 11 …

"We don't have much time," Mara said. "The Twins want the Circlet. They're keeping Dalmeet until I bring it to them."

"And to think I was starting to feel sorry for them locked up like that," Ethan spat.

"It's all my fault," said Mara. "I'm so stupid."

"You are not stupid," said Hiroko.

"I am."

Ethan felt the desperation as she turned on herself, but he couldn't tear his eyes away from the marks on her pale skin.

"I agreed to it because they said they knew where it was. They said they would tell me. So I agreed. Then everything went to hell. And now they've got Dali, and I still have no idea where the Circlet is."

Why make wounds with such complex, deep curves? Observations clicked into place. That curving line was familiar. *12, 13, 14 …* The puzzle consumed him, suppressing his anger at the Twins. This was something to solve. Something he could do.

How do I know that shape?

He bent nearer. The cut along Mara's right flank zigzagged over her hipbone, dropped toward her ass in club-like shape, then sliced across the top of her leg. The cut turned sharply midthigh in a vaguely boot-like shape.

15, 16, 17 …

I'm so close.

On the right side of her rib cage, two vaguely circular wounds dripped blood. *They look like …* What was it? *Almost like … That's it!* Ethan strode from one side of the room to the other, smacking his fist into the palm of his other hand. "Islands! Fucking islands!"

Mara and Hiroko stopped talking, their attention riveted on his frantic pacing.

"What's wrong?" asked Mara.

"I am so pissed. They … shit … I can't believe they …" He gestured his arms frantically over her damaged body. "You … look at you …"

"I know it looks bad," Hiroko said, "but the wounds are totally superficial."

He couldn't get the words out. Instead, he pointed to Mara's naked hip.

"Come on, Ethan," said Mara, forcing a laugh. "It's not like you haven't seen a girl's ass before." Hiroko fumbled for the sheet to cover Mara, but Ethan ripped it out of her hand, tossing it to the floor.

"Look!" Holding his finger a hairsbreadth from her skin, he traced the two islands. "Ireland! England! And here," he said, pointing to a cut slicing under her right breast, "is Norway. Denmark. The whole freaking coast."

"By the Blade—" Hiroko cursed. "I see it now." She pointed to Mara's ass. "That's Spain, and Italy's on your thigh."

Mara twisted her body to see what they were seeing. Fresh droplets beaded up on the cuts.

"Don't you get it?" Ethan roared. He was so angry now that he felt the pressure of tears behind his eyes. "Those pigs! Those barbarians! They … they … My god, Mara, they've turned you into a map!"

THIRTY-SEVEN

AEDA

GANEM FORTIFICATION ON THE OUTSKIRTS OF ISTANBUL, TURKEY

R and Ganem snapped his fingers and one of the many pregnant women in his household scurried to clear the tea things. "Your scientist arrived. Would you like to see him?"

Aeda nodded, though she could hardly tear her eyes away from the view across sloping farmland and into the sprawl of Istanbul. The roof of the High Council compound was a speck near the Bosporus. After the explosion at the lab, she had decided to move Paul Layil to a more secure location. It amused her to have him here, right under Armaros's nose.

But her amusement barely scratched the surface of her irritation. She was ready to move. *Now!* Three days she'd been waiting for Matthias de Alba to clear the way. A gnawing hunger mushroomed inside her.

"Come," said Rand, handing Aeda her fur coat. "It's cold in the lower levels."

Rand Ganem was a broad-shouldered, swarthy First Born who had spent decades buying land and building this solar-powered, self-sufficient estate. A casual observer at the bottom of the gated drive would see nothing but a bank of windows and a hint of metal roof. They wouldn't know that the structure was a twenty-thousand-square-foot underground warren protected by earth from most anything short of a nuclear attack. Thick metal doors could be lowered to shield the windows as well. His family could survive for months on production from their hothouses, chicken coops, and stockpiled supplies.

Aeda did not know how Rand could bear to copulate with the human women, but at least he had the good sense to keep them segregated, subservient, and very productive. Rand led her past several classrooms filled with his Offspring. The youngest were doing calisthenics in formation. The older ones were being drilled in military tactics by a brawny male instructor.

Beyond the classrooms, they passed dormitories for the children. Crisply made bunks lined the white walls. No posters of pop stars or basketball players. The only decorations were the symbols of the Eleven and inspirational quotes from the Offspring Giovanni Rocco, the most prolific philosopher to argue against the Covenant.

"How many children do you have now?" she asked.

He grinned. "Oh, you know ... *as numerous as the stars of heaven and the sands on the seashore ...*"

Aeda completed the verse. *"... and your descendants shall seize the gates of their foes."*

At the end of the corridor, Rand stopped at a steel door and tapped his password into the code lock. The door swung open, revealing a guard monitoring the security feeds from the two-level prison.

"The women are housed four to a room on the upper floor," Rand explained. "Those who have proved reliable work in the house. The others ... well ... they maintain themselves in prime condition for pregnancy."

As they traversed the upper level, Aeda peered into the women's rooms, which were cluttered, cramped, and full of human detritus. She wrinkled her nose at the smell of sweat and musk.

"The men are below," Rand continued. "Much more difficult to manage, of course. The women will do anything for their babies. But what can I do?" He shrugged. "I have daughters as well as sons."

At the last cell, Rand stopped.

Dr. Layil was hunched over a desk scribbling furiously in a notebook. At their approach, his hand froze on the page. The look he gave Aeda was venomous.

"Where's Mara?"

"You're getting all paternal on me."

Paul rose and strained against the bars. Aeda heard the metal bend and screech. She raised one thin eyebrow at Rand. "Will it hold?"

"Yes," he assured her, "but we can electrify the enclosure if that makes you feel better."

"Do it. He's second generation."

Rand flipped a switch, and the current flowing through the bars sent Paul flying across the cell. He was on his feet immediately, shouting, "Where is she?"

The murmured sounds of the other inmates ceased.

I don't know. I wish I did.

She tilted her lovely face, appraising him. "I'm sorry, Paul. My head of security killed her." Aeda watched the muscles in his face tense. A wash of red swept over him, but the man kept his anger in.

"It's touching," she murmured, "to see how much you really care. Maybe you shouldn't have thrown yourself so fully into your work."

Paul twitched, skewered in place by her words.

This is why one should never have children.

"She's made you weak, Paul."

"I won't work for you anymore. Not another minute."

We will see about that.

A wide smile spread across her face. "Rand," she said, without taking her eyes from Dr. Layil's face, "are your older children ready for a tactical exercise?"

"Of course. What did you have in mind?"

"The *Pro Lapis Astra* monastery in Portland. There's a boy there ..."

Paul paled and leaned heavily against the back wall of the cell.

"Kill him."

"But the Covenant," Paul stammered.

The Covenant is ending.

"I wouldn't worry about old-fashioned proprieties," Aeda crooned. "In a few days, it won't matter. What you should be worrying about is me."

THIRTY-EIGHT

ETHAN

THAI AIRWAYS FLIGHT EN ROUTE TO BRUSSELS, BELGIUM

Ethan's overhead light was the only one on in the near-empty plane. It was just after two thirty in the morning, and he was wide awake. Hiroko slept in the window seat next to him, swathed in a lavender blanket. Across the aisle, Mara spread across an entire row of seats, all limbs and sprawl.

Everything about Thai Airways was pastel, including the flight attendants in tidy suits the color of Easter eggs. When they'd boarded in Bangkok, Mara had tried to lift their spirits by holding her arms at stiff right angles and walking on tiptoes without bending her knees. "Hello," she said in a cheery, plastic voice. "I am Barbie. Welcome to my pretty plane."

He'd tried to laugh, but nothing changed the ugly facts.

Dalmeet is gone and Max is beyond help.

Mara had gone to the Twins hoping to make a deal, and instead, those monsters had sliced every bay and peninsula of the European continent into her flesh. The worst wound was on her right hip. A deeply carved eye with a mouth in the center marked the location of the ancient city of Bruges. Hiroko had held a cloth to the spot for ten minutes before it clotted.

Mara had asked the Twins if they knew the location of the Circlet of Moments. They could've just said Bruges, right? But no, they threw a tantrum and tore her to bits.

And poor Dalmeet. Ethan wondered how Mara could pity the Twins. As they'd snuck out of the monastery, she'd said they were like her—things that weren't supposed to be born. *I hate them.*

Ethan watched Mara sleep in the dim light of the cabin. She'd raided Dalmeet's bag for clothes, exchanging her bloodied rags for a pair of his khakis, rolled up to her calves, and an untucked, white button-down with sleeves that covered her gauntlets. Mara shifted, whimpering in her sleep as her clothes chafed the cuts on her body.

Ethan stood and stretched, glancing up and down the aisle at the other sleeping passengers. He pulled another lavender blanket from the overhead compartment and spread it over Mara. Ethan wished he could rest, or better—take his board to the concrete maze of ramps and bowls under the Burnside Bridge and skate. It would be good to have a break from thinking for a while.

The eye-mouth inscribed on Mara's hip told them more than the presumed location of the Circlet. It told them whom they would face in Bruges. The relic they needed was in the hands of the Hidden Eye, an ancient fraternity of humans dedicated to eradicating Offspring from the face of the earth.

But how do we find you assholes in Bruges?

The online searches he'd run on the Hidden Eye while they drove to Bangkok had yielded nothing. That fact alone told him how dangerous they were. Hiding one's tracks online was no easy task. Hate groups usually like to spread their vitriol. Operating below the radar meant they were organized and focused on covert action rather than bombast.

They have to communicate somehow.

Ethan figured it was through symbols rather than words because visual images were easier to hide in the avalanche of pictures on the Internet. Before the plane had taken off, Ethan had again mobilized the computing power of YouKnowMe, throwing processing power behind the memory-intensive image recognition searches he needed them to do.

The eye-mouth is out there, I know it.

It would be buried in some tourist's online travel album or an obscure academic's navel-gazing musings.

I will find them.

The search was running. For now, he could only eat airplane peanuts and wait.

And watch Mara sleep.

His fingers itched to touch her. He'd seen her nearly naked and had even traced the cut lines from her breast to her belly, but he couldn't reach his hand across the aisle and stroke her cheek. The steady rhythm of her pulse marched alongside his own. She rolled over, and Dalmeet's dress shirt fell open, revealing the curve of her breast. Ethan ached for her, but he pushed away his desire.

1, 2, 3, 4…

After the Binding, he didn't plan to take anything she didn't offer. And the chance of her dropping her defenses and daring closeness… Well, he thought he had a better chance of winning the X-Games.

Ethan pulled the tablet from his backpack. He'd taken a screen shot of *CLOAKED*'s last play so he could puzzle it out inflight, even with the Wi-Fi shut down. Maybe that would take his mind off things.

Or maybe not.

Between his moves and those of *CLOAKED*, the game had yielded a random but freakishly weighty list of words: *INNOCENTS SUFFER CORRUPT JUSTICE*. The connections were not easy to ignore.

CLOAKED's last move had been *BLAME*.

Ethan connected *RIGHT* to the *R* in *CORRUPT*.

That didn't take long. So much for distraction.

He laid his tablet on the seat and slugged back the last of his ginger ale, wishing it were an energy drink. He could practically hear Hiroko lecturing him about the utter toxicity of those so-called sports drinks, but he would drink jet fuel if it kept him focused and awake. Maybe he would read the new Gaiman book he'd pulled down on his e-reader.

Ping!

Ethan snatched up the tablet.

CLOAKED had hooked *WRONGS* onto the *G* in *RIGHT*.

Wasted another S, you dumb-ass. He was sorting the possibilities in his hand when alarm bells started going off in his head. *What the ...?* Ethan double-checked the Wi-Fi. It was definitely disabled.

How had CLOAKED managed to play?

Ethan stared out the window, half expecting to see his mystery opponent perched on the wing *Twilight Zone*-style. This game was off-kilter in too many ways. Ethan scanned his letters and tossed down the first word he saw: ZEST on the T of GUILT.

Ping!

Stacking two letters, *ZEST* turned into *PAST*.

This should not be happening. Pulse racing, Ethan scanned the cabin. *Could CLOAKED have set up a private network on board?* Everyone else on the plane was asleep. Ethan counted until his heart slowed. *Okay, fine. Let's see where this is going.*

He played *SECURE* on the *S* in *PAST*.

Ping!

No sooner had Ethan slid his letters into place, his word was transformed into *SECOND*.

Ethan set *DANCE* on the *N*.

Ping!

CHANCE.

And then *CLOAKED*'s name vanished from the in-play queue. Ethan wiped his forehead. The cabin felt tight and hot. He reviewed *CLOAKED*'s words: *WRONGS PAST SECOND CHANCE.* Combined with his first move and rearranged, the message commanded his attention.

RIGHT PAST WRONGS.

SECOND CHANCE.

This is no game.

As if to punctuate his thoughts, the plane hit a rough patch of air and dropped a few feet. Ethan's stomach heaved into his mouth, and he held back bile. Several other passengers jolted awake, gasping. The plane leveled, but Ethan remained painfully aware of how insignificant they were hurtling along at thirty thousand feet.

THIRTY-NINE

DALMEET

OUTSIDE OF TIME

It was easier when Dalmeet kept his eyes closed. The ever-changing landscape gave him near constant motion sickness. Whatever the Twins wanted or dreamed grew into a reality made of sand. When they changed their minds, the world disintegrated.

When the rushing sound of moving sand slowed, Dalmeet rolled over on his side and risked opening his eyes. Bright sand filled his field of view. *Thank the Blade it's not moving.* He pushed himself up. The Twins were nowhere to be seen. He ventured a deep breath, then another, hesitant to do anything that might call attention to himself.

At first, he'd tried to befriend them. Dalmeet knew what it was to be unwanted and unwelcome. At least he'd grown up with freedom, something the Twins had never known. But their whims were devastating. Sometimes they upended the ground and replaced it with air just because they could. And they took things from him. Personal things. Memories.

Dalmeet shuddered.

A bit of black poking out of the sand caught his eye.

My dastar.

He crawled toward the cloth, remembering how it had been ripped from his head when the Twins recreated their capture by the Eleven. *I felt sorry for them then.* That was before they took Mara. *Where is she?* Dalmeet hoped she had returned to the fabric of time. An ideal hope. *She's probably dead.*

He unburied the length of cloth, shaking the sand out of it in a crystalline cloud. *I'm as good as dead.* He pressed one hand to his chest and wished for the hundredth time that his heart was beating. The Twins' hunger for knowledge of the world inside of time was rapacious. They knew nothing of boundaries, of the sacred space of an individual mind. *I cannot withstand them.*

From his long-lost life inside of time, a memory of Momar returned. "You are Singh," his uncle rumbled. "Never forget that."

Dalmeet stared at the cloth draped over his arm, aware of the weight of his hair against his back. "I am a Singh," he repeated. "I am a Singh." Slowly, he pulled his fingers through the knots in his hair, tugging them free. He twisted it back and wrapped the turban in place. "I am a Singh."

Lilya's voice in his ear was like a punch to the gut. "What are you doing?"

He flinched. They always came like that, without warning. That was when they wanted things.

I am a Singh.

"Why do you wrap your hair?" she demanded.

Weariness filled Dalmeet. "To show I am a Sikh."

"Your hair is very long."

I am a Singh.

"Yes."

"Why?"

Dalmeet felt her breath on his shoulder and fought the urge to step away. "So I will have the strength to endure unto infinity."

I do not think I will have the strength, Uncle.

"I want to feel it," Lilya announced. When he didn't respond fast enough, a sand golem with monstrous hands tore off the turban, nearly wrenching the hair from Dalmeet's head. Lilya insinuated her body against his, running her skeletal, bloodless fingers through his long hair.

I am a Singh.

I am a Singh.

I am a Singh.

After a lifetime—or was it only a second?—Eleon was there, pushing into Dalmeet's consciousness.

"What is music? Sing! Again!"

Eleon pulled melodies from Dalmeet until he thought he was poisoned by the insipid pop songs Eleon favored.

I am a Singh.

"What's a car?"

"How do you drive one?"

Harvesting a memory, they recreated the precipitous streets of Seattle in sand. Taan was teaching him to drive a stick shift. Dalmeet lurched on the clutch, stalled on a steep hill, rolled backward inch by inch as Taan called him *dumb-ass* and *jerkwad* and *loser.*

I am a Singh.

The Twins were voracious.

"Show us drunk!"

Dalmeet puked cheap beer and tequila, wishing he were drunk enough to pass out.

I am a Singh.

FORTY

MARA

BRUGES, BELGIUM

What's next?" Mara said, stopping under a store awning to get out of the sleet. She pulled the collar of her motorcycle jacket up around her neck. "I can't wait to get out of here."

Bruges was a bad-weather cross between *Pirates of the Caribbean* and a renaissance fair. The tourists crowding the sidewalk were eating it up. Mara fought the urge to shove them and their stupid umbrellas out of the way. They'd been walking through wintry rain for hours. Every step caused the clothes Mara had pinched from Dali to shift and scrape across her cuts. Her flesh burned and her feet hurt.

Squeezed in beside her, Ethan and Hiroko pored over a map of Bruges.

"Let's go to the linguistics institute next," said Hiroko.

"The curiosity shop is closer," Ethan countered.

Jet-lagged and sleep-deprived from trains, planes, and automobiles, Mara leaned against the brick wall, too tired to see straight. They'd been to an old theater with the eye-mouth carved on its cornerstone, a jewelry museum displaying a Victorian eye-mouth pin, and the famous Belfry of Bruges, where they found the symbol in medieval graffiti. Their last stop had been a Moroccan teahouse full of mosaic tables with the eye-mouth rendered in glass tiles—blood red, ice blue, and pearly white. Revolting but at least they'd had ten minutes out of the cold.

I just want to be warm.

She didn't really care anymore where they led her.

When she'd woken on the plane, Ethan had gone all cryptic on her, talking about second chances. *Like I believe in that crap anymore. Mom's a zombie. Dad's an asshole. My brother's never waking up. Dali's gonna die.* She bit the insides of her cheeks to keep from crying.

Or losing it.

Mara couldn't shake the feeling that she was the problem. *Nothing I touch turns out right.* She could feel the volatile mixture of her bloodlines as if her veins were filled with explosives. Ethan and Hiroko weren't safe around her. It wasn't a question of *if* her control would lapse; it was *when*. Dali said the Circlet would stabilize her abilities, but he was gone and couldn't help her do it.

Ethan must have read her mind because he shoulder-bumped her. "We'll get him back. We will. I know it."

"Yeah," she murmured, not believing him for a second. "Let's go."

The next location required a half-mile walk toward an increasingly fishy-smelling canal. "This is it," said Hiroko. "Feel it out, Mara."

The gauntlets were quiescent on her arms. No hint of Offspring flickered through her veins. Would there be a time when she could stop worrying about getting someone killed? *Probably not.*

"Nothing," she said.

"Good. What do you make of this?"

Two curiosity shops stood side by side on the ground floor of a skinny, three-story building. They shared a common wall and each had a carved wooden sign hanging out front—no words, just an image like those used in medieval times. There the similarity ended.

On the left-hand sign was an angel with flowing hair and outstretched wings. On the right was an eye-mouth swallowing white feathers. The two shops were locked in mortal combat.

Mara gaped. "Holy cow, Batman."

"Think that's a coincidence?" Ethan asked.

"Not on your life," said Hiroko.

Mara pointed to the dorky angel. "Is that supposed to be us?"

Hiroko nodded, looking nauseated. "Humans that came into contact with the Eleven made up all kinds of crazy explanations—spirits, angels, demons, whatever." She flapped her hand dismissively. "You should see all the Area 51 stuff."

"I'll check this one out," said Ethan, reaching for doorknob for the eye-mouth place.

"Better you than me," Mara replied as she followed Hiroko into the other shop.

The place was crammed with angel everything—books, paintings, knickknacks, jewelry. There were avenging angels, guardian angels, child angels, angelic angels. She picked up a cross-stitched wall hanging depicting a winged woman against a deep blue background. Embroidered in flowing pink letters, it read, "Why does the night sky sparkle? Because each star is a jewel carried by an angel!"

She held it out to Hiroko. "Seriously? Gag!"

Hiroko stifled a snort.

"*Hallo. Welgekomen,*" said a stooped man with pale gray eyes and a wispy, white combover.

"Uh ... hi?" said Mara, hoping English would work.

"May Angels touch you," he lisped, switching to English.

What's the appropriate response to that?

"And you too?" Mara ventured.

The man broke out in a huge smile. "Come, come, let me show you some wonderful things. Do you know that the angels speak to us in numbers?"

Mara gave Hiroko a *please save me* look through a display of crystal figurines. Hiroko pointedly ignored her, examining a rack of socks printed with spiraling rows of hand-holding seraphim.

"I had no idea angels did math," Mara said.

The man chuckled and held out a bowl of smooth rocks, each etched with a single-digit number. "Don't look. Just take three and we'll see what they say to you."

"I don't know ..."

"Dear American lady, I am a spiritual healer and ascended master of the angelic realms. Come now. Choose. Choose."

"We really have to go," said Mara. "My friend wants to look next door."

The ascended master's face went pastier—if that was possible. He looked as if Mara had said Hiroko was going next door to drown puppies. "But you mustn't," he said, grasping Mara's shoulder in a bony hand. "Evil is behind that door."

And this is perfectly normal?

"Sorry!" Mara shook out of his grasp and headed for the door. "Come on, Hiroko."

"Wait!" wailed the man, shaking the bowl of rocks. "At least draw the stones before you go?"

Anything to shut him up. The rocks were smooth and warm, as if each one had ridden awhile in the pocket of a cowboy's jeans. She palmed three and held them out to the ascended master.

He leapt back, spilling half the rocks out of the bowl. "Angels preserve us! Three ones? That never happens!"

Mara dropped the rocks into his jittering hand. "People say that a lot around me."

Time to go. She ushered Hiroko through the door.

As they crossed the threshold, the man called after her. "Watch your thoughts, young lady. The angels—they will make your thoughts manifest! They ..." The door slammed shut.

Mara turned to Hiroko. "I'm not scary. Tell me I'm not scary. Am I scary?"

"That man was insane."

"You didn't answer my question." But both the question and Hiroko's answer vaporized as soon as they entered the second shop.

"Oh my freaking god," said Mara.

Ethan was standing beside a wall display of gruesome sculptures. Each piece was lit from below, deepening the shadows on the garish figures. Gladiators speared angels. Samurai beheaded them. Amazons burned them alive.

And the angels ... Mara wasn't entirely sure that they were supposed to be angels. Sure, they had wings—black bat wings. Instead of the beatific smiles of the angels next door, their eyes smoldered red black.

Turning away from the gnarly display, Mara scanned a bookshelf. "*Humanity Is for Humans. A Crime for the Ages. The Interference of Angels.* What is this shit?"

Before Hiroko could respond, a rough voice spoke in heavily accented English, "May I help you?" They turned to see an old man with skin the color of dried dates.

Mara recognized him instantly. How could you miss a man in a red fez? Earlier that day, he'd been in the tea shop with the eye-mouth tables. He wasn't Offspring, but his probing look made Mara glad her jacket covered the bumps on her shoulders.

"First, I see you in the teahouse," he said. "Now here in my shop." He inclined his head to the merchandise as if he stocked fancy umbrellas or Coach bags. "Tell me ..." His words prodded at her. "You have a special interest, yes?"

Ethan stepped in front of her. "I'm an exchange student from America, and I'm doing a project on symbolism. I'm very interested in this." He picked up a bronze medallion the size of a quarter upon which shone the raised outline of the eye-mouth dangling feathers. "I'd never seen anything like it until the teahouse. I texted my instructor, and he told me about this shop."

"Ah," said the man with a sigh, the threat in his posture relaxing. "He told you of the symbol's meaning, then?"

Hiroko shifted nervously, bumping Mara in the very spot where the eye-mouth was carved into her hip. Mara couldn't suppress a grunt of pain. The man's eyes darted to her as she turned it into a cough. Sidling sideways to avoid giving the man a glimpse of her back, however well camouflaged, Mara pulled

Hiroko over to admire a dark oil painting that covered half the shop's wall.

Come on, Ethan. Work your magic.

"I've studied eye symbols like these," said Ethan, pointing to a rack of glass amulets in the shape of a huge, blue eye. "Talismans against the evil eye, right? Then there's the 'Eye of Providence' on American money, the Egyptian Eye of Horus, and of course, the Nazca sun-eye."

Nazca sun-eye? Is he making this shit up?

"The eye sees. The mouth devours," intoned the man in the fez.

Out of the corner of her eye, Mara saw Ethan nod like that totally made sense.

"The Unholy walk among us pretending to be holy. The Hidden Eye—the Eye behind the Mouth—finds the Unholy. Or so they say." The man tacked a curious chuckle onto the end of his sentence.

This guy totally believes his spew.

"You are here for the museum tour, yes?"

"Absolutely," said Ethan.

"Come along, then. Come along all of you."

I want to get out of here.

Fez Guy's crap about devouring gave her the creeps, but she fell into step as Ethan and Hiroko followed the man to the back of the shop. A red velvet rope cordoned off a narrow set of wooden stairs going down. A slotted box sat on a stand beside the stairs with a carefully lettered sign—*Suggested donation 5 euros*—in six languages. He waited, looking everywhere but at them, until Hiroko slipped the requisite bills into the slot. Then he beamed, removed the rope, and led their descent.

Before Ethan followed him, he whispered to Mara, "Anything?"

She shook her head. No Offspring were nearby, but that didn't mean they were totally safe, either. At the bottom of the stairs, Fez Guy ushered them into the museum, if you could call it that. Really it was a long narrow hallway lined with glass cases.

"Begin here." The man gestured to his left. "And continue around." Ever dutiful, Ethan leaned in close for Fez Guy's steady stream of commentary.

Mara shuffled in line behind them.

"Look at this!" Hiroko hissed as they leaned into the first case.

It held a marked-up map of ancient Africa and a painting. The captions were in French, German, and Flemish, none of which Mara could read, but the image was enough to root her to the spot. Twelve figures, pain twisting their faces, were pinned to the ground by frightful, razor-edged metal wings.

"That's supposed to be the Dead Vlei in Namibia," Hiroko whispered, "when the Eleven were embodied."

Mara pointed to the nomadic Africans depicted around the edges of the painting. "They look pissed."

"I know," said Hiroko, crinkling her nose. "But that's not right. I was taught that the early peoples welcomed the Eleven."

The next case held Stone Age African implements and another image. This one depicted the ancient Africans as slaves laboring under cruel, alien-looking masters. One, clearly meant to be Azza, forced them to carry severed wings toward a forge manned by a cruel-faced Tamel.

"Maybe it wasn't such a warm welcome," Mara said.

"Or maybe this museum is full of lies."

The eye sees. The mouth devours. Maybe one person's lies were another one's history.

This museum made it pretty clear to Mara who Fez Guy called the Unholy. He was talking about her ancestors. He was talking about her! She shivered. Everything about this narrow space menaced her.

Relax. You could take him.

But he hated her—or would hate her if he knew what she was. She had to get out. Mara's skin crawled. It was all she could do not to turn tail and run up the stairs, but something drew her to a display on the opposite side of the room. Each step closer to it increased the quaking sensation in her limbs.

I don't want to look. I don't want to look.

She was pulled closer. Glancing over her shoulder, she saw the others still clustered by their guide. Around her, dust motes seemed to stutter and stop. *Not now. Not here.* Like in the charnel house with Dalmeet, Mara was aware of the thin boundary between time and not-time.

As soon as she reached the case, the gauntlets clenched hard against her forearms. A round band of dark metal rested on a velvet display stand. A ripple quivered through the band and Mara's gauntlet responded in kind.

I know that relic.

She'd seen it in Armaros's memory.

She'd seen it recreated in sand by the Twins.

She'd know it anywhere.

The Circlet of Moments.

FORTY-ONE

ETHAN

BRUGES, BELGIUM

Every time Ethan edged away from the man in the fez, his guide scuttled closer, reeking of sweat and apricots. "Look here, look here," he droned, tugging Ethan's elbow to direct his attention to the display case. Ethan snuck a glance at Mara. She was standing very close to a case near the bottom of the stairs with her hands pressed against the glass, her breath fogging its surface. Ethan's heart thumped hard against his sternum.

Something's freaked her out.

"Here you see various methods for extinguishing the Unholy ..."

Ethan looked back at the display.

"... drowning, burning, crushing ..."

And I have a pretty good idea what it is.

"... hanging, suffocation ..."

The man's sour breath enveloped Ethan. He itched to leave the dim, low-ceilinged room. *Focus! There might be something here that can help her.*

Ethan forced himself to listen, desperate to extract clues from the hodgepodge of archaeology, anthropology, and pseudoscience the dude was slinging. He was slightly incoherent, but his hatred for Mara's people burned through the rhetoric. It slithered down Ethan's spine like poison. Increasingly rapid breaths swept through his lungs, and Ethan realized that it was Mara's frenetic energy that rose in him like a tsunami.

He was dropping into a crouch and bracing himself for impact well before the explosive crash of glass and metal. The man in the fez shrieked. Ethan whirled toward Mara, flinching as shards of glass skittered in every direction. As he launched himself toward her, Mara pumped her fist in the air, and he saw, clenched in her hand, a narrow crown of dark metal.

Holy hell, she found it!

Exhilaration surged through him. Ethan bolted up the stairs after Mara and Hiroko. He was only halfway up when he was jerked backward, his shirt biting into his throat. The pressure of the guide's hand on the back of his coat wrenched Ethan around. He swung punches wildly, gyrating his body to escape the man's meaty hands.

"You are one of them," the man growled and then began to shout in a torrent of frantic Flemish. Ethan couldn't believe the man's strength. One wiry arm was around his neck now and he could neither yell to Mara nor free himself.

The sudden, loud bang of a trapdoor in the floor flying open sent Ethan into a panic. He thrashed with renewed strength, flinging the museum guide into the young man emerging from the floor. Ethan caught a glimpse of shiny metal—*a gun?*—before he raced up the stairs after Mara.

"The mouth devours!" the man yelled after him, and he could hear boots on the stairs as he burst out of the shop into the rain. Mara was at the end of the block, panting hard and stuffing the Circlet into her backpack. Next to her, Hiroko beckoned wildly, shouting for him to hurry. He ran, screaming, "Go, go, go! They're coming!"

Footsteps pounded behind him—four, maybe five pursuers.

Pushing himself to top speed, Ethan fell into stride with Mara and Hiroko.

Crack—a gunshot zinged off the brick building next to them, sending a plume of red dust in the air. A chunk ricocheted, grazing Ethan's shoulder.

"Son of a bitch!"

Mara slid in a puddle of slush and bounced off a parked Citroen, leaving a dent in the yellow door. They sprinted through the narrow alleys of Bruges until Ethan's sides stabbed with pain, but he kept pace with Mara and Hiroko, pushed beyond normal human limits by the blood of the Eleven in his veins.

Crack—a bullet grazed the roof of a nearby car, sparking on impact.

Twisting through the rat warren of streets, they tried to throw off their pursuers, but every alley seemed to loop back on itself. Canals forced them to change directions constantly. It was a city without logic, and seemingly, without escape.

Bullets flew around them.

Mara swerved hard right, and Ethan followed. The tight walls on either side gave way to another damn canal. A crowd of tourists bundled against the cold snapped photos of the historic buildings on either side. Mara skidded into them, sending a woman in a red coat splashing into the water. Amid shrieks in a babble of languages and the confused crush of the crowd, Ethan grabbed Mara and Hiroko by their hands and dragged them toward a pedestrian bridge a hundred meters on.

Traffic snarled and sirens blared.

For a moment, Ethan thought they'd lost their pursuers in the tangle of people, but gunfire hit the canal in a barrage of miniature geysers. The deep, concussive boom of a larger gun cut through the screaming, and one wail rose in the silence.

Someone's been hit.

Pushing harder, Ethan pelted toward the bridge with Mara and Hiroko on his heels. They tore onto it as another round of bullets hit the stone railing, ricocheting everywhere. Hunching low, they hustled across the bridge.

"We can't outrun them," he panted.

On the opposite side of the canal, traffic streamed past, the drivers unaware that a full-on strike force was heading for them. Ethan scanned the traffic, stretching for some idea, any idea that could get them safely away. "We need wheels."

Crack—a bullet pounded into the railing beside Hiroko. The shooters thudded onto the bridge. Ethan spotted a motorcycle with a sidecar driving by. "Mara, look!" he yelled. "The bike!"

The three of them vaulted over a traffic barrier, exposing their upper bodies to fire from the bridge, and ran full out for the bike. Ethan's lungs burned, and his legs were on fire. Every second, he anticipated bullets burying deep into his flesh. Darting through two lanes of traffic, Ethan dove straight at the chest of the goggled driver, bowling him off the saddle. The bike stalled. Ethan rolled off the stunned man and regained his footing. Mara straddled the bike, revving it back to life, urging Hiroko into the sidecar. Ethan vaulted on behind Mara, wrapping his arms around her waist as she accelerated. Looking behind, he saw four men. Three of them stopped traffic while the fourth steadied a shotgun on his arm.

Mara bent low over the handlebars, weaving through traffic.

Ethan watched the barrel of the gun swing toward them. *Faster, faster.* Cars were peeling off the road and soon there were no obstructions between them and the man with the gun. *Faster!* They were still within range.

BOOM—a spattering of shot zinged off the back of the bike and sidecar. Searing pain stabbed through his left calf. Hiroko let out a loud whoosh of air and slumped forward in the sidecar.

"Hiroko!" Mara shrieked. Bending over to the healer's crumpled form, she caused the vehicle to swerve wildly.

"Drive!" Ethan shouted. It was the only word he could shape through the red-hot explosion in his calf. Wooziness loosened his grip, and he wobbled precariously.

"Ethan—"

He clutched at her waist, berating himself. *She can't know.*

The world was tilting at odd angles. Ethan forced himself to focus on the upper rim of the sidecar's windshield until the nausea subsided. Hot fluid poured down his leg, but he ignored it. Keeping one arm around Mara, he reached for Hiroko. At the speed they were traveling, he couldn't do much more than place a hand on her back, but it was enough to know she was breathing.

"She's alive," he yelled into the icy wind.

Mara was starting to sob. "I'm sorry. I'm so sorry."

The pain in his calf pulsed with every jolt of the cobbled street. He leaned his cheek on Mara's back. "You're doing fine. Good job, baby."

"What's wrong?" The fear in her voice cut through the pain in his calf.

He wanted ... No, he needed to help her keep it together. Ethan forced himself upright. "It's okay, Mara," he said, enunciating each word. "We need to get someplace safe so we can check on Hiroko."

Purely by accident, Mara had ended up on a major road heading west out of Bruges. She pushed the bike harder and within minutes they were driving through farmland.

"Are they still behind us?"

"No," he assured her. "It's okay."

"Stop saying that," she barked. "Nothing's okay."

He couldn't argue. Not with blood filling his shoe. Not with Hiroko unconscious. When Ethan spotted a decaying building, he directed her toward it. At least they could hide and be protected from the nasty weather.

Mara eased the bike onto the rutted track and directly inside the abandoned barn. When she cut the engine, Hiroko's head lolled alarmingly to one side. Muttering a string of expletives, Mara hurried to her.

Ethan sucked in his breath, trying to figure how he could dismount. Putting weight on his left leg was out of the question. Awkwardly, he pulled his right leg around the front of the seat and gingerly lowered his weight onto both feet. If he could just get a look at the wound, wrap it up or something, she wouldn't have to know.

"Ethan, get over here. I need you," said Mara, staring at her blood-covered hands.

Ignoring the pain, he shuffled around the rear of the bike. Three jagged holes in Hiroko's jacket revealed where she'd been hit—just above her right kidney, her right shoulder blade, and on the left side of her back. Wincing, he helped Mara ease their friend out of the sidecar and onto the dirt floor of the barn.

"Hiroko?" Mara called. "Can you hear me? Hiroko!"

An exit wound on Hiroko's abdomen was furiously oozing blood. Ethan lowered himself to the ground and pressed the puncture with the flat of his hand.

Hiroko's eyelids fluttered.

"Hiroko!" Mara practically pounced on her. "Tell me what to do."

Hiroko licked her dry lips. "Take ... the Circlet ... to ... Armaros."

Mara tensed. "We're doing that together. Tell me how to doctor you up."

Hiroko shook her head, the grit under her head scraping like bone on bone. "Make ... her ... go," she wheezed at Ethan, taking hold of his hand more tightly than he would have thought possible. As she squeezed, her eyes widened. "You've ... been shot."

Damn healers. How'd she always know everything?

"What?" squeaked Mara. "You're shot?"

"No biggie." *At least I hope not.*

"Let me ... see it," Hiroko said.

"Nah, you're the big show here."

Her mouth quirked up at his lame attempt at humor.

"One in … my kidney. One … in my lung. Nothing … to do." Her speech was peppered with coughs, and blood was starting to trickle from the corner of her mouth.

"No," moaned Mara, entwining Hiroko's left hand in both of hers. "You're strong. You're brave. You have to be all right."

Hiroko lifted Mara's hands to her lips and kissed the battered fingertips. Then she forced Mara's flattened hand to replace Ethan's on her belly. "Press hard. I need time," she winced. "Now Ethan. Before it's too late … let me see … your leg."

How can I refuse her?

Ethan shifted his body so his left leg was near the side of Hiroko's head. Rolling up his pant leg and shoving down his blood-soaked sock, he revealed a leg looking like a bad cut of beef.

Behind him, Mara muttered furiously. "Time. More time. Turn the blood."

Beside him, Hiroko struggled at first to lift her arm, but when she started to palpate his calf, she strengthened. Maybe Mara was doing it—giving Hiroko's body the chance to heal itself. Instantly dizzy from pain, Ethan pressed his hands against the ground so hard that gravel bit into his palms.

"The bullet … passed through," Hiroko whispered. She licked at the blood on her mouth. Mara had worked herself into a frenzy, pleading for more time, begging Hiroko's body to respond, but more and more blood seeped through her fingers, running down Hiroko's sides, puddling on the ground.

"It's not working!" Mara screamed. "Help me!"

"Mara," Hiroko said, "time cannot heal everything. Let me go."

Ethan lay his hand on Hiroko's shoulder. Her breath grew shallower and shallower. If only his hand could say all the things he wanted to. This woman had taught him so much. She'd welcomed him. Made him feel a part of her world. Warmth radiated from Hiroko's palm, evaporating the pain in his calf. Was that how friendship felt? Like safety?

"What are you doing?" he asked.

"One ... last ... cure," she whispered.

A distant vagueness swam in Hiroko's dark eyes. "Hold on," he begged. "Please stay with us." Mara wept over Hiroko's wounds.

Around them time seemed to freeze. Not by any gift of Armaros but through the curse of loss. The muscles in his calf knitted together. The weeping blood was rerouted into fresh, new-grown capillaries. Delicate pink skin swept over the raw, angry flesh.

The pain vanished.

Her hand fell to the ground, and the light fled Hiroko's eyes.

FORTY-TWO

MARA

IN THE BELGIAN COUNTRYSIDE

The edges of Mara's vision swam in shadow. Her breath came in short, shallow pants. Nothing was clear in the grimy barn. Darkness was pooling on the dirt, dribbling from Hiroko's lips, and coating her hands. A shaft of watery light filtering through a hole in the roof lingered on Hiroko's heart-shaped face, her motionless chest, and her rigid neck.

Ethan moved slowly into Mara's field of view. His icy hands wrapped around her wrists, trying to force her palms away from Hiroko's blood-slick torso.

"Stop it," she snapped, biting at the air in his direction like a tortured dog. "We have to keep pressure on it."

"Mara." His voice was tender and soft as he tugged at her hand.

She batted him away, and when he moved, it was as if all warmth had left the barn. Shivers shook her like a rag doll. The dark tunnel thickened, clotting her vision. Mara squeezed her eyes shut against a wave of dizziness. *I will count to ten. I will open my eyes. I will wake up. Hiroko will be fine.*

Somewhere near her, Ethan moved, scraping against gravel.

Mara opened her eyes.

Ethan's fingers stroked Hiroko's face, closing her eyes.

Seconds ago, Hiroko had danced in those eyes. Now they were glass beads—flat, fractured, and empty.

"Don't," Mara began, "she needs to see."

Ethan ignored her. Tears poured down his cheeks as he took Hiroko's limp hand in his own. Mara closed her eyes again, as if not seeing could block out knowing. Taut and clenched, Mara's muscles confined her, and in that prison of her body, she knew—of course, she knew—that Hiroko was dead. She'd have to be an idiot not to know it. If she could beat or batter or dominate that truth into falsehood, she would.

But her steady, dear friend was gone all the same.

Grief tore at Mara, clawing its way through bone and gristle in heaving sobs. Shuddering, she wept like she was bleeding out. Loss obliterated her. Everything she touched had died or shriveled or warped. Hiroko and Momar were dead. Dali—*wry, uppity Dali*—was lost outside of time. And Max—*sweet little brother*—she might as well have taken a chainsaw to her own heart because he wouldn't survive, either.

Every person she'd loved and needed ... gone. And for what? For someone else's stupid war? A stab of hatred knifed through her anguish. She hated all of it, the lumps on her shoulders, her freakishness, this world the Eleven had wrought. The eye-mouth was right. They—and she—were Unholy.

They'd killed Hiroko for the crime of being Offspring, and Hiroko was as far from Unholy as anyone could be. *It should have been me.*

Mara reached into her backpack with blood-smeared hands. She pulled out the Circlet, trying to crush it in her hands. On her forearms, the gauntlets kicked and bucked against her destructive intent.

The metal bit into her hands.

They killed her for this fucking Circlet.

Grief burst out of her in a strangled roar. She hurled the horrible thing as far as she could into the dark recesses of the barn. It glittered as it arced through the rafters, disappearing amid a flurry of startled pigeons.

Ethan sprang to his feet, scrabbling on the dirt, tripping over rotten boards as he tried to track the Circlet's path. He peered after it, mapping the trajectory of its fall.

"Let it go!" she screamed. "I hate it!"

He stood with his back to her, sobs sweeping through his body in heavy gasps. When he finally regained control and turned to her, Ethan was utterly unguarded. "It wasn't your fault."

Another great, rolling wave of emotion caught her. This one tender and lush on the heels of grief and fury. *Ethan.* His name filled her. In this past month of running scared and fighting hard, she'd learned to read him. A tilt of his head meant he was gnawing on a problem. A triumphant crinkle around his eyes told her he'd unearthed the solution.

She knew what he meant when he said it wasn't her fault.

It meant he loved her.

He shouldn't, but he did anyway.

He came to her and pulled her to her feet. Mara leaned into his arms, battered and doomed. It was only a matter of time before he was collateral damage. Ethan held her tight, pressed his lips to her forehead, then turned her toward the darkest corner of the barn. "You need to go get the Circlet. Use the gauntlets. I'll stay with Hiroko."

She forced herself out of his arms and stumbled in the direction Ethan had pointed. Her leaden limbs pushed aside rough timbers. Within minutes, her palms were full of slivers. Rats scurried into still darker shadows. The pigeons rustled and resettled on their gloomy perches.

What's the point? The Circlet won't bring Hiroko back. We're done for—all of us.

Mara was caught among Aeda, Armaros, and the Twins. They'd splayed her out, ready to be quartered into bloody hunks. No matter how much she wanted to walk away and try for normal, everything about her old life was gone. Nothing good was on the horizon.

As Mara kicked debris aside, she felt a hardness rising. It blocked and stoppered the fissure that Hiroko's death had cracked into her. Her gauntlets pulled her hands downward. Her fingers touched metal exactly where Ethan said it would be.

It's an ugly thing.

Her friend was dead so that Armaros could have her prize. Mara no longer harbored any hope for Max or Dali, but she would do what Hiroko had asked. *Armaros can have her damn Circlet. I want nothing to do with it.* She'd take the Circlet to Armaros and then … In her fierce grip, the Circlet shrunk to the size of a bracelet, then a ring. As Mara slid it onto her finger, her anger flared.

A plan was forming.

You won't approve, Hiroko.

She knew what she was going to do after she gave the Circlet to Armaros.

I'm going after Aeda Moreau.

Aeda first, and then one by one, they'd all pay. She had nothing left to lose. And if she went down in the fight, well … that would be one problem solved for everybody else.

Mara retraced her steps through the barn. Looking up, she saw Ethan and Hiroko in a patch of pale winter sun. He eased Hiroko's messenger bag from around her body, removed his jacket, and folded it into a makeshift pillow for her head. He smoothed Hiroko's hair back the way she liked it and then crossed her slender hands over her belly. From this distance, Hiroko looked peaceful.

I want you happy and whole.

She wiped a fresh rush of tears from her face.

Ethan was kissing Hiroko's forehead. Mara caught her breath.

I love him.

She knew it—fiercely, protectively, hungrily.

How had she not realized it before?

How had she let that happen?

Mara drank in the sharp angle of his jawbone, the rich color of his skin, that crazy mess of curls, those mahogany eyes. He was perfect, right in all the ways she was wrong.

And then she had everything to lose.

Again.

FORTY-THREE

The dim bluish glow of Petra's laptop was the only light in her room. She stared at the screen. *So many names.*

Rhianna Lynne

David Scopes

Susan Haidar

Matthew Chen

Abby Reed

Marrit Jones

Louis Chappelle

A'Ishah Kalil

Janelle Potts

Essie Cohn

Brian Wang

Derek Holmes

Petra thrummed her fingers on the desk. *Too many names!* These twelve—recent unsolved missing persons from Portland, Oregon—represented only a fraction of the disappeared. She had lists from every city in which Aeda and Sinioch Moreau had a business presence: Seattle, San Francisco, and Los Angeles as well as Chiang Rai Province in Thailand and Hokkaido in Japan.

At last tally, she was up to one hundred and seven names in total. She pushed back from her desk, pacing the long way, six strides from one wall to the next. *One hundred and nine,* she amended. No one had seen Paul and Veronique Layil for over a year, and their boy had been poisoned. Coincidence? Petra had seen too much human violence to believe that. Six more strides brought Petra back to her desk. A swipe of her fingers sent her list of names scrolling into a gray blur.

How are they linked?

The disappeared were Christians, Muslims, Jews, Buddhists, Taoists, Shintoists, and atheists. They were rich, poor, and middle class. Male, female, all races, all ages. Seventeen of them, including Derek Holmes and Essie Cohn, were minors.

By the Sacrifice! Children!

No doubt a skeptic would argue that the list was full of runaways and parental abductions, the mentally ill and crime victims. *Some of them, probably, but not one hundred and nine!*

Petra needed to know how many were Offspring.

Because the Eleven lived so long, their family trees were immensely complicated. Many of their children, all half siblings born of different human parents, were born centuries apart, and the family lines of the Eleven were spread around the world. In the old days, when each family was linked to a Scribe line, records were well kept and transferred in confidence to the Keeper of the Lines.

Even five hundred years ago, it would have been possible to consult the Keeper and find out who on Petra's list were Offspring. Petra shook her head, perceiving anew the cracks in her world. Nearly all the Scribes were gone. The Keeper herself was ancient, and the Eleven were fading fast. Even Petra had to acknowledge that soon Armaros would return to the Before.

Sadness welled up in her, but Petra pushed it away and jabbed the print button. She would take the names to the Keeper of the Lines and see if she recognized any of them. It was a long shot, but her only shot. If more than one or two on that list were Offspring, then Petra's suspicions would be confirmed, and she'd have one more piece of evidence against Aeda Moreau.

As the list of the disappeared churned out of the printer, Petra tried not to think of a world without Armaros. It would be a world with no place for her.

FORTY-FOUR

ETHAN

IN THE BELGIAN COUNTRYSIDE

Ethan sat next to Hiroko's body with his head on his knees.

It wasn't supposed to be like this.

"I'm sorry," he whispered. "I'm so sorry." He flexed his left leg, which was virtually free of pain. One last gift from Hiroko. *My friend.* "I'll get you home. I promise."

Ethan pulled his tablet out of his backpack, and once he'd broken into a nearby network, he called the only person he could think of—Abbot Greb. While he explained the help they needed, Mara emerged from the shadows of the barn covered in dust and cobwebs. She held out her hand to show him the relium band and sat cross-legged in the dirt. Concluding his call but leaving the connection open, he set the tablet on the ground and slid his free arm around Mara.

"Abbot Greb promised to send someone."

"Okay." Mara picked halfheartedly at the splinters in her palm.

It seemed like they sat there forever.

Ethan's mind was paralyzed. No number sequence came to him. No safety net. Nothing but the changing angle of light in the doorway, the biting wind through the cracks in the walls, the increasing chill of Hiroko's body, and Mara's warmth against his side.

He had no idea how much time had passed when the tablet alerted him to an incoming call. He pulled it onto his knees. "Yes?"

"Oh, thank the Blade you've answered," said a woman in heavily accented English. "Is this Ethan Skylar?" Before he could even grunt a response, she continued, "Is your location still secure? The Eye? Have they tracked you?"

"I don't know. I don't think so."

"We're on our way. Send me your location and wait for us."

As if we would leave Hiroko.

An hour later, they heard vehicles outside.

"Offspring," said Mara, wiping the tears that had flowed on and off while they waited. "You talk to them. If anything feels off, I'll kill them."

Ethan watched her face turn steely as she concealed herself to one side of the door. Half of him wanted to shake her, to bring back the tears and the softness around her eyes. The other half was equally murderous so he said nothing but rose stiffly and stood between Hiroko and the door. *Right now, only Hiroko matters.*

Car doors opened and closed.

A brief exchange in French revealed a woman and two men, but only the woman entered. She stood backlit by the dove-gray sky, blinking against the dim interior.

"I'm Julia Beaumont. Abbot Greb sent me." Ethan nodded, recognizing her accent from the phone call. "We have to hurry. The Eye has people in the police."

"How do we know we can trust you?" he asked.

"We? I only see you." She took two more steps into the barn. Out of the glare, he could see that she was about his mom's age, her graying hair in a twist at the nape of her neck.

She knows Mara's here.

"I'm going to turn around," Julia continued, pulling her rain jacket off her shoulders, "so you can see my back." Stumps protruded under her tight brown sweater. "I'm Offspring, not the Eye." As she spun slowly, she saw Mara, nodded once, and continued until she again faced Ethan. "They will find us."

Mara stepped into the light. "You may be Offspring, but how do we know you're on our side?"

"I'm not sure I know what you mean," said Julia.

A wave of exhaustion swept over Ethan. "Look," he said, rubbing his temples, "the only Offspring I trust right now is Mara, but we need your help with our friend so we're going to go with you." Mara started to argue, but he took her hand and squeezed it. "We're running out of options."

Instantly, the woman barked a command in French. Two men entered carrying a pine coffin. Ethan felt his stomach lurch. *I don't want Hiroko in there.* But he moved out of the way so they could set it in the dirt beside her body.

"We'll do it," said Mara.

She pushed aside the coffin lid and gestured for Ethan. He slid his arms under Hiroko and lifted her leaden body. No trace of the healer was left in that shell. He picked up his jacket and replaced it under her head. Mara straightened Hiroko's limbs and bent to press her lips against her forehead. When she rose, her face was a mask. A low, cold fear settled in Ethan's stomach. *She's leaving me too.*

The pine lid squealed as Mara pulled it over the coffin.

Ethan fought the urge to rip it off and break it into splinters. *We have to stick together.*

But hadn't they already failed? Dalmeet and Hiroko both gone ... *It's only a matter of time before we all go down.*

His hands curled into fists. *I am not going to lose Mara.*

Julia led them outside. Ethan stood awkwardly near the back of the truck while the two men lifted Hiroko inside, hid the motorcycle, and raked dirt over the bloodstains in the barn.

We are easily erased and easily separated.

Mara stood a few feet away, but she might as well have been on another planet. Jacketless in the sleet, Ethan shivered, but it was loneliness that shook him to the core.

"Where are you taking her?" Mara demanded, refusing to let Julia close and lock the back of the truck.

"We'll take Hiroko to a funeral home and then arrange to fly her body home to Denver." *I didn't know she was from Denver.* "Abbot Greb has already spoken to her family."

I never asked.

"Into the car," Julia urged. "We've been here too long already."

Ethan could hardly put one foot in front of the other, but somehow he managed to get into Julia's Fiat. *Did Hiroko have a brother? A sister?* The car bounced along the pitted access road. *1 plus 1 is 2. 1 plus 2 is 3.* Julia pulled onto the highway toward Brussels. Ethan pressed his forehead against the cold glass and the scenery blurred into a wash of gray and green before his eyes.

2 plus 3 is 5.

3 plus 5 is 8.

No one spoke until Julia parked in front of a row house flanked by a bakery and a florist.

"Where are we?" asked Mara.

"My apartment," she answered, leading them up a narrow flight of stairs to the top flat.

Through the numbing wall of numbers he'd erected, Ethan took in the book-lined studio. Near the windows facing the street were a bed and a couch. In the rear, the kitchen overlooked a narrow alley. They'd entered in the center, where Julia had a round table cluttered with papers. A bicycle leaned against one wall.

He walked to the window. *It's so normal.* People in the bakery below were buying bread. The florist was arranging hothouse roses. *Hiroko is dead.* How could life just go on like normal? *I want it to stop.* If he were Mara, if he had the Circlet, he would freeze everything and mourn.

Julia handed Mara a towel and clothes, gently directing her to the bathroom. "Get cleaned up, dear." She draped a blanket around Ethan's shoulders, and he realized he was still shivering. "I'm going to borrow some clothes for you from my neighbor."

As the door clicked behind her, Ethan looked at himself. Dried blood flaked off his hands. His pants were stiff with it. He sat on the edge of the couch until it was his turn in the shower, and then stood in the hot spray counting for a long time.

Later, over warm bread, cheese, and a steaming mug of lentil soup, Julia talked about getting them a flight home. Home sounded good—filthy apartment, drunk mom, and all—but Ethan knew they weren't going home. Mara had promised Hiroko that she would take the Circlet to Armaros. That meant getting to Turkey somehow. Ethan wished Julia would leave them alone so he could talk to Mara. She hadn't met his gaze since they left the barn. He'd never seen her so drained of fight. Where was that snarl? He wished he knew what she was thinking. *We have to do the right thing.* But what the hell was that?

The gears in Ethan's brain felt completely stuck.

If they gave the Circlet to Armaros, Mara would be free, and maybe that old woman did know how to help Max. Everyone talked about her like she was some kind of god. Maybe she could. Of course, that would mean the end of Dalmeet. The Twins said they would free him in exchange for the Circlet. If he was still alive. Maybe.

If any of them could be trusted.

That was a big if.

FORTY-FIVE

MARA

BRUSSELS, BELGIUM

Mara cupped her hands around a mug of lentil soup, but in spite of the garlicky steam on her face, Mara felt like the marrow of her bones had frozen. Julia was talking, but the words rolled right over her. Ethan kept trying to get her attention, his eyes full of questions, but Mara kept her head down, twisting the ring on her finger.

She'd made the decision in the shower. She had to leave for Istanbul—soon and alone. Mara wasn't sure how long her resolve would last, but she knew Ethan wasn't safe as long as he was with her.

He should go home. He still has one.

Not wanting him to guess her intentions, Mara had left her gauntlets off, but she'd stowed them in her backpack and set it by the couch. As soon as she found an opening, she could grab it and go.

The sooner he forgets me, the better.

Julia's cell phone rang. While she talked, Mara kept her eyes fixed on the soup. When she hung up, Julia said, "I need to make the arrangements for your friend. I'll pull out some blankets for you. Be comfortable. Sleep. You're safe here. We'll get you home soon."

As soon as she left, Ethan began pacing.

Mara wondered if she should bolt.

Finally, he stopped by the window and rested his head against the frame. "Are we taking the Circlet to Armaros?"

I am taking it. You are going home.

She'd be damned if Ethan was going down with her.

It was completely wrong to love him.

Everything about her was wrong. *Unholy.* What an ugly word.

He'd never leave her, she knew. No, she'd have to be the one to do it.

For his own sake, she had to get him out of here, but first …

First, she wanted him. She wanted to feel love in fingers on skin. She wanted his arms wrapped around her.

Ignoring his question, she went to him, interlaced her pale fingers with his darker ones, and leaned into his body. She slid a hand around the nape of his neck and looked into his dark eyes. She saw a quick succession of expressions flicker through them—surprise, worry, need. It shocked her to realize that he had learned to read her too. He bent his face into the curve of her neck. When he spoke, his breath caressed her skin.

"You can't get rid of me, Mara Layil."

She was grateful that he couldn't see her face. She wouldn't lie, but she wouldn't answer, either. "Will you step outside of time with me?" she asked.

His body shuddered, his desire matching her own, but he pulled away, cupping her face and urging her to look at him. "What about Armaros and the Circlet? We have no—"

"Time won't pass," she interrupted. "Nothing will change while we're gone. Please, Ethan, I need …"

Her words trailed off in his half-hungry, half-wary eyes.

He pulled her tight.

It was answer enough.

She paused long enough to feel his heart pounding against her body. Outside of time she wouldn't be able to relish the way its steady beat measured out his allotted time. She loved that sturdy rhythm.

I have to leave him to keep him safe.

But not yet.

FORTY-SIX

MARA

OUTSIDE OF TIME

Mara turned inside the circle of Ethan's arms. He kept them around her waist as she slid the ring from her finger and held it before them. She pulled gently on the ring. The metal rippled and grew.

"How do you know what to do?"

His low, husky tone reminded her of wool jackets and warm bread. Desire pulsed through her. How did she know what to do? Did he mean using the Circlet or ...? She couldn't help a grin from spreading across her face. Truth was, she ran on instinct and intuition—just like always.

"I watched Armaros do this," she said, answering the obvious question, if not the subtext.

"Is it safe?"

"No."

She wondered if that would change anything.

"Okay."

I guess not.

Once the Circlet was as wide as the span of her arms, she raised it overhead and lowered it around them. As the nexus of the Circlet passed, she felt like she'd been moving at an enormous speed and had thrown the brake.

Anything or rather *any when* was open to her.

She could step back into the expanse of time at any point, or she could remain outside of it. With a stab of fear, she sensed the brutal, ever-shifting layer of the Twins and yet another pang of grief for Dali filled her. But sadness would wait for her inside of time. Right now, she gave herself one small moment free of loss.

There were infinities outside of time. She chose one and when the Circlet touched the ground, Mara led Ethan across the band before reforming the ring and placing it on her finger. Unlike the gold sands and white sky of the Twins' domain, they stood upon a vast expanse of pale green moss, soft and springy. Like when she had been with Armaros, the horizon curved up, but in this case, it merged with a silvery blue sky. A thin mist hung in the air, warm and suffused with the light. It caressed her cheek with a honeyed touch.

With a wave of her hand, the moss underfoot undulated, and with her raised arms she drew forth trees. A ring of silvery trunks surrounded them, a canopy of pale green leaves arched overhead.

Mara couldn't remember ever feeling so peaceful.

Turning back to Ethan, she saw his hand pressed hard against his chest.

"It'll come back," she said. "I promise."

Panic faded from his beautiful, perfect features.

His belief in her was staggering.

"I'm sorry," he said.

Sorry? She stared at him. *What could he possibly have to be sorry for?* She was the one who'd dragged him into one mess after another.

Ethan brushed his lips across the inside of her wrist. A sparking sensation leapt up her arms, and she caught her breath. If her heart hadn't already stopped, it would have then.

"I'm sorry," he whispered, "because I didn't mean to fall in love with you."

Mara's lips twisted in a crooked smile. "Damn you. Always causing trouble."

"Nah, that's your job, Mara Layil."

"I ...," she began, but he stopped her.

"My life has sucked for a long time. You know that. My dad left. My mom drinks like a fish. I've been really lonely. But I have always tried to hang on to one idea about the future—that maybe it won't suck as much as the past."

Tears rose in Mara's eyes, prickling against her self-control.

I've brought him nothing but trouble.

She tried to step out of his arms. "I'm being selfish. I shouldn't have brought you here."

He kept her close and traced the curve of her cheek, leaving a fiery, shimmering wake.

How can I leave him?

"You," he said, eyes crinkling at the corners, "do not suck."

But I do. And it will.

It was selfish to bring him here even if it was what they both wanted. And Mara did want him. Was it such a bad thing to get what she wanted this one time?

"Do you ever shut up?" she asked.

Ethan let out his breath in a silent chuckle and slid his hands down her back. They stood a moment, his lips resting on her brow; then he kissed his way along her hairline, a whispering touch on the top of her ear, his tongue along the curve of her jaw.

The glowing mist swirled around them.

Mara moaned and slid her hands under his shirt. Hunger roared through her, and she devoured his mouth, stroked the taut muscles of his back. Mara shrugged out of her borrowed shirt and helped Ethan unbutton his. Her cheek nuzzled against the smooth skin of his chest, she inhaled the smell of him—summer rain and oiled leather. She lifted her face and found his mouth again.

He was everything she'd ever wanted.

Everything she'd ever needed.

For a moment, he pulled away from her, leaving an aching absence on her lips.

"Is this what you want?" he asked, his voice rough with his own need.

Want?

There were not words for this kind of want.

She pulled him down on the soft carpet of moss and straddled him. Holding his face, she said, "You, Ethan Skylar, are exactly what I want."

She was drowning in her own desire.

Mara found his ear, the hollow of his neck, and the place at the base of his throat where his pulse should have thrummed.

They were hands and mouths and flesh and fire.

They were outside of time, and nothing lay between them any longer.

There was only the unlikely way they fit together and the union that redeemed them both.

FORTY-SEVEN

ETHAN

BRUSSELS, BELGIUM

E than woke face down on the floor.

He couldn't tell if his eyes were open or closed. Dust from a rug filled his nose. He tried to push himself over, but his arms wouldn't work. Blackness squeezed his peripheral vision, and the floor pitched beneath him.

Maybe he'd had a stroke.

He wrestled with his tongue. "M ... Mara?" he croaked.

Nothing.

Where is she?

Grunting with effort, Ethan tried his arms again and managed to push himself over against the couch. Had they been attacked? Perhaps he'd had a head injury. He didn't recognize this place—an apartment full of books—or these clothes—a plaid button-down and black jeans.

Faulty bits of information flashed through his brain. A man who smelled of apricots. A motorcycle. Gunshots. Something wrong with his calf. Ethan touched it with one unsteady hand and felt the newly healed skin of a deep, round wound.

He'd been shot and so had Hiroko.

Sadness rushed over him. She'd been shot and killed.

How could he have forgotten that?

Where is Mara?

Ethan pulled up the corner of his shirt to wipe sweat from his face and smelled the rich, fruity sweetness of her. Scattered images of light and heat and hands skittered through his mind. Had Mara borrowed his shirt?

He lay against the couch, panting.

Had she been kidnapped?

He clutched his chest. His heart was beating, the steady rhythm of it pounding through his confusion.

He also knew that his heart had stopped!

He remembered that. But when? How?

No wonder he felt terrible.

Why would she leave me?

Ethan struggled to haul himself onto the couch. He closed his eyes and breathed deeply, cycling through the Fibonacci sequence until he remembered the lentil soup and Julia Beaumont and Mara sitting at the table with him. His eyes flicked open. There on the table were three mugs and the end of a loaf of bread.

Mara had been here with him. Dazed as he was, he knew it, and despite the head injury or whatever it was that was making him so loopy, he knew exactly what she was doing. Mara was taking the Circlet to Armaros in Turkey.

I need to get to Turkey!

Slowly, control of his body returned, though not any memory of what had happened between eating soup and waking up plastered to the floor. Eventually, he got up, cleared the table, and did the dishes. Perfectly normal, right? To clean up a kitchen that belongs to some foreign woman whom you've met over the body of your dead friend.

Maybe he should just go home.

Given Mara's penchant for ass-kicking, he doubted very much that he'd been conked over the head and she'd been nabbed. *She left you, asshole. Hell, for all you know, she was the one who clocked you.*

Ethan paced around the small apartment, torn between worrying about Mara and feeling sorry for himself. Maybe it was true that she didn't want him, but he'd absorbed her stubborn streak and made it his own. If she wanted him gone, she'd have to tell him to his face.

Julia didn't seem to be around, and Ethan was too amped up to sleep, so he pulled his tablet out of his backpack on the off chance Mara had tried to leave him a message.

Nothing—not that he really expected it, but it was still a punch to the gut.

Hope is, after all, far different from expectation.

It's a misunderstanding, that's all. I'm supposed to be with her.

Drumming his fingers against the battered table, Ethan pulled up flight info between Brussels and Istanbul, noticing that even an economy ticket would leave him with next to nothing in his bank account. *Ditched and broke in Belgium.* No flights were scheduled for the next twelve hours so he logged in to *Stack & Scatter*, hoping for diversion.

CLOAKED's last series of moves still baffled him. *RIGHT PAST WRONGS. SECOND CHANCE.* Whatever hack his opponent was pulling, it was damn impressive. What wrongs needed righting? Who was getting a second chance?

Not me, apparently.

Ethan connected *TREE* to the *E* in *POWER*, a play from very early in the game. He'd long since given up on high-point moves. Understanding the hack was more interesting.

Ping!

There was *CLOAKED*, right on schedule, stacking *F* onto Ethan's word—*FREE*.

Ethan used the *W* in *WRONGS* to connect *TWIST*.

Before Ethan could blink, *TWIST* became *TWINS*.

FREE TWINS.

Ethan dropped the tablet on the table like it was on fire.

Holy shit! Free the Twins?

"What the hell is going on?" he muttered, wondering if his tablet was booby-trapped.

He scanned the apartment, listened at the door, and sidled to the window to stare at the dark street. He was alone. Mara's absence filled the silent rooms. Ethan's fear morphed into anger. *Who does he think he is trying to tell me what to do?*

Ethan snatched up the tablet and threw himself into a hack of his own.

After *CLOAKED* had managed to play without wireless on the plane, Ethan had delved into the code behind *Stack & Scatter* so he had a framework from which to start. The game wasn't that complex, and after twenty minutes, he'd managed to manipulate his own letter distribution.

A move for the offense.

He hadn't been able to shake the feeling of being watched so after he changed the nine letters in his hand to the new ones he wanted, Ethan glanced around the room. "Ready?" he whispered and played them all.

It was easy enough to find attachment points for three short words.

WHO

ARE

YOU

His play was highlighted against the array of words on the screen. *Show me what you got.* His hand autofilled with nine random letters. Ethan stared at the screen, daring *CLOAKED* to answer. *Play, damn you. CLOAKED's* user name taunted him, but his opponent didn't play. Ethan had almost given up in disgust when the nine letters in his hand disappeared. He blinked at the empty letter cache as one by one, they were replaced.

R U A I I D A G D

He squinted at the screen. *What are you trying to say?*

Reordering the letters, he could make *GIARDIA* or *DRUID*. He doubted that was what *CLOAKED* was trying to say. The answer would require all the letters, of that Ethan was sure. No single word could be made from those nine letters so he began looking for multiple words, all with connecting points on the board.

This is it.

If he could unravel this clue, Ethan would know the identity of *CLOAKED*, and if *CLOAKED* was talking about freeing the Twins, then whoever he or she was might be able to help Dalmeet and Mara. Excitement pounded through Ethan. The word *GUARD* popped out at him from the smattering of letters.

This is promising.

Hadn't the Amyclaean Guard been chasing them until Armaros called them off?

Is that part of the answer?

If he used *GUARD*, that left two *I*s, a *D,* and an *A.* There wasn't a stand-alone word there. Ethan paced a tight circle around Julia's table. At every pass, he stopped and scanned the entire game board, hoping that something new would jump out at him. His first throwaway word *GIARDIA* niggled at him. He tried to ignore it because really, what did some parasite that made people sick have to do with the Twins and righting the wrongs of the past?

That message, at least, was crystal clear. Whoever *CLOAKED* was, he thought the imprisonment of the Twins was dead wrong. He'd called them *INNOCENTS* and riffed on *CORRUPT JUSTICE*. His directive couldn't have been more to the point: *FREE* the *TWINS*. Urgency rose in Ethan's mind. Right now, Mara was on her way to Armaros. That old hag wanted the Circlet to keep the Twins trapped. But what if that wasn't the right thing to do? What if *CLOAKED*'s way was better? *Who is he?* The question pinballed around Ethan's head as he paced.

GIARDIA

GUARD

The answer was right in front of him.

Ethan rearranged the letters and built on the *N* in *TWINS*.

GUARDIAN

What was left? An *I* and a *D*. The solution might as well have been in technicolor.

"Yes!" Ethan yelled.

Stacking the *D* on *BLAME* gave him *BLADE*.

And the *I*? Ethan could stack it on any other *I*.

All nine letters were down. The answer to his question plain as day:

I

BLADE

GUARDIAN

The instant Ethan signaled the end of his play, the game went dark.

A surging wave raced through his blood.

"Let's go, shall we?" asked a low, rumbling voice.

Ethan whirled toward the sound, knocking over his chair with a bang. A man in a hooded cloak was watching him from the corner of the apartment. The pieces were falling into place too quickly for Ethan to feel surprise or fear. The person standing before him changed everything.

"You're not dead."

"I guess not." A trace of humor skirted the rough, craggy features of the man's face.

"You want Mara to free the Twins."

"Justice will be served, Pythagoras," said the man, pulling down the hood and giving a mocking nod.

"I'm Ethan."

"Oh, I know, Ethan Skylar, I know. I suppose you've figured me out, smart guy like you." The man commanded the space around him. He was lean and muscled with thick, black hair rippling to his shoulders. Though he looked close to fifty, Ethan knew he was far older than that.

"You're Tamel," Ethan said, "one of the Eleven. They call you the Blade Guardian."

"And your Mara is on her way to Armaros with the Circlet of Moments."

My Mara? Ethan's cheeks burned as a half-remembered image of flesh on flesh filled him. He hoped his skin was dark enough to hide it.

"You need to convince her to free the Twins."

"She's afraid of them."

"She should be. Free will is terrifying."

Ethan considered Tamel's messages throughout their game. "I believe in second chances."

Tamel shifted his weight, exposing the intricate, folding blade at his hip. "Some things cannot be undone." The heaviness in his words was suffocating. "If they could ... well, we'd be living in a very different world."

Ethan was gasping for breath when the pressure in the room changed again. The weight was gone, replaced by an expansive boundlessness, a swirl of infinite space, and comfort laced with longing. It reminded him of Mara, and he did not ever want to leave.

But the man spoke and once again Ethan was only himself. "Are you ready to go?"

Ethan reached into the side pocket of his tablet case and drew out the relium scalpel that Toru had sunk into Mara's flesh. He felt the way the handle pulled tight to his hand, drawn by the relium in his blood—in Mara's blood.

With an absolutely steady hand, he held it out to Tamel. "Max Layil deserves his second chance. Help him, and I'll go with you."

FORTY-EIGHT

PETRA

HIGH COUNCIL CHAMBER, ISTANBUL, TURKEY

Petra rarely begrudged the loss of her voice, but she wished she had it now. The High Council compound was awash in rumor and suspicion. Two days ago, Aeda Moreau had arrived in Istanbul. She had not yet turned up at the High Council, choosing instead to stay with Rand Ganem in his bunker full of women. A ripple of disgust wrinkled her face. *What about the Covenant, you beast?* If forced impregnation wasn't a violation of human free will, she didn't know what was.

Petra might have given Aeda a chance—innocent until proven guilty and all that—but not now. Everyone knew that Rand Ganem wanted revolution, but if Aeda was part of his rebellion, Petra could not figure out where she fit. The woman claimed to have brought definitive proof that the Layil girl was stalking and killing Offspring. Petra thought of her list of names. Of the one hundred and nine people on it, the Keeper of the Lines had identified at least seventy as Offspring. *Seventy!* With the proportion of Offspring in the general population at far less than one percent, Petra had to agree with Aeda on one thing.

Someone was attacking Offspring.

I must be the only one not convinced it's Mara Layil.

Everywhere Petra went, groups of people were huddled and whispering, always whispering. From the knife range in the practice yard, Petra could hear them.

"Armaros is losing her powers."

"Armaros weakens."

"Armaros is dying."

How easily loyalties waver. Petra wanted to scream her protests and argue her case. She didn't like Mara Layil. In fact, she thought the girl undisciplined and self-serving. But to doubt Armaros ...

The Time Weaver shouldn't have to explain herself.

Petra hungered to speak. "Believe Armaros. Trust Armaros," she wanted to say to every person she saw, but she couldn't. Armaros herself had taken Petra's voice and turned her into a shield.

Petra left the practice yard and headed for the High Council chamber. She would try once more to make Armaros see the danger.

The great chamber was empty.

Petra stood a moment before the statue of the White One, thinking about sacrifice.

The Eleven could not have made their way on Earth without the sacrifice of the White One. She had freed the rest of them. Like the White One, Petra believed that there were things worth sacrificing for. That is why she had joined the Guard and given her voice.

She walked around the room, determined to wait for Armaros. The echo of her boots made it impossible to think. On impulse, Petra sat and pulled them off before resuming her circuit.

The slick marble felt cold through her socks.

She remembered sliding on this very floor as a child, playing chase with her cousins. The descendants of Hrminir gathered every ten years in Istanbul, and that particular reunion, she'd been seven. Her grandfather, a jokester always up for a prank, had organized the kids in a game of hide-and-seek. A sure-fire way to get the Crimson Scribes in a tizzy.

Hide and seek.

That's exactly what I need to do. I am her shield.

Petra grabbed her boots and tiptoed to the wall behind the ring of thrones. She ran her fingers along the marble, trying to find her grandfather's favorite hiding place. It was here somewhere.

It must be lower. I was smaller then.

Crouching, she made another circuit around the room. *There!* Her fingers found the tight-fitting door. Petra edged it open with her nails. The marble panel concealed a cubicle.

Plenty big for a cot.

Concealed in intricate carvings on the outside of the panel were several peepholes. From within, she could see without being seen, and since Armaros spent nearly every waking moment in this room, Petra could do what her gut was telling her to do—watch, wait, and protect.

I am her shield.

FORTY-NINE

AEDA

GANEM FORTIFICATION ON THE OUTSKIRTS OF ISTANBUL, TURKEY

Following Rand Ganem down a windowless, concrete hallway, Aeda couldn't shake the impression that Sinioch walked beside her, his long strides matching her own. After years of planning and preparation, their day had come.

You should be here to see it, my love. The way has been prepared.

Rand unlocked the room he'd dedicated to her use and left her alone. Aeda pulled the door nearly shut, leaving the lights off. All that remained was for Aeda to wake her sleeper. A sliver of light glinted off the refrigerated case. She caressed the slick metal surface, closing her eyes and allowing the thrill to rise in her.

The Covenant will end!

Now more than ever she wanted Sinioch. They were supposed to do this together. Aeda swept back her long hair and her grief along with it. This was no time for emotion. The woman in stasis was Aeda's evidence against Mara and the distraction she'd need to end the Eleven once and for all. The relium garrote in her pocket pulsed against her thigh, eager for blood.

Aeda fingered the latch, and the top opened with a hydraulic whoosh. The form inside was motionless. *You are the first to rise, my beauty.* She touched the woman's face and realized that they resembled one another—dark hair, pale skin, fine features. Gazing in that rigid mirror, Aeda shivered as if she were the one entombed.

Until this moment, it hadn't occurred to her that she might not survive the day. She'd filled the hole left by Sinioch's death with revenge at whatever cost, but looking at the woman in the case, Aeda realized she wanted to live.

Not just to watch her enemies suffer but to build something triumphant, to shape a future for every Offspring strong enough to seize it. *We have been held down too long.* Aeda reached for the control device, fingers tingling in anticipation. She would wake her weapon.

By the Blade, it is time for revolution!

FIFTY

Show me again," Eleon whispered into Dalmeet's ear as he slid his sinuous body against Dalmeet's back.

By the Blade, they were everywhere!

He shuddered but maintained his cross-legged meditation stance. It didn't do any good to move. They always found him. Dalmeet focused on his breath and the single sentence that he clung to outside of time.

I am a Singh.

Eleon's skin burned against his back. Dalmeet's shirt was long gone, torn to shreds by the winds outside of time. Lilya sat cross-legged in front of him, mimicking his meditation pose. She stroked her long finger down his cheek, leaving a sizzling, oily wake.

"Show me!" the boy demanded, pressing his body harder against Dalmeet's. "I want to know *kiss*."

I am a Singh.

Eleon dug deeper into Dalmeet's mind.

The first line of the Blade Guardian's blessing came to him—*As you wielded the Blade of the Sacrifice, may my knife fly true.* His fingers itched for the hilt of his kirpan. He would send it true, by the Blade, straight into Eleon's heart if he could, but the boy had long ago taken the kirpan.

He had taken everything.

Over and over, Eleon wanted to inhabit the memory of Dalmeet's first kiss.

He'd been fifteen. Uncle Momar had taken him and Taan to southern France for a summer of language practice. Tired of his brother's constant taunting, Dalmeet had taken to ditching lessons and walking the quiet roads near the villa they'd rented.

One afternoon he found himself on a road that wound into the hills and dead-ended at the edge of a river. A battered green Citroen was parked by the bank, and Dalmeet could hear the sounds of laughter and splashing. He followed the noise upstream until he found the swimming hole. Two boys and a girl, all about his age, were roughhousing in the water.

Without hesitation, they'd pulled him into their easy circle. It seemed to Dalmeet, who wore the downtrodden seriousness of the constantly passed-over, that Chloe and her cousin, Philipe, never stopped laughing. Chloe's boyfriend, Renard, had brought wine that he served in China teacups and lobbed sweet oranges at them all while they swam.

When Chloe and Renard started to chase each other through the rolling wheat field bordering the stream, Dalmeet and

Philipe collapsed on the picnic blanket still snorting with laughter. Dalmeet would never forget lying on his back, wondering how a sky could be so blue and distant and liquid and close all at the same time. He would never forget the sudden shade as Philipe's face blocked out the sun. He'd shaken his drenched curls like a dog, sending spray over Dalmeet's face.

And then he'd kissed him. Warmly, full on the lips, and with utter confidence.

Philipe.

Dalmeet emerged from the memory, his mind released by the Twins as quickly as they'd taken possession of it. Eleon's hand was on the hard bulge in Dalmeet's pants. He rolled away. Disgust replaced desire, the memory ruined. It had been a kiss freely given, a kiss that said *you are worthy*. Yet the Twins kept taking it again and again and again.

Dalmeet fought the urge to retch.

I am ...

... gone.

FIFTY-ONE

ETHAN

THE FORGE OF TAMEL, BENEATH THE DEAD VLEI, NAMIBIA

Sweat poured down Ethan's chest. Every breath was a stew of smoke and fire, more liquid than air. In the blink of an eye, Tamel had transported them from the apartment in Brussels to a cave deep beneath the Dead Vlei. Narrow shafts in the rock brought air and scant light from the surface, casting shadows on the blackened walls.

The roaring heat from Tamel's forge stifled him like a blanket of coals. Ethan thought it might be possible for his blood to actually boil. He'd stripped to the waist and was standing as far back from the forge as he could get. He didn't know how Tamel could bear the inferno. Ethan was sure that if he took a single step closer, he would incinerate on the spot.

"Her blood protects you," Tamel growled.

"Uh …," Ethan stammered, "are you reading my mind?"

Tamel was carving a ring of concave depressions, each the size of a BB, into a palm-sized piece of solid diamond.

"I listen," he replied, "and I feel the blood of Armaros within you, Scribe."

"I'm not her Scribe."

"Close enough."

Tamel had melted down the scalpel of Otohime and was pouring it into the mold in a fiery thread. The corded muscles in his soot-streaked arms constricted as he controlled the flow. Filled with molten relium, the mold resembled a necklace of pearls embedded in solid diamond.

With extreme delicacy, Tamel carried the mold to a vat of water next to Ethan.

"Shut your eyes," he grunted, "or the steam will blind you."

Even through closed lids, Ethan could see the white-hot image of the relium pellets scorched into his retinas. The cloud of steam that billowed over them nearly suffocated Ethan in spite of Mara's blood in his veins.

Ethan had no doubt that Mara had changed him. In the presence of Tamel, his blood surged and raced. Relium relics appeared to know him. His body had responded to the healing gifts of Hiroko more like Offspring than human. But more than the Binding, knowing her had rewired his perception of the world and crazily, confirmed his faith—that the future didn't have to suck, that he could be different, that second chances could turn out right.

"Why do you want Mara to free the Twins?" Ethan asked, opening his eyes now that the steam had cleared.

"To right past wrongs."

Oh, come on ... That is seriously cryptic.

Tamel laughed, his humor tinged with bitterness, and again, Ethan was convinced the man could read his thoughts.

"They're dangerous," said Ethan.

"Yes."

"And they're angry."

Tamel fixed him with a glare that rooted Ethan to the ground. Sweat stung his eyes, but he could not lift a hand to wipe it away. "They committed no crime," Tamel said, "and I was told to kill them. When the rules become more important than the lives they govern, something needs to change."

Then why did you wait so long?

Tamel stepped closer, the bulk of his muscled body threatening to crush Ethan, but he stood his ground. "Why now?" Ethan demanded.

Tamel swung away from him and pulled the diamond mold from the water, which had nearly boiled away. "There are only two people capable of freeing them. One is Armaros and the other is your Mara." He tipped the slate gray relium pellets into Ethan's hand. Still warm, they rocked back and forth, matching the ebb and flow of his blood.

"The Twins are unpredictable," said Ethan.

"So's Mara. It's your job to convince her to do the right thing."

Ethan looked at the pellets in his palm. Upon their roiling surface, he seemed to see Dalmeet and Max. Their faces shifted in the firelight—first wracked with pain, now smooth as a summer day. It was still possible that Mara could save them both, but even in the oppressive heat of the forge, Ethan felt a chill. Freeing the Twins would change everything.

Fifty-Two

PETRA

HIGH COUNCIL CHAMBER, ISTANBUL, TURKEY

Armaros had been sitting so long at the foot of the White One that Petra wondered if she'd fallen asleep. Her mentor only used her throne during official business. Sometimes Armaros paced the chamber, her footsteps echoing faintly, but more and more frequently, she would rest next to the carved likeness of her sister-self, one fine-boned hand stroking the silken surface of the marble.

Petra tried to wrap her head around the millennia that Armaros had lived. She had known the infinite Before. She had seen the world change in both inspired and catastrophic ways. She had outlived her brothers and sisters.

The emptiness of the other thrones must haunt her.

In the twenty-four hours since Petra had entered the hidden room behind the thrones, she'd tried to imagine what it was like when the thrones were full, when the joined presence of the Eleven had filled the space.

I wish I had known that time.

What she really hoped was that she would not have to witness the end of the Eleven. It would be too cruel to have to watch the death of everything she held most dear. Armaros had buried many children. *I want her to bury me.* But when Armaros lifted her head, the sadness around her eyes made Petra ashamed of that thought. *If I love her well enough, I should let her go. Just not now. Please, not now.*

Petra shifted in her hiding place, searching for a more comfortable position, when Armaros sprang to her feet. Petra snapped to attention. The air in the middle of the room began to shimmer, mirage-like. The shimmering grew until Petra could almost see the layers of time fracturing. A spot in the center pixelated, and the pixelation grew steadily from a pinprick to a circle of disturbed space the size of a dinner plate; then it was as big as a truck wheel. Still expanding, it became a door.

Stepping through the floating ring, the Layil girl appeared out of nothingness. With a swipe of her hand, the pixelated region shrunk and disappeared. Petra had a fleeting glimpse of a dark ring, which the girl slid onto her finger.

Armaros, still unmoving, stared at her.

Mara Layil looked much smaller than she had on the train two weeks ago.

She looks beaten.

When they'd fought, she'd been ferocious, full of the brash confidence of someone who thinks she can have it her way.

Now the girl was cagey, shifting her weight from one foot to the other.

Like prey.

Maybe she didn't know where the hit was going to come from, but she knew it was coming. Pity bloomed in Petra's chest. The girl was too young to be crushed.

But to surrender? Petra would not have chosen that humiliation.

What would Armaros do with the girl? Would she call on Petra to serve justice by knifepoint? Petra found that thought unsettling.

The girl is nothing. Armaros is everything.

"You have found my Circlet. Well done." Armaros's praise, though not directed at her, sent a quiver through Petra. She would give anything for that warm sentiment to fall on her, but Armaros's words seem to diminish the Layil girl even more.

"Well done?" the girl repeated, her words hard and mocking. "My friend is dead. Killed for this!" She thrust her left hand toward Armaros, and Petra could see the ring rippling and Mara's arm trembling as if holding an enormous weight.

Armaros inclined her head. Petra felt the sweet wave of her sympathy crash through the room. "I am sorry about the healer."

The girl clenched her fists. "Her name was Hiroko Mori."

"I know her name, and I, too, know loss."

The girl's face twisted in a rage-filled scowl.

Maybe she is the killer they say. Petra's fingernails cut into her palms as she forced herself to wait and watch.

"I am the last of my kind," Armaros continued. "I have outlived more sons and daughters and lovers than you can possibly imagine. Yet I have borne that pain and served the greater good."

"I don't care about the greater good." Petra caught the tremble of sadness behind the girl's tough words. "I've lost every single person I've ever loved."

Armaros nodded as if those losses were her own. Petra felt a renewed stab of worry that she could really, truly lose Armaros. She would be orphaned and adrift.

Impossible! Armaros had lived for centuries. She would keep living. She was strong. She was like the sun. *My sun.*

"Loss is hard, child, but you must bury them and find the strength to go on."

Petra suppressed a gasp. Was Armaros speaking to the girl or to her?

Now the girl bristled with fury. "GO ON? What's the point? There's nothing left for me."

"Open your eyes, girl!" Armaros snapped. Petra felt the angry thrust of power reverberate through the room. "This is not about you and your friends. The schism in our world has grown so great that we are on the brink of war. Do you understand that?"

The truth of it took Petra's breath away. Armaros knew, and she believed that Matthias and Aeda were planning something.

"I don't care about your idiotic war. I've brought you the Circlet." She wrenched the ring from her finger and thrust it at Armaros. "Now do what you said you'd do. Help my brother, and we'll be even."

Petra choked back a cry of recognition—*the Circlet of Moments.* She had new respect for the girl who had so freely given up such a powerful relic.

"Even?" Armaros plucked the ring from Mara's hand with a chuckle. "You're not that naïve, Mara Layil. We don't just shake hands and walk our separate ways. You broke the Covenant, and you will absolve your sins by ..."

"Absolve my sins?" The girl's voice rose to a shriek. "I didn't ask for any of this. I just want to help my brother. Fix him and I'll stay here. I'll do whatever you want."

Petra tensed, ready to reveal herself and fly to Armaros's side, but the girl's manic energy drained from her. She stood limply before Armaros, who turned the ring over and over, finally holding it gently and pulling on it until the metal stretched like a rubber band. When it had morphed to the size of a crown, the metal quivered back into solidity.

"I am going now," Mara whispered, turning toward the door, defeated and exposed.

Petra knew that Robaire and Semo guarded the other side. She'd been unable to countermand Matthias's order to post them there. They were under orders to capture the girl on sight, but she knew how easily accidents could happen. Outside the door was death.

Thanks be to the White One, I will not have to mete out justice.

Petra immediately regretted her weakness. Mara Layil deserved better.

"Mara," said Armaros, "I know you're not fond of rules."

The girl paused.

"As long as one of the Eleven lives, the Covenant will hold, no matter how cracked it has become. But once we are gone, the peace will break. War will come unless there is someone to renew the Covenant."

The girl resumed walking.

"You have been to see the Twins," Armaros continued. "Upon my death, they will be unleashed. They are chaos. They could destroy this world."

The girl whirled around. "Make them free my Scribe."

"The Twins crave. The Twins devour. They are havoc and mayhem. Your Scribe is probably dead. The first of many to die if they are freed. Do you want more blood on your hands?"

The pain on the girl's face was tearing Petra to the bone. "I've given enough," said Mara, her voice choked with tears.

"The only way to stop them is for you to control this." Armaros held out the Circlet, her voice soft, but commanding.

"You will take my place. You will keep the Twins outside of time. You will keep the peace."

Disbelief filled Petra. *Impossible! No one can take the place of Armaros—especially not this wild girl.* Mara Layil looked as desperate as Petra felt. She was a cornered rabbit, staring down the maw of the fox. "I don't want this," she said.

"No one wants the responsibility of ruling, but someone has to do it. You are my blood. And besides ..." Armaros's voice went steel-hard and cynical. "Everyone wants power. Now take it!"

"I don't want it!" the girl yelled. "I just want to be left alone."

Armaros brought Mara crashing to her knees with a sweep of her hand. The force of it swept through the marble separating them, and Petra's knees crumbled as well.

"Please!" Mara begged.

Armaros held the Circlet over Mara's bowed head. The girl fought violently, the tendons in her neck protruding as rigidly as the relium bars piercing Petra's.

"For the sake of the White One," Armaros commanded, "you will do the right thing."

She thrust the Circlet onto Mara's brow and then a blade flashed in Armaros's hand, slicing the air like a thunderbolt.

And the girl screamed.

FIFTY-THREE

T *ime!*

Mara's body shrieked for time—to evade, to run, to prepare. But Armaros had been creating time for centuries. It was hers to command. Mara was a baby, barely able to walk.

She was out of time.

Armaros's relium blade slit Mara's throat from chin to clavicle, opening the entire length of her carotid artery in a single, white-hot flash. A disembodied scream tore from Mara's mouth. In one lucid moment, she expected the terrible shriek to be followed by a hot wash of blood, soaking her clothes and sucking her life out with it.

But time froze around her, paralyzing her every motion. Her eyelids clung to the round whites of her eyes like tiny hands. Her throat seized up around speech. Blood congealed in her veins. It was as if her body had died around her. A fiery speck of her spirit was trapped in her corpse, unable to writhe free.

Strangely, there was no pain. In fact, the absence of all sensation scared her more than anything else.

Unable to move, barely able to think, Mara could only watch as Armaros bent toward her until they were nose to nose.

I don't want to die.

Though there were damn good reasons to let go. Going dark would be an easy out from all the shit, yet the speck of her soul that burned in her petrified body yearned toward life. With targeted precision, the best part of herself drew forth her greatest strengths. She began to walk her past, every remembered day layered in this space of no-time. The living and the dead together.

Momar putting Band-Aids on her perpetually scraped knees, training her in *gatka*, slipping her licorice jelly beans when her energy waned. Max, at four years old, reaching for her with chubby arms, crawling into her bed when he heard her troubled dreams. Hiroko, clucking over her wounds—a friend like no other. Dali, her perfect foil, refusing to let her take herself too seriously. And there was Ethan, offering himself to be her padded room and safe house, as if his lips and hands and arms could hold the evils of the world at bay.

But neither the living nor the dead could stop Armaros.

She raised the blade again, its edge sharp enough to cut through time itself.

This is it. Screw you and screw Aeda and all the other bitches. Mara wished she could yell it to the sky so they would know she wasn't dying easy. *Screw you!*

Armaros swung the knife in a broad, unstoppable arc and brought it down …

… not on Mara's chest, but on her own arm. She flayed the paper-thin skin and split her flesh down to bone. Grimacing, Armaros held her slashed forearm to the wound on Mara's neck, and a crimson torrent of blood flowed horizontally across the space between them, driving directly into Mara's veins.

Time, like a defibrillating shock to Mara's heart, jolted back into action.

Pain came with it.

Mara's every sense was decimated by agony. Blind, deaf, dumb. Pain erased her physical presence so that even touch was gone, burned away in the wake of molten metal that was the blood of the Eleven. As it pulsed through her veins and arteries and drilled its way through delicate capillaries, Mara's mind contorted with resistance, but it was useless. Armaros rolled through her. Centuries of memory ate away at Mara's self like an acid bath devouring her layer by layer.

A lifetime of experience flashed by like flotsam carried upon the river of pain. Five thousand years of birth and death, love and destruction engulfed Mara.

Burning! Suffocating! Exploding!

Armaros was overtaking her.

Soon there would be nothing left.

Mara struggled to shape one last thought before the darkness took her.

I want my own life.

FIFTY-FOUR

PETRA

HIGH COUNCIL CHAMBER, ISTANBUL, TURKEY

When Armaros turned the knife on herself, Petra leapt from her hiding place, heedless of secrecy or caution. She couldn't cross the room fast enough. Horror poured through her like the cold grip of a nightmare. Petra's stomach churned as the ruby swath of blood rushed from Armaros's arm into the girl's neck. As one, Armaros and the girl crashed to their knees. The old woman gripped the young one's shoulders with age-spotted, claw-like hands, their bodies linked by the terrible, insistent current.

For thirty years, Petra had guarded Armaros, ever watchful for attack. Never once had she considered that Armaros might harm herself. Petra had sworn to keep her alive, damn it. To protect Armaros was the sole focus of her existence.

She can't die on my watch.

Petra slid to the ground beside Armaros.

"Please," she moaned.

"I am not dead yet, my Petra." Armaros's voice wavered, but her body remained rigid and conjoined with the girl's. "I am about to be freed." A silver glow suffused her ancient face with the bloom of vitality. "I am truly mortal now. This is what the Eleven wanted all those years ago."

A warm wetness—*blood?*—coated Petra's cheeks. *Not blood but tears.* It had been so long since Petra cried that she could hardly recognize them. Deep in her bones, Petra knew that Armaros was dying, and the thought of a world without her cut Petra to the core. Everything she knew and loved and defended was connected through her. This bit of refuse, this Mara Layil, was wrenching Armaros away.

"I'll kill her," Petra swore, drawing her knife from its sheath on her belt. "I will avenge you."

"Petra, my sweet." The warmth of summer swept over her. "You cannot kill her," said Armaros. "She is me now—reborn of the Eleven."

FIFTY-FIVE

MARA

HIGH COUNCIL CHAMBER, ISTANBUL, TURKEY

Mara was being swallowed whole, raw material for the alchemy of Armaros. A slide show skittered through Mara's field of vision. Every second, a new scene appeared before her. The Eleven in the ochre expanse of the Dead Vlei. The High Council chamber crowded with Offspring. Armaros wrapped in a man's embrace.

Mara knew these scenes, though she could not understand how she knew them.

I don't want to watch this movie.

Trying to think was like coercing rust-sealed gears to move.

This is no movie, idiot.

She was on her knees, the marble hard beneath her, the iron grip of powerful hands holding her motionless. *I can't move. Is this my body?*

A giantess with blond hair and broad features crouched near her. *My Petra.* The woman was crying. *The bitch from the train. How do I know her name?*

The sweet smell of jasmine tickled her nose. She became aware of the person kneeling in front of her. She knew that face too. It was her own.

My self. My sister-self. My mirror image.

Wait, that doesn't make any sense.

I am Mara Layil!

Pain redoubled within her. *I can't survive this.* She was being assaulted, swallowed by the will of Armaros. *Who will I be?*

Eighteen years she'd been alive.

I don't want to die.

She twisted against the hands that held her. *I want my life.*

Moments from her own past became intercut with those of Armaros. A hospital room. Her mother cursing her birth and refusing to hold her. Her father's eyes, always measuring and finding fault. Her high school math teacher calling her selfish and self-absorbed. The girl in group therapy yelling "bitch."

But damn it, it's my life. Mara wanted the freedom of her own mind. If that meant she constantly fucked things up, so be it. At least she fucked them up her way.

More of Armaros's memories avalanched through her. The stench of bodies in a mass grave. The unfettered abandon of flight. The last breath of Tur'el, her brother-self.

I am Mara Layil.

THAT is Armaros.

Mara fought, pitting the insignificant speck of herself against the force of Armaros.

Like rushing floodwaters choked with debris, Armaros's life attacked her tiny refuge, battering her until Mara knew nothing of the world but toughing out pain.

How long?

Forever.

Never.

There is no such thing as time.

Max and Momar. Hiroko and Dali. Ethan.

When there is no time, no one is ever truly gone.

Ethan. Dali and Hiroko. Momar and Max. Little Max.

The pressure eased a sliver.

Mara felt her chest heave.

The raging cataract of Armaros's blood was starting to ebb.

Mara's life was hers for the taking.

My life.

Mine.

Me.

The rapid-fire slide show of Armaros's history ceased. Mara re-emerged in her body. Someone was weeping. Her neck burned, but less so with every passing second. Armaros was squeezing Mara's upper arms so tightly that she couldn't feel her hands. If her hands were still tethered to her body.

The scent of jasmine swirled around Mara.

She understood.

She'd been metamorphosed.

Armaros's blood eddied through her veins, carrying memories and carrying power. The gash on her neck was healing, sealing the legacy of the Eleven within the confines of her body.

I am not alone.

The weeping woman was Petra, the most trusted of Armaros's guards. Armaros herself, wan and weak, kneeled before Mara. Daylight cascaded into the High Council chamber, catching a floating strand of silvery hair.

Once again, time began to warp around them. Mara was falling outside of time.

"Get control," Armaros rasped. "You must not drift."

Control? How do you control the rush of wind or sweep of sunset?

"Child! NOW!"

The command tethered her.

"When my blood has fully supplanted your own, you will be as one of the Eleven. Only you will be able to hold back chaos. The barriers that keep the Twins outside of time must be restored. Use the Circlet of Moments."

Mara's awareness shifted to her head where a writhing band of relium clung to her brow. The Circlet itself was not heavy but weighty with moments, with centuries. Under its pressure, she nodded.

"That's a good girl," said Armaros. Then she collapsed in Mara's arms.

Fifty-six

AEDA

HIGH COUNCIL CHAMBER, ISTANBUL, TURKEY

No one approached Aeda as she entered the outer courtyard of the High Council compound. Urgency consumed her, but she slowed her pace to match the jerky, forced steps of her hooded companion. A thrill rippled through her. Sauntering into the Covenant's stronghold with her prize at her side ... Ah ... this was justice. Sinioch would be avenged, and the High Council would be hers to command.

Soon, my love.

Aeda urged her companion toward the chamber.

The Crimson Scribes were conspicuously absent. Matthias had promised to call them together for some procedural nonsense, and he seemed to have done it. *Excellent.* That meant fewer eyes and fewer self-sacrificing fools to throw themselves in front of Armaros. Aeda wanted a precision strike, though it pained her to lack an audience for her triumph.

In a thousand years, no one had attempted to assassinate one of the Eleven. Who in their right mind would attack Armaros?

The proscriptions of the Covenant were too ingrained, the powers of the Eleven unassailable.

Times are changing. Aeda fingered the relium garrote in her pocket and glanced at the slight figure by her side. *We will change everything.*

Robaire and Semo stood guard outside High Council chamber. In spite of the best efforts of that insufferable Petra Adler, Matthias had managed to get them on duty at the same time.

"Is Armaros inside?"

Robaire nodded.

"Alone?"

Again, he nodded.

"Give me your knife," she said to Semo. The big man's hands flew protectively to the hilt at his waist. An Amyclaean without a relium blade might as well be naked.

Let him be naked.

Aeda slapped his hand aside, plucked the knife from its sheath, and handed it to her companion. The bone-white hand that received it was terribly delicate. As a weapon, she was still imperfect, but as a distraction, Aeda thought she would do the job. Aeda steadied herself, forcing tears into her eyes. She would approach Armaros once again as a grieving supplicant, begging justice for the woman at her side.

For Sinioch.

Aeda knew how it would play out. Armaros would be shocked to see the familiar face under the hood. She'd be horrified at the woman's condition and even more so as Aeda insinuated Mara Layil was to blame. The old witch would raise her gnarled hand to the gaunt cheek. Damn, if she wasn't always stroking somebody on the cheek. Aeda hated those constant ministrations, but in this case, they would be to her advantage. Armaros would lean in, close, then closer.

It will be the last thing she does.

Aeda fixed a mask of concern upon her face and pulled open the door.

FIFTY-SEVEN

MARA

HIGH COUNCIL CHAMBER, ISTANBUL, TURKEY

Still reeling at her changed nature, Mara cradled Armaros. Her great-grandmother's body reminded her of a broken bird. She felt the warm pressure of Petra's arms around her and heard the woman's heaving sobs. In the wake of pain, Mara was hollowed out, afraid to move lest she crack into bits like old porcelain.

I don't know what to do. Her thread of consciousness was drawn very thin.

Yes, you do. Dense, textured fragments of Armaros's mind still dominated her thoughts.

Mara shoved them away. *I need to rest.* Mara's eyelids slid closed. *Petra will keep me safe.*

Suddenly, the Circlet contorted again Mara's brow, and her gauntlets rippled violently. Her exhaustion vanished. Mara's eyes shot to the door as Aeda Moreau, lithe and predatory, strode forward. She was flanked by a hooded figure, lurching forward with an odd, uneven gait.

Mara's every sense was on high alert.

"Take Armaros," she whispered to Petra.

I must stand.

Her body was ill-weighted, as if she were on a planet with different gravity, but there was a responsiveness to her limbs that hadn't been there before. She achieved upright and took in the utter shock on Aeda's face.

"You?" Aeda spat, her eyes darting from Mara to Armaros's body.

Mara waited, not trusting herself to operate something as basic as vocal cords.

Recovering her composure, Aeda threw back her head and crowed. "You killed the last of the Eleven!"

"She did not!" Petra flung the words at Aeda. Mara felt her own surprised response intermixed with that of Armaros. The old woman was touched by the way her Guard rose to Mara's defense.

"You've come for Armaros," Mara guessed, "to kill her and start a war."

"Well, I didn't come for a street rat like you," Aeda sneered, "but now it would seem I owe you my thanks." Mara shifted her weight, testing the reliability of her legs as subtly as possible. "You saved me the trouble of taking on the old bat." Out of the corner of Mara's eye, she saw Petra place Armaros's body safely behind the row of thrones. "Now I can give you my full attention," Aeda continued. The threat was clear. Petra responded immediately, rejoining Mara with her knife drawn. "How precious. You have a watchdog."

"I don't want any trouble," said Mara.

That really made Aeda laugh. "Since when have you avoided trouble, Mara Layil? Finally growing up, little one?"

"I never wanted trouble," Mara repeated. "I was protecting my brother. I didn't mean to kill Sinioch."

All humor drained from Aeda's face, and she tensed. "But you did, didn't you?"

"Look what you did to my brother!"

The gauntlets pulsed a warning, and Mara flexed, preparing for an attack.

"I almost forgot," Aeda said, all sugar. "Since we're on the topic of family, I brought a little something to show Armaros, but really, it's far better if I give her to you."

Aeda snapped her fingers, the crack echoing off marble, and the hooded figure shot toward Mara, her extended blade flashing. As she leapt onto the dais, the hood flew off, and Mara was absolutely, completely unable to move.

The face was less rigid than the last time Mara had seen it, and her head had been shaved, but the woman's once lovely features were instantly recognizable.

"Mom!" Mara's strangled cry filled the room.

Petra dove into Veronique, deflecting the blade plunging toward Mara's chest. Both of them went sprawling across the floor. Mara watched them tumble, stunned.

Maybe her mom didn't love her, but she wouldn't try to kill her, would she?

Ignore her, maybe—but kill her?

Her mother shoved Petra into the base of Armaros's throne with a guttural cry. She fixed her empty eyes on Mara. A flat, transparent pouch filled with dark liquid was attached to the left side of her shaved head. A tube snaked from it straight into her skull.

What have they done to her?

All Mara wanted was to rip off the hideous thing. Even as her mother lumbered toward her, Mara couldn't tear her eyes from the gruesome device.

"Move!" Petra yelled.

Reeling, Mara barely had time to block with her gauntlet as the knife slashed. Her mother spun away, turning to attack Mara's other side. All the time, Aeda laughed. "Isn't family wonderful?"

Mara parried the blows and dodged behind thrones. Her mother's limbs jerked as if Aeda's control was incomplete, but she was fast and accurate. All Mara could do was yield ground.

I can't attack my own mother.

The pouch had to go.

The thing was a parasite sucking away every last trace of her mother.

I want her back.

Mara had nearly convinced herself that being alone didn't matter, that it was for the best, but it was a lie. She wanted them all back—her mom, her dad, and most of all, Max.

The next swipe of the knife sent Mara spinning, and a pulse of red obscured the vision in her right eye. Trying to staunch the wound, Mara's fingers skimmed the Circlet. Understanding jolted through her. She had Armaros's relic and her skill. She hadn't wanted it, but By the Sacrifice, she would claim it now.

Behind her mother, Petra clambered to her feet, readying her knife.

I must do it before anyone else gets hurt. Mara stopped giving ground. Instead, she slid into the stream of Armaros's experience and stepped straight into her mother's line of attack. Raising her arms wide, Mara enveloped her mother in the embrace of frozen time.

Petra shouted.

Dust shimmered in the air.

Her mother was as motionless as a mannequin in the mall of the damned. Her knife hung in the air inches from Mara's neck. With the power of the Circlet amplifying Armaros's blood, Mara could conduct seconds, minutes, centuries. She could hold her mother to that singular point for eternity. Mara plucked the relium blade from her mother's fingers and handed it to Petra.

Aeda roared and sent a wave of force rolling toward the ceiling. Great chunks of plaster and marble crashed down around them. Mara felt herself yanked free of the dust and rubble.

She nodded wordlessly to Petra, and shoulder to shoulder, they moved on Aeda.

The thunderous collapse had finally been enough to alert the men outside. Mara recognized the two from the train, and in her mind, Armaros named them. Robaire and Semo. Petra changed course.

Is she joining them?

Mara didn't know if they were for or against her.

Petra answered that in a clash of knives as she fought to keep the men at bay.

Every fiber of Mara's being stayed focused on Aeda. They circled one another in the space beneath the statue of the White One. Something dark and whiplike snapped in Aeda's right hand.

A relium relic as deadly as my own.

Mara's blood galloped through her limbs at the resonance of all the relium in the chamber. Her gauntlets roared with the rhythm. Aeda sent the garrote flicking toward her. Before Mara could think, her gauntlets responded. Blades sprang forth, deflecting the sinuous noose. Mara jumped backward.

She did not want to do this. Not like it happened with Sinioch. *I don't want to kill again.* Especially now, suffused as she was with Armaros's memories. Mara could see Aeda as a girl, a teenager, a young woman at her wedding. Armaros loved her. Armaros wanted her to live.

Aeda lunged toward Mara.

Mara sprang away and tried to capture Aeda as she had her mother, but Aeda barreled through the frozen web of time, burning it away. She was fearsome, driven by revenge. Mara did not want to get close enough to see what she could do to flesh.

Aeda sent another section of the roof crashing down.

Mara rolled under the shelter of the White One's wings, barely avoiding being smashed. Through the haze of marble dust and the shafts of light cutting down from the ruined ceiling, Mara saw Robaire and Semo press their attack on Petra. The big woman sent Robaire tumbling off the edge of the dais, but even as he fell out of sight, he hurled his blade, and it took Petra behind her knee.

Blood spurted from the wound, and Petra crumpled. As she hit the ground, she met Mara's eyes. Ignoring Semo's great bulk bearing down on her, Petra flung both knives at Aeda. One blade thudded into her thigh, but the other, deflected by Aeda's spinning garrote, went skittering across the marble floor. A protective surge pulsed through Mara, and the shock wave emitted from her hands sent Semo flying across the room.

A chunk of the destabilized roof hit Mara squarely on the shoulder. Mara heard the crunch of bone. Aeda jerked the knife from her thigh and turned on Mara, forcing her to the ground. Her gauntlet took the force of the blow. Twisting hard, the blades caught, metal on metal squealing until the knife flew from Aeda's grip.

Straddling Mara, Aeda flexed the garrote. It bit below Mara's chin, raising drops of blood in a ruby choker. Her lungs burned. Her vision wavered. The crazed fire in Aeda's eyes sent a surge of desperation through Mara. She writhed and twisted, trying to free her arms. She couldn't go much longer without air. Gathering all of her energy into one last, violent burst, Mara thrashed one arm free; the gauntlet slithered over her hand and she sent her fist straight into Aeda's sternum. The force threw Aeda backward, arms flailing, into the plinth of the White One. Gulping air, Mara scrambled after her.

Finish this now!

There was no turning back. Mara steeled herself for it, gauntlets held high, but she lost her balance again when the doors to the chamber collapsed inward like wet cardboard. The tremors sent more of the ceiling crumbling down.

A great chunk smashed into the White One, cracks spiderwebbing through the statue. One wing cracked at the shoulder joint. As though in slow motion, the carved marble fell through glittering clouds of dust like an ax straight toward Aeda's neck.

FIFTY-EIGHT

ETHAN

HIGH COUNCIL CHAMBER, ISTANBUL, TURKEY

Ethan stood beside Tamel on a thick wall high above a courtyard in tumult. People swarmed toward a building with ornate double doors. Yells and shouts cascaded through the crowd.

"An attack!"

"Call the Guard!"

The noise rose, bouncing off the stone walls and reverberating as hundreds of people poured into the open space below him. The sound of weapons being drawn reminded Ethan of giant insects furiously snapping their mandibles. The newly bared blades, many of them relium, send a frisson of warning through him.

A gray-haired man standing in front of the doors pumped a fighting staff in the air. "The girl has killed Armaros!" he yelled, cutting through the cacophony. "We must defend the Covenant! Death to the violator!" Around him, others took up the cry.

"Death! Death! Death to the girl!"

The girl?

It had to be Mara. Ethan scanned the crowd.

Where are you?

Without warning, Tamel grabbed him by the scruff of his neck and leapt over the crowd. Never in all his years as a skater had Ethan ever caught air like this. He flew. The Blade Guardian's cloak billowed around them, sending a new surge of shrieks through the crowd. They cleared the entire length of the courtyard, landing hard in a cloud of dust. The gray-haired man fell to one side as Tamel kicked down the doors.

Massive holes had been blasted in the ceiling. Piles of white marble sparkled, making the gruesome tableau in the center more awful than it already was.

Bodies everywhere.

The twisted form of a dark-haired woman lay beneath a broken statue. Another woman with some electronic contraption bristling from the side of her bald head was standing weirdly frozen with an arm raised as if to strike a blow. Two Amyclaeans lay amid the rubble, and near them, the body of an old woman.

Tamel's hand pressed harder on the back of his neck, and Ethan could feel the tension coursing through him.

Mara!

The only person Ethan cared about was crouching beside a blond woman lying in a spreading pool of blood. Mara slit the woman's pant leg with the blade of her gauntlet and touched the wound behind her knee, her gore-splattered face contorted in concentration. Instantly, it ceased spurting blood. The pain on the woman's face eased.

Mara rose and turned toward the commotion at the door.

She was different. Not only battered—he was used to that—but there was an aura of strangeness to her that he did not know.

He felt momentarily strangled. *Who is she?*

Ethan shook free of Tamel's hand.

He knew her, damn it!

"Mara!"

Sprinting around the piles of rubble and the fallen bodies, Ethan was sure that if he touched her, he could bring her back. As soon as he reached her, Ethan pressed his lips to her forehead, breathing in sweat and blood and marble dust. The stiffness of her body melted, and he heard the quiet hiss of blades retracting into her gauntlets. His own body reacted to hers more strongly than he thought possible, but there was a new strangeness about the way she sent his blood racing.

"You're not supposed to be here," she murmured into his neck.

"Shut up."

A small laugh escaped her but was lost in a renewed cry from the crowd. A crush of people forced their way through the doors, wailing at the sight of Armaros's body and raging against the destruction all around.

"Murderer!"

"Death!"

Ethan whirled to put himself between Mara and the mob.

The Blade Guardian stood exactly where Ethan had left him, and the expression on his face was equal parts fury and grief. His brooding eyes flicked from Armaros to Mara and back again.

The bloodthirsty clamor was rising.

Tamel bore down on Mara, drawing the Blade of the Sacrifice from beneath his cloak. His battered knuckles flexed around the hilt. With a flick of his wrist, the middle section of the collapsible weapon swiveled down and snapped into place. The end section followed in the blink of an eye. The joints vanished.

A ripple of recognition swept through those gathered.

"The Blade Guardian!" someone cried.

"He lives!"

"Blessed be the Sacrifice."

Others took up the call.

"Step away from her," Tamel commanded, pausing less than a sword's length from where Ethan stood.

"She didn't kill Armaros," Ethan said, hoping it was true.

"My last of my sister-selves lies dead," Tamel raged, "and she is to blame."

Tamel raised a scarred hand and slammed Ethan into the wall across the room, advancing on Mara. Ethan scrabbled for purchase on the slick floor. He had to get to Mara before it was too late.

"Mara!" he yelled.

Tamel raised the Blade of the Sacrifice. The age-old metal pulsed with a dark, otherworldly glow.

Mara lifted her arms, palms up, her face calm and untroubled.

"Fight," urged Ethan. "You always fight."

But she didn't.

Instead, she said the last thing in the world Ethan expected to hear.

She said, "Brother, I missed you."

FIFTY-NINE

HIGH COUNCIL CHAMBER, ISTANBUL, TURKEY

Mara saw with her own eyes and Armaros's memory.

Her brother lived.

Joy more intense than any she had felt in centuries soared through her.

"My brother," Mara said, "I did not think I would see you again in this world."

A tremor shook Tamel's sword arm, but otherwise he was granite. "You are no sister of mine."

How I love him!

The gray-haired man pushed through the crowd. "You killed Armaros."

Mara's head swiveled toward him. Through the filter of Armaros's memory, she knew him too. "How convenient for you, Matthias, to blame me. Which one of these," she gestured to the thrones, "did you plan to sit in when I was gone?"

Tamel placed the centuries-sharp Blade against her neck. "I will know the truth. What has happened here?"

"Kill her," Matthias urged. "Look to your sister."

All eyes turned to Petra, who still shielded the body of what had been Armaros.

I am your sister. The Blade against her skin sang to her blood. *How could I ever fear you?* She locked eyes with Tamel. "I will show you what happened."

Slowly, she raised a supplicant's hand.

He nodded, granting permission.

She closed her hand around Tamel's wrist. His pulse slammed against her fingers, and their minds joined in an echo of the Before. Mara rewound time to the moment when Armaros had begun the blood transfer and showed him everything.

When she released him, Tamel sheathed the Blade and cupped her cheek. "Sister."

He reminded her of Max—as much as a world-weary warrior could resemble her favorite fan club of one.

A warm, familiar hand touched her arm. "Mara?"

Blood dribbled from a split in Ethan's lip.

"It's okay," she said.

And it was—or would be.

Her brother lived.

Ethan nudged her again. Mara tore her eyes from Tamel's familiar features to look at Ethan. He offered her his hand. A quiver ran up Mara's spine at the sight of that hand. It had known the terrain of her body so completely.

"I shouldn't have left …," she began.

"Look," Ethan interrupted, extending his hand as if he held a baby bird. She peered into his cupped palm. Two dark pellets lay against his skin. Her Circlet flexed in response.

Like the tumblers in a lock, each thought fell into place.

Hope staggered her.

"Relium?" She breathed the word as a prayer and a question. "For Max?"

"And your mom," said Ethan.

"And Mom," she repeated.

"Not so fast," said Tamel, enveloping Ethan's hand in his own. "Sister or not, you owe me. Life for life."

You owe me. Mara knew that voice from her own memories. "It was you on Toru's island."

"Yes," Tamel answered, "and we made a deal."

"What do you want?"

"Free the Twins."

Sixty

DALMEET

OUTSIDE OF TIME

Blowing sand sucked at Dalmeet's limbs. His clothes had nearly disintegrated. His hair hung in ragged mats. Sharp-edged grains caked his cracked lips and swollen eyes. The Twins had probed his mind and had stolen his memories. He wouldn't last much longer.

I am nearly gone.

He would welcome the end.

The strength of the cyclone grew until it sucked him aloft, spinning his body around and around. At the vortex were the Twins. He'd never felt them this agitated. Their emotions were a conflicted jumble of fear, fury, and anticipation, all pouring through him like acid.

Dalmeet couldn't fathom what had upset them nor did he care.

The relentless sand drove into his flesh like poisoned needles.

He could no longer remember the absence of pain.

Let me go.

Please.

The tornado ceased as quickly as it had started. Dalmeet hung high above the sand for a split second; then he was in free fall, a scream torn from his lips. He crashed with bone-shattering impact at the feet of the Twins.

SIXTY-ONE

*F*ree the Twins?

Mara's insides writhed like the sands outside of time.

"But they're monsters," she blurted.

"It is time to right the wrongs we did. They deserve a second chance."

That's all I wanted—a second chance to make things right.

The will of Armaros surged within Mara and hijacked her voice. "You don't know what you ask. We'd unleash chaos upon this world. The Covenant must stand. Our world deserves the strong hand of justice."

Mara's head twitched violently as she suppressed Armaros's commanding presence. She had to maintain control of her own thoughts. Ethan tried to approach her, but Tamel had his hand—and Max's future—trapped in his battered fist.

I am responsible.

To my brothers. To my lover. To my Scribe.

Petra and the other Offspring pressed close around them.

I am responsible for all of them now.

Armaros had said, "No one wants the responsibility of ruling, but someone has to do it."

Are we ruled by laws or by our own convictions?

We chose free will, and the rules rose up around us.

"Now is the time to decide," said Tamel.

I don't want to rule anything. I want the ones I love.

A fierce happiness filled her. *I can save Max and Dali.*

Armaros fought back. *Eleon and Lilya will destroy the world around them.*

Mara felt the sun on her face and the cold, crisp air of winter. She breathed deeply. Eleon and Lilya were unpredictable and impulsive. Maybe she should sacrifice Max and Dali to a five-thousand-year-old bargain, but chaos didn't always mean destruction, did it? The world was changing.

Mara looked to Ethan. "I don't want to do the wrong thing."

"I know."

"What if I ruin everything?"

"What if you don't?"

What if I don't?

How could she have ever thought time hurtled forward like a train?

Instead, the past, the present, and the future spiraled around each other.

Nothing was set in stone.

There were such things as second chances.

Mara drew Tamel and Ethan to her. She grasped the Circlet from her brow and pulled on it. The air in its center shimmered like the surface of a lake rippled by a breeze. The Circlet expanded into the now familiar oval doorway through which she could already see the shifting dunes outside of time. Unnaturally flat light poured from the doorway. Far off in the distance, she saw two specks of pure white brilliance.

The Twins are coming.

Lilya and Eleon sped toward her on a sand road that dissipated behind them. Eleon was carrying something. Mara squinted, trying to bring the image into clearer focus.

Not something—someone.

"Dali!" she cried. "They've got Dali!"

"Is he dead?" Ethan asked.

She'd assumed he would be but maybe not. A sensation like wings fluttered through her chest. Mara rose on the balls of her feet, poised to run to him, but the Blade Guardian held her back.

"You must not let them have the Circlet. Whatever happens, close the breach and take the Circlet with you. Understand?"

With Armaros's memory, Mara saw the day the Twins were sentenced, the grief on their mother's face. She ached for the Twins and for Azza, who fell that day.

Mara's heart pounded.

Ethan pressed against her.

"Beware!" Tamel yelled to the crowd behind them. "They are coming!"

The luminous bodies of the Twins filled the breach.

They were naked as before, and Dali, her sweet Dali, nearly so. His clothes hung in strips from his emaciated body, but against the ghostly opalescence of the Twins' bodies, his copper skin was reassuringly solid.

His breath came in short, shallow rasps.

He's alive!

Mara wanted to shout and pump her fist in the air, but the dangerous, hungry look upon the faces of the Twins silenced her.

When they stepped through the Circlet, Mara felt dread settle on the gathered crowd.

No one moved. No one spoke.

The blank white eyes of the Twins seemed to look everywhere and nowhere.

They released Dalmeet, and Ethan jumped forward to catch his body.

"Mara Layil," they intoned.

The force of their will penetrated her.

Even as she reached for the Circlet and closed the way outside of time, she shuddered.

By the Blade, what have I done?

Book three in the Angel Punk Saga trilogy is coming soon.
Please visit angelpunksaga.com for more information.

ACKNOWLEDGMENTS

Like all good things, The Angel Punk Saga is possible only through the hard work and support of many people.

First, to Amber J. Keyser, author of *The Hunt for Mara Layil*, for all you have done to bring Mara and the rest of the characters in this saga to life. Your love and care for the story and people in this world shines through your words on the page.

To Julie O'Connell who adapted the Angel Punk screenplay into the first book, *Offspring*. You jumped right into this existing world and helped us bring it to others.

Without the original concept and ongoing dedication of Devon Lyon, Kevin Curry and Scott Bernard Nelson, none of this would have been possible. Sometimes crazy ideas come together to create new worlds!

Huge shout out to Eric Doebele, Jack Phan, Jake Rossman, Chris Weilert, and Matthew Wilson for being early believers in this story and project. All of your help and support over the years manufacturing inertia has been invaluable.

Jennifer Stangel's work navigating the complexities of the publishing world is the reason you're holding this book or reading it on your electronic device. For that and being a believer in the project from the beginning, she gets eternal gratitude.

For the investors in The Angel Punk Saga, without you this would have never gotten off the ground. Thank you, thank you, thank you.

A hearty 'Huzzah!' goes out to the book cover artists, Steven Barker and Amelia Harp, for bringing their unique visions of the world to life.

To Shannon Wheeler for his generosity in sharing knowledge about the comic and publishing world, we offer a toast of rich, black coffee. And Levi Moroshan for believing in the project and bringing his photo talents to the table so many times.

A special thanks to the Angel Punk comic art team who brought Mara and the rest of the characters to life visually, including Val Mayerik, Bob Wiacek, Steve Olliff, Brian Snoddy and Tom Orzechowski. Also, our art team intern Sarah Cloutier added so many incredible images to this world.

ABOUT THE AUTHOR

Manuscript by Amber J. Keyser

Visit angelpunksaga.com for author and creators' biographies. Want to learn even more about the hidden supernatural world of Angel Punk? Then be sure to also visit the website's blog and art pages for additional, in-depth material, a free short story, and a downloadable PDF of chapter one from both Offspring (book one) and The Hunt for Mara Layil (book two).